THE DEMONS HAVE WON,
AND IT'S OPEN SEASON . . . ON HUMANS.

Gazing west across the valley, Max saw the autumn trees blaze in a final flash of red and gold as the sun dipped below the opposing ridge. He turned to make the steep, slow walk back to camp.

But something blocked his path.

It was a human being. A boy.

He was roughly the same age as Max. His shirt was ragged and his shoes were worn as if he'd been living in the wild for months. Max held up both hands and bowed his head in greeting.

To his surprise, however, the boy did not respond. He merely stood, rooted to the spot and trembling, as though in shock. Only now did Max discern that the boy was gasping, struggling to catch his breath.

"I'm a friend," said Max calmly, showing his empty palms.

Thud, thud.

Max started at the ugly, nearly simultaneous sounds. The boy staggered half a step, his eyes fixed upon Max. From his chest protruded two arrowheads, whose tips trickled with green witch-fire. The boy staggered, his eyes fixed upon Max; then he fell forward onto the slope.

Max watched as stones rolled down the slope, loosened by whatever was now trodding heavily down the mountain. Something green bobbed uphill: an arrowhead wreathed in the same green flame as those that had killed the boy. As the flame came closer, Max saw its light reflected in three eyes—pale tiger's eyes—set within the face of a horned rakshasa. It was Demon Lord Vyndra.

THE TAPESTRY · BOOK 3

THE FIEND AND THE FORGE

WRITTEN AND ILLUSTRATED BY

HENRY H. NEFF

A YEARLING BOOK

Text, map, and interior illustrations copyright © 2010 by Henry H. Neff
Cover art copyright © 2010 by Cory Godbey

All rights reserved. Published in the United States by Yearling, an imprint of Random House Children's Books, a division of Random House, Inc., New York. Originally published in hardcover in the United States by Random House Children's Books, New York, in 2010.

Yearling and the jumping horse design are registered trademarks of Random House, Inc.

Visit us on the Web! randomhouse.com/kids

Educators and librarians, for a variety of teaching tools, visit us at
RHTeachersLibrarians.com

The Library of Congress has cataloged the hardcover edition of this work as follows:
Neff, Henry H.
The fiend and the forge / Henry H. Neff.
p. cm. — (Tapestry ; bk. 3)
Summary: Reeling from a personal tragedy but determined to stop the demon Astaroth, twelve-year-old Max McDaniels sets out from Rowan, where magic and nature flourish so long as the people do not oppose the demon, and travels through the preindustrial nightmare Astaroth has created using the Book of Origins.
ISBN 978-0-375-83898-9 (trade) — ISBN 978-0-375-93898-6 (lib. bdg.) —
ISBN 978-0-375-89295-0 (ebook) — ISBN 978-0-375-83899-6 (pbk.)
[1. Magic—Fiction. 2. Demonology—Fiction. 3. Books and reading—Fiction.
4. Witches—Fiction. 5. Schools—Fiction.] I. Title.
PZ7.N388Fie 2011 [Fic]—dc22 2011002129

Printed in the United States of America

10 9 8 7 6 5

First Yearling Edition

*To
Danielle Raymond Neff,
my life and love*

CONTENTS

THE
FIEND AND THE FORGE

ROWAN ACADEMY

~ 1 ~

THE MOON HAS A FACE

It was not the warm sun or the bleating lambs that woke Max McDaniels. Rather, it was the soft patter of little feet—sly, terribly eager feet—that converged upon him as he lay amid the ripening corn. Max kept still while the first of his visitors hopped onto his chest. He did not stir at the second or third. But once the twelfth clambered up with an exasperated *peep*, Max cracked an eye and smiled.

Twelve goslings stood upon him. Downy heads bobbed; inscrutable eyes glistened like wet pebbles. With a sudden, triumphant *honk*, the boldest stepped forward and tapped its hard little beak on Max's breastbone. The others followed suit, and soon Max writhed and chuckled beneath the Lilliputian assault.

"Ouch!" he exclaimed, shooing at them halfheartedly. "I'm awake!"

The pecking continued.

"MAX!" bellowed a shrill female voice.

Several crows took flight as a plump white goose crashed through the cornstalks and into Max's row, looking frantically from side to side.

"There you are!" exclaimed the goose. "Sleeping away like a lazy bottom!"

"Bottoms can't be lazy, Hannah," murmured Max. He plucked the last of the marauding goslings off his stomach and placed it on the ground, where it promptly resumed its indiscriminate pecking.

"Like-a-lazy-bottom!" sang the goose, aspiring to an operatic tremolo.

"Bravo," said Max, rising to his feet.

"Thank you," replied Hannah, curtsying. She waddled forward and gave him a motherly once-over. "Max, there are a gazillion things to do, and you should know better than to sneak off for a handful of winks."

"I've been working late every day for a month," protested Max, emphasizing the point with a bleary yawn.

"Excuses, excuses," retorted Hannah. "Stoop down a bit, dear." Max bent over in silent resignation while the goose flicked bits of dirt and hay from his shirt and smoothed his dark hair into a respectable shape. She sighed. "You of all people should know how special tomorrow is. . . ."

"I do," said Max. "I'll do my part."

"You'll do your part *now*," she said pointedly. "On the double!"

The matronly goose buffeted Max forward with her powerful

wing and whistled for the goslings to fall in line. They did so dutifully, and the group now formed an orderly column as they marched through the cornfield. When they arrived at the Sanctuary's main clearing, Hannah flapped her wings excitedly. "Nearly all back to normal and pretty as a picture," she crowed, gesturing toward the rebuilt Warming Lodge.

The long, low building seemed almost to bask next to its small lagoon. Its timbered walls were clean and smooth. There was no trace of splintered wood or blackened stone, nothing to suggest that this very building had been recently reduced to embers.

"Hmmm," said Max, privately thinking that Rowan Academy, while largely rebuilt, would never be "back to normal." Only six ~~imal~~ ~~o~~. Astaroth's armies had rampaged across the school's ~~rm.~~ pus, burning its forests, razing its structures, and ~~the~~ its flocks as they marched upon Rowan's final refuge Many lives had been lost. It was Max who ultimately them, fighting on alone until the only remaining option urrender the Book of Thoth to the Demon that coveted ad been a wrenching decision, but Astaroth had seemingly his word and fulfilled their bargain. The monstrous armies re spirited away, and Rowan had been left in peace, battered and broken, but free to rebuild at its own pace.

By any standard, that pace had been remarkable. Using magic and muscle, crops were planted, stone was quarried, forests were raised, and herds restocked. The Sanctuary's broad plain was now thick with grain fields, lush orchards, and grazing herds that were hemmed by a broad forest that sloped up into the mountains. Max inhaled the September air and spied a family of shimmering pixies as they skimmed toward a yellowing oak.

It was not just the Demon's peaceful withdrawal or recent glimpses of notoriously shy pixies that roused Max's curiosity.

There were other changes, too. Since Astaroth had claimed the Book, Max had felt the world thawing—as though the Earth had clomped in from the cold, stamped snow from her boots, and settled by a comfortable fire.

"A new age is beginning," he muttered.

"It sure is, honey," remarked Hannah brightly, herding her goslings toward the Sanctuary gate. "And just like I predicted, Mother Nature was due for one."

"Can you feel it, too?" he asked. At times he wondered if he was particularly sensitive to such things. Max McDaniels was a son of the Sidh, a hidden land where gods and monsters slumbered amid the hills. As the child of an earthly mother and an Irish deity, Max straddled a tenuous line between mortal and immortal. Within his blood coursed rare sparks of the Old Magic, pr[...] forces that could make Max as wild and powerful as a st[...] Hundreds of enemies had given way before Max during [...] Siege of Rowan.

"Of course I can feel it," replied Hannah, her head bobbi[...] in time with her step. "Things growing, the air brimming a[...] crackling with magic. It's like a ray of sunshine on my beak! You [...] have to be a ninny not to feel it."

"Do you believe Astaroth's behind it all?" asked Max.

"Who knows?" The goose shrugged. "But I'd wager that onc[...] he got his hands on the Book, he's been changing a thing or tw[...] Can't say it's ruffling my feathers, either."

"So you think things are better?" asked Max, feeling somewhat defensive. He had been expecting fire and brimstone following Astaroth's victory, not a peaceful, bountiful summer. The quiet was unsettling.

"Around here they are," Hannah concluded. She spread her wings and puffed out her chest to absorb the autumn sunshine. The goslings imitated their mother. "Anyway, I've done what I was supposed to do: find you and direct your lazy bottom back toward the Manse. So, you go mow lawns or weed gardens while this goose gets her groom on!"

"Excuse me?" asked Max.

"Deluxe feather tufting, Swedish beak massage, and a pedicure," explained Hannah. "The dryads owe me big-time. Big-time! So be a dear and watch the goslings while you do your chores. You know they just love it when you babysit. Mind you, L'il Baby Ray's been wheezy, so don't let Honk play too rough. And Millie's not allowed any sweets since she's been a very naughty gosling, and . . ."

Max's eyes glazed over while Hannah recited a litany of special instructions for each of her fidgeting, utterly indistinguishable children. Once Millie's pesky skin irritation had been addressed, Hannah waddled away, greeting a nearby work crew with the amiable ease of a big-city mayor. As soon as she disappeared, Max felt a sharp peck on his shin. The goslings were jostling at his feet. Implacable stares met his own.

"Mind your beaks," said Max, and with that he led them toward a mossy wall and the stout wooden door that separated the Sanctuary from the rest of Rowan Academy.

A symphony of sounds greeted them as they made their way through the tunnel-like arch of interlaced trees. Hammers, saws, shouts, laughter, and innumerable other noises blended together in a happy hum of endeavor. Emerging into daylight, Max saw hundreds of chattering students and adults touching up the stables' trim and fitting the last planks for a riding pen, where palominos pranced and whinnied. The invigorating air smelled of fresh paint, autumn leaves, and the sea. Max felt a rumbling in his stomach and toyed with the notion of stealing into the kitchens for a bite. . . .

But duty called. He led the goslings along a path that skirted round the stables and past the orchard until they arrived at the Manse, Rowan's central building and Max's home. Cutting across a garden, Max gazed up at the Manse's noble entrance with deep satisfaction. Charred stones had been salvaged and scrubbed to a spotless gray, shattered windows had been replaced, and welcoming smoke puffed once more from the many chimneys adorning the steep slate roof. Most pleasing, however, was the line of rowan trees that graced the drive once again. During the Siege, the Enemy had uprooted them and hacked them to splinters. Yet now they stood tall, crowned with creamy white blossoms as though no vye, goblin, or ogre had ever touched them.

A hag *was* touching them, however. Bellagrog Shrope was a massive specimen, some two hundred pounds of globular flesh cajoled into a dress intended for a smaller being. Her skin was gray, and her dress was brown; the combined effect was suggestive of some sort of enormous, dusky vegetable that had been uprooted and unwisely endowed with teeth. These teeth—these gleaming, triangular teeth—now chewed thoughtfully upon the hag's upper lip while she shuffled through a stack of papers. One of the goslings uttered a frightened *peep*.

The hag ceased her shuffling. Straightening, she gave the air an audible sniff. With a slow swivel of her head, she fixed the goslings with a pair of bloodshot crocodile eyes.

"Hello, darlings," she murmured. Stooping to the ground, she extended her arms. "Come and give ol' Bel a kiss!"

The goslings huddled close to one another, forming a soft, trembling mass. The hag repeated her invitation but to no avail.

At length, she rose and gave a deep chuckle. "Guess I ain't as cuddly as their ol' Mother Goose!"

"They're just shy, Bellagrog," Max lied, privately applauding the goslings' judgment.

"Sure they are, sure they are," said Bellagrog, scratching absently at her belly. "Anyway, it ain't them I been waitin' to see. It's you. I got a schedule to keep, Max, and yer puttin' me behind. Can't have it, love, can't have it. . . ."

Max ventured forward and stood next to the hag, peering over her shoulder while she riffled through her papers and scanned them like a stern accountant.

"Now, because I like ya, I'm going to give you some choices," she said. "No septic duty for Rowan's hero." She blinked and gave a snort of laughter. "'Septic doody' . . . that's a good one, Bel! Right witty, you are. Anyhoo, Max, we need ya doing stonework at the gates, shelving books in the Archives, or oiling seashells for the feast. What's it gonna be?"

"What about Old Tom?" Max inquired, scanning the seemingly endless list of remaining tasks. "Can I work there instead?" Max had a special affinity for Old Tom and had dearly missed its ringing chimes these past months. The academic building had been badly damaged during the Siege. In fact, Max himself was responsible for cracking the ancient bell housed in its clock tower. He felt a twinge of guilt over this and liked to work on its stately, weathered edifice whenever possible.

"Access to Old Tom is restricted until the celebration," replied Bellagrog coolly.

Max turned to view the building several hundred yards away. Stories of scaffolding were draped in white, wrapping the building as if it were an enormous present.

"What's going on?" asked Max.

"Information regarding Old Tom is to be distributed on a need-to-know basis," said the hag, examining her talons. "You don't need to know, and now you is making me regret my generous offer. . . ." She flipped the page, and Max glimpsed the word *sewer* in the heading.

"Seashells," he blurted. "I'll work on the seashells."

"Right, then," said Bellagrog, penciling his name next to others. "Off ya go. Work up an appetite for tomorrow's party. I know I am. . . ."

Bellagrog grinned at the goslings. Ignoring her, Max led his little charges to the broad expanse of grass and gardens that served as Rowan's central quad. On one sizable square of lawn, clusters of children were polishing colossal seashells with rags dipped in round tubs of yellow goop. Some of the seashells were no bigger than a beach ball, while other ancient specimens loomed as large as mail trucks. The yellow goop was a thickened form of phosphoroil, and as the waxy, pungent substance was applied to the shells, they began to give off a soft glow, like gargantuan fireflies. The effect was diminished by daylight, but even so, a golden haze hovered above the lawn as though El Dorado lay beneath. Max stepped past a giggling group of children and sized up an imposing nautilus.

For the better part of two hours, Max polished the shell. It was monotonous but satisfying work as he burnished each smooth, curved section to a natural gleam until the oil saturated its surface and it began to emit a phosphorescent glow. While Max worked, the goslings were reasonably well behaved. They seemed content to gaze at their ghostly, distorted reflections in the shell until Honk managed to roll—or plunge—into a tub of phosphoroil. While Max scrubbed the indignant bird, a shadow fell over him.

"Well, what have we here?" chuckled a familiar voice.

Turning, Max saw Dr. Rasmussen, the deposed director of the Frankfurt Workshop. The hairless, nearly skeletal scientist grinned at Max from behind his thin spectacles. Some dozen adults accompanied him.

"Ladies and gentlemen," said the engineer, "please allow me

to introduce Max McDaniels. The young man visited the Workshop last year, but given the circumstances, I fear that many of you did not get to meet him. Let's amend that now."

Max nodded at the strangers as they were named. They did not return his greeting but merely stared at him with expressions of cold curiosity. Putting aside their rudeness, Max was surprised to see members of the Workshop at Rowan, much less in the company of Dr. Rasmussen. The Workshop was a techno-centric society—a scientific faction that had splintered off from Rowan long ago and now lived within a network of self-sufficient subterranean cities. Until the previous year, Jesper Rasmussen had been the Workshop's director, but his colleagues had driven him out on Astaroth's orders.

Since that day, Rasmussen had taken refuge at Rowan, offering his technical expertise. Unfortunately, his expertise was accompanied by his arrogance, and thus requests for his input had dwindled. He was now Rowan's most sullen dignitary.

"When did they arrive?" asked Max, looking past Rasmussen at the visitors.

"This morning," replied Dr. Rasmussen. "They're here to . . . make amends."

"With you or with us?" asked Max, keenly aware that the Workshop had done nothing to resist Astaroth's assault on Rowan or the world at large. For all Max knew, they had now sworn allegiance to the Demon. Rasmussen ignored the pointed question.

"Does Cooper know they're here?" asked Max.

"Yes, yes," muttered Rasmussen. "Everyone here has the requisite authorization. Thank you for making sure, however." He offered a prim smile to his colleagues. "Wherever would we be without the endearing insolence of teenagers?" He elicited one feeble laugh. Shooting Max a peevish glance, Rasmussen beckoned his colleagues along. They began to follow until one of them—an angular, humorless-looking man—abruptly stopped.

"What is that mark, Jesper?" asked the man, pointing at Max's wrist.

Dr. Rasmussen frowned and peered closely at the crimson tattoo of a red, upraised hand.

"Hmmm," mused Dr. Rasmussen. "Agent Cooper has the same one, I believe."

"You did not mention anything about a mark," said the man, sounding aggrieved.

"What is he talking about?" asked Max, snatching his arm away from Rasmussen.

Rasmussen offered no response but merely scrutinized the tattoo for a few more seconds before waving his colleagues on again. The group departed, with the exception of the man who had first observed the mark. He stood rooted to the spot, allowing his pale, watery eyes to wander over Max's face and body without a hint of hurry or embarrassment. Max might have been a laboratory rat.

"Why don't you just take a picture?" Max snapped.

The man blinked, as though Max's question had jolted him from deep contemplation. Strolling closer, he rested his hands upon his knees and leaned forward until his thin, impassive face hovered only inches away.

"And why would I do that?" the man whispered. "I can see you whenever I want."

Straightening, the man offered a curious smile and then walked briskly away to rejoin his colleagues. Max felt a reflexive surge of anger as he watched them go; he despised the Workshop and its smug representatives. Still, it was a peculiar comment. Max had never seen the man before and was unlikely to do so again. While he puzzled over this, it suddenly dawned on him that these very representatives were from outside. The Workshop was based in Europe. Surely they would know the status of various governments and cities; they would know what was happening in the wide world beyond.

"Hey!" called Max, running after them. "Hold on."

He caught up to them as they were climbing the Manse's broad steps. Rasmussen tried to hurry the group inside, but they had already stopped and turned in response to Max's breathless call.

"How is the rest of the world?" Max asked. "What's going on in Boston? Or Berlin? Or Paris!"

He was met with silence. Clearing his throat, Rasmussen glanced at his colleagues. An olive-skinned woman in a pale gray suit shook her head, and Rasmussen's thin lips tightened.

"Max, do yourself a favor and forget about Paris," he said softly. "It's forgetting about you. . . ."

Before Max could ask another question, Rasmussen had turned away and the adults continued inside. Following after, Max watched them cross the foyer and funnel into the hallway leading toward Ms. Richter's office.

With a sigh, Max tossed his rag from one hand to the other, nodding hello to an elderly couple as he made his way back to the field of shells. As he approached the nautilus, he saw that a man and woman were sitting near its base.

"We were wondering if you'd come back," chuckled the man.

Nigel Bristow and his wife were sitting with the goslings. While Mrs. Bristow soothed the panic-stricken birds, the sandy-haired recruiter wagged a chiding finger.

"God help you, Max, if Hannah learns you left her darlings unattended."

"Oh!" said Max, reddening. He hurried over to the wicker basket where the couple had arranged the goslings upon a mound of folded laundry. Max made a quick head count and breathed a sigh of relief. "I'm sorry, Nigel," he said. "I was only gone a couple of minutes."

"And presumably that was long enough for this irascible fellow to give himself a phosphorescent makeover." The middle-aged man sighed and scooped Honk up into his hands.

"No, he did that while I was here," explained Max. Despite Max's hasty cleaning, the gosling was still glowing, the oil's effect even more apparent in the fading daylight.

Nigel and his wife exchanged bemused glances.

"The Workshop is on campus!" said Max, changing the subject. "Here visiting Rasmussen. That's why I left—to see if they had any news of the outside world."

"There will be many visitors over the next few days, Max," said Nigel, frowning. "I assumed you knew this."

"Don't tell me the witches are coming, too," moaned Max, but Nigel shook his head.

"No," he said. "Not the witches. After all that happened last year, the witches are forbidden on these grounds. Are you certain Ms. Richter hasn't spoken to you? I know she had been intending to."

"Nobody tells me anything," said Max. "According to Bella-grog, things are on a need-to-know basis, and apparently I don't need to know."

Nigel looked thoughtfully at Max. Placing Honk back in the basket, he turned to his wife. "Emily, would you take these little ones back to Hannah's nest? Max and I need to have a chat."

Once Max had promised to put on a sweater and pay a visit to the Bristow's cottage, Emily kissed her husband, hefted the basket, and strode off with a swish of her skirt.

All around Max and Nigel, people were beginning to gather up their things—saws, hammers, spades—as the smell of cooking wafted across the grounds. Max and Nigel strolled against the tide of hungry workers, out toward the windy bluff that over-looked the Atlantic. As they approached, Max saw a lone figure kneeling at the base of a marble statue.

The statue, like countless other decorations and even buildings, was a new addition to Rowan's campus. With all the activity of the preceding months, Max had not yet stopped to look at it. The statue was of a man, tall and bearded, standing upon a rough pedestal of black granite. Despite the majesty of cold marble and the figure's scholarly robes, the subject had a feral, unkempt appearance. His hair was tangled, his beard was uncombed, and his strong hands seemed almost to rend his book rather than cradle it. Max thought he looked like Poseidon, as huge and wild as the sea.

"It's beautiful, Greta," said Nigel, stopping to appreciate the looming work. The kneeling woman did not turn, but kept her attention on the pedestal's bronze plaque. Her navy blue robes told Max that she was a Mystic of middling rank. Her hands betrayed her age, but the bronze plaque revealed nothing. It was blank.

"Is that you, Nigel?" croaked the Mystic.

"It is," he said, "but don't let me interrupt you."

"Nonsense," said the old woman, consulting her notes. "He's almost finished. . . ."

The Mystic spread her fingers and whispered beseeching words of transformation. The bronze began to churn and bubble, and as the sun's final rays sank into the west, elegant letters were raised in the thick metal. Leaning closer, Max saw a familiar name emerge.

ELIAS BRAM
1598–1649

With a grunt, the Mystic rose slowly to her feet and stood on tiptoe to pat the statue's foot. Gathering up her things, she nodded a polite hello to Nigel and Max and came to stand by them so she could appraise her gleaming creation in its entirety. She gave a sudden cackle, a gleeful fit of artistic satisfaction.

"Handsome devil, isn't he?" she said, winking at them. Bidding the pair good night, the old Mystic hobbled back toward the Manse, taking one of the garden paths and swinging her lantern like a girl.

Once the woman had gone, Nigel looked at Max with a decidedly boyish, mischievous expression. "Last one up's a sorry loser!" he exclaimed, and dashed toward the statue in an attempt to heave himself onto the massive base.

Max did not join Nigel in this game but merely watched. He admired the man's determination, but it was a mortifying spectacle. There were pitiful leaps, hoarse curses, and several agonizing moments when Nigel's meager arms failed him at the pivotal instant. Eventually, Nigel simply clung to the granite, occasionally kicking his legs like a dying frog.

"Would you like a hand?" Max offered.

"If you insist," gasped Nigel.

Knitting his fingers together, Max boosted him up. Seconds later, the two were seated on the far side of the statue, their backs resting against the stone drapery of Bram's robes. Breathing heavily, Nigel fished for a handkerchief and mopped his brow.

"Ah." He exhaled, scanning the tranquil sea. "A bit trickier than I'd imagined, but we're up and I was first! You may have youth and vigor, Max, but it will never be a match for age and treachery!"

"Please," said Max, rolling his eyes. "But, Nigel, should we be sitting on this thing? I mean, Greta just finished it."

"What stuff!" scoffed Nigel, refolding his handkerchief.

"I'm disappointed in you, Max. Every student should know that statues are meant for sitting. If we're to endure their terrible old faces leering at us, the least they can do is offer shade or a comfortable perch."

Max grinned. "Should we write our names on it?" he asked, twisting to examine the spotless marble.

"A noble impulse," said Nigel. "But for the moment, we shall stick to sitting."

Settling in against the cold stone, Max folded his arms for warmth. The moon was rising. It was nearly full, its pale light shining on a lone seagull skimming over the ocean's swell. As if reading Max's thoughts, Nigel spoke in his warm English tenor:

"The moon has a face like the clock in the hall;
  She shines on thieves on the garden wall,
  On streets and fields and harbour quays,
  And birdies asleep in the forks of the trees."

"I've heard that before," said Max. "But I can't remember when."

"It's from a nursery rhyme by Robert Louis Stevenson," said Nigel. "One of my favorites."

"My mother used to read that to me," said Max. "Or at least I think she did." He searched memories of his old house in Chicago and those quiet evenings when he was burrowed in his bed. It seemed a lifetime ago.

"Yes, well, I'll be reading it to many a young one," said Nigel.

"What do you mean?" asked Max. Nigel and Emily Bristow had no children.

"Career change, Max," said Nigel. "I'm sorry to say my recruiting days are over. I'm going to be a teacher. Given how things stand, it looks as though the refugees will be permanent residents here, and thus Emily and I have volunteered for one of the kindergarten classes."

"But if you're doing that," Max wondered aloud, "who will be testing Potentials?"

Nigel smiled, but there was an unmistakable tinge of sadness in his eyes. "No one, Max," he replied. "No one will be recruiting or testing Potentials. Those days have passed. We lost the war and must live by Astaroth's rules."

Max sat in confused silence. Of course, he knew they had lost; none knew better. But he hadn't considered all of the implications. Rowan had spent the past six months furiously rebuilding, and it had been Max's assumption—his expectation—that they would resume the great struggle against Astaroth when they were able.

"And what are those rules?" he asked quietly.

"Oh, I've only been told the ones pertinent to me," said Nigel. "No more recruiting; no leaving Rowan until our borders are finalized and we're given permission. That's why it's important that someone speak to you before . . ."

Nigel appeared nervous, tapping his fingers against his knee and glancing at his watch.

"I can't imagine what you went through last spring," he said at last. "A boy your age having to fight alone. It is because of you that Rowan has even had the opportunity to rebuild. We owe you a debt we can never repay."

"Nigel," laughed Max. "Out with it, already! What are you getting at?"

Swatting irritably at an insect, Nigel took a deep breath. His words were slow and deliberate. "Max, there will be a contingent of demons arriving here tomorrow—"

"What?" exclaimed Max, sitting up.

"Let me finish," Nigel pleaded, his voice calm and taut. "This is precisely why I wanted to speak with you. Max, I love you like a son. But you have a terrible temper, and tomorrow is not the time for it."

Max glared at Nigel. Wary of illustrating the man's point, he slowly willed himself to stillness.

Nigel nodded appreciatively and continued. "The demons will be arriving tomorrow, led by one of Astaroth's lieutenants— one called Prusias. They are coming as a token of goodwill—"

Max could not resist a scornful laugh.

"As a token of goodwill," repeated Nigel, ignoring the interruption. "And to formalize the ongoing terms of our arrangement. They have promised to treat us with respect, and we have done likewise. Do you understand me, Max? This is how peace is made."

Silence ensued, and the two sat while the waves lapped at the beach below. Max was angry—he found the idea of hosting demons insufferably repugnant—but he was curious, too. It seemed tomorrow would bring answers to many of his questions. He pondered this until Nigel blurted something that Max did not catch.

"What?" Max asked.

"Emily and I are going to have a baby," repeated Nigel. He spoke more slowly this time, but the words still tumbled out. "In March. You're one of the first to know."

"Congratulations," said Max, unsure what else to say. It was an unexpected shift in their conversation.

"Yes, well, it changes one's outlook on life and one's priorities," said Nigel. "Like any parent, I want my child to have the best chance she can have—a chance to make her own way and survive in the new way of things."

"So you're having a girl?" asked Max.

"Well, we don't know yet, of course," said Nigel, smiling. "But Emily has her hunches. Can you imagine a baby in our house, Max? It will be such a precious thing! Emily is beside herself, and I . . . well, I didn't know if we'd ever be so lucky."

Nigel's appeal resonated more powerfully than anything Ms. Richter could have said. Max's initial interpretation had been wrong; this was not a cowardly plea for meek compliance but the protective instinct of an expectant father.

"I'll behave myself," said Max solemnly.

"Thank you," replied Nigel, allowing himself to exhale. He patted Max's hand before peering casually over the edge of the pedestal. "You know, I've never really been one for heights. . . ."

"Nigel, we're six feet off the ground."

"Yes, well, there's the precipice, too," he argued, gesturing impatiently at the nearby bluff. "A fellow could trip and roll right off the edge. They'd probably never even find the body."

Max thought it would take quite a determined roll to traverse the twenty feet of flat, manicured lawn. Hopping down from the statue, he turned and offered a hand to his friend.

"Not that you need it," said Max.

"Quite right." Nigel sniffed. "It's simply a civilized courtesy."

"How did you ever pass physical training?" asked Max.

"Never underestimate the power of a well-chosen bribe."

Once Nigel was deposited safely on the ground, the two rounded the statue and gazed upon the Manse once again. All of its windows were alight, a remarkably cheery sight considering the smoldering hulk it had been months before.

"Ah," said Nigel. "Supper beckons, and you shall marvel at the bizarre combinations Emily's eating these days. Pork chops and chocolate; ice cream with mustard. You'd think we're having a hag."

"You go on ahead," said Max. "I'm going to stay for a bit."

"Are you sure?" asked Nigel. "The 'Bottomless Pit' passing up a meal!"

"I'll come in soon," said Max. "Just ask my dad to put something aside for me."

"Will do," Nigel promised. "I'm glad we had this talk, Max."

Max nodded and waved good night. As Nigel's footsteps faded, Max realized that the campus was still, and he became intensely conscious of the crashing surf, the creaking trees, and the dry leaves that skittered across the flagstone paths. He glanced at Old Tom, its gables, walls, and tower still cloaked in secrecy. Sighing, Max thrust his hands deep in his pockets and turned to face the statue once again.

The marble planes of Bram's face were sharp, the set of his jaw defiant. It occurred to Max that he knew only the broadest strokes of the man's history: the Last Ascendant who sacrificed himself at the Siege of Solas. Rowan's teachers spoke of Bram with such reverence that Max thought of him not as a man, but as an idea whose abstract benevolence was akin to St. Nick or the tooth fairy.

The figure before him did not look benevolent, however. He looked dangerous. Max was aware that his roommate, David Menlo, believed Bram to be the greatest Sorcerer in human history. While Bram's powers may have been vast, they had not been enough to keep him from Astaroth's reach. When Solas fell, the Demon had spent his remaining energies consuming him.

Max felt an unexpected surge of affection for the stern visage. He thumped the pedestal with his fist and glanced up at the towering figure.

"I'll bet you wouldn't welcome a demon to your door," he whispered.

The statue stared stoically ahead, and Max sighed. The marble positively gleamed in the clear evening, and Max rocked back on his heels to stare at the moon. It had risen nearly to its zenith and seemed to hover directly above the campus, shining a spotlight on Rowan and its quaint little doings.

"The moon has a face, indeed."

~ 2 ~

AN EMPTY BED

When Max finally returned to the Manse, it was well past midnight. He was not alone as he wound slowly through the orchard; a lymrill accompanied him. While Max mused on demons, his charge bounded ahead, thrusting its broad snout into the dewy underbrush.

The lymrill's gait was peculiar on flat ground, akin to a badger's rolling waddle. Its powerful hindquarters and enormous claws suggested that it made its home in trees or rocky burrows. Although it could not speak like some other charges, the lymrill was an intelligent creature that communicated by means of its mewling calls, bushy tail, and coppery quills. A sharp ridge of these quills lined its back, serving not only as a daunting defense, but also as a telltale indicator of mood. At the moment, they were not smoothed into a lustrous, tranquil coat but had flared in bristling protest. Max saw their points glinting beneath a street-lamp as the animal prowled impatiently.

"You wanted to come, Nick, so don't whine," said Max.

Nick mewled and began digging his claws into a nearby flower bed.

"Stop!" hissed Max, shielding himself from a shower of dirt and stems. "Those were just planted!"

Soil was churned and flowers flew until Max succumbed and fished a metal bar from his pocket.

"Last one," he said, offering the small ingot on his palm. The lymrill abruptly ceased his mischief and padded close so that he could retrieve the treat as gently as a spaniel. Nick's otterlike face relaxed into a more agreeable expression, and his whiskers trembled with pleasure as he settled back on his haunches and swallowed the bar down.

It was a remarkable thing to watch a lymrill eat. While Nick hunted vermin with a sudden, insatiable ferocity, he was consid-erably more delicate with the minerals and alloys required by his unique metabolism. Metal objects were typically swallowed whole rather than chewed—even objects as large as an antique, and apparently expensive, toy train. How Nick managed to swallow these items, much less digest them, was a mystery. But there was little doubt that the metals made their way into each tooth, claw, and quill. These parts of his anatomy were harder than steel and made an adult lymrill truly formidable.

But nature's gifts were bittersweet. Throughout history, scholars and alchemists had hunted the lymrill to near extinction, eager to discover and exploit the composition of its pelt. To Max's

knowledge, Nick was the last of his kind—and thus Max felt justified in spoiling him.

Historically, Rowan's charges—mystical creatures entrusted
to student care—were confined to the Sanctuary and only permitted beyond its borders on very special occasions. Since the
Siege, however, this policy had been relaxed. It was no longer
unusual to find a faun dozing in the Manse's gardens or a gruff
talking hare monopolizing tables in the Bacon Library. Nick's
motives—aside from a natural impulse to be where he should
not—involved Max's bed. It was a comfortable bed, and the
lymrill had come to prefer its soft mattress and downy comforter
to his arboreal habitat. Once he was placed upon it, Nick took
great pleasure in tunneling beneath the blankets and wriggling
about until he reached the footboard and plunged into sleep.

Nick was eager for that bed and, indeed, so was Max. The
pair crept inside the Manse's doors, crossed the dim foyer, and
wound their way up the spiral staircase to the dormitories. When
they arrived at room 318, Max unlocked the door and ushered
Nick inside with a stern directive to be quiet.

He needn't have bothered. David Menlo was still awake.
Max's roommate was on the lower level of the large, domed
observatory, the top of his blond head just visible amid piled
books, beakers, and arcane contraptions.

Peering up at the room's glass dome, Max noted that the view
had shifted to exhibit the night skies of the southern hemisphere.
Hydra twinkled, remote and beautiful, from beyond the curving
glass. Threads of golden light connected the constellation's stars
until they gradually unraveled and faded, only to reappear and
illuminate Leo moments later.

While Max loved the observatory and its tranquil beauty, he
knew better than to think it had been magically configured for

him. In fact, he had not even been present when the room had been reconfigured following the Siege. It had happened one day over the summer while Max was doing carpentry down the hall. He happened to poke his head inside what had been a charred mess and had found David sitting comfortably by the fire, sipping coffee from his favorite thermos. The room had been restored down to the last detail, from the octagonal table at its center to the gleaming armoires and luxuriant bookcases.

Max did not begrudge David's initiative to configure the room on his own; he used the room and its singular qualities in ways that Max did not. There had been many nights when Max awoke from a dream to find his roommate standing upon the central table, studying the dome's wheeling contents as though they were a puzzle, a cipher containing secrets great and terrible.

Walking down to the lower level, Max saw that David's attention was not on the heavens but on a boiling beaker. David's brow was furrowed, and the whole of his being seemed to focus on the mixture, which issued a weak trickle of white smoke. Unblinking, he plucked several red flower petals from a small wooden box.

A sudden, brilliant flash of light caused Max to yelp and Nick to bolt back up the stairs. Crowning billows of thick crimson smoke now poured forth from the beaker. They spread throughout the room with a noxious odor that made Max gag.

"Phew!" he cried, snatching an atlas and waving the vapors away. "David, what are you doing?"

"Testing something," replied David distractedly as he scrawled in his notebook. "It's late. I thought you were sleeping at your dad's." Glancing up, he caught sight of Nick peering down from the top stair and pawing at his nose. David put down his pen and waved his hand; the spreading smoke condensed into a stream and funneled into the fireplace and out of the room.

Collecting Nick, Max approached the table, stepping gingerly past innumerable manuscripts and scrolls and the forbidden grimoires that David had a tendency to borrow. Settling the lymrill onto a leather chair, Max leaned close to peer at David's concoction.

Within the beaker frothed a rose-colored liquid, which surged and splashed against the glass. Tiny golden bubbles rose in double and triple helixes, evaporating with a hiss that sounded very nearly like a human sigh.

"What is it?" Max asked, leaning closer.

"Oh, a pet project," replied David, plugging a stopper in the potion and removing it from the burner. He placed the beaker next to several others that contained similar contents—roiling liquids that ranged in hue from vivid scarlet to murky plum.

"So it's a secret!" teased Max.

"If you like," sighed David. "It gets tedious having to explain oneself all the time. Between Ms. Richter, Kraken, Boon, and every other self-proclaimed Mystic on this campus, I'm asked questions all day long. I hope you don't mind if I come here for a break from questions, Max. I need it."

Max glanced at his friend. It was not like David to brush him off. There was affection in David's tone—a weary plea for understanding—but an unmistakable impatience simmered beneath.

"No worries," said Max. "I won't even ask you what those are. . . ."

He gestured toward a small mound of red flowers that lay upon a rumpled cloth. He had never seen such flowers before—on campus or even within a textbook. They had seven bloodred petals that were veined with gold and spiraled out from a black pistil. Max reached to touch one.

David lurched to his feet. "Don't!" he cried, snatching the flowers away.

A wave of searing heat issued from David's body as though a furnace door had been opened. Papers blew from the tabletop, their edges curling as they floated slowly down to the floor.

Max froze as though he'd been caught plundering a cookie jar. For a moment, he simply stared at his roommate. David appeared equally shocked and leaned heavily against the table, refusing to meet Max's gaze. After several seconds, he regained his composure. With careful, deliberate motions, David folded the cloth over the crimson flowers and placed the bundle in the wooden box. Closing its latch, he cleared his throat.

"I'm working on things, Max, and some of my projects can be very dangerous. Please don't touch anything unless I specifically say it's okay."

Max stood tall and glowered down at his roommate. "I'm not a little kid, David. And I live here, too."

David's face fell, and he gave Max an imploring look. "No, no, that's not what I meant," he said meekly. "Of course this is your room—our room." Frazzled, he began gathering up armfuls of singed papers, diagrams, and books. An awkward silence ensued until David slid a final sheaf of notes into a tattered volume entitled *Seeking Lazarus*.

"I'm sorry, Max," he mumbled. "I know how that must have sounded."

"It's okay," said Max, trying to shrug it off. He placed another log in the fireplace and joined Nick in the leather armchair.

The beakers and tubes were stowed in a velvet-lined case and, along with the boxed flowers, were placed in David's enchanted backpack. Max stroked Nick's quills, trying to remember and catalog the many questions that plagued his mind.

"Ah," said David, easing into the opposite chair and swinging his legs onto the ottoman. "I have messages for you. They were slipped under the door."

From the pocket of his cardigan, David retrieved a crumpled wad of notes.

"Who are they from?" asked Max wearily.

"Hmm," said David, scanning the folded pieces of stationery. "I believe Julie, Julie, Julie . . . and, yes, one more from Julie. Unless Connor has also taken to signing his notes with little pink hearts. Would you like me to read them to you?"

"No!"

David handed over the notes, and Max read them, blushing, while his roommate grinned and stoked the fire.

"And what does Julie have to say?" asked David.

"Nothing," said Max hastily. "Er, she wants to meet us for breakfast tomorrow morning."

"Yes, I'm sure I figure prominently in her plans," said David mildly. "But I won't be able to join you."

"What do you have to do?"

David said nothing but glanced at several drawings lying on the table. Max saw that these were a variety of summoning circles—intricate, powerful diagrams used when summoning malevolent spirits. Max had seen David use them before and knew such things were incredibly dangerous.

"David, have you been summoning . . . things?"

David's pale blue eyes flicked over to meet Max's. "You don't need to worry about me, Max," he said coolly.

"But demons are dangerous," cautioned Max.

David glanced at him as if mildly amused. Pulling back the sleeve of his sweater, he revealed the stump where his right hand used to be. Astaroth had taken that hand—devoured it—to punish David at their first meeting. Laying the remainder of his limb on the armrest, David stared at the soft, puckered skin of the wound and sighed.

"I know very well that demons can be dangerous. I also happen to think they are profoundly misunderstood."

"I see," said Max, shifting Nick's heavy body to his other leg. "And so Connor being possessed last year and nearly killing you was just a big misunderstanding."

"Don't be ridiculous," said David, waving off the sarcasm. "I just mean the idea of demons as terrifying bogeymen is a fairly modern misconception and gets us nowhere."

"But you said once that even imps were demons and that—"

"I know what I said," interrupted David testily. "My point was not to 'demonize' them but to warn Connor that even an imp may possess abilities of which he should be aware. I assume you realize that the very term *demonize* illustrates my point."

"Which is?"

"Because demons are different from us, people have tended to classify them as a generic family of creatures that should be reviled, feared, avoided, or even worshipped," he said. Clearing his throat, he spoke with the stentorian gravitas of a Roman orator. "They shall emerge from the sea, with skins of metal and the limbs of beasts, and we shall appease them as gods returned. . . ."

"Do demons really have skins of metal?" asked Max, leaning forward.

"No," said David, smiling. "That's how the Aztecs described Cortés and the conquistadors when they arrived at Tenochtitlán. The Aztecs mistook the Spaniards' armor for their skin, and the horses—the Aztecs had never seen horses—for the lower part of the soldiers' bodies."

Max blinked. "David, what do conquistadors have to do with anything?"

"Before we project all our fears on the idea of demons

inhabiting our world, Max, I think we should try to understand them," said David, settling deeper into his chair and sipping from his thermos. "Objective understanding—without blind prejudice and ignorant stereotypes."

Max began to argue, but David did not seem to hear him. Whenever he drifted into one of his quiet reveries, David's soft, round features assumed the contemplative expression of a much older person.

"Life is a competition," he said softly. "Whether you believe it's a Darwinian struggle for resources or a spiritual proving ground makes little difference to our problem. The fact is that another species—an intelligent, very powerful species—has taken control of this world. You can choose to view them as fiends from the pit, celestial wanderers, or just another iteration of Cro-Magnons edging out the Neanderthals."

"Are you going to fight them?" asked Max.

David fixed Max with a stare that offered very little in the way of an answer. Easing up from his chair, he swung his back-pack onto his shoulder and shuffled upstairs.

"Good night, Max," he said wearily. "Be sure to keep your promise to Nigel. Tomorrow is very important."

Max grunted good night and heard the familiar sound of sliding rings as David drew shut the curtains around his bed. Yawning, Max scooped up Nick and lugged the heavy animal to his own bed.

It was only when Nick was snoring against the footboard and Max was sinking into sleep that David's parting comments finally registered: *Keep your promise to Nigel.*

Max had not mentioned the promise to David.

Slipping quietly out of bed, Max crept to the brass railing and stared across the room to where David's bed was hidden behind its dark curtains. Suspicions rose and fell like the ocean's cold swell. Max squinted at the summoning papers below, scripted in David's spidery hand.

Max had seen demonic possession firsthand. His best friend, Connor Lynch, had succumbed to it the previous year. While he knew a lowly imp could hardly possess a Sorcerer so learned and powerful as David, Max also knew that his roommate did not bother with lowly imps. David was primarily interested in the Spirits Perilous, those ancient, immensely powerful entities that constituted a sort of royalty among their kind.

Astaroth was one such being. Perhaps Prusias was, too. . . .

You're a member of the Red Branch, Max reminded himself. *You promised Cooper that you'd protect David from any danger. It's your sworn responsibility. . . .*

Max reflected on this sentiment and felt his cheeks grow hot with shame. He scratched at the tattoo on his wrist and glanced across the room at David's bed. Sleeping behind those curtains was one of the kindest, gentlest souls Max had ever known. He would not reach out to David because of any oath or assignment; he would offer his help because David was his friend.

Max padded along the curving walkway of the upper level. The room seemed cold, and the only sound was the soft ticking of David's clock. As Max drew near the curtains, he paused and became aware that his heart was thumping wildly in his chest. For several awful seconds, he imagined that beyond the curtains was not David's sleeping form, but Astaroth's white face smiling in the darkness. The hairs on Max's neck stood on end. Steeling himself, he parted the heavy curtains.

"Sorry to wake you, but—" Max stopped and caught his breath.

There was no demon lurking in the darkness, but there was no David, either. The bed was empty, the pillows cool to the touch, and hardly a crease marred the silver moons embroidered on the blanket.

~ 3 ~

THE HAGLINGS

The next morning, Max yawned and picked halfheartedly at a bowl of congealing oatmeal. He had hardly managed any rest the previous evening, instead lying for hours and straining his ears for any indication of David's return. There had been none. When Max had finally drifted off, his sleep had been plagued by the same dream that had haunted him for years. While he replayed its details in his mind, he gradually became aware that something was bobbing before him.

"You are getting sleepy, very sleeeeeeeeeeeepy," said a coy voice with an Australian accent.

"Huh?" said Max, blinking at the spoon that was swinging before his eyes like a hypnotist's pendulum.

"Really, Max," sighed Julie Teller, putting down the spoon. "You're turning into a zombie. Here I've been prattling away about tonight's bonfire and the start of classes, and all you can manage is 'Huh?'"

"I'm sorry," he said, reaching for a carafe of coffee. "I didn't really get any sleep."

Julie scooted around the dining table to sit next to him on the bench. A smile shone on her tan, freckled face. Her sparkling blue eyes looked at Max attentively, and she took up his oatmeal in her hands. Steam began to rise again from the bowl, and in a few seconds it was piping hot.

"There," she said, setting it back down. "Now your breakfast's edible, and you can tell me why you're not getting any sleep. I'd love to think it's just sweet dreams of your fabulous girlfriend, but I have a sneaking suspicion that it's something else. . . ."

Max debated whether to share anything about David's mysterious experiment and odd disappearance. He decided against it, reasoning that he needed a great deal more information before he started any rumors, and if he told Julie, the rumors would spread like wildfire. She meant well, but Julie reveled in gossip—from the salacious to the mundane—and often used her position as Rowan's photographer to feed her inquisitive nature. If she knew that David was off on secret errands, Julie was liable to set up a stakeout.

"You know me," he said. "Just excited for class to start."

"I'll bet," said Julie. "Oh! That reminds me." She reached across the table and fished through her bag for a pair of envelopes. From the official stationery, Max saw they were class schedules.

"I picked this up for you," she said, handing one to Max.

It had already been opened. "I got into Honors Devices, so it's going to be tricky, but I think we can have lunch together outside Old Tom on Wednesdays and Fridays."

Max glanced at his class schedule. It was handwritten—all of the school's computers and networks had been destroyed during the Siege. From a technology point of view, Rowan had essentially been placed in the nineteenth century.

"Hmmm," he said. "Chemistry, Applied Mathematics, Conjurations and Enchantment, something called the Art, Literature, and History of Empire, Devices I, and . . . what the heck is this?"

"That's what I was going to ask you," she said quietly. "I've never heard of that before and am a little curious why you're listed as the teacher."

Max peered closely at the paper, his eyes zeroing in on his name written in smooth navy ink:

ADVANCED COMBAT TECHNIQUES—LEVEL X
MAGGIE ROOM 222—M/W/F—16:00–17:30
INSTRUCTOR: MAX MCDANIELS, RED BRANCH

"I don't know anything about this," he breathed.

"Well, the registrar does," said Julie. "I tried to switch my schedule to take it. She laughed and told me that every single Agent has already tried to register. Apparently, I'm not even qualified to be on the waiting list."

"This doesn't even make sense," said Max, craning his neck to see if any teachers were present. Several tables over, he spied Miss Boon breakfasting with Agent Cooper. He and Julie hurried past the thick stone pillars and the bustling tables of students and families. As they approached the pair, Max saw that Miss Boon and Cooper were not alone. A gray-brown hare was on the table, holding a pair of spectacles as he stood on his hind legs and harangued them. Miss Boon's expression was polite and attentive, but Cooper's cold blue eyes were wandering.

"Do the math, you silly girl!" exclaimed the hare in an imposing Scottish burr. "We need more scribes. I need a hundred more scribes this very afternoon! I've got all the Highland hares chipping in—even the bumbling clans—but you know perfectly well that our paws aren't well suited for—"

"Tweedy," said Miss Boon calmly. "You know that I'm as sympathetic to the situation as anyone, but I need to clear your request with the Director."

"Fiddlesticks!" cried Tweedy, hopping up and down in exasperation. "And exactly when can one make an appointment with her? I've submitted dozens—hundreds—of reports, suggestions, and queries to her office without receiving a single response!"

"I'm sure you have," said Cooper, maintaining a straight face.

"Is that sarcasm, you monosyllabic buffoon?" retorted the hare, turning to glare at the Agent's pale, disfigured face. "I wouldn't expect *you* to understand, but I thought Hazel was a woman of education and refinement. . . ."

For a second or two, Max thought the defiant hare's mouth might have gotten him into serious trouble. But Cooper's scarred features merely writhed into a small, uneven grin. Pulling his black knit cap over the shiny burns on his head, the Agent eased up from the table and winked at Miss Boon.

"Me go now," he said evenly, stepping aside so Max and Julie could take the open seats next to the young Mystics instructor.

"I'll see you later, William," sighed Miss Boon as Tweedy raised his paw to make another point.

"Continuing," said the hare briskly, beginning to pace. "Even with Mystics, I've calculated that we still need approximately five hundred additional volunteers working in twelve-hour shifts to have a chance—a *chance,* mind you—of making the merest dent in the job."

"What job is that, Tweedy?" asked Julie.

"Oh, nothing important," retorted the hare, bristling. "Only salvaging the accumulated knowledge of some five millennia. But why should we worry ourselves that Proust and Hume and Aristotle and Archimedes are all fading into oblivion? I'm shocked that Agent Cooper isn't more concerned over the imminent demise of his pulpy spy novels or whatever godforsaken trash occupies his leisure hours."

"Tweedy," snapped Miss Boon. "That's enough."

"What are you talking about?" asked Max.

"This!" shrieked the hare, pushing a thick book on musical theory toward them. "I'm talking about this, boy!"

Max scanned a page of dense paragraphs and charts. It appeared to be comparative analysis of string instruments and the sound frequencies they produced.

"I don't get it," said Max, looking at Julie, who merely shrugged.

"The print, the print!" cried Tweedy, pointing with his paw.

Max saw that the print was a mild gray on the clean white paper, as though it had been bleached in the sun. Looking closer, he saw that some sections were, in fact, difficult to read.

"Maybe it's just old," suggested Max, trying to calm the irate hare.

"Idiots!" shrieked Tweedy. "I'm surrounded by idiots! I'll have you know, young man, that this is my personal copy. This book has been meticulously maintained, and two short weeks ago, its print was as rich and fine a black as any in creation. Now it's fading by the day!"

"Did you spill something on it?" asked Julie soothingly.

"All the books are fading!" thundered the hare. "With the

exception of handwritten manuscripts, everything is vanishing! Every scrap of paper that's seen the business end of a printing press is fading to little more than wee wisps of ink! When I think of the formulas and musical scores and equations and reproductions— Oh! It's enough to make a hare weep!"

When it dawned on Tweedy that Shakespeare—beloved, worthy Shakespeare—might also fade to indistinguishable blank volumes, he began to hyperventilate.

Miss Boon stroked the trembling hare's fur. "You'll have your volunteers," she promised. "I'll find them, or I'll see if David Menlo can brainstorm a better spell to quickly copy the books. At the very least, we know you've memorized Shakespeare for us."

The hare's small paw patted her hand appreciatively. "That's true," he acknowledged. "The Bard is safe. Thank you, Hazel—I knew I could count on you."

Clutching his book to his tufted chest, Tweedy hopped down from the table. Miss Boon watched him go, her mismatched blue and brown irises following the hare's hurried progress out of the hall. When he began bounding up the steps, she pursed her lips and rubbed her temples.

"Sometimes . . . sometimes I wish things could just be how they used to be." She sighed and glanced warily at Max and Julie and the schedules they clutched. "What can I do for you two?"

"Well, you're my adviser," said Max slowly, "and I have something funny on my schedule. It says here that I'm teaching a class?"

"Dear Lord," she moaned, running her fingers through her short brown hair. "Max, this is all my fault. I was supposed to give you this last week. Things have been so absurdly busy in preparation for tonight's events that it completely slipped my mind. Please accept my apologies. If it's any consolation, I don't think any significant preparation is involved—no syllabus or reading lists to compile. It's my understanding that the Agents simply want to study the techniques that you learned in the Sidh." She rummaged through the bag at her feet and produced a small stack of papers.

Max unfolded and read the first of several handwritten pages. It appeared to be an employment offer and a contract for services rendered.

Julie looked over his shoulder. "Max will be part of the faculty?" she asked.

"Yes," said Miss Boon. "If he chooses to accept."

"Can a C student be on the faculty?" asked Max, incredulous.

"You're not teaching physics, dear," said Miss Boon delicately.

"Why is he being paid in gold?" asked Julie, pointing at the final paragraph.

"What other currency would you suggest?" asked Miss Boon. "Cattle? Land? Wheat? Salt? You're aware, of course, that the very word *salary* stems from the age when soldiers were given an allowance of salt. . . . If Max would prefer another means of compensation, I can speak to the Director."

"What about plain old dollars?" inquired Max.

"And where do you intend to spend those?" retorted Miss Boon, cleaning her glasses. "The value of paper money is only as stable as the country that issues it, Max. And to my knowledge, there is no government of the United States. If I were you, I'd take the gold—managing a herd of cattle might be a headache."

"What if I don't want to teach a class?" asked Max.

Miss Boon shrugged. "Then I suppose you'll be assigned to physical training along with your classmates. It meets at six each morning."

Max promptly snatched up the pen near Miss Boon's teacup. "And so where exactly do I sign?"

"Bottom right."

"It's funny," said Max, carefully signing his name. "With everything that's happened, you wonder why we even bother with classes and school."

Miss Boon stiffened. Retrieving her pen from Max's hand, she rapped it once on the table and fixed him with a hard stare that made him sit up straight.

Her words arrived in a shrill staccato. "We 'bother' with classes and school because they mean civilization, Max McDaniels. Civilization. Don't you ever forget that. Now, if you'll excuse me, I have five hundred volunteers to find."

"I wonder if we should postpone tonight's bonfire," Julie mused.

Miss Boon stopped in midstride and spun on her heel. "No, Julie," she said. "It's important that the students have an opportunity to celebrate this evening. While I'm sure it will be lovely, you will have to enjoy it without Max's company. All teachers are required to attend a council following the feast."

"But that's not fair," protested Max.

"Welcome to the faculty, Agent McDaniels," said Miss Boon. "You'll find that being a teacher has many rewards, but an enviable social life is not one of them. Good day."

For several minutes, Max and Julie sat in silence, taking turns reading the letter and its accompanying details. Apparently, a respected family of domovoi—obsessive, gnomish creatures—would oversee all payments, weights, and measures. They had been handling such tasks for centuries and, despite the reputations of their distant cousin, the carefree leprechaun, domovoi accountants had an impeccable reputation for careful fiscal management.

"I forgot to ask about vacation," said Max, trying to cheer up Julie.

"The only good thing about this," she said, trying to manage a smile, "is that you'll be flush with funds. I'd rather we had a dance, though. I mean, I know someone has to show up at this council or whatever it is, but Miss Boon didn't say how long someone had to be there, right? Maybe someone could sneak away at, say, ten o'clock and come dance with his sweetie?"

"Absolutely," said Max.

"Good answer," said Julie. A genuine smile had returned to her face, and she blew Max a kiss goodbye as she left for her morning chores.

Grabbing a slice of pumpkin bread, Max chewed thoughtfully as he strode toward the kitchens. He had not seen his father the previous day and knew Scott McDaniels would be there—dicing, slicing, marinating, broiling, mashing, and baking in preparation for the evening's feast. As he walked, he noted just how chaotic the rebuilt Manse had become. The dining hall was teeming with people—nursing mothers, grandparents, students, teachers, Agents, robed Mystics, and even the occasional faun. Max pushed through the swinging doors.

As he did so, he felt the door hit something. Whatever it was, it was small—the door gave only a brief shudder before continuing smoothly on its hinges. Peering inside, Max's heart nearly stopped when he saw a diapered toddler sprawled upon its back and weakly kicking its legs.

"Oh!" Max gasped, hurrying inside to help the child. As he knelt down, he saw his father's broad back hunched over the sink, where he was peeling potatoes. "Dad!" he cried. "Give me a hand—there's been an accident!"

"She's fine," said Mr. McDaniels evenly. He did not even bother to turn around. "Just make sure her mask hasn't fallen off," he added, reaching for another potato.

Still panicked, Max ignored his father and made to scoop up

the baby. An unexpectedly strong grip seized his finger, and as he hoisted the baby up, he found himself staring into an angry pair of black beady eyes.

It was a hagling.

The hagling couldn't have weighed more than ten pounds, but Max was taken aback by the creature's strength and determination. Pudgy gray arms flailed about, while a pair of three-toed feet bicycled furiously through the air. Its black hair had been gathered up into a pink-bowed topknot that rose like an antenna from a gourdlike head. As Max stared, the hagling's small eyes began to well with tears. It stopped its struggles and made a pitiful bawling sound while pawing weakly at the crude leather muzzle that had been fitted over its mouth.

"Poor thing," muttered Max, cradling the hagling against his chest and pulling at the tightly fitted mask so he could slide it past its peninsular chin. As he did so, he became aware that a number of dark little shapes had appeared in the doorway to the inner kitchen. A cluster of additional haglings stood there watching him. Some of the creatures were in diapers; others wore pinned towels, and two had forgone clothes entirely. All had been fitted with leather masks. They tottered closer as Max's hagling intensified its bawling and scrabbled miserably at the muzzle. It appeared to be choking.

"Dad," Max said angrily. "You think you could give me a hand?"

Mr. McDaniels put down his knife and turned just as Max wrenched the muzzle off.

"Max!" he exclaimed. "Don't!"

It was too late.

As soon as Max removed the muzzle, the hagling abruptly stopped its crying. Tiny, asymmetric features smiled to reveal a single sharp tooth that projected from its upper gums like an ivory can opener. With a bloodcurdling shriek, it launched itself at Max while the others converged like piranhas.

While Max staggered around the kitchen, he was vaguely aware of his father's shouts, the haglings' panting, and the jarring crash of broken crockery. The bulk of his attention, however, was focused on the sharp tooth that pecked about in a desperate attempt to draw blood. While the one hagling clung ferociously to his neck, the others had fastened themselves to his legs like barnacles or pushed against him as though trying to topple a tree. His father hurried over to help, but Mr. McDaniels slipped on a broken plate and crashed heavily to the floor. He shrieked as several of the haglings abandoned Max and swarmed over him like army ants.

"Oi!" bellowed a voice, thundering above the din.

The hagling at Max's neck froze while those at his feet promptly released him and scattered to the far corners of the room. With a sudden, violent jerk, the remaining hagling was wrenched off Max's chest. Recovering his breath, Max saw that Bellagrog was holding the little creature casually by the topknot. The hagling gnashed and spat at the enormous hag, but Bellagrog appeared far more concerned about Scott McDaniels. Extending the struggling hagling to an arm's length, Bellagrog grunted and heaved Mr. McDaniels to his feet.

"Sorry, love," she sighed, brushing away shards of broken plates. "You in one piece, Max?"

"I'm fine," said Max, keeping a wary eye out for any haglings he'd missed.

"Good, good," muttered Bellagrog. She pivoted on a thick-soled shoe to eye each of the cowering haglings. The one held captive by its topknot had stopped struggling and hung limp in sour-faced resignation.

"Line up!" bellowed Bellagrog. Instantly, they hurried from

their corners to form an orderly line against a wall of cupboards. Seven haglings arranged themselves by height, leaving a space in the middle, presumably reserved for the plump, unfortunate creature now swinging by her hair. Bellagrog raised her up so that the two were at eye level.

"Whatchoo doin', nipping at Max?" she demanded. "Whatchoo got to say?"

The hagling glanced sideways at Max. "I is sorry for nippin' at ya," she muttered in a hoarse undertone.

"Does that answer, Max?" inquired Bellagrog, fixing him with her bright crocodile eye.

"Of course," he replied. "Bel, please, put her down."

"Right, then," muttered the hag. With an unceremonious heave, she flung the hagling over her shoulder. As Max gaped, the little creature arced through the air and collided with a stack of serving trays piled atop a high shelf. Everything—shelf, trays, and hagling—crashed to the floor.

"Bel!" cried Max, but the hag merely waved him off and stepped squarely in his path as Max sought to rescue the little creature.

"Don't interfere," growled the hag. "Five's got to learn her manners."

From amid the pile of trays, the hagling's small face emerged. Flinging aside a tray, she adjusted her diaper and marched with a fierce, defiant expression to join the others against the wall. The hagling appeared not only uncowed, but also utterly unhurt.

"Whose children are they?" asked Max, breathing a sigh of relief.

"Mine!" exclaimed Bellagrog proudly. "Dropped this litter last night after I tucked in. Thought it was just a case of the midnight breezies, but I shoulda known better. Passed 'em in my sleep, and the adorable rascals almost got the best of me!

Almost . . . but I woke up and learned 'em, didn't I? And now here they are! Nine little haglings, pretty as pie!"

Max scanned the row of hideous, petulant-looking creatures that were staring insolently at him from behind their muzzles.

"Did you say nine haglings, Bel?" he said at last. "Um, I count only eight."

"Eight, nine—what's the difference?" Bellagrog shrugged, scratching at her belly. "Anyway, we gots to keep 'em muzzled till they learn how to mind their nippers."

"Er, should someone clean this up?" asked Mr. McDaniels, gesturing weakly at the scattered trays and shattered ceramics.

"You're sweet to offer, but let their auntie get it." Bellagrog sniffed. "It's Bea's job, love."

At that very moment, Bellagrog's sister arrived in the outer kitchen. Bea Shrope, affectionately known as Mum, had been working at Rowan for decades, but her tenure meant nothing to Bellagrog. While Max did not know all the intricacies of hag culture, he had divined that it was deeply hierarchical and that the grandeur of one's given name was a surefire indicator of status. Bea was no match for Bellagrog in girth or title, and thus the latter had ordered Mum about since arriving the previous year.

"What's Bea's job?" Mum asked, offering a hesitant, inquiring smile. Her small reddish eyes gazed about the room until they finally settled on the fidgeting haglings. "Oh no!" she gasped, nearly backing out of the room. "I didn't know you were expecting, Bel. . . ."

"Neither did I!" chortled the larger hag. "But here they are, and as their aunt, you've got responsibilities."

"They're your problem, Bel!" Mum shrieked, fleeing to the inner kitchen. "I have enough to do!"

"Hag Law, Bea!" roared Bellagrog, folding her stout arms like two crossed hams.

There was a curse and the sound of a wooden stool being shoved aside before Mum reappeared in the doorway. As though resigning herself to some unspoken duty, Mum now curtsied to the haglings, who tottered toward her and began to climb up her skirts until they were safely nestled in every serviceable nook and perch upon her person. As Mum's burden increased, her legs sagged and her nose inched ever closer to the ground until she could only waddle about like a bloated, crabby raptor.

"There," said Bellagrog with an approving nod. "Was that so hard? I got to have my hands free for my own responsibilities, don't I?"

Max's spirits sank with Mum's posture. "What about the, um, father?" he asked.

At this, Bellagrog's amusement escalated to hilarity. Even Mum wheezed with laughter, leaning against a nearby table. Max turned fire red.

"What?" he demanded. "What's so funny?"

Bellagrog wiped away a tear. "God bless ya, Max! I ain't laughed so hard in ages! Ya see, there ain't exactly no Mr. Shrope, love. Hags is all female."

"But," said Max, wrinkling up his nose, "then how do you . . ."

"Drop a litter?" asked Bellagrog. "It's one of nature's secrets. When haglings is needed, you just pop out a dozen or so."

"And they come . . . out . . . ready to walk and talk?" asked Mr. McDaniels.

"Sure do!" declared Bellagrog proudly. "This lot came out knowin' their knots, too! Almost had me all trussed up in a jiffy! Bwahahahaha!"

"Mum, have you ever had any haglings?" Max asked.

As soon as the words left his mouth, he knew he'd made a terrible mistake. Mum frowned and sank under the weight of her clinging nieces.

"No," she said quietly, unsnagging a hagling's tooth from her beaded necklace. "Not yet."

"Nature knows her business," said Bellagrog with brisk authority. "Some hags is breeders—others ain't."

"How many children do you have, Bel?" asked Mr. McDaniels.

"Couldn't say, couldn't say," replied Bellagrog, plucking at her chin. "Dropped maybe a hundred or so, but they gots a tendency to scatter. Guess I'm not the motherin' type. Shoot, I ain't even named but two!"

"But you just called that one 'Five,'" said Max's father.

"They all get numbers," murmured Mum. "Just numbers till they reach their teens, and then they gets named proper. It's bad luck otherwise."

In Max's opinion, simply being a hag seemed bad luck from the very beginning. Given their ravenous siblings and voracious parent, there seemed few safe harbors for the three-toed creatures clinging to Mum. He was amazed that any managed to reach their teens and earn a proper name.

"Anyway, enough blabbing," said Bellagrog, plucking up her clipboard of assignments. "I assume you're here for yer next job."

"Oh," said Max. "Not really—I mean, I've got a lot to think about. . . ."

Bellagrog turned to contemplate him with an expression of amused incredulity.

"You is having a joke with Bel, ain't ya?" she sniggered, cocking her head. "Surely, Handsome Max ain't trying to weasel out of chores the day of the big feast! Ain't no way my Max has got the guts to tell a working hag what dropped a dozen babies last night that he's 'got a lot to think about.'"

"There are only eight," Max reminded her.

"Who's counting!" roared Bel, ambling toward him and thumping the clipboard.

"Well, I just learned I'm going to be teaching a class," said Max hastily, thrusting his papers at the glowering hag. She snatched them from his hand, her red-rimmed eyes devouring the contents.

"What's that?" asked Mr. McDaniels. "You're going to be teaching?"

"Yup," said Max proudly. "A combat class for the Agents. And they're going to pay me in gold!"

Scott McDaniels whistled at this and held out his hand to Bellagrog for the sheets. The hag's face darkened as she read the final lines of the contract, and she practically flung them at Max's father.

"Off ya go, then," she said in a husky voice. "I ain't in charge of faculty jobs."

"Ho-ho!" crowed Mr. McDaniels, reading the letters. "My boy's a full-fledged professor!"

"I don't know about that," said Max, reddening. "I'll just be teaching some things I learned."

"Well, we got work to do, Max," huffed Bellagrog. "Mum, get the girlies in their aprons and teach 'em to roll out the dough. Scott, I need you on the lamb—let some of the refugees peel potatoes. A few of those grannies are right quick with a peeler."

"Will do, will do," said Scott McDaniels cheerfully. He washed his hands, looking over his shoulder to speak to Max. "Do me a favor today?" he asked. "Look in on Connor and make sure that he's planning on coming to the feast. David too. I've hardly seen 'em, and it'd be nice if they joined us."

"I will," said Max. "At least I'll make sure Connor comes. David's . . . pretty busy these days." Max shrugged at the weak excuse. "I'm going to head out, Dad."

As he left, Max took one last look around the kitchen. He sighed and wished Bob were there, hunched on his enormous stool and working culinary magic with his gnarled fingers. But Rowan's chief chef—a reformed Russian ogre—had yet to fully recover from injuries he'd sustained during the Siege. Eight little haglings staggering about with rolling pins were a poor replacement for Bob's calm, comforting presence.

Max glanced at his watch as he took the stairs. It was still midmorning, and these days Connor often slept past noon. Walking briskly down the dormitory corridor, Max decided against knocking on Connor's door and instead veered into his own room.

The observatory dome had brightened, and the stars were but faint glimmers against a smooth wash of middling blue. Max had not expected to find David, and he was proven correct. His roommate's bed had not been slept in—there was nothing to indicate David had been there since his mysterious disappearance.

Padding downstairs, Max kindled a fire and stifled a temptation to snoop through David's things. He couldn't help scanning the desk, however, and his eyes came to rest on a particularly imposing tome. He recognized the title—*The Conjuror's Codex of Summons* had gotten David into trouble before.

The carven lead cover rolled smoothly back on its hinge. Licking his thumb, Max paged through the heavy sheets of parchment, his eyes scanning a host of strange names and images. As he perused the pages, he saw that the headings were in rich black ink and the handwritten passages were not suffering from any of the curious fading that had so disturbed Tweedy. Max paused at a page detailing a marid before arriving at the desired entry.

"Know thy enemy," he whispered, staring at an intaglio print of Astaroth's emissary, Prusias.

The image of the demon stared back. The artist had depicted

him with pale cat's eyes that shone like a pair of gemstones against his dark, handsome features. Wealth surrounded Prusias; he sat upon heavy sacks that spilled coins at the seams. Fingering a jewel-encrusted goblet, the demon seemed to beckon at the viewer in invitation, gesturing at an empty chair across a laden table. Max wondered if the demon really looked like the barrel-chested, richly robed nobleman in the picture.

By sunset, he would know.

~ 4 ~

TEN SILK SAILS

The fire had faded to embers and Max was still reading. He slouched low in his warm chair, propping the grimoire against his knees as he studied accounts from those who had summoned Prusias throughout the ages. There were many. Prusias was apparently a great favorite among those seeking wealth. He was popular not only because he was skilled at procuring riches, but also because he was considered amiable. The writings portrayed a jesting, curious connoisseur of humanity and its wants. Unlike Astaroth, Prusias liked being summoned.

At the promised hour, I saw the demon through the eastern window—a dark figure among the white birches that Lizzie loves in springtime. Cloaked and hooded was Prusias, and I must confess that terror overwhelmed me when I first beheld the demon and witnessed his approach. My servant fled the room, and I was left alone within the witching circle that the stranger had drawn upon the floor. I feared the servant might wake my Lizzie and spoil all my loving plots, but he merely shut himself in the cellar, and there may he rot. At the demon's knock, the stranger rose and it was she who admitted him to my home. A fiend did I expect—a horror worthy of Dante! But it was a handsome lord who ducked beneath the doorway, and it was my pleasure to offer him such nourishment as I was able. At last I found courage enough to speak.

The demon listened most graciously, offering fair comment on each of my petitions. Jacob's house and lands shall be mine as should have been so when Father died. Prusias has promised them to me and further tells of silver spoons buried within its accursed nursery. These, too, shall be mine once Jacob and his harlot have been driven off. All this the demon hath pledged to do, though I dare not press about particulars.

Max read many such stories concerning petty feuds, coveted heirlooms, and bloodstained jewels plucked warm from an owner's hand. It was disturbing reading. Whenever Prusias was involved, wealth was reallocated in grisly fashion. Those who summoned him invariably praised his services and then labored for the remainder of their account to justify their good fortune.

There was one exception, however, and Max had returned to the passage several times. The entry was transcribed from a journal entry Elias Bram had made during the winter of 1647.

My researches point ever to Astaroth. I cannot find the Demon, but I know he is lurking. I see him in the page's smirk and hear him in the minstrel's words. His works are in the marketplace and on the theater stage. He is here. I have climbed the Tower and called to him with Orkney stones, but the Demon is strong and answers not my summons. I fish for Leviathan with naught but hook and string. Thus it was this evening that I turned to his vassal—a fiend called Prusias.

Blessings to Solomon, who hath plumbed these depths before me, for Prusias did arrive at the appointed hour, if not the appointed guise. The demon intended murder, which surprised me, for that is not his reputation among those who prize him. He did not take shape within the inscribed circle, but had concealed himself within my apprentice. Young Pieter had knocked and entered to place my supper upon the table when I saw the demon in the child's eyes. I grew angry at this trespass and drew Prusias forth. The demon hath learned a painful lesson. I am hopeful that the boy shall recover, but to harbor a Spirit Perilous is a grievous thing for one so young. Most pressing is how Prusias evaded the Terms of the Summoner, for in such things I do not err. A great evil is brewing.

Upon exiting the boy, the demon fought and I have broken him. He crawled within the circle and, for a fleeting moment, I did see his true form writhe upon the floor. But I blinked and thus beheld only a pagan king wrapped beneath a rich black cloak.

Under great pain, Prusias confessed that all beings of the Old Magic are bound by one or more geis—strictures to be obeyed lest their subject come to ruin. Astaroth's geis confines him to the truth. Should the Demon lie, it will be his undoing and the pleasures of this world shall be denied him. Therein resides our chance, and may Fortune favor us.

But my findings are bittersweet. Since boyhood, I have known that the Old Magic lives within me. Thus I, too, may be bound by geis. I must learn its nature lest I, unknowing, sow the seeds of my own destruction and leave great works unfinished.

As for Prusias, it was nearly dawn when I dismissed him. The wretched demon bared his teeth and dragged his limb, swearing vengeance before he became as a carrion bird and departed through the window. The morning was grim and gray, and I fear that every sleeper in the town below was cruelly wakened by the demon's cry. I pray no newborn heard that sound, for it was not a fitting welcome to the world.

"Hi there," said a voice behind Max.

Max yelped in surprise, then flung the horrific grimoire aside and leaped up from his chair. He whirled to see David Menlo standing on the observatory's lowest step.

"Oh no!" laughed David. "I'm sorry to surprise you." He stooped to retrieve the grimoire.

"It's okay, it's okay," said Max, waving him off and pacing about. "You just startled me."

"Reading up on Prusias?" inquired David.

"Yeah," said Max, recovering his breath. "It kind of spooked me."

"Understandable," said David. "But I'm happy that you've been learning about Old Magic and geis, Max. I'm sure you realize the importance."

"That I have a geis? Yeah, I thought of that," said Max.

"I have never wanted to pry about your time at Rodrubân," said David delicately, "but did Scathach or Lugh ever mention anything that sounded like it could be a geis?"

Max went to his dresser and fished through his top drawer for the brooch Scathach had given him when he had finally departed that strange castle in the Sidh. He ran his fingers over the clasp and the smooth ivory sun on its face and tried to recall the many days he'd spent there.

"I don't think so," he concluded. "I only saw Lugh once, and he barely spoke to me. Scathach and I spent lots of time together, but she never spoke about a geis. The only thing I can think of is what she said when I left."

"And what was that?"

"'Never forget you are the son of a king,'" said Max, remembering the inexplicable sadness with which Scathach had uttered those words.

"Hmmm," mused David, placing the grimoire on the table and sliding into the other chair.

"You'd think they'd be more specific if breaking a geis was a matter of life and death," Max laughed. David merely frowned and prodded weakly at the fire. "What time is it, anyway?"

"A little past four," replied David, rising to trudge back up the stairs.

"I have to get ready," muttered Max. He turned to peer at his face and unruly hair in the wardrobe's mirror. As he did, he spied David's reflection as the smaller boy stopped to stroke Nick. David's typically pale complexion now bordered on the cadaverous. Whatever Max's roommate was doing, it was taking a heavy toll.

"Are you coming to the feast?" asked Max, striving for a casual tone. "We can see Prusias together."

David sighed, padding off toward his bed. Max heard his voice from the railing above.

"I have seen Prusias, but he has not seen me. I prefer it that way. Give my best to your father and the others. I'll be with you in spirit."

Once again, Max heard David's curtains close. He could only guess whether his roommate was in bed, decoding the heavens, or stealing off to Neverland.

Twenty minutes later, Max had scrubbed his face, combed his hair, and brushed his Rowan jacket until it was a smooth, navy perfection. A few deft loops of his tie, a final glance in the mirror, and he slipped out the door with Nick in tow.

The hallway outside was in pandemonium as students crowded into the corridor, abuzz with excitement over the reopening of the school and its attendant festivities. Some adults were interspersed throughout the throng, parents cooing over their sons in formal uniform or grandparents fumbling for cameras. They might have been attending a graduation, and Max wondered if these madly grinning parents—or even his fellow students—knew how strange the evening might prove. A contingent of demons was coming to Rowan, and yet arms were looped and poses were struck while shutters clicked.

Hoisting Nick up from underfoot, Max crossed the hallway to knock at Connor Lynch's door. There was no answer, and after Max had knocked a third time, he turned to leave. Just then, the door opened a crack and he heard a man speaking from beyond. It was a deep voice, tinged with an Eastern European accent.

"I never promised it would be pleasant, Connor. It is your choice to make, but you know where I stand."

The door swung farther open, and Max looked upon a man whose green eye was paired with another so deathly white it might have been a pearl peering from the socket.

For a brief moment, Max and Peter Varga merely stared at one another. Despite their many meetings, the prescient's eye still managed to give Max a jolt. Peter, or "Ronin," as Max had been introduced to him, was an imposing middle-aged man with short black hair and handsome, if hollow, features. Despite Peter's height, his injuries now caused him to stoop so that Max looked down at him as he filled the open doorway.

"Hello, Max," said Peter, offering his hand.

Max merely nodded. "Is Connor in there?" he asked, looking past Peter into the room.

"He is," replied Peter, stuffing his hands deep in the pockets of his blazer. "It is late notice, I realize, but would it be possible to join you and your father at the feast? I've missed our visits."

"Our table's full," said Max coolly.

"I see," said Peter, lowering his gaze. "I won't keep you, then. Enjoy yourself, and congratulations on your appointment to the faculty. I look forward to your class."

"Thank you."

Peter brushed past him and hobbled down the hallway, trailing a wake of silence as visitors caught their very first glimpse of Rowan's remaining prescient and his ghastly eye. Normally, Peter walked with a cane and this had evened out his gait on his morning walks around the campus. Today he was without this prop, and he limped down the hallway, muttering apologies to those obliged to step aside.

That Peter could walk at all was a minor miracle. His back had been broken while rescuing Max and the kidnapped Potentials from the Enemy. As Max watched Ronin hobble down the corridor, he stifled a surge of conflicting emotions. The man had saved his life, but Max also held him responsible for the disappearance and premature death of Max's mother. Years ago, Ronin had sought out Bryn McDaniels in Chicago and had hurried her off to the Sidh so that she might someday aid her son when he arrived in that mystic land. Ronin's vision had been accurate, and Mrs. McDaniels had guided Max and David to the Book of Thoth, but the Sidh was not a place for mortals, and her stay had sapped her youth. By the time Max found his mother, her years had been spent and she was a very old woman. Bryn McDaniels had managed to leave the Sidh with her son, but died soon after.

As Ronin disappeared down the hallway, Max frowned. What possible reason did Peter have to visit Connor? Setting Nick down, Max pushed through the open door.

Connor Lynch's room was a snug cabin crowded with four bunk beds and a single desk that looked out upon a sunlit meadow. When set against the Manse's many exotic, often magnificent bedrooms, it was a conspicuously humble abode, but Max found it cozy. There was a fire burning, and the room's pine walls warmed to a rosy glow as the waning sunlight streamed through the open window.

The sun's rays fell directly onto Connor's face as he sat on one of the lower bunks in a T-shirt and jeans. Many clothes were strewn about his bed, including his Rowan uniform. Connor was hunched over, staring at his shoes while his fingers clenched the side of his head, their tips buried in his chestnut curls.

"Hey," said Max, kicking Connor's foot. "Are you having a fashion show in here?"

Connor gave an obligatory grunt, but Max saw that he was deeply troubled.

"Throw on your uniform," Max said. "You're having dinner with my dad and the Tellers."

"Sorry," replied Connor. "I don't think I'm going to the feast, Max. And if I do, I've got to sit with my family."

"They can join us," said Max. "Or we'll join you—but let's get going."

"Ah," said Connor, closing his eyes. "I know what you're trying to do, and you're a good mate. But you and I both know that my family's not joining the McDaniels duo for supper anytime soon. . . ."

Max nodded. He had expected that answer. Connor's family blamed Max for Connor's troubles the previous year. These troubles had included possession by an imp named Mr. Sikes and his captivity during the Siege. While possessed, Connor had stabbed David Menlo and dispelled the enchantment that had hidden Rowan from the Enemy. These actions, and the still-unspoken horrors he had suffered while being held hostage, had rendered him but a sad echo of the cheerful, jesting boy he had been.

"Well, we didn't really want you to join us, anyway," said Max, plopping down on the desk chair and doodling on a pad. "Have you ever seen yourself eat? You're worse than Nick."

The lymrill peered up at the mention of his name, a sock dangling from his mouth. Connor managed a wan smile and leaned forward to retrieve his uniform jacket from the floor. He plucked a stray thread from the sleeve and smoothed it on his knee.

"I don't think I should go."

"Have you seen Lucia lately?" Max asked brightly. "She'll be there, and if you come, I promise to sic my dad on Mr. Cavallo. He'll be stuck talking about Bedford Crispy Soup Wafers all night!"

Lucia Cavallo was a strikingly beautiful classmate whom Connor had pursued since arriving at Rowan. Like Connor, Lucia's relatives had taken refuge at the school. Most conspicuous among her family was Mr. Cavallo, who watched his daughter like a territorial rooster and had become something of a terror to Lucia's would-be suitors.

"That *is* a tempting offer," said Connor, cocking an eyebrow and regaining a glimmer of his old, mischievous self. He sighed and stood up from the bed, crossing the room to open one of his roommate's trunks and retrieve clean boxers, dark socks, and a dress shirt. "Tell you what, Max. You iron those trousers and I'm your man."

"Do you just borrow your roommate's clothes whenever you feel like it?" asked Max, retrieving an iron from a cupboard while Connor slipped into the clean white shirt.

"Pretty much," quipped Connor, staring at his tongue in a small mirror. "Stefan's always good for a clean shirt, and Lord knows he owes me for his snoring."

"I'm sure he does it just to needle you," replied Max, squinting with concentration as he ran the iron along the trousers' faded crease. "By the way, why was Peter Varga in here?"

"Ol' Blinky?" laughed Connor, peeling his lid back from his eye. "Oh, he visits now and again. Always lurking behind corners and having his say, I guess. He's been pestering me since last spring."

"About what?" asked Max, setting the iron down and fixing Connor with a sharp glance.

"That's my business for the time being," said Connor. "I'm still turning things over. Let's just say I hope a fiend in black don't sail in off the sea."

Max instantly thought of his readings and the many descriptions of Prusias.

"Connor, a fiend in black is coming to Rowan. Tonight. A demon named Prusias."

For a moment, Connor said nothing, but Max saw the blood drain clear away from his round, ruddy face. Chewing his lip, Connor beckoned at Max to toss over the ironed trousers.

"They're not quite finished," said Max, eyeing his sorry attempt.

"No matter," said Connor. With a deep, steadying breath, he expanded his chest like a bodybuilder. Appraising his mirrored profile with an approving air, he smacked his stout belly and exhaled. "Tonight I am a man of wit, warmth, and charming disarray. The wrinkled pants are a stroke of genius, but a cunning detail in my master plan—"

Max hurled the wadded pants at Connor, who abandoned his monologue and fell back onto his bed. Minutes later, the two were hurrying down the hallway.

Outside, Rowan glittered like a city of the Sidh, all gleaming stone and light beneath deepening bands of twilight blue. Old Tom's scaffolding had been removed, and the building's clean stone façade stood exposed, much like a patient freed from gauze and plaster.

"Poor fellow looks almost naked, no?" joked Connor.

Max had to agree. Without its ivy, the stately academic hall looked somehow younger—its gray stones lacking the marks of age and the twining leaves that had draped its shoulders like a shawl. What it had lost in character, however, it had gained in brilliance. The building appeared nearly luminescent, lit from beneath by floodlights the size of kettledrums. Thousands of students and refugees laughed and chattered among the gardens, strolled among the shells, and clustered upon the steps of Old

Tom and Maggie. Connor tugged on his arm and pointed toward Julie, who was beaming at them and squeezing past a pack of bearded scholars.

"Finally here!" she exclaimed as she bounded up the Manse steps. She gave Max a kiss and embraced Connor. "Your dad sent me to look for you. We've got a table in the orchard—a bit too close to those Workshop stiffs, but at least we're by Hannah's nest. Where's David?"

"Not coming," said Max with curt finality. "Are we supposed to sit down?"

"In a minute," said Julie. "Everyone's supposed to gather here for a special announcement. By the way, Connor, what look are you going for? Casual transient?"

"Charming disarray," said Connor, shooting his cuffs. "Nailed it, didn't I?"

"Well done," said Julie.

The three stood on the steps, pressed against the railing while more people streamed out of the Manse and from the woods, out onto the paths that led to the Sanctuary. Among the crowds of people, Max saw domovoi; fauns; red-capped lutins, tiny elfin creatures wearing long knit caps; and even Orion, a Syrian shedu, clopping along with several children on his back. Fluttering his tail, Nick left them and waddled out among the partygoers, falling into step with a Himalayan münchel. As the stars began to peek from the evening sky, everyone gathered on the quad, which was ringed by the tall white statues of past luminaries. Max felt a pinch on his elbow and saw Julie pointing up at Old Tom's tower. A figure stood on the small balcony outside its gears and clockworks. It was Ms. Richter.

Rowan's Director raised her arm, and a single white light rose from her outstretched hand like a tiny star. The light grew and grew, bathing the campus in brilliance, until all conversation ceased and all eyes were focused on the balcony. When she spoke, her amplified voice rang clear and true across the campus.

"Ladies and gentlemen, children, and Sanctuary residents, I welcome you as we celebrate the reopening of Rowan Academy and acknowledge the tireless efforts you have made on our behalf."

Max cheered and clapped along with thousands of others as he scanned the multitude for a glimpse of his father.

When the crowd had quieted once again, Ms. Richter continued. "On this evening, we also wish to welcome representatives of the Frankfurt Workshop and those representatives from Blys who will be arriving shortly. I know you will treat them with the utmost courtesy, as is due and proper."

This announcement was greeted with scattered applause, quizzical looks, and a buzz of muttered questions.

"What the heck is Blys?" asked Connor, but Julie shushed him as Ms. Richter resumed.

"As much as we honor these emissaries, however, this evening is not about them. It is about us. For six months, we have been confined to this campus while we repaired, rebuilt, and rehabilitated. I am happy to say that within the week, the gates shall be opened once again and you may come and go as you choose."

Thunderous applause. Many in the audience were anxious to search for family or, like Max, were consumed by curiosity regarding the state of the outside world.

Ms. Richter raised a hand of caution. "We would urge you, however, to be patient just a little longer until we have had an opportunity to scout our new borders and assess the safety within them. As we all know, things have changed."

Max had never seen so many people stand in morbid silence.

He could only imagine the myriad of thoughts and emotions that surged through the crowd. Their governments were gone, their homes had been abandoned, and their loved ones were lost to fates unknown.

"But some things," continued the Director, "some things remain the same. Tonight, Old Tom's bell shall ring once more to open this school and remind us of our sacred duty to kindle a light—however small—on this beloved earth. Like others before us, we shall be a city on a hill, a beacon to those requiring shelter from the storm. We are no longer students, faculty, refugees, or guests—we are citizens of Rowan. At this time, I would like to invite one of our own to strike Old Tom's bell and bless this new chapter of our history."

Max gaped as an enormous head poked out of the dark opening that led to Old Tom's clock tower.

It was Bob.

Even at a distance, Max could see the Russian ogre's craggy grin as the crowd burst into cheers. A bandage still covered his knotted head, but Bob had managed to dress suitably for the occasion. Straightening to his full height, he dwarfed the Director. He offered the crowd a shy, awkward wave before stooping low to whisper something to Ms. Richter. The Director kissed the ogre on the cheek, and the two turned to gaze up at the enormous clock face above them.

When the hands were nearly poised to strike six o'clock, Bob ducked beneath the arched doorway and disappeared inside the dark clockworks. The crowd hushed and drew a great, collective breath. With smooth precision, the clock's slender hand closed over the twelve and it was officially six o'clock.

Old Tom rang.

Max's eyes filled with tears as the chimes resonated across the broad campus. The sudden clamor startled a pair of birds from their nest beneath the tower's weather vane and, as the rich sounds reverberated in Max's ears, he had a sudden desire to be a student again. It seemed very important that he read in little nooks, discover the world's secrets, and shape his life into something of beautiful purpose. He relished the thought of chalk and blackboards and worn wooden seats and the crack of a new book's spine. Schoolwork, which Max had always regarded as a tedious chore, now seemed a monumental privilege. He glanced at Julie, whose eyes were also wet and shining. The moment, the campus, and the world seemed to brim with possibilities.

The feasting tables also brimmed with possibilities. As Connor went off to find his family, Max and Julie joined the slow procession of those whose tables were situated behind the Manse. These tables were arrayed amid the orchard trees, which for reasons unknown, had not been touched by the Enemy during the Siege.

These sacred trees, their boughs heavy with golden apples, were awash in light supplied by hundreds of lanterns and candles placed on stout barrels or set within twisted wreaths of autumn leaves. Max inhaled the fragrance of apples and candle smoke while the music from a satyr's reed pipes and a domovoi's fiddle soothed his soul like a warm bath. Julie waved to her family, who were seated at a table with Mr. McDaniels, Hazel Boon, Cooper, and the Bristows. As Max greeted everyone and claimed a seat on the end, he noticed that Nolan, Rowan's chief caretaker in the Sanctuary, was kneeling by Hannah's nearby nest. The man was engaged in conversation with the goose, whose every feather trembled with indignation.

"So, I have it on your word that those things—those hideous, godforsaken things—understand that they are not to get within a stone's throw of my nest?"

"Yes," replied Nolan wearily. "They've been muzzled and Bellagrog has promised—"

"Ha!" shrieked Hannah, stretching her neck. "As if her word counts for anything! That hag would be first in line to gobble up my babies." The goose's voice dropped to a conspiratorial whisper. "For heaven's sake, Nolan, she gobbles up her own! My goslings are practically defenseless, and poor Honk's still glowing. He can't even hide in the dark!"

Max felt a twinge of guilt at this and glanced sheepishly at the downy lightbulb peering from Hannah's nest. He tried to focus on Julie's six-year-old brother Bill's latest masterpiece: a crayon drawing of Max fighting a vye. Max found the drawing's crude labels indispensable, for he had been depicted with red skin, and he absolutely dwarfed the vye, which looked like a black bunny sporting enormous teeth. Nevertheless, Max proclaimed the drawing a great success and the boy positively beamed.

Max turned his attention to Miss Boon, the Tellers, and his father, who was regaling Cooper with stories from his college football days. Throughout the meal, however, he could not help but crane his head about.

"You want to find Bob, don't you?" asked Julie.

"Yes, I do," said Max, stealing a sip of his father's wine and wiping his mouth.

"Well, go on, then," whispered Julie. "My mom's complaining about my aunt, and I've got to nod and agree for the next half hour. Try to make it back by dessert!"

Max grinned and excused himself, swinging his legs over the bench and striding past a low table where four red-capped lutins were absorbed in a game of poker. Ducking beneath a branch, Max made his way past several more tables before he saw the Workshop members arranged around a large, circular table on the patio near the French doors that led to the Director's office.

Rasmussen appeared pleased and sleepy as he held court at the Workshop table. While Bellagrog refilled Rasmussen's wineglass, Mum scurried about, clearing plates and scraping crumbs off the white tablecloth. Spaced about the table's periphery were the haglings, standing at attention like tiny soldiers. Each of the little monsters wore old-fashioned maid costumes that had been starched to near immobility. Max heard Bellagrog chortle.

"Right you are, sir," she said in reply to a pudding-faced engineer. "They are indeed an obedient lot. Hags and their haglings are happiest when serving their betters. Why, me sis and I were over the moon to learn we'd be waiting on Your Excellencies this evening. Over the moon!"

Max paused a moment. Bellagrog was refilling glasses rather quickly, and her statement that she was tickled to "learn" that they'd be waiting on the Workshop was pure nonsense—Bellagrog had assigned the jobs. Max changed course and approached the table, bending close to whisper in Rasmussen's ear. The man was giggling about an optics experiment he'd conducted as a teenager.

"Can I have a word?" Max hissed.

"What is it, boy?" asked Rasmussen, not even bothering to look up. Max glanced behind and saw a muzzled hagling glaring at him. Bellagrog had also paused midpour and swiveled her crocodile eye toward them.

"It's private," said Max. "I insist."

Rasmussen's smile glazed over. "Very well," he said, dabbing at his mouth and rising from the table. "Colleagues, excuse me for but a moment. This young man 'insists' on a word."

Max ignored the laughter and marched Rasmussen past the watchful haglings and onto the grass. Rasmussen glared impatiently at Max and tapped his watch face.

"Stop drinking," Max ordered.

The man blinked and refocused, staring at Max with a bleary mixture of annoyance and incredulity.

"The hags are trying to get you drunk," Max continued. "They're up to something. Do you honestly think they've forgotten that their cousin Gertie is on display as a specimen in your museum?"

"Drivel!" retorted Rasmussen, shaking his head. Gazing at Max with a knowing, indulgent smile, he wagged a sticklike finger. "You are sentimental, Max McDaniels, and thus you overestimate their sentimentality. You'd make a very poor engineer, I'm afraid. They are hags, boy. *Pediwora terribilis* is no more sentimental than a lizard."

At this, a small gray hand reached up to tug at the man's dinner jacket. Max and Dr. Rasmussen looked down to see one of the haglings peering up at them. A hoarse voice rasped through the leather stitching that covered her sharp, solitary tooth.

"Does the kind sir wish Number Three to fetch an after-dinner drink?"

"No, my good hagling," said Rasmussen magnanimously. "Lead me to it. I'm in the mood for a fine, velvety cognac . . . just the thing before one meets a demon face to face!"

The man laughed, but Max saw a very real tinge of fear pluck at his features, and his smile concluded in a nervous tic. Without a word of farewell, Dr. Rasmussen allowed Number Three to lead him back to the table, where his colleagues were making loud, unsteady toasts to each other's good health and fortune.

Swallowing his disgust, Max rounded the Manse and jogged toward the academic quad, where he suspected Bob was sitting. It was not hard to spot the ogre. He was at a table beneath the rowan trees, his wheelchair flanked by a pair of moomenhoven nurses. Bob's bandaged head glistened with tiny beads of water from the misting fountain nearby. Sipping tomato soup from an enormous tureen, he nodded politely in response to an inquiry from Monsieur Renard.

Max poked Bob on the shoulder and grinned.

The huge head turned, and for a moment, Max thought the ogre had forgotten him. Bob's small blue eyes merely blinked at Max in quiet curiosity, peering at him as though he were but a colorful little bird that had hopped from a nearby copse. Soon, however, Bob's warm, leathery hands reached out to envelop Max's. The ogre beckoned one of the moomenhovens to reposition his chair so he and Max could face one another.

"It is my Max, no?" he rumbled, gently patting Max's hand as though it were a rabbit. "Bob sees not so well these days."

"It's me," said Max, noticing that Bob was thinner, his legs mere shanks beneath his trousers. The attack last spring had taken an enormous toll on the aged ogre. But one would not know it from Bob's warm, toothless grin.

"It's so good to see you, Bob," said Max. "How are you feeling?"

The ogre shrugged. "Bob is tough. He will be making éclairs and soufflés in no time."

"So you'll be back in the kitchens next week?" Max asked.

"Tomorrow," said the ogre with gruff decisiveness, glancing pointedly at one of the attending moomenhovens. "The kitchen needs Bob."

"Yes, it does," said Max. "Have you met the haglings?"

Bob frowned and nodded, leaning close. His mottled, papery skin smelled like soap and ripe apples. "Be extra good to our Mum. She needs you. Bellagrog is . . . difficult. Promise Bob you will visit his little Mum."

"Of course," said Max.

"Good boy."

Apparently this was the end of their visit, for the drowsy

ogre's eyelids fluttered, and he released Max's hand. Closing his eyes, the ogre knitted his fingers together and looked like a hopeful, pious boy on Christmas Eve. As his great head began to dip, one of the moomenhovens deftly whisked away his napkin while the other strained to swivel the casters beneath his chair. A moment later, Rowan's chef was snoring while his nurses grunted and wheezed with the effort of rolling him off to bed.

The dinner was coming to a finish, and Max saw that many of the younger children had already abandoned their tables and were running about, flinging pinecones and generally doing their best to distract the still-conversing adults. Overhead, the stars were twinkling, and the air nipped with September chill. As Max strode back toward his table, the sky was suddenly illuminated. He turned and saw a fading bloom of golden fireworks.

They had come from the sea.

Max hurried toward the ocean, weaving between the emptying tables, joined by hundreds of other people all trotting down the garden paths and across the lawns to form a line along the rocky bluff. Another burst of golden fireworks filled the eastern sky, expanding like a rose before arcing back to earth with a glimmering hiss. Up ahead, Max heard cries that something had been sighted—a ship was moored out in the Atlantic.

As Max squeezed through the crowd, he discovered that the commotion was dissipating to an eerie silence. Unable to find a suitable vantage point, he clambered onto the pedestal of Elias Bram's statue, ignoring the scowling disapproval of a nearby Mystic. Peering out over the spectators' heads and the blue-black waves, Max saw a ship the likes of which he had never imagined.

At first glance, the ship's dimensions nearly overwhelmed the senses. Even a rogue wave—a tidal monstrosity—would hardly daunt such a vessel, and Max doubted it had been crafted for earthly seas. The gargantuan ship resembled a modified galleon, with brightly illuminated portholes lining its sides at irregular intervals and heights. Ten masts the size of redwoods protruded like spines from a deck whose entirety was lost to the night fog. Upon these masts were white silk mainsails, stretched to taut, voluminous perfection by the onshore breeze. The bright moonlight revealed that each sail was embroidered with an intricate design, some sort of symbol. At first, Max thought it might be Astaroth's seal; however, instead of the Demon's mark, this circle enclosed twined sheaves of grain that overlapped one another to circumscribe three smaller circles that might have been coins. From his earlier reading, Max recognized it as the seal of Prusias. In surprising contrast to the ship's staggering grandeur, a slender rope was all that tethered it to the dark rocks of Brigit's Vigil.

Boom!

More crackling fireworks were fired from a long cannon on the bow, arcing high before they exploded in a dazzling brilliance that briefly turned the sea to gold. Several children nearby clapped their hands before their parents hushed them. While the fireworks faded, the enormous galleon sat motionless in the swell. Max felt someone's fingers lace through his; Julie had climbed the pedestal to join him.

"Are those demons?" she asked quietly. "I heard Miss Boon talking."

"They are," Max said, frowning.

"How many do you think are on that thing?" she asked.

"Fewer than you might guess," he replied. "They're here to talk, not to fight."

"Why bother bringing a ship so big?" asked a nearby man, holding his daughter.

"To intimidate us," Max replied simply.

"It's working." Julie shivered as tatters of night fog swept in off the ocean.

~ 5 ~

GILDED GRÀVENMUIR

The wind moaned and torches sputtered as demons climbed the stony steps to Rowan.

At Cooper's direction, Max had joined the rest of the Red Branch in ushering the crowd away from the bluff and the winding paths to the Sanctuary. He had promised Julie he would join the bonfire when he could, then returned to the cliff to stand among those who remained—assorted Mystics, Agents, faculty, and scholars, along with the visitors from the Workshop. They watched as a longboat launched from the galleon to cleave across the breakers, torches illuminating the smaller craft's progress to the rocky beach below.

As the demons climbed the long stairs to the cliff's top, Max realized that his breath was becoming short and shallow. Was it fear? he wondered. He mused on the huge ship moored off the coast, the silent procession of unknown visitors, and concluded that yes, he was afraid. But he was angry, too. It had been Max who had dug a grave for Jimmy, who had looked after the boy's bathroom, giving outdated haircuts and drenching the unwary in cologne. The merry domovoi had been discovered in a horrific state following the Siege. The little man had done no harm, and yet now he lay beneath a bed of tulips near the Manse's north wing. These visitors, or their servants, had killed Jimmy as he struggled to join the others in the Sanctuary.

His fingers twitched, and he felt the slow churn of sickening force begin to quicken within his body. A tremor ran through him, and he dropped to one knee.

"What's the matter, Max?" asked Cooper, coming to his side.

"This is sacred ground," croaked Max, glancing beyond the Agent at Bram's statue, where he had promised Nigel that he would behave. "The demons shouldn't be here."

Cooper's face remained a mask of stern appraisal. "You're in the Red Branch," he said, pulling Max to his feet. "Master yourself."

Max nodded but found that his heart was beating wildly within his chest. He inhaled the cool night air and focused on the fire that had been built in the center of two large arrangements of seats. The fire was building, sending sparks up into the night and casting an amber glow on the faces of Rowan's people as they took their places. Ms. Richter was seated in the center of the first row, her face grave as she stared out toward that point along the cliffs where the demons would emerge. Heading toward the bonfire, the pair took their seats, with Cooper sitting at the Director's right.

"You are the son of a king," Max whispered to himself, repeating Scathach's parting words. Cooper glanced at him but said nothing. Max closed his eyes and repeated the mantra in his head. All around him, he could hear the hushed, nervous conversations and antsy creaking of chairs.

And then all of it stopped.

Max opened his eyes and saw two identical standards rise above the crest—Astaroth's circular seal perched upon long wooden staves. The banners fluttered in the night breeze as their bearers came into view and began a silent procession across the lawns.

Throughout the Enemy's approach, Max sat utterly transfixed, his attention focused upon the nightmarish things that bore Astaroth's flags. The standard bearers were taller than men but thinner, gangly beings whose faces were hidden behind great mummers' masks. These masks—crude and primal—were fashioned to resemble a great ram or bull, and they extended a full six feet from the shoulders of the creatures as they glided across the lawns, trailing their patchwork robes. Max found them horrifying—pagan dolls that had been jolted to life and set to a dark purpose.

A growing phalanx of other strange creatures followed.

Max did not find the armored ogres strange, or even the wolfish vyes, whose feral eyes gleamed in the firelight. The rest were presumably demons, and they were much more varied in appearance than Max might have imagined.

Some met Max's expectations—powerful, diabolic figures with curving tusks and fearsome, militant faces. Others, however, appeared meek and scholarly, including one chinless, peach-colored imp no larger than a toddler. Compared to their ogre and vye guards, the demons were richly dressed. As they approached, the very air before them seemed to shimmer as though a great, noxious heat was emanating from the motley host.

When the masked standard bearers reached the arranged chairs, they stopped and stood at attention. For a moment, utter silence reigned as Rowan's residents merely stared at the demonic entourage.

Finally, Ms. Richter stood and spoke. "Peace is made in quiet times when the crows have left and the earth is still. Rowan bids you welcome."

A booming cackle erupted from the throng. There was a sound of small, merry bells, and the ogres and vyes and lesser demons stepped aside as something made its way toward the center. The laugh sounded again—an abbreviated, cheerful bark, as if the owner struggled to restrain himself.

"Ms. Richter, you do us too much honor," exclaimed the voice. "Your greeting has a poetic lilt, the pleasing rhythm of spellwork. . . . We have not crows in the barrens of my homeland, but I shall send some there, and they shall be known henceforth as harbingers of peace, not war."

An enormous man-shaped figure strode beyond the standard bearers and leaned his bulk upon an ivory cane.

Compared to the other demons, Prusias was decidedly human in appearance. As in the accounts Max had read, his guise was that of a huge, powerfully built nobleman gone to seed. His chest was broad and barrel-shaped, and he was clad in a rich black tunic. His legs were disproportionately small and slender, comparative stilts to the bulk of his upper body. His handsome features were deep and pronounced, as though sculpted by a bold, assured hand. He was olive-skinned and deeply tanned, and his every crease and wrinkle suggested a persona inclined to laughter. The demon's face and expressions were defined by scale. His was a face suited for the stage. A wild mane of black hair and a long braided beard heightened the dramatic effect. Despite his kingly attire, Prusias exuded the air of a tribal chieftain rather than that of refined royalty. Set within the hollowed eye sockets, however, was a pair of round blue cat eyes—a startling reminder of his demonic heritage.

The peach-colored imp hopped forward and cleared its throat. "May I present Lord Prusias, Exalted Ruler of Blys, Defender of the—"

"Enough, enough," growled Prusias, shooing the imp away. "We are among friends—such formalities are unnecessary. There will be time for introductions later, but Gabrielle Richter I already know. Where is the one called David Menlo?" inquired the demon, scanning the crowd. "My lord specifically bade me to extend his greetings."

Heads turned and whispers coursed through the crowd.

"He is not here," said Ms. Richter, her voice admirably measured. "He is unwell."

"It grieves me to hear it," said Prusias, smiling. "I had longed to meet him. And where is the other child of the Old Magic, so I may greet this champion?"

All of Rowan turned to Max, who closed his eyes and wished that he were far, far away. At Ms. Richter's bidding, Max stood, the moonlight falling full upon his face. One of the demons—a tall, armored rakshasa standing behind Prusias—bared its teeth and cocked its head in surly appraisal.

"*Caia, Prusias!*" exclaimed another demon, a beaked creature with the wide, staring eyes of a lemur. "*Lihuar connla nehunt ün homna. Connla breargh ün Sidh.*"

"*Vey, miyama.*" Prusias nodded, speaking to the demon as though it were an inquisitive child. "But it is not polite to speak in tongues before our hosts."

The staring demon bowed by way of apology and retreated a step.

"What did it say?" asked Max, returning the stares of the demons that crowded and jostled to gape at him.

Prusias suppressed their chatter with an irritated glance. "To her eyes, you do not seem human," explained Prusias. "In the moonlight, your aura shines and flickers like those from our realm . . . and others. Are you certain you're not a demon, Max?"

For several seconds, the startling question merely hung in the air. Finally, Prusias winked. Round, jovial features contorted into an amused grin as he offered Max a courteous bow. Max did not return it.

Several of the demons gasped, and a palpable tension saturated the air. Max felt Ms. Richter's eyes boring into him.

Rising slowly, Prusias's eyes flicked up and met Max's own. "This will not do," said Prusias, cocking an eyebrow at Ms. Richter. "The conquered must have manners."

"Max," said Ms. Richter, her voice preternaturally calm. "Please greet Lord Prusias appropriately so we may begin this important business."

Max turned and looked at her, but she might have been a character in a film. She was not real; she did not truly exist. Her eyes pleaded with him, but she seemed to grow dim. There was a drumming in his ears—a thousand drums and a thousand calls and a thousand horns that stirred the Old Magic within his blood.

"I am not conquered."

Something was pulling at his arm. It was Cooper. Max merely looked at him; he might have been a child. Leaning down, Max pointedly removed the man's hand.

"Max McDaniels does not speak for Rowan, Lord Prusias," said Ms. Richter, standing to bow low. "I offer our sincere apologies. He is still a boy."

Max glared at Ms. Richter, but her attention was fixed upon Prusias, who watched these events unfold with a patient, watchful air. The demon offered a modest, understanding smile, but his eyes gleamed with a lingering malevolence. At length, he shrugged and his shoulders shook with a sudden laugh.

"Do not trouble yourself, Director," he exclaimed, beckoning her to rise. "This is a time for celebration and merrymaking! I sympathize with our young friend—it is always thus after such misunderstandings arise. Let us turn to the tasks at hand. There are several points of order before our celebration can begin in earnest. With your permission, Max, may I share Lord Astaroth's terms? They are most generous."

Max stared at Prusias. The demon leaned upon his cane and returned the stare with a calm, contemplative expression that suddenly made Max feel that he was being childish. Slowly, Max took his seat.

At Prusias's command, the demons were seated in the first row of chairs across the fire from Rowan's senior representatives. There were about a dozen of them, some armored in elaborate suits of mail, others sleek and robed. Behind them stood the vyes and ogres, huge and grim, flanked by the standard bearers.

"Where is our charming messenger?" asked Prusias, beaming, as he turned to address his entourage.

One of the vyes loped forward, tugging gently on a leash to pull something that had been hidden behind the mountainous row of ogres. Max sat up. It was a middle-aged woman—at least that was her appearance. She stooped along, dressed in the gaudy silks and curling headdress of a jester. The woman's graying hair was matted with sweat, and her simple, uncomprehending eyes stared about her surroundings. She clutched a large obsidian scroll tube with trembling hands.

Prusias smoothed the woman's hair and whispered something in her ear with a kindly, paternal air. Sliding the gleaming tube out of her hands, he patted her on the head and she was led back to her place, where she sat on the lawn and dug her fingers in the grass.

Leaning on his cane, Prusias eased himself into the chair opposite Ms. Richter. He gave a broad grin and drummed his fingers on the case.

"The Four Kingdoms salute you," he said. "And I am honored to speak for them." Unscrewing a silver cap from the black tube, he removed and unrolled a long scroll whose dense script was penned in red ink. Prusias held it up and tilted the parchment so he could read by the firelight.

"The realm of Rowan shall be vast!" he proclaimed, his voice rising so all might hear. "Once you agree to the terms and sign the document, this land shall be yours. Rowan shall govern its own affairs and flourish here in a haven and harbor of its very own. . . ."

For a moment, Prusias sat in silence. His eyes, sapphire orbs suffused with an inner glow, wandered over the assembled Rowan and Workshop dignitaries with an expression of patrician magnanimity.

"And what are these terms, Lord Prusias?" asked Ms. Richter, breaking the silence. At her words, Prusias blinked and reexamined the scroll.

"There are but seven, I believe," he purred, twining a braid of beard about his finger. "Seven Sacred Edicts are all that your people must follow to guarantee our lord's goodwill. They are most reasonable."

Prusias pivoted in his seat and craned his neck to look around the campus and the night.

"As you have undoubtedly noticed, our Lord Astaroth has been cleansing the world of its accumulated filth and disease. Once again, the air is pure, the soil is rich, and the oceans teem with life. Mankind may begin anew under the tutelage of wiser, gentler stewards. This is Year One."

"Is that an edict, Lord Prusias?" asked Ms. Richter.

"An observation." The demon smiled, returning his attention to the scroll. "The first edict concerns Rowan's lands, sovereignty, and safety. Rowan shall constitute a fifth kingdom under the reign of Astaroth. Its lands shall range from these shores west to the Appalachian Ridge, north to the Great River, and south to the Algonquin Chesapeake. Within these boundaries, Rowan may govern its own affairs and rule its denizens as it sees fit. No demon lord or aspirant shall invade these lands or harm its inhabitants under pain of death."

There was a murmur of relieved approval among Rowan's dignitaries.

"Is our safety guaranteed outside these lands?" asked Ms. Richter.

"Alas," said Prusias, "our lord shudders at the thought of unreasonable promises. As I said, no demon may wander these lands unbidden, and we shall not make war upon you. If one of your people should leave these borders, they are subject to the whims and fates of the world."

Max did not like Prusias's casual shrug or the way the demon's eyes became blank and unfocused whenever he was interrupted with a question. When considering his response, Prusias also had the habit of smoothing his beard and compulsively wetting his red lips. The effect was a revolting, predatory contrast to his smiles and diplomatic speech.

"We must look after ourselves," confirmed Ms. Richter. "Please continue."

"Many inhabitants of Rowan are blessed with mehrùn—the gift of 'magic,' in your tongue. As possessors of this gift, many of you may remember the earlier days, and thus you may keep whatever tomes and lore survive the Fading. However, the second edict is this: It is forbidden to transport any book, document, or written word whatsoever beyond the borders of this land. We shall consider the act to be a severe provocation. . . . Is this understood?"

Ms. Richter nodded like a schoolgirl receiving a strict lecture.

"Excellent," chuckled Prusias. "Edict three: It is forbidden to teach reading, writing, or history to humans beyond Rowan's borders." The demon's face became grim, and his gaze moved from face to face, lingering among the scholars. "Let me impress upon you the gravity of edict three, my friends. Should you teach reading, writing, or any history whatsoever to any human beyond these borders, the lives of the teacher, pupil, and every human within one hundred leagues may be forfeit. Is this clear?"

A silence ensued.

"We shall consider this," said Ms. Richter at length. Max had never seen her look more miserable.

"By all means," said Prusias, resuming his pleasant demeanor. He skimmed the dense parchment until he found his place once again. "Here we are . . . edict four. While the inhabitants of Rowan are free to live and prosper, its borders are hereby closed. No one shall enter without the explicit approval of our ambassador. Rowan and its representatives are further forbidden to seek other humans who have been born with mehrùn. To do so invalidates this contract."

"But they're immortal!" Max hissed to Cooper. "They'll keep us in here like zoo animals until we've all died out and faded to dust."

Cooper's mouth tightened, but he said nothing and motioned for Max to be quiet.

"Edict five," continued Prusias, "concerns the mystic arts of summoning. This branch of mystic study is hereby ended. All works that detail the summoning of demons—of se'irim, shedim, afrit, jinni, ahriman, lilin, marids, asura, devas, daitya, rakshasa, nephilim, vetalas, drudes, imps, and all other absurd names that humans attribute to our kind, including those nobles you have named 'the Spirits Perilous'—must be removed from your teachings and destroyed. The summoning of demons is hereafter forbidden."

"But how shall we gain knowledge?" whispered one of the scholars to his neighbor.

Prusias apparently heard this, for he abruptly turned and addressed the mortified speaker. "How, indeed?" he inquired. "I suppose, my friend, that you will have to pry such secrets on your own. You can imagine how tedious it has been for many of my kind to answer your beck and call throughout the centuries and pay in pain for doing so. Scholar, teach thyself!"

Prusias jabbed at the bearded, bespectacled scholar with his ivory cane and chuckled at the joke, but the man squirmed beneath the demon's penetrating gaze and did not meet it. Max wondered at Prusias's cane. It seemed a strange prop for one so powerful. Why did Prusias use one? Was it a tool to play upon one's sympathies? Years ago, a disguised vye had used a cane to deceive Max into believing she was old and feeble. But somehow Max did not think that Prusias's cane was a ruse. Max recalled Bram's account: *The wretched demon bared his teeth and dragged his limb, swearing vengeance. . . .* Was Prusias still injured from his encounter with Elias Bram? Max turned and gazed at the statue and the wild, glaring face of its subject. Bram had given his life so that the refugees from Solas might survive to found another school. And here was Prusias sitting as plump and pleased as a feasting Falstaff. Max could only imagine Bram's outrage.

"Our lord has issued edict six in the spirit of lasting peace," intoned the demon. "Rowan shall not seek revenge upon the witches who, in turn, relinquish any and all claims regarding the contract known as 'Bram's Oath.' This vendetta is over, and the witches have been granted their own lands within Lord Aamon's kingdom."

"Very well. And the final edict?" asked Ms. Richter.

"A simple one," replied Prusias, smiling. "Also in the spirit of peace. Any new inventions, emigration, or interkingdom trade must be submitted, reviewed, and sanctioned by Lord Astaroth's embassy."

"And where is this embassy?" asked Ms. Richter.

Prusias stood and stretched, gazing about the campus quad. His eyes finally settled upon the smooth lawn beneath his feet. He tapped the grass gently with his cane.

"Right here should do," he said, sounding oddly detached. "Yes, upon this very spot."

The demon rose to his grand height and walked in a slow circle around the cropped grass he had touched with his cane. He appraised it and then glanced at the grounds about them, lingering upon the statue of Bram.

"Upon this very spot," he whispered again, wetting his lips.

The demon's gaze locked upon Max as he raised his cane high and then plunged it deep into the soft earth.

A screeching sound tore the air asunder, like lightning striking metal. Along with those around him, Max clapped his hands to his ears and fell back as the ground began to groan and buckle. His chair toppled over, and he found himself scrambling for purchase upon the cool grass, whose substance seemed to sift and change beneath his hands. Where Prusias had struck the ground, Max saw gurgling torrents of crimson blood stream from the soil as though Rowan itself were a writhing, wounded thing. From this spot, this singular point, coursed a wild, jarring force, wave upon wave of Old Magic that issued from the embedded cane like ripples in a pond. These ripples seemed to bend and warp the surrounding earth and air, twisting the elemental matter into a new form.

As Max watched, the grass beneath his fingers turned hard as the blades knitted together, smoothing and receding until they were as marbled stone. The Old Magic within him seemed to claw and twist like a wild animal seeking to escape its cage.

The earth howled and wailed as sheer walls of rock and soil were raised about them, blocking out the night and the moon and Old Tom's tower. Higher and higher these walls rose, spilling bits of rock and soil as stony tendrils arced to form a sort of rib cage. Vines spilled forth from stone and interwove to form tapestries and paintings; musty toadstools became luxuriant divans; and the tongues of the bonfire were snatched by invisible hands and used to fuel lanterns and candles set within the grottos of what was rapidly becoming the richest, most splendid entry hall Max had ever seen.

Nature's shrieks and wails died away. The subterranean rumbling subsided to quiet as the hall smoothed its rough edges into crisp, cosmetic perfection. His whole body trembling with energy, Max looked about and sought to gauge whether Cooper or Ms. Richter had been similarly affected.

They had not. Instead, this display of Old Magic, this casual gesture of creation, had shocked Rowan's leadership into gaping silence. Not a protest was uttered. Instead, Ms. Richter and the rest merely craned their necks and stared about a hall whose frescoed ceiling and gilded walls rivaled Versailles'.

Max stared at Prusias, who seemed to sense Max's gaze and emerged from his heavy-lidded, trancelike state to offer a most unsettling smile. The demon snatched up his cane and rapped it hard upon the marble floor, shattering the eerie silence. Max leaned forward to look for Ms. Kraken. He had once overheard a lecture during which the elderly Mystics instructor had said that the amount of magic needed to create a thing far exceeded the energy required to destroy it. Max could not imagine the stores of magic that Prusias must possess.

Max finally spied Ms. Kraken, whose folding chair had been replaced with an antique settee that she shared with Miss Boon. Both women looked terror-stricken, their bodies leaning away from the demon so that even their feet were curled under them as if the very ground were poison.

Max swallowed. To sit quietly and listen seemed a better option than it had before.

Old Tom struck nine o'clock, and from his seat, Max could see the white clock face, rippled and distorted, through an enormous stained-glass window. Prusias waited out the chimes and bid the grim standard bearers remove themselves to the back of his entourage, which were in turn seated comfortably amid the many chairs and couches. When the chimes ceased, the demon turned to again address Rowan's representatives.

"I bid you welcome to our embassy," he said, bowing low. "It shall be named Gràvenmuir—'the Watcher,' in your tongue. Here our representatives shall keep a ceaseless vigil on Rowan's safety, hear whatever petitions may arise, and maintain peace between our kingdoms. I trust you have no objections."

"No," said Ms. Richter.

"If I recall correctly, Director, you had expressed some reservations regarding edict three," said Prusias, leaning forward and wetting his lips. "Do you still require time to consider it, or shall we conclude this business with your signature? Our lord is most insistent about contracts, and I should take it as a personal favor if you would . . . humor me." The demon smiled, but his eyes remained unblinking, unfocused.

Ms. Richter turned to her senior advisers—Kraken, Nolan, Vincenti, Watanabe, and others. The careworn replies and nods were unanimous, and Ms. Richter stood to approach Prusias, who held out the scroll expectantly. An imp approached with ink bottle and pen, and the scroll was signed.

"There!" boomed Prusias, snatching the scroll away almost before Ms. Richter had finished. He swiftly rolled it up and tamped it down into its obsidian case. "All finished. My secretary shall provide you with a copy. Now, we may bless this hall—bless Gràvenmuir as we should and celebrate peace between our peoples."

The demons clapped, the vyes howled, and the ogres roared while creatures—hunched, larval-eyed servants—emerged from a doorway bearing platters of food and flagons of wine. The creatures hurried around, offering joints of beef and mutton and other fare to Rowan's people, who stood about as awkwardly as students attending their first dance. Max furiously waved away one of the creatures once it had approached him for a second time. As though he sensed a breach of etiquette from afar, Sir Alistair Wesley appeared at Max's side.

"It's poor form to refuse food from a host," the instructor whispered, taking a goose leg from the platter and thrusting it into Max's hand.

"But I don't want it," growled Max.

The smile never left Sir Alistair's face as he nodded to a passing demonness. "Young man, you will behave yourself. You will eat that goose with relish and you will smile. In other words, you will act like a gentleman and stop endangering our entire community."

Grimacing, Max sniffed at the goose and managed a peevish bite. With an exasperated sigh, Sir Alistair glided toward several Workshop representatives as though they were dear friends.

When Sir Alistair glanced over as though to invite Max to join them, Max stooped quickly on the pretense of tying his shoe. While he crouched, a pair of enormous black boots came to a halt mere inches away. Glancing up, Max saw Prusias towering above him.

"No need to kneel, my boy," chortled the demon, waving him up.

As Max rose, nearby conversation hushed and then nearly ceased altogether. Up close, Prusias seemed even larger, easily seven feet tall and over half that span across his barrel chest. An enormous hand, laden with heavy gold rings, seized Max's and shook it. The strength in that grip was terrifying. With a smile, Prusias pulled him closer so that he was nearly pressed against the black brocade of the demon's tunic. Max felt a terrible, searing heat emanate from the demon's body, as though beneath his fleshy guise, Prusias was naught but flame. His other hand lifted Max's chin, forcing him to stare directly into the demon's face.

"It is most refreshing to meet the 'unconquered,'" said Prusias softly. "I thought I must suffer Alexander's lament—'no worlds left,' and so forth. It is refreshing to discover at least one back that is yet unbowed. Come to Blys, brave Max, and my subjects shall travel for miles to look upon you."

"At the pillory or the gallows, my lord?" asked Max innocently.

At this grim humor, Prusias laughed—a fine, piratical roar that made his great body shake. Releasing Max's hand, he smoothed the banded braids in his beard and studied Max's now-impassive face. Periodic chuckles overcame him like aftershocks, and small, perfect teeth—a child's teeth—gnawed at the demon's lips.

"Ah, I like you, Max," replied the demon, winking. Looking past him, Prusias called jovially to Ms. Kraken and made his way toward her. Despite his smiling air, when Prusias crossed the hall, even the other demons parted, as do lesser fish when a shark glides into their waters.

As Max watched Prusias go, he noticed that many servants among the demons' entourage were now clearing furniture away from the hall's center. Silken cushions and bronze braziers were arranged around the perimeter to form a great ring some fifty feet across. When the braziers were lit, Prusias's voice boomed out with the jesting tones of a ringmaster.

"Gather round!" he said, beckoning. "It is time for us to celebrate this occasion with médim. Please be seated while I acquaint you with its ways."

Curious, Max watched as everyone present ceased their conversations and moved to claim a place among the cushions. Max took a seat near the back, scooting over as Nigel squeezed in next to him.

"Remember your promise," Nigel whispered, looking anxious.

Before Max could reply, Prusias extinguished the hall's many lights with a sweep of his cane. The coal-burning braziers provided the only illumination, and in these dimmer surroundings, the demons' eyes gave off an eerie gleam. The heavy smell of incense filled the room. Prusias loomed within the circle's center, and such was his presence that Max almost forgot that he was still at Rowan. The demon seemed not only master of the hall, but of all that might lie beyond it. His deep voice echoed slightly as shadows danced upon the gilded walls.

"Our kind," he explained, "celebrate gatherings or the settling of disputes with sacred contests that we call médim. With these, we honor the Great Gifts from our Maker and those who have mastered them. The contests of a médim may vary, but they are always chosen from the three great arts—alennya, amann, and ahülmm. In your tongue, these are the arts of beauty, blood, and soul. We begin with alennya. Who shall champion Rowan in music and poetry?"

Prusias waited expectantly while Rowan's Mystics and Agents glanced anxiously at one another. Several tense moments elapsed before Ms. Richter stood.

"Lord Prusias, we are unfamiliar with these traditions and I daresay we have not designated any champions of such things."

Several demons audibly scoffed, and Prusias's expectant grin disappeared.

"This is most unexpected," he replied. "I'd been told you were a cultured people. Is there not a worthy musician among all these assembled mehrùn? If not, I am deeply ashamed for you. . . ."

The ensuing silence was almost unbearable. Rowan was giving the painful impression that it was not merely uncultured, but cowardly.

"Someone step forward," Max moaned quietly.

At last someone did. It was Nolan, the man who oversaw Rowan's Sanctuary, who stood from a group of teachers. As he entered the ring, it was clear that Max was not the only one whose pride had been injured.

"Give me a fiddle and I'll give you a match!" the man shouted angrily.

Nolan's spirit was contagious. Mystics and scholars, Agents and teachers all sprang to their feet and roared their support. None clapped or cheered louder than Max.

"Excellent!" crowed Prusias, his disappointment vanishing. "No simpering here—bring this good man a fiddle and let us hear his soul in every note and chord!"

A violin was fetched and Nolan immediately set to testing its strings and tune. There was an intense look of concentration on the man's weather-beaten face. Once satisfied, Nolan nodded to Prusias, who had settled back onto his cushion. The hall became silent.

Nolan tapped his foot three times and began to play. He'd chosen an old Irish tune and played it as rough and raw as the violin would allow. Faster and faster he sawed at the strings, while Prusias looked on in delight. At last, just when Max feared the strings would snap, the chords converged into a single note of simple, mournful purity. The note held, then trembled, and finally died away.

"Bravo!" thundered Prusias, leading the applause. He strode across to shake Nolan's hand. Looking spent but proud, Nolan stood aside as Prusias invited his own contestant into the ring.

The demons' champion was a delicate, fox-faced demonness whose kind was known as kitsune. She wore a red kimono and seemed to glide to a gilded chair that had been set in the center of the ring. A vye brought forth an unfamiliar instrument. It was akin to a standing bass, but taller and more slender. While the vye set it into a stand, the kitsune flexed and stretched her long, slender fingers. There was something peculiar about her hands, and Max gasped.

"She has seven fingers on each hand!" he hissed, elbowing Nigel. "That's unfair!"

Nigel shushed him as Prusias resumed.

"Your man has done you proud," the demon observed. "We honor him for sharing his gift and sparing Rowan an unseemly showing. Now we shall see if Lady Akiko and her belyaël can match such a spirited performance."

The hall grew silent once more as Lady Akiko closed her eyes and placed her hands in precise arrangement upon the instrument. Giving the belyaël a soft, collaborative tap, the demonness began to play.

The resulting music was not merely beautiful, but strangely hypnotic. Lady Akiko's fingers were almost a blur along the belyaël strings. As she played, each hand's dual thumbs deftly flicked beads up or down the many strings, altering their tension and imbuing the instrument with a range far beyond anything Max had ever heard. The piece was intensely moving, a rapid patter of notes interrupted by brusque chords and a simmering dissonance. Max's hopes sank—the kitsune's hands were blessed with seven fingers and each danced with superhuman dexterity. Nolan was a skillful amateur, but the demonness seemed born to this single purpose.

Lady Akiko had undoubtedly earned the victory, but Max still complained when Prusias announced his verdict.

"Of course he picked his team to win," he griped to Nigel. "And how can you judge something like that? It's totally subjective!"

The same could not be said for the rest of the médim. While there were other contests subject to Prusias's judgment, the majority were coldly objective affairs that left no doubt as to the demons' superiority. Natasha Kiraly—a swift runner and member of the Red Branch—was beaten badly in a race around the hall. Archery was utter humiliation as a demon lord named Vyndra shot three bull's-eyes before Rowan's Agent had even nocked his arrow.

Max practically writhed with frustration. Already there had been several matches he believed he could have won or made a better showing in than the competitors Ms. Richter chose. The médim was proving that the demons were not only stronger and faster, but also more skilled and cultured. Music, archery, fencing, poetry . . . the demons dominated them all, and their growing exultation was unbearable. As the losses accumulated, Max became mutinously silent.

"Hang in there," Nigel whispered.

"By tradition, unarmed combat is the médim's final contest," said Prusias. "It is the oldest of all the contests and the primary sport of amann, the arts of blood. Who shall be Rowan's champion?"

Even as Prusias said this, the demon turned and fixed his eyes upon Max.

"Ignore him," said Nigel. "Cooper will handle this."

Indeed William Cooper had already risen and was making his way toward the ring, removing his black cap to reveal the white scalp and its patchwork of pale yellow hair. Prusias cocked his head at the Agent's approach.

"Madam Richter, is this truly Rowan's champion?" inquired the demon. "I'd heard so many tales of Rowan's little Hound, and yet he has skulked behind his elders throughout this entire médim. . . ."

Max almost leaped to his feet, but Nigel gripped his arm and pleaded with him to sit.

"Don't take such obvious bait," he warned. "Remember your promise."

Max nodded, but his fingers twitched and trembled.

With a sigh, Prusias turned to address Lord Vyndra. "I had thought to put you forward once again, but I question whether the man is worthy. I leave the decision to you."

The great rakshasa had been sitting stoically amid his lieutenants. He was a proud, fearsome-looking demon, resplendent in burnished mail that shone like coppery scales. Three eyes were set within his horned, tigerlike head, and each was gleaming as though a furnace blazed behind them. Rising, he came forward to tower over Cooper.

For several moments, the demon looked Cooper up and down. But then he stooped to look the Agent directly in the eye. Cooper bore this strange inspection for a full minute before Vyndra shook his head in disapproval.

"He is afraid," declared the demon. "I will not meet him as an equal. Grahn can humble this pretender."

Max seethed at the sight of Vyndra turning his back on the leader of the Red Branch. Between warriors there was no greater sign of disrespect. It was a grave insult, but Cooper merely stood quietly, his hands clasped before him.

Returning to his seat, the rakshasa gestured lazily at one of his lieutenants, a potbellied demon with tusks and four hairy arms that looked capable of ripping a man in two. Max gaped at the new challenger.

"Dear lord," muttered Nigel as the creature practically leaped into the ring, howling with such fury that the hairs on Max's neck stood on end. Cooper went about preparing himself, pulling off his shirt of nanomail, revealing a wiry, pale torso that was criss-crossed with scars. Grahn howled again as vyes removed his thick iron breastplate. Four muscled arms, each thicker than an ogre's, began to shake and snatch at the air as though grasping and throttling an imaginary adversary.

"Nigel," Max breathed. "I should be the one in there. Cooper shouldn't be doing this."

"Cooper can look after himself," croaked Nigel, looking faint. "Do not interfere."

"But—"

"But nothing," snapped Nigel. "Now sit still and tell me what's happening. I don't think I can watch. . . ."

"The rules are simple," said Prusias. "No weapons, no magic, no murder. Combat ceases upon the loser's submission. When the bell sounds, let the amann begin."

Many of the demons were now puffing eagerly from hookahs as Prusias took his seat. The air was thick with a smoky haze and the amber light from the braziers. Grahn howled again and paced a mere arm's length from Cooper, whose hands were clasped while he stared at the rug at his feet. The man's posture suggested a prisoner resigned to execution rather than a willing combatant.

The demon settled into a bristling crouch as though every muscle and nerve were coiling for a sudden, devastating assault. The hall became still and unbearably tense.

When the bell sounded, Grahn leaped.

Max had never seen Cooper move so fast. With a blurred sidestep, the Agent evaded the demon's grasp and delivered an exquisitely timed blow to his temple. The resulting crack made the audience jump. Even Max had to swallow his cheer when he saw the result.

Grahn lay in an unmoving heap on the ground.

Had Cooper killed him?

For a moment, even the Agent seemed uncertain. Rounding on his heel, he shook the impact from his fingers and stared at his prostrate opponent. Grahn was splayed in an awkward heap, oblivious to his comrades, who were bellowing at him to get up. Vyndra watched the scene with cold disgust, but Prusias seemed genuinely amused.

"Do you submit, Grahn?" called Prusias in a mocking tone.

One of the demon's arms twitched. Then another.

Max's attention shifted to Cooper. While the Agent watched to see if Grahn would rise, he tentatively shook and flexed his fingers. Max groaned—he was sure the hand must be broken.

"What's happening?" asked Nigel, his hands clapped over his eyes.

"Cooper knocked him flat," replied Max. "But now he's hanging back and letting the demon recover. Why doesn't he just finish him?"

But the Agent did not press his advantage. To Rowan's collective dismay, Grahn regained his senses and clambered to his feet. The left side of the demon's face was swollen, his piggish

eye sealed shut with caking blood. He tottered drunkenly, staring at Cooper all the while. Finally, Vyndra roared at the demon in their own language and Grahn gathered himself and went on the attack.

Once again, Cooper hit him with a blow that might have killed a lesser opponent. This time, however, Grahn managed to keep his feet and stagger through the punch to bear down upon Cooper.

Max heard Miss Boon's shriek as the Agent was wrenched violently off the floor. Four arms encircled him, hugging him against Grahn's chest as the demon howled and crushed him like a rag doll.

"He'll break his back," muttered Max, horrified.

"He submits!" cried Miss Boon. "He submits!"

"The combatant must submit," Prusias reminded her, his eyes fixed on the contest.

Again and again, Grahn shook Cooper in sudden, horrifically violent fits. The Agent's body had gone limp, and Grahn cackled.

"Does the little man surrender? Does he submit, or does his skin go up on Grahn's pretty wall?"

When it appeared the Agent would speak, the demon ceased the throttling. But Cooper merely grinned while blood ran down his nose. Tightening its grip, the demon howled and wrenched him up again.

"SUBMIT, WILLIAM!" cried Miss Boon, her voice hysterical.

Time slowed to an excruciating crawl. Max could not bear to watch. Cooper would never submit—he had far too much pride. Max bolted to his feet, determined to intervene.

But even as he did so, Prusias spoke.

"That is enough, Grahn."

The demon abruptly ceased, but swiveled his savage head toward Prusias in disbelief.

"Yes, that is enough," reiterated Prusias calmly. "The man is unconscious and cannot submit. No deaths will mar this médim."

Howling, Grahn tossed Cooper's body aside. The Agent's body crashed into one of the braziers, where he lay still. Miss Boon rushed to his side.

"A pity," Prusias observed, gazing at Max. "A pity that your man was hurt while Rowan's champion cowered in the shadows."

It was too much to bear. His face burning with shame, Max wriggled free of Nigel's grip and bolted to his feet. He knew he was making a spectacle of himself. He knew he was disobeying orders. But he did not care. It was bad enough that Rowan had meekly signed a treaty and been humiliated throughout the médim. But seeing Cooper beaten to a pulp while he sat idly by was too much by far.

He stormed across the hall toward the doors where the silent, masked standard bearers stood. They stood aside to let him pass. Once outside, Max ran from the embassy as though the Furies themselves pursued him.

~ 6 ~

QUILLS AND SCROLLS

Dashing between Maggie and Old Tom, Max followed a serpentine path into the dark woods that skirted the northern edge of Rowan's campus. Panting, he pushed onward, intent on putting as much distance as he could between himself and the shameful médim at Gràvenmuir. The image of Cooper lying motionless haunted him, and he found he was in no mood to join his classmates at the bonfire. He ran faster.

Soon Max found himself in unfamiliar territory. He had never wandered this far north of the academic quad. He registered a distinct change in the air, as though the atmosphere were charged with something wild and elemental. Sweat cooled upon his skin as he slowed to a jog and glanced sharply around his sur-roundings. He was seemingly adrift in a sea of trees—gargantuan trees that appeared as though they'd been planted during a forgotten, primordial age. Their trunks were laden with moss that dampened the air and created an eerie sort of amphitheater. Max stopped to listen.

The silence was conspicuous. No calling bird, no scurrying creature disturbed the pervading stillness. Max became aware of his heart thudding within his chest. Breathing deeply to steady himself, Max took in a heavy scent of damp earth, wild herbs, and fallen leaves. The trees were so dense where he stood that he felt he'd stumbled into a thicket of deepest midnight. For several moments, he simply stood and breathed and listened, content to be just another inhabitant of the forest. In such darkness, Max could not see his wrist or the Red Branch tattoo that marked him.

He wandered deeper into the woods, far from any path he had ever walked or even seen on a Rowan map. Eventually Max came to a clearing, and he looked up to see a mammoth oak, standing alone amid a moat of dense undergrowth. From the deep recesses of the tree's leaves came occasional flickers of light, like a crown of winking stars along its branches.

As Max approached, these lights abruptly disappeared and all was quiet, but he could feel the presence of life—vibrant, watchful life—all around him. The forest was listening, and he felt very much the intruder.

Conjuring an orb of blue flame in his palm, Max peered about the clearing, leaning against the ancient oak tree.

"The fire burns me."

Max jumped at the voice—a deep, female voice that spoke in Greek. As quick as a wink, he snuffed the illuminating flame and glanced around the towering trees to find the speaker. He needn't look far. The oak tree shuddered, and a face emerged from the craggy patterns in its bark. A pair of beautiful eyes blinked at him, wet and shining.

"I didn't mean any harm," replied Max. "I was just . . . looking."

"I know," replied the spirit, not unkindly. "But we fear fire, and it is not welcome here."

"I'm sorry," said Max, squinting to better see the visage, which seemed to shift and ripple within the trunk, as though the oak were molten. A wild, willowy form stepped forth from the tree, and Max found himself staring at a dark woman with almond eyes, nettled hair, and glistening, reticulated skin that blended with the leaves and branches.

"Who are you?" breathed Max.

"I am a dryad," replied the wild spirit. She tilted her head and stared at Max, her expression curious. "My name I keep. And what are you?"

"I'm a human," explained Max. "A student at Rowan."

"A student, perhaps," mused the dryad. "But you are no human. I see stars upon your brow. Are you a spirit-child? Are you a demon?"

"I don't know what I am," Max replied in a hoarse, empty voice.

"How strange not to know," replied the spirit. "I have only just awakened, and yet I know myself."

"What do you mean, 'awakened'?" asked Max.

"I have been asleep," she explained. "The dryads have long been slumbering deep down among the world's roots. But many are waking again. We have been recalled to life by the Great God."

"What Great God?" Max inquired.

"The Great God who called to me and said my truename," replied the dryad.

"Not Astaroth . . . ," said Max. His mood darkened with this new evidence that the Demon had been very busy with the Book of Thoth and the secrets it contained.

"Yes," said the dryad, blinking slowly. "That was his name. I heard him whisper it unto me. . . . But is it wise to so boldly speak the name of the Creator?"

"Astaroth is not the Creator!" snapped Max. "He's a demon playing God!"

At this outburst, the dryad retreated several steps until her body had merged smoothly with the tree trunk. Her emotions seemed to totter between anger and confusion.

"What else would I call the one who breathed the life spark into me?" she hissed. "Who are you to proclaim knowledge of the Creator? You who do not even know what you are! I am a dryad. The one who gave me life is Astaroth! And Astaroth has returned to make the world beautiful and whole."

"No," said Max wearily. "The Demon has fooled you."

Long seconds passed while the dryad considered this.

"Perhaps I am foolish," she said. "Few pass this way, and I have need of a friend to explain this strange new age to which I have awakened. When last I walked, hags and their ilk feared the humans, yet tonight I have seen hags bear a man aloft as though he were the Great God!"

Max frowned at this unexpected image. A cold, sinking sensation began to pool in his stomach.

"You saw hags?" he confirmed slowly. "Hags carrying a man into the woods?"

"Yes," said the dryad. "I thought it was a festival, for the hags sang and danced, and the man seemed most excited. He wriggled like a fish and made the most peculiar shrieks."

"Oh no," said Max. "Was he a thin man? Hairless?"

"I believe so," replied the dryad.

"Where did they take him? Tell me quickly!"

The dryad pointed northeast, and Max was off, running through the woods, as swift as a deer. He called thanks to the dryad and promised to return someday.

As Max's search led him back toward the coast, the forest gave way to a night sky that roiled with great, pearly clouds. The surf roared from below the chalky cliffs as Max threaded through the tall fir trees that dotted the coast, searching for any sign of the hags and their abducted quarry.

At last he found a sign, but it did not bode well. Some hundred yards ahead, a dilapidated cabin stood in a clearing of packed earth. Within that clearing, a cooking fire was heating an enormous black cauldron and casting eerie shadows upon the clearing as the haglings leaped and danced in a merry circle around it. Mum was inside the circle, tasting the broth and bouncing in time to Bellagrog's singing. Keeping to the shadows, Max crept closer and was able to hear the hag's rough, tuneful voice as it rose above the crashing surf.

"Cut a potato, make it two.
Add some carrots, some celery, too.
One pinch of salt, a dash will do.
Let's make a Ras-mus-sen stew!

He slipped us once, but now he's caught.
We told him we'd forget him not.
Stoke that fire, heat that pot.
Revenge is a dish that's best served hot!"

Linking their arms together, Mum and Bellagrog clinked their wineglasses and struck up the song again. They cackled as one of the haglings lobbed a potato into the cauldron, sending up a splash. Max was revolted by the thought of Jesper Rasmussen cubed into mouthfuls and stewing in the pot. Crouching against the tree, he pondered his options.

If Max reported the hags, the entire Shrope family might be exiled from Rowan. While he did not much care if Bellagrog or the ferocious haglings were sent away, he cared very much about Mum. Mum was a hag, yes, but she was his hag. Bob's, too.

Max glanced back at the cauldron. The damage might be done, but he did not have to sit by and permit the hags to consummate the feast. Stretching forth his hand, Max focused on the fire and began to absorb its crackling energy into his body. The singing, capering hags seemed at first oblivious as the cooking fire died away, its bright flames retreating into the stacked firewood. When naught but a thin smoke trickled forth, Bellagrog ceased her singing.

"Oi!" she cried. "Ain't you listening, wee ones? I said 'stoke that fire, heat that pot!' This here pot's gone cold as Nan's headstone! Get some kindling and warm 'im up again!"

While Max debated how best to handle the situation, the haglings set about gathering more kindling from a neat stack by the cabin. Another poked a stick into a lantern until it smoked and caught fire. Meanwhile, Mum turned her attention to the stew's other fare, expertly peeling more carrots and potatoes. With a deft flick of her wrist, she tossed them over her shoulder.

The resulting splash was expected—what followed was not.

One of the potatoes flew back out of the cauldron.

It was a sorry, wobbling flight, and Bellagrog watched the spud come to a rolling stop on the packed earth. The potato was not alone, however. More vegetables shot out of the cauldron— carrots, onions, and an entire bulb of garlic—as though the stew had initiated a full-scale revolt. Grinning, Bellagrog hefted an enormous ladle in her meaty hand and tested its weight. Waddling over to the pot, she peered inside.

"Bwahahahaha!" she cackled. "Come have a look, Bea! Doc's still kickin', he is. Ooh, but he's a feisty one! Well, I can be feisty, too!"

Max was horrified. Bellagrog managed to land three clanging blows upon the still-alive-and-struggling engineer before Max seized her wrist. Shocked, the hag merely gaped at him as Max pried the ladle out of her grip and flung it away.

"So help me, Bel," muttered Max, moving Bellagrog aside and peering into the cauldron.

Stuffed inside was Dr. Rasmussen, bound and gagged and up to his nose in chicken broth. The man looked nearly insane with panic. Peering up at Max, he tried to scream but managed only a stream of bubbles that sent carrot slices bobbing away.

"Take it easy, love," cooed Bellagrog behind him. "Ain't nothin' happenin' here but Shrope family business. . . ."

"Bellagrog, put down that cleaver before I get really angry," Max growled, catching sight of the hag's sinister shadow. The bloated hag cursed and hung the tool back on her belt.

"Max, don't be angry," pleaded Mum.

"Angry?" thundered Max, wheeling on her. "You're cooking him alive!"

"Well, he's very stringy," Mum explained. "We needed to let him soak on a low simmer for two hours before—"

Max waved off her explanation and turned to their half-cooked, frantic prisoner, whose skin gleamed as red as a boiled lobster. The man screamed bloody murder as Max reached in and lifted him out of the broth.

"I'm sorry," Max whispered. "I know it hurts. . . . Just maybe try not to shriek so much."

It was no use. Even when cooling, Rasmussen was as pink, naked, and inconsolable as a newborn. Once his gag had been removed, he howled while Max set him gently on the ground and carefully removed his bindings. Even the slightest touch triggered a wince and a wail.

"I—I want them all arrested!" Rasmussen chattered, clinging to Max while wisps of steam rose off his body. "The little ones, too—they're the worst of all!"

"Shhh," said Max, trying to gently pry the man's arms away.

"They ambushed me!" sobbed Rasmussen. "Just before the meeting . . ."

"Shhh," Max whispered, easing him to his feet. "Let's get you back to the Manse. Easy does it. One step at a time. There you go."

"You're interferin' with Shrope family business!" thundered Bellagrog, her gray face flushed dark with fury. "Don't make me put ya on the list, Max!"

"Forget 'Shrope family business,' and stuff your list," muttered Max. "You'll be lucky if you're not marched to the front gates when the Director gets wind of this."

"Bel made me do it," simpered Mum, clasping her hands behind her back.

"Shut yer mouth, Bea," growled Bellagrog, gathering her haglings about her. The squat, ferocious things said nothing but clung to their mother's starchy skirt and glared at Max as he helped Dr. Rasmussen waddle away from the cauldron. As Max led the engineer back down the coast, Bellagrog's voice—almost incoherent with choked rage—rent the night air.

"This ain't over, Rasmussen! The Shropes never forget!"

The horror-stricken engineer let out a wail and waddled faster.

They had almost reached the Manse before Rasmussen realized he was naked.

By the time Max left his scalded, self-conscious patient in the moomenhovens' care, it was nearly dawn. He was exhausted but still far too charged for sleep. Instead, he ambled about the quiet

Manse, flitting like a shadow through sprawling rooms and intimate parlors. Occasionally he passed a domovoi or a fellow insomniac, but the huge, rambling house was largely still. The Manse had not yet awakened to the new chapter of its existence. Directly across from the Manse, separated by several hundred yards of grass and garden, was Gràvenmuir.

Walking outside, Max gazed at it from the Manse steps. The building perched against the cliff's edge like a great black vulture. It was a dark, Gothic structure whose pinnacles and steep roofs swept up toward the sky like a many-pointed crown of iron. Its stone was weathered, and its spires were twined with black ivy as though it had stood upon the wind whipped coast for centuries. Rowan's buildings—gleaming and newly built—appeared the newcomers. While Gràvenmuir's exterior was dark, its windows were alight and the interior gleamed like molten gold against the gray dawn. The building's front doors stood wide, spilling light onto the dark lawn. By all appearances, the demons' embassy was open for business.

Max turned on his heel and closed the Manse's heavy doors behind him.

Climbing the winding stairs, he continued to traverse many long hallways until he approached the Bacon Library. Its door was open, and from within he heard frantic scratching sounds, as though Rowan's entire student body were madly scribbling to finish a final exam. Peering inside, Max saw a most curious sight.

Suspended in midair above the tables were hundreds of slender black quills. Before each quill was a stack of parchment, an ink bottle, and an open book whose pages turned on their own. Guided by invisible hands, the quills copied away like overcaffeinated scriveners. Upon one of the tables, two Highland hares were engaged in quiet conversation next to a flickering candle stub.

"I don't see why we need to stay, Dalrymple," moaned a young tawny specimen with tufty ears. "The quills work just fine on their own."

"They need someone to give 'em fresh ink now and again," replied his long-whiskered elder. "Anyway, Tweedy said that Mr. Menlo wants us to supervise 'em so he can be told straightaway if there's any problems."

"He's just a student, for all love," yawned the sleepy hare. "Since when do students give the orders at Rowan?"

"Student or not, Hamish, that boy might just have saved us from another Dark Age. I'll sleep once I know the classics have been copied fair. Be still now. . . ."

Max glanced once more at the scribbling quills and backed quietly out of the library. The mention of David rekindled his curiosity. Where had David been throughout the evening? Prusias might have been less haughty and the médim less humiliating if Rowan's greatest Sorcerer had bothered to show.

Stealing down the hallway, Max hurried to his dormitory wing. Unlocking the observatory, Max entered his room and saw that two letters had been slipped beneath the door. The first note was a plain scrap of paper that had been folded in half.

MAX, COME FIND ME FIRST THING IN THE MORNING. LOTS TO TALK ABOUT. DIRECTOR WANTS TO SEE YOU BEFORE SUPPER.
                                        —COOPER

P.S. I'M FINE. DON'T LOSE SLEEP OVER IT.

Max exhaled with relief and turned to the second letter, whose peach stationery and graceful script were very familiar.

Well, I waited up as long as I could but finally gave up. Where are you?!? Everyone's been guessing and gossiping nonstop about the demons, and I was hoping someone would fill us all in before we were herded through the back door of the Manse. No one will let us go out on the quad. Honestly, the place is under lockdown! Anyway, the aforementioned certain someone is now in unspeakable trouble and owes another certain someone a dance.

Just teasing. I think you're very cute and neat and hope that we can spend some time together tomorrow. Lunch in the Sanctuary? Sweet dreams.

—Julie

Max grinned and tucked the note back in its envelope. Closing the door behind him, it seemed that the room's glass-domed sky and faint constellations triggered the weariness within him. Yawning, he glanced at David's bed, but its curtains were closed and he did not hear his roommate's peculiar, whistling snore. Despite his recent anger at David, Max dearly wished he were present. David had such a logical way of looking at things and could always unravel Max's mental knots with a few penetrating questions. Gazing up at the wheeling stars and then around the room's many nooks, Max wondered where David's secret door was hidden.

Max knew it would not be visible—no twinkling veil to the outside. But he might feel it—after all, Mystics left traces, and he could sometimes perceive magic like a faded stain. He strolled to David's side of the room.

When he came to the moon-stitched curtains that hid his roommate's bed, he paused, guilt plucking at his conscience. David was an intensely private person, and Max was painfully aware that his trespass was a gross violation of privacy. He tried to see things from David's perspective. Despite Max's great and growing abilities, it was David Menlo who bore the world's hopes upon narrow shoulders and a borrowed heart. Max was not asked to enchant copying quills or to raise buildings from rubble or to scry the dark corners of the world for a glimpse of far-off happenings. These things fell to the frail blond boy who shared this room and who maintained that he had good reasons for the secret errands that had been occupying his time.

While Max had many confidants—his father, Bob, Cooper, even Hannah—it suddenly struck him that David was very much alone. When David had arrived at Rowan, the only family he acknowledged was a very sick mother back in Colorado. To Max's knowledge, this mother had abandoned David, whose early letters had been stamped "return to sender." David had borne this as he bore so many things—with a quiet stoicism that belied his youth. Of course, Ms. Kraken or Ms. Richter or any of the scholars would have been thrilled to serve as a surrogate family, but Max knew that David did not look to them for such things. He looked to Max. In all other matters, David Menlo kept his own counsel.

But there were times, Max reasoned, that one could not keep his own counsel. David admitted that he had seen Prusias before . . . but where? Max's thoughts flitted faster through his mind. David knew things, yet he refused to answer very reasonable questions. David was experimenting with substances that might be dangerous to Max. David had been summoning things, and this was now a strict violation of Astaroth's edicts.

Max thumbed the edge of the silken bed curtains. David had been using his secret exit in search of answers; perhaps Max could, too. For all he knew, David was in great peril. Max would have failed his friend and violated his oath if he did not go searching for David. He glanced at the Red Branch tattoo upon his wrist. It was his solemn duty to protect his evasive roommate . . . for everyone's good.

Max pulled the drapes aside. Despite his nagging conscience, he stepped into the space beside David's still-unused bed and peered about in search of a door, some subtle gateway to the outside world. Far off, Old Tom rang seven o'clock while Max jostled the bed, searched beneath it, and flung blankets about in a desperate quest for David's elusive door. He found naught but crumpled parchment, a Rowan sweater, and an empty bottle of crusted ulu blood—a rare substance priceless for its ability to translate arcane languages.

Max slouched dejectedly on the bed. He was not only guilty of violating David's privacy; he had further failed to find anything of use. Sighing, Max simply sat still for a moment until something moved within his peripheral vision. Cocking his head, he stared at the headboard, whose mahogany grain was swirling in and out of focus as though viewed through an adjusting lens. Jumping to his feet, Max stood at the bedside and exulted in the thrill of discovery as the dark grains snaked into discernible letters. This same thrill evaporated, however, when the letters joined to spell out a snooper's ultimate nemesis.

PASSWORD?

"Menlo!" blurted Max. "Colorado . . . Maya . . . Ulu . . . Richter . . . Sidh . . . Cobbler . . . Sorcerer . . . Ice cream . . . no, no, no!"

The last utterance was not a password attempt, but an exasperated reaction to the headboard, whose message had begun to fade. Letters became clusters of dark grain, and soon the headboard had returned to its original state. Max rapped it, but nothing happened.

"So close," he moaned, sinking his head onto David's pillow.

He gazed up at the magnified constellations overhead. Cassiopeia shimmered into view, followed by Perseus, and then Cetus. Max blinked as the golden threads that comprised the mythical sea monster dissipated into tiny motes of light.

When Max awoke, he was in his own bed. Propping himself up on his elbows, he saw that he was still wearing his shoes and that a glass of water had been placed on his night table. Swinging his legs over the bed, he pushed through his drawn curtains and looked out over the rail to the room's lower level.

David sat at the table, methodically writing in his journal. Max marveled at how David had adapted to the use of his left hand, which was now as dexterous as the one he had lost. The pen moved quickly, and David rocked back and forth as he was wont to do when deep in thought. Taking his glass of water, Max padded down the stairs.

"David, I'm sorry I tried to pry into your things," he said hoarsely. "It was wrong."

David did not respond immediately, but instead pushed back from his seat and ambled over to his armoire to remove a battered shoebox. Opening it, he dumped a pile of baseball cards onto the table and sorted through them. Finding the one he sought, he plucked it up.

"Come and have a look," he said, holding it between his fingers.

Max peered at the card, which showed the faint image of a slugger in the midst of a ferocious swing. It looked like an over-exposed photograph.

"This was my favorite card," said David. "I used to collect baseball cards back in Colorado. We didn't really have any money, but the cards were cheap and you got some chewing gum with every pack. Whenever I had a dollar to spare, I'd ride my bike down the hill to Twill's Tobacco Shop and Sundries," he said with a nostalgic smile. "I'd imagine it's long gone now. Anyway, I loved the anticipation. I'd buy my dollar's worth and pedal as fast as I could to a spot by the river where I could sit and get away from all the headaches at home. I'd open each pack and chew the gum and turn over each card like it held my fortune. Most of the cards were junk, but one day I found this. . . ."

"Is it really valuable?" asked Max.

"No," laughed David. "It was worth ten bucks maybe—but it was better than anything I'd ever found. Money was tight at my house. My mom couldn't work, and the neighbors took advantage of her. They knew when she'd got her government checks, and they'd always show up with some story about how they needed a loan just this one time. But it was never just one time. And they never paid her back."

"Why?" asked Max. "Why did she keep giving them the money?"

David stared at the card. "My mother is handicapped, Max," he replied carefully. "Her IQ's not much higher than sixty. It wasn't a very hard thing to fool her."

Max nodded in understanding, but inwardly he reeled. It was exceedingly rare for David to mention anything about his past life, but he had alluded to his mother once and to the fact that she could not really take care of him. Max had always assumed she was very ill or was an alcoholic.

"Well," David continued. "One summer, one of the neighbors—Mr. Bailey—came by with a broken teakettle and sold it to my mom. I was afraid of Mr. Bailey and hid behind the couch, watching him look through her wallet and count her money. He told her it was her lucky day—his teakettle was worth two hundred dollars but he'd let her have it for the ninety-three dollars she had on her. Well, Mom handed over the money, and Mr. Bailey laughed and told her she was one sharp cookie."

"David," said Max quietly. "That's awful."

David only nodded. "That was all the money we had, and the welfare check wouldn't arrive for another week," he explained. "There was no food left in the house. The next day I sat and watched her open the refrigerator and frown and then go through her purse. She did it six or seven times. She never really made the connection that the money was gone and we couldn't buy any more food. The next week was horrible. She got so hungry that she'd just sob and lie on the floor. When she finally fell asleep, I'd take out this baseball card and study it under the lamp. I could have sold that card, Max. Mr. Twill would have given me ten dollars for it. But I didn't."

"So what did you do?" asked Max.

"When it got dark, I'd scrounge through the neighbors' trash for garbage," David replied, placing the card facedown on the table. "I fed my mother dog food, Max, but I got to keep this baseball card."

Neither spoke while David scooped the cards back into the box.

"Everyone does shameful things," said David, breaking the silence. "It was wrong for you to invade my privacy. It was wrong for me to keep that card. I'm sorry for what I did. I know you're sorry, too."

Max looked sharply at his roommate. "To be honest, David, I'm only sorry I got caught. I want to know what you're doing."

"And I'd like to tell you," answered David. "But that's not going to happen."

Max frowned and searched his friend's face for any indication of a chink in the armor, a latent willingness to share. There was none.

"I met Prusias," said Max heavily. "You always seem to know everything, so I assume you know about the embassy outside."

"Yes, I do," said David. "Prusias is a bigger fool than I could have hoped."

"Well, I'm glad you think so," said Max. "He doesn't come across that way. He issued the edicts and raised Gràvenmuir with a single twirl of his cane. I've never felt that much magic in one place before. It was scary."

"Exactly!" said David, brightening. "Forget the edicts for a moment—they were utterly predictable. Oppressors always make rules restricting people's movements, communication, history, teachings . . . Hitler, Stalin, Pol Pot. What was *not* predictable was Prusias's impatience to flaunt his newfound power. That's a real weakness, Max. That's something that can be used."

"What do you mean?" asked Max. "What newfound power?"

"Max, Prusias is a powerful demon, but he's one whose entire history has been concerned with wealth and its accumulation. What he did tonight is well beyond anything that's ever been documented. I could not do what Prusias did tonight . . . and neither can he."

"But then how . . . ?"

"You said it yourself," said David, grinning and pushing a tin of cookies at Max.

"The cane," Max mused aloud. "The energy did seem to come from the cane. So the cane is some sort of artifact?"

"I believe that cane harbors a very powerful ingredient," said David. "It's a boon for Prusias, and one that's bound to create some profound jealousy among his rivals. Just between us, I think a page from the Book of Thoth has been embedded within that cane. Prusias is too arrogant and impulsive to realize that his display of power was bound to raise questions at Rowan and beyond. I'd bet his rivals have already heard all about last night's fireworks and are adjusting their plots accordingly."

"What rivals?" asked Max. "What plots?"

"The rulers of the other three kingdoms," replied David. "I don't believe that Prusias is the most senior or powerful among the four demonic rulers, but he was chosen to represent Astaroth on this mission. And he has just showcased a conspicuously powerful gift. Lord Aamon won't like that. Neither will Lilith or Rashaverak. Forgive my saying so, but the only redemption Prusias had last night was provoking you into acting insubordinate. You made Ms. Richter look as if she doesn't wholly speak for Rowan."

"How do you know about that?" asked Max.

"Because I was there."

"What?"

David merely nodded and closed his journal, placing the pen on top.

"If it makes you feel any better, his evening wasn't a total success. I'm sure he's disappointed that you didn't just charge into the ring."

"He almost got his wish," Max admitted, frowning at the memory. "I hate Prusias."

"If it's any consolation," muttered David, "you're not the only one he tried to bait tonight."

"What do you mean?" asked Max.

"Did you see that woman among the demon entourage?" he asked. "She wore a jester's costume and brought the edicts to Prusias."

Max nodded.

"That was my mother."

~ 7 ~

SHARPS, FLATS, AND SELKIES

David Menlo would not elaborate upon this revelation. He betrayed no glimmer of emotion as Max peppered him with anxious questions about Mrs. Menlo, her current whereabouts, or her presumed danger among the demons.

The discussion was over.

Showering and dressing, Max made his way out of the dormitories and into a residential wing that housed some of the senior faculty. Cooper's apartment was located somewhere nearby, but Max had never visited the Agent before. He peered at doors and nameplates until a helpful Mystic pointed him toward a plain wooden door at the end of a narrow hall. When Max knocked on the door, he was happy to hear Cooper's familiar Cockney accent.

"It's open."

Somewhat hesitant, Max entered and saw Cooper sitting at a small writing desk. The Agent's room was no silken palace—or even Connor's humble cottage—but rather was the picture of Spartan simplicity. Glancing at the bare walls, Max wondered whether the space had even been configured. In one corner was a bedroll, a bookcase, a desk, and a dented steamer trunk.

"How are you feeling?" he asked, glancing at the bandages wrapped around Cooper's hand.

"Bit knocked about," grunted the Agent, smearing a balm over his skinned knuckles. "Grahn's got quite a grip, but I been through worse."

"I'm sorry I ran out," said Max. "It's just—"

Waving off the apology, Cooper covered his knuckles with a final bandage. Flexing his fingers, he stood. "That's not why I asked you here," he said. "Take my seat. I want to show you something."

Walking over to the trunk, the Agent removed a deck of playing cards and sat cross-legged on the floor. Neatly halving the deck, he began methodically shuffling the cards.

"Do you know how a con works?" Cooper asked.

"What?"

"A con—a confidence game," replied the Agent, cutting the deck and shuffling faster. "Well, a confidence game is played between sharps and flats. Sharps are predators; flats are prey. Now, most cons have three stages, Max. The first of these stages is called the pledge. The pledge occurs when the sharp gets the flat to buy into the basic premise of the game. The pledge is very important, as it sets the stage for the rest of the con. For example, a card game . . ."

Cooper's hands became a blur. He cut the deck again and shuffled, flicking a stream of cards from one hand to the other.

"The second stage," he continued evenly, "is called the turn. The turn occurs when the sharp permits the flat to glimpse something unexpected. This lures the flat into thinking he's clever and catching on. Every flat wants to think he's a sharp; a good con lets him believe it."

As he spoke, Cooper periodically flashed an ace from among the cards—procuring them as though at will. It was a clever trick, but Max's quick eyes saw that the Agent always managed to palm them, separating them from the rest of the cards until they were needed.

"I get it; I get it," said Max wearily. "You're hiding cards and are going to deal yourself an unbeatable hand."

"No," said the Agent. "Not quite. You're forgetting about the third stage of a con, Max. That third and final stage is called the prestige. The prestige occurs only after the flat's been duped and is convinced that he's in on the trick."

Something tapped Max on the shoulder.

Whirling around, Max saw Cooper's scarred, impassive face looking down at him. The Agent tapped a sheathed knife once between Max's disbelieving eyes before placing the weapon on the desk. Stepping past Max, he stooped to examine his illusory double, which continued to shuffle and deal as though nothing had happened. With a sharp snap, Cooper dispelled the illusion.

The thought of being a flat reddened Max's cheeks.

Cooper merely shrugged. "It's no fun to be conned," the Agent acknowledged. "My point was to show you that you ain't always in on the trick. There's an old saying in poker: 'If you can't spot the sucker, the sucker's probably you.'"

"So you're calling me a sucker?" growled Max, his temper kindling.

"No, mate," replied Cooper calmly. "You're not a sucker, but you're an impulsive whelp. Let's take last night—"

"I want to forget all about it," said Max. "Why didn't you just finish Grahn when you had the chance?"

Cooper smiled.

"I don't like getting my nose pulled any more than you do," replied the Agent. "Neither does the Director, I might add, but last night was not the time to lay our best cards on the table. If the demons think we're a sorry bunch, so much the better. . . ."

Max gaped.

"You lost on *purpose*?"

"Those were my orders," said Cooper, shrugging. "Truth is, I almost botched it. That Vyndra got me so fired up, I hit his boy with everything I had. Damn near killed 'im, I think. Director would have been mighty displeased if Grahn hadn't come to."

"Why wouldn't you let me in on the plan?" asked Max.

"Because you're an impulsive whelp," repeated Cooper. "Personally, I don't think you could have let yourself lose. And then there are other possibilities. . . ."

"Like what?"

"Like Vyndra, Max," replied the Agent. "Grahn was just a brute, but Vyndra's right dangerous. I think if you'd gone into the ring, Vyndra wouldn't have left things to Grahn. He'd have had a go at you."

"So what?" snapped Max. "I'm not afraid of him."

"Maybe you should be."

"We're in the Red Branch," said Max proudly. "We shouldn't be afraid of anything."

Cooper frowned at this and walked to the other end of the room.

"We *are* in the Red Branch," he acknowledged. "And that means we sometimes have to go places others cannot. Most times those places are dark and the things in them can be scary. Pretending otherwise doesn't make one brave, Max. It makes one a fool."

Max did not reply. His attention drifted to the bookcase where a curious object akin to an ostrich egg sat upon the topmost shelf. Cooper merely watched as Max took up the gleaming oval and rubbed its oily surface. The object was covered in some sort of membrane that slid beneath Max's fingers.

"Is this an egg?" Max asked, cradling its unexpected weight in both hands.

"Turn it over," Cooper suggested.

Max did so.

His gaze fell upon an enormous bloodshot eyeball sporting an iris of cobalt blue. Max promptly dropped the gruesome thing. It landed with a surprising crack and rolled to Cooper's feet. The Agent picked it up and placed it back on its stand within the case, swiveling the iris so that it did not face them.

"Where the heck did that come from?" asked Max.

"Fomorian giant," muttered Cooper.

"Oh," said Max. "The one on the Isle of Man?"

"That's the one," said Cooper.

"Señor Lorca mentioned him," said Max quietly. "He said that's how you . . ."

"Lost my face," said Cooper curtly.

"I guess you hurt him pretty bad, too," said Max.

At this, the Agent actually laughed. "Who knows? Fomorians—or at least this Fomorian—have any number of eyes. My memory's a little foggy on it all. Half my face was burned . . . just smoldering scraps, really. I figure it aimed to just bite me in half and end things. But once I got close enough . . ."

Max winced as the Agent made a savage wrenching motion with his hand.

"What happened?" whispered Max.

"Couldn't say," replied Cooper, shrugging. "When Lorca found me, I was unconscious and cradling that eye like my first-born. Anyway, now I've got a souvenir to remind me that it's okay to be afraid."

The Agent smiled, but there was unmistakable pain lurking beneath. Max remembered the photos he had seen of Cooper before the incident; William Cooper had been a handsome man.

"Can't the moomenhovens . . . you know, heal your wounds?"

"They tried," replied Cooper. "The Fomorian is Old Magic—old as roots and rocks. His works don't just go away. Since you seem to know something of the story, I guess you know why I went looking for him."

"Señor Lorca said it was to have the giant fix Cúchulain's spear," Max replied.

"That's right," said Cooper. "I, too, was an impulsive whelp."

"Why?" Max asked. "What was so impulsive about trying to fix the *gae bolga*?"

"Everything," replied Cooper, staring at his hands. "I'd just been admitted to the Red Branch. I was taken down to the vault to choose my weapons. Vilyak and the others showed me Cúchulain's broken spear—told me it was the Red Branch's greatest treasure. The others couldn't even touch it; the *gae bolga* burned their skin or screamed and wrenched itself out of their hands. At first, I couldn't touch it, either. But I kept trying and found it would let me hold it for a minute or two. The pain would come eventually, but it was all the encouragement I needed. I'd read the stories, Max. . . . Thought if I fixed that spear, it would make me invincible. I got greedy. And I paid."

The Agent scowled at the memory. He blinked.

"Anyway, last night's médim and my scrape with the Fomorian aren't the only reasons I asked you here. Now that we've signed

Astaroth's treaty, our scouting expedition will begin. The Red Branch heads out tomorrow morning. I'm splitting the twelve members into six pairs. You'll come with me."

"Where will we be going?" asked Max.

Cooper unrolled an antique hand-drawn map of North America. While the eastern coast was meticulously detailed, the interior was nearly blank. Max's eyes scoured the document out to its frayed and tattered edges. There were no labels. It was almost as if America had never been discovered.

"Where's New York?" asked Max, squinting. "And Boston?"

"That's what we aim to find out," replied Cooper, tapping the map. "All the modern maps are fading. The scholars have their theories, but no one's been off campus to test 'em."

"David's been off campus," Max said.

"No one's been off campus," repeated the Agent. "We've got posts at every exit."

"My mistake," said Max said.

"We'll travel on horseback south along the coast and then west," he said, returning to the map. "You're excused from classes and your teaching responsibilities until we return. This is the Director's highest priority."

"When do you think we'll be back?" asked Max, thinking of Julie and his pangs to join his friends during the upcoming school year.

"Two weeks," mused the Agent, rubbing patches of blond stubble. "Maybe three. Depends on what we find."

By the time Max left Cooper and the Manse behind, he was feeling better. Despite the brooding presence of Gràvenmuir, the lawns were teeming with people. Determined to adopt his mentor's resolve, Max ignored the dark spires and instead set a brisk pace toward the Sanctuary, where he knew Julie would be waiting.

An unexpected sight greeted him on the far side of the Sanctuary's gates. All along the broad border hedge, and extending down toward the lagoon and Warming Lodge, were a host of stakes and pennants. Among these markers, hundreds of humans, domovoi, and even the odd satyr ambled about, measuring distances, tying colored ribbons to various stakes, and consulting with a professorial man with white hair and a neatly trimmed beard. Max hurried over.

"What's all this, Mr. Vincenti?" asked Max, stepping aside so some huffing domovoi could pass with a wagonload of timbers.

"Max!" exclaimed Mr. Vincenti, shaking his hand warmly. "I'm glad to see you out and about after last night's . . . well, all the excitement. Apologies for the mess, but we're breaking ground on a new township—one inside the gates."

He unfolded his broadsheets and let Max have a closer look. Scanning the documents, Max saw beautifully rendered drawings of a village with winding, cobbled lanes and quaint little buildings and alleys. Scanning the key, he read aloud: "'Cobbler shops, tanneries, weavers, blacksmiths, dyers, wheelwrights' . . . it's like a whole city!"

"It will be," said Mr. Vincenti proudly. "As you can imagine, we now need to make everything ourselves using older means and methods. Everyone will be trained in a trade and put to work. Fortunately, we're salvaging old techniques from books, and many of the Sanctuary residents are a godsend. The dvergar can mold metal like clay. . . ."

"Why can't we just replicate modern technologies?" asked Max. "I mean, I realize things like engines and printing presses have disappeared, but can't we re-create them?"

"You're lucky you even remember them," said Mr. Vincenti. "Most of the refugees have already forgotten they ever existed. Even I'm getting foggy on some things."

"That's so strange," Max muttered. "You've been an engineer all your life and you can't remember how things work? I mean, what if you looked at a schematic or something?"

"I've tried," said Mr. Vincenti, shrugging sadly. "No matter how often David's quills copy the blueprints for industrial technologies, they fade in minutes. By now the originals have all gone blank. Even when I tried to memorize a schematic, I couldn't retain anything longer than a few seconds. It's maddening—like a fish darting just out of reach."

"And that's all due to Astaroth?" asked Max.

"Astaroth and the Book," confirmed Mr. Vincenti. "With it, he can reshape the present however he chooses. At least he's wise enough to leave the past alone."

"What do you mean?" asked Max. "He's taken away all those inventions. We're *living* in the past."

"He's taken them away from us," said Mr. Vincenti. "But he hasn't stricken them from the Book entirely. He hasn't made it so that they never existed. To do that would be to change the course of history, and those consequences are too unpredictable."

"Is this going to give me a headache?" asked Max. "David once tried to talk to me about time travel and my head hurt for days."

"I'll keep it simple," said Mr. Vincenti, smiling. "Let's say I possessed the Book and used it to remove certain medicines from human history. I don't mean just making them vanish from shelves, Max, but eliminating their existence in both past and present. Well, that would fundamentally change the course of history, wouldn't it? What if my grandparents had only survived childhood due to those medicines? My parents might never have been born, and thus I would never have been born! And if I'd never been born, how could I possess the Book and remove those medicines now?"

"Here comes that headache," Max moaned.

Mr. Vincenti laughed. "Needless to say, you can see that even a very minor change to the past might result in endless outcomes. I can't imagine Astaroth would take such risks. After all, if he was foolish enough to *alter* the past, he might well lose control of the present. No, I think he can exercise all the control he wants by reshaping the present and causing memories of the past to fade."

"Will people even remember that Astaroth is our enemy?" wondered Max, recalling his conversation with the dryad.

Mr. Vincenti gazed out over the Sanctuary, which was thriving with life, energy, and the combined effort of humans and creatures that had previously tottered on extinction. The man shrugged. "If he leaves us alone, I might be willing to forget on my own."

The statement disturbed Max. He spied Julie lounging with her friends down by the lagoon and handed the blueprints back to his teacher.

"I'd better be going, Mr. Vincenti. Thanks for the lesson."

"Have fun," replied the teacher, turning his attention to a pair of waiting dvergar—slate-skinned dwarfen creatures with white eyes and bronze ringlets in their beards.

Max jogged down the slope toward the lagoon and sneaked up behind Julie, putting his hands over her eyes.

"Guess who?"

"Hmmm," she mused. "Is it Tweedy? A hagling? No, no . . . the voice isn't deep enough. It can't be Max. . . . Max McDaniels is far too busy to be hanging out with mere students."

"Ha-ha," said Max, flicking her earlobe.

She giggled mischievously. "Come squeeze in," she said, scooting over so Max could sandwich in between her and several other girls. "You got my note?"

"Yup," said Max. "I'm really sorry I couldn't make it to the bonfire, but stuff came up."

"That's putting it mildly," said one of the other girls. "A black castle just sprouted up across from the Manse! Did you see it happen?"

"I did," said Max softly.

"And you met Lord Prusias?" asked another, closing her book.

Max nodded, curious at the tone in the girl's voice. She sounded dreamily envious.

"Was he handsome?" she asked.

"He's a demon," replied Max coldly, "not some celebrity."

"Well, I heard he's handsome," the girl said defensively. "And wealthy. I read a story about him in last year's Summoning course. Some people think he was the genius behind the rise of the Medici in Florence. Handsome and smart!"

Max was aghast. "Am I missing something?" he asked, turning to Julie. "Are we seriously discussing how handsome Astaroth's ambassador is? Please tell me we're not."

"Of course not," said Julie quickly. "But you have to admit that all these changes are kind of exciting. We're living in a new world, Max! You can't blame someone for wanting to know what's happening. There's a new race . . . a new royalty that's being introduced. Who wouldn't be a little curious?"

"I guess," said Max. "Well, if you want to know what's happening, I can tell you that you won't be reading about Prusias in Summoning anymore. Summoning has been banned."

"We know," said Julie, gesturing toward a stack of bound sheaves of parchment. "All Summoning materials have been pulled from the course books."

"Still," said the girl, her eyes twinkling, "I've heard that Prusias likes to be summoned. You just wade to your waist in water and say his name three times."

"No," said another girl, "I heard you drop a coin into a well and whisper some sort of rhyme."

"I wouldn't do those things," cautioned Max. "Even the other demons were scared of Prusias."

"What's he like compared to Astaroth?" asked the other. "You've met them both, haven't you?"

Max did not know what to say to this. He was exceedingly annoyed by the question—it seemed to make light of grave matters—but the subject did intrigue him. He remembered his conversation with Astaroth at a crossroads in the far-off Sidh. He envisioned the Demon's white face, the smooth hair that framed it like black silk . . . the jesting, merry eyes that seemed perpetually amused. Compared to the imposing swagger of Prusias, Astaroth was almost delicate, effete. And yet Max knew that Astaroth's shimmering visage was but a mask. Behind those crinkling eyes, Max had glimpsed a terrible, unblinking will—a will that was beyond human understanding and that merely chose to cloak itself in a slender, smiling form.

"Prusias may call himself a lord, but Astaroth really is some kind of royalty," said Max quietly. "He's—he's like a lonely star that has fallen to earth and will burn it all away. . . ."

"I didn't know you were a poet," teased Julie, leaning into him.

"I'm not," said Max, gazing at a shiny lump of gray rock jutting out of the lagoon. "But I just don't know how else to describe— What the heck is that?"

The rock had begun to move and was turning a slow, majestic circle about the lagoon, bending the reeds and lifting its head to peer benevolently at the children who now waded into the shallows, clapping and pleading for a ride upon its gray-brown back.

Max gaped.

It was a selkie, nearly the size of a school bus. Blubber was spread generously across its broad frame in great, rippling mounds. The selkie's carriage was proud, and it cruised about the languid waters like a pleasure yacht. Raising its nose high, it sniffed the air once, twice, and then issued a low *barooooom*ing call that sent two herons flapping away.

"A new selkie," said Max, standing to watch as the creature coasted toward the lagoon's farther bank.

"A *male* selkie," said Julie.

Max raised his eyebrows.

"I've never even heard of a male selkie," he reflected. "Where are Frigga and Helga?"

"Off somewhere freshening up, probably," said Julie. "His arrival has sent them into a tizzy. They've been fetching His Highness fish all day."

"His Highness?" asked Max.

"Sir Olaf the Insatiable, Lord of Leisure," said Julie, rolling her eyes.

"You're making that up," said Max.

"I am not," replied Julie. "And believe me when I say I've got it right—Sir Olaf is a stickler for proper address. Either title will suffice, but he prefers them both."

"Wow," said Max, kicking off his shoes and sitting down once again. For the next twenty minutes, he deflected a nonstop flurry of questions from Julie and her friends about the previous evening.

Then Old Tom chimed four o'clock and Max groaned.

"I have to go," he said apologetically. "I have a meeting with Ms. Richter."

"But you just got here!" said Julie. "And I wanted to show you something. Are you free after dinner?"

"Sure thing," said Max.

"When does your meeting start?"

"A minute ago!" called Max over his shoulder, waving good-bye and dashing toward the tunnel.

* * *

Ms. Richter's office had changed considerably since the Siege. Gone were the computerized maps and backlit screens that tracked all manner of Agent activity. Gone, too, were the electric lights, air-conditioning vents, and even the gleaming miniature of a Bugatti—a toy from childhood—that had adorned the elegant desk. Instead, light came from many candles, a breeze cooled the room from a crack in the French doors, and the world—what remained of the known world—was mapped on a cream-colored tapestry upon the far wall. Yet all evidence suggested that this was still a room where councils were kept and decisions were made.

Max gathered that one such decision was imminent, as there were four chairs placed before Ms. Richter's desk and three were occupied. Ms. Richter sat behind her desk, fixing him with a frank expression.

"I'm sorry," said Max. "I lost track of time."

The Director motioned for him to sit, and he hurried to fill the empty chair between Dr. Rasmussen and the two scowling hags. Mum patted Max's hand, but Bellagrog did not even glance up. Instead, she sagged lower in her seat, folding her meaty arms across her chest.

"Please continue with the account of your assault, Dr. Rasmussen," said Ms. Richter coolly.

"Assault?" spat the engineer scornfully. "It was nothing of the sort. It was murder—attempted murder! As your guest and a representative of the Frankfurt Workshop, I demand justice."

"Humbug!" protested Bellagrog. "The tipsy drunkard tripped and fell in me broth!"

"Lies!" said Dr. Rasmussen. "Your children . . . your—your swarming abominations carried me off! They heaved me into that pot and shut the lid on my head!"

"Where's yer proof, ya silly creature?" demanded Bellagrog,

snapping her fat fingers at him. "I won't have the Shrope family name dragged in the gutter by this lunatic. I won't have it!"

"Are you insane?" cried Rasmussen, waving his bandaged arms about. "I'm red as a lobster! I'm half-boiled and bandaged! McDaniels was there—he saw everything!"

"Is this true, Max?" asked Ms. Richter evenly. Max turned to look at Mum, who was staring at her floral skirts and fighting tears.

"What would happen to the hags if it was?" asked Max.

"That's not the issue at present," replied Ms. Richter. "Can you attest that the hags abducted Dr. Rasmussen and tried to cook him?"

"Of course he can!" shrieked Dr. Rasmussen.

"Be quiet!" snapped Max, glaring at him. "I warned you to keep away from them, didn't I?"

"Just answer the question, Max," said Ms. Richter calmly. "Did you see the hags abduct Dr. Rasmussen?"

"Well," said Max carefully. "Technically, I didn't see them abduct anybody; I mean, he was already in the pot—"

"That's true, Director!" interrupted Bellagrog. "Max found that nitwit right after we did! Good thing for the doc that we were all there to save him. . . ."

Ms. Richter raised an eyebrow and glanced coolly at Bellagrog, who abandoned her tale and returned to her indignant scowl. The Director's attention shifted back to Max.

"Need we discuss the difference between being forthright and being honest? I expect both and would ask that you abandon the clever semantics. Do you believe that the hags abducted Dr. Rasmussen with intent to eat?"

Seconds ticked off a wall clock. Mum began to sob while Max fidgeted and looked helplessly about the office. With an apologetic glance at Mum, he opened his mouth to speak.

"I demand a trial!" roared Bellagrog.

"Excuse me?" asked Ms. Richter.

"A trial," hissed the hag, leaning forward. "A trial by our peers. Ya gots to give us one, Director—it says so right in your little rule book!" She thrust a quill-copied tome at the Director.

Rowan Academy: Common Law and Customs.

"I don't think a formal trial will be necessary," said Ms. Richter wearily.

"Oh, really?" cackled Bellagrog. "Well, I do! And it says I'm entitled to one right there in Article Three, Section Four—top of the third paragraph! I know my rights, Director, and I'll be damned if I sit by and let you run roughshod over 'em!"

Ms. Richter rubbed her temples before consulting a calendar on her desk.

"Very well," she said. "We'll conduct your trial three weeks from today. Mr. McDaniels will be traveling for some time and cannot appear before then. I presume that is sufficient time to prepare your defense, Bellagrog?"

"Plenty of time, Director, thankee," replied the hag, apparently mollified.

"This is an outrage," whispered Rasmussen. "I—I can't be expected to stay in this magical petting zoo for another minute, much less three weeks. . . ."

"Then you will forgo your opportunity to testify, and we'll be obligated to drop the case," said Ms. Richter.

Bellagrog chuckled with satisfaction and knit her fingers across her broad belly.

Steadying himself, Dr. Rasmussen leaned forward and glared at her. "I demand round-the-clock protection!" he declared.

"Given the circumstances, I think that is a reasonable request," said Ms. Richter. "We'll see to your security."

"That's defamatory and prejudicial!" roared Bellagrog,

smacking Ms. Richter's desk. "If a bodyguard's following this fool around, what's a juror gonna think? Why, they'll convict the Shrope sisters before we gets our day in court!"

"Bellagrog," said Ms. Richter, a warning note in her voice. "You have requested a trial and received it. Dr. Rasmussen has requested protection and will receive it. That is fair, and that is all. You are dismissed, and you are suspended from kitchen duties until this matter is settled. That goes for you, too, Mum."

The smaller hag burst into tears. "But Bob is just easing his way back," Mum said. "He can't manage on his own!"

"We'll see that Bob gets all the help he needs," said Ms. Richter reassuringly.

Once Bellagrog had slammed the door, Ms. Richter sighed and jotted a note on a piece of stationery. Folding and sealing the note, she let it slip out the window, where it skimmed away as though a bird in flight. Easing Dr. Rasmussen out of his seat, she escorted the beet-red man toward the door.

"It's best if you return to the healing ward, Jesper," she said. "That letter was for Agent Eames, who will meet you there. She'll take good care of you until the trial."

"But what are her qualifications?" inquired a panicky Dr. Rasmussen. "D-does she have real-world experience with hags?"

"Yes, yes," said Ms. Richter, easing Dr. Rasmussen out of the room and closing the door firmly. She sighed again, then turned back to Max. "Can I get you anything to drink?" she asked. "Water or lemonade?"

"No," said Max. "I'm fine, thank you." He sat in uncomfortable silence as Ms. Richter took her seat only to rearrange the wild-flowers in a vase.

"I'm sorry I disobeyed orders, Director," Max blurted. "I didn't mean to do the wrong thing—I only wanted to help Cooper."

"I know," she replied quietly.

"Are you angry with me?" he asked.

"How shall I answer that?" she chuckled, and leaned in to sniff the flowers. "Max, put yourself in my shoes. I have just signed a treaty with our conqueror, witnessed the creation of a demonic embassy on our lands, and endeavored to embark on a new Age of Discovery. That keeps me busy. Furthermore, I have a school to run, and Rowan's facilities must be expanded while we find homes or jobs for thousands of refugees. You might say I'm swamped and reasonably conclude that it tries my patience when I must put everything aside to deal with insubordinate teenagers and legally savvy hags." She paused and sighed a third time. "I take it that Cooper imparted a valuable lesson earlier today?"

"Yes," replied Max. "He taught me about sharps and flats."

"Good. Right now I need scalpels, Max. Not hammers."

Max nodded.

"But that's not all I need," she added. "Max, I would like to know what David Menlo has been doing."

"I don't know," replied Max.

"Max, I'm sure you can appreciate the necessity for full disclosure. I do not delude myself that we can restrict David's movements or activities, but we should at least collaborate."

"Can't you just call him to a meeting?" asked Max.

"He doesn't answer," she said, frowning. "He's withdrawn entirely. What does he do in that room of yours?"

"I don't know," said Max. "Honestly, Ms. Richter. David keeps everything a secret—he says he needs it that way."

The Director sighed, brushing a stray strand of silver hair from her forehead. "That poor soul might jeopardize all my plans," she muttered.

"What if he's thinking the same thing about you?" asked Max.

Ms. Richter's eyes flashed up. "Thank you, Max. That will be all."

* * *

Supper had hardly begun when Julie took Max's hand and led him from the dining hall. The two stole out of the Manse and across shadowed walkways, where lanterns flickered in the twilight. They laughed and crunched leaves underfoot, hurrying toward the Sanctuary and whatever secret spectacle Julie wished to show him.

Within the Sanctuary, the sky deepened from azure to indigo. Stars twinkled above the looming mountains.

"Let me just see if Nick's in the Warming Lodge," said Max. He had not seen the lymrill since the feast and was curious that his charge had not come calling within the Manse.

"He's not in the Warming Lodge," said Julie assuredly, looping her arm within his.

"How do you know?" asked Max, scanning the clearing for any sign of Nick peering from behind a rock or among the tall grass. The lymrill loved an ambush.

"Oh . . . just a hunch."

Max pestered her with questions, but she refused to answer as they wound their way up into the forested foothills that bordered the broad clearing. Where one path split into several, Julie took the one veering north. Once they'd climbed a few hundred yards, she stopped and peered about.

"I think that's it," she said, crossing over to a young sapling. Max saw three thin lines marked in one of the branches, and Julie put a finger to her lips. Taking his hand, she led him off the path and into the resin-scented trees. They arrived at the base of a towering beech whose bark had nearly been stripped and scored away.

Julie leaned close to whisper in Max's ear. "After the bonfire, I was upset that you didn't show," she said. "Camille and I went for a walk, and I saw Nick near that tree I marked. I called to him, but he ignored me. I thought it was weird—he usually comes right over when I call. I decided to follow him—I thought he might be sick. Well, he sniffed the air and paced around, then suddenly bolted up this tree!"

"Is he okay?" asked Max, growing concerned.

"See for yourself," said Julie, pointing to a thick branch some twenty feet above.

Gazing up, Max spied the faintest hint of sharp, glinting quills among the branches. When Max called, he heard a familiar mewl. There was a stirring in the branches, followed by a sprinkling of bark and discarded rodent tails. Lifting the shutter on her lantern, Julie sent a beam of light up into the tree.

Max gasped as not one but two pairs of eyes were illuminated.

"He's better than okay," Julie laughed. "He's in love!"

For a full minute, Max gazed with quiet pleasure at a sight he thought he'd never see. Next to Nick perched a second lymrill, a silvery female who shone as fine and bright as the moon.

~ 8 ~

HERE BE MONSTERS

Descending the tree headfirst, Nick leaped the final ten feet and landed with a thump to circle Max and Julie. Smoothing his quills into a gleaming pelt, Nick brushed against them with feline affection, pausing occasionally to peer up at the female who still lingered amid the branches. Mewling, Nick stood on his hind legs and hooked his claws into Max's sweater, ripping the wool.

"Hey!" said Max, swatting vainly at the sturdy creature.

"I think he's telling her that you're family," laughed Julie.

The female lymrill mewled in kind and stirred from her perch to ease cautiously down the trunk. While the female sniffed at Max, Julie shone the light upon her, illuminating a slim, sleek form that suggested something like a ferret. Unlike Nick's coppery quills, the female's brightened from bronze at the base to silver at the tips. The needle-sharp tips alternately bristled and smoothed as she acclimated to the humans. Her amber eyes peered up at Max as she sank back on her haunches and issued a low growl, shaking her thick tail like a maraca, as Nick had done years before. Max braced himself for what he guessed would come next.

Sure enough, the sleek head darted forward and nipped his outstretched hand, drawing blood.

"Ouch," muttered Max, shaking his injured hand.

"Why'd she do that?" asked Julie, coming closer to examine the bleeding wound.

"To let me know she can," Max replied. "Nick did the same thing when he chose me."

"That looks pretty bad," said Julie, gathering wild rose hips from a thicket. Crushing the bulbs between her hands, she began to whisper a mild healing spell when Max stopped her.

"It's okay," he said, holding up his hand and wiggling his fingers. "All better."

"I don't understand," said Julie, blinking as she inspected his hand by the lantern. "There were at least four deep punctures. How did you do that?"

"What can I say?" quipped Max, petting the female lymrill, who now gnawed placidly on his shoelace. "I'm a fast healer."

Julie's eyes fell upon the pale scar that traced a thin, straight path from Max's cheekbone to his chin.

"Why didn't that one heal?" she asked.

"I don't know," he responded, shrugging. "I got it while I was training in the Sidh. Scathach caught me when I was slacking."

"And who's Scathach?" asked Julie, raising her eyebrows.

"A woman," replied Max. "She lived at Rodrubân."

"How old was she?" asked Julie.

"No clue," said Max, laughing. "Time doesn't work the same way there. She looks young, but she could be older than YaYa. She's been training warriors for ages."

"Hmmm," said Julie, stooping to stroke Nick, who had been pacing about her feet. When she spoke next, her voice was unnervingly casual. "Was she pretty?"

"Very," replied Max, reflecting on his last glimpse of the raven-haired woman standing atop Rodrubân's ivory towers. Even in silhouette, Scathach's strength and sorrow were evident in subtleties of poise and posture. "Beautiful, even."

An awkward, lingering silence ensued. At length, Julie sighed and pulled Nick's head close to her own, kissing his otterlike muzzle. She laughed.

"Really, Max," she said. "You should spend more time with Sir Alistair. If you don't have the good sense to lie and declare her a shambling, wheezy thing, then you should simply call her 'cute.' *Cute* is manageable. *Cute* is nonthreatening."

"Point taken," said Max. He stroked the female lymrill's whiskers and sought to change the subject. "I guess we need to give you a name. What should we name her, Julie? I think we should call her Eve—you know, since she might be the only female around."

"Nick and Eve?" muttered Julie. "I think not. My vote is for Circe."

Scouring his memory, Max hit upon the *Odyssey* and remembered its isle-dwelling sorceress—the one who transformed men into swine. He wondered whether Julie was trying to tell him something.

"Fine," he said evenly. "Circe it is."

As if taking to her new name, Circe nuzzled Max and curled

into a ball, ignoring Nick, who had ventured over to nibble at her flattened ear.

"So," Julie said, "anything else you want to tell me about this Scathach? Better now than tomorrow at lunch with all my friends prowling about for gossip."

"I'm not talking about Scathach or anything that happened in the Sidh," said Max firmly. "And I can't talk about anything tomorrow, anyway. I'm leaving at sunrise for a few weeks."

Julie stood in the golden lantern light, plucking at a slender bangle. "You're joking," she said, her voice barely rising above a whisper.

"I wish I was," said Max. "The Red Branch is heading out to explore Rowan's territory. We can't be sure any of the old maps are accurate. Everything's uncharted now."

"But what about school?" protested Julie with a disbelieving laugh. "What about the class you're teaching?"

"I'll catch up when I get back," replied Max.

Biting her lip, Julie's eyes darted about as though searching for possible loopholes. When they finally met his, their light had dimmed.

"And when did you plan to tell me this?" she asked stiffly.

"Tonight," said Max softly. "Don't be angry. I just found out myself."

"I see." Julie hugged him. Her cheek was warm and wet, and it lingered a moment against his until finally she broke away. "Should I leave the lantern with you?"

"No," said Max. "You take it."

She nodded and walked away with the lantern dangling at her side. Its warm yellow light receded until it passed beyond a stand of aspen and finally disappeared. Kneeling, Max held Nick and Circe close and simply listened to the forest. The moon was high, the night was full, and the lymrills paced with hunger.

"Happy hunting, you two," he muttered. Emptying his pockets, he left several small ingots of iron on the dewy grass and strode up into the hills, where the trees thinned to reveal a broad sweep of the plain below.

By sunrise, Max was seated on a stool in Rowan's main kitchen, stirring his oatmeal and gazing forlornly at the coffee mug that Scott McDaniels had placed before him.

"If you can wait a few minutes, there'll be fresh milk," his father said, rinsing his hands in a basin of wash water. He sighed and sank heavily onto the opposite stool, glancing at a handwritten list of the day's recipes. A pantry door closed behind Max, and he turned to see Bob lumber out, hefting a sack of barley. Apart from his injuries, the ogre looked haggard, and Max guessed that he had heard all about Mum's and Bellagrog's troubles. The ogre rumbled hello, but squeezed past into the inner kitchens and closed the door behind him.

"Is Bob okay?" asked Max.

"Oh, he's all right," replied Mr. McDaniels, pouring himself a cup of coffee. "Worried about Mum. Of course, we'll be shorthanded without the hags, but we'll manage—plenty of applications to work in the kitchens. Everyone's eager to earn their bit of gold now that everything's gonna cost 'em."

"You're charging now for food and stuff?" asked Max.

"We will be," replied Mr. McDaniels. "The farmers can't work for free, Max. They need money to buy tools and clothes and everything else. We do, too."

"How much for the coffee?" asked Max with a weary grin.

"It's on me, moneybags," said Mr. McDaniels.

"I thought you were saving up to buy me a car," Max joked.

"What the heck is a car?" asked his father, looking up. "Is it expensive?"

"It's nothing," said Max, his smile fading. "Forget about it. Anyway, I need your advice about Julie. Do you think she was breaking up with me?"

"Nope," said his father. "But she might be considering it after you just let her go off alone."

"But I thought she wanted to be alone."

"No," mused his father. "She wanted you to go after her. She wanted you to show that you cared about her feelings and that you'll miss her these next few weeks."

"Well, it's too late now," said Max, glancing at the morning sun peeking through the windows. "Why couldn't she just say what she meant? Why couldn't she be direct?"

"She *was* being direct," chuckled Mr. McDaniels. "She was just speaking a different language. Girls and boys often do. Anyway, she's not the only one who'll miss you, kiddo."

"I know—I'll miss you, too. Will you be all right?" asked Max.

His father managed a "sure, sure" as he creaked up and arranged clean coffee mugs on a tray to be taken out into the dining hall. Fishing for his wallet, Mr. McDaniels pressed something into Max's hand. It was a small, blank piece of paper, cracked and bent as though it had been handled many times.

"I'll be fine," rumbled his father. "By now I'm used to you disappearing out into the blue. But I have a favor to ask while you're out on your expedition."

"What's that?" asked Max, still studying the blank paper.

"If you happen to find a pretty spot—a tree or a little hill by a lake—would you bury this for me?"

"Sure," replied Max, "but what is it?"

"A photo of your mother," explained Mr. McDaniels. "This is the last one to fade. Got none left now, and it's torture plain and simple to hold on to them. They're all blank and white like Bryn never even existed. I've gotten rid of the others, but I want the last to be somewhere out in the world, sleeping somewhere nice. Can you do that for me?"

"Of course, Dad."

The two said their goodbyes, and Max took the faded photograph of his mother, wrapping the paper in linen and slipping it inside his woolen coat.

Minutes later, Max had slung his pack over his shoulder and walked out the Manse's front doors. Waiting beneath the rowan trees, near the fountain, were a dozen saddled horses stamping the morning dew from their hooves. Cooper sat astride a champing Appaloosa and held the reins of a glossy black Arabian.

Hurrying down the steps, Max nodded to the Red Branch and began tying his pack to the Arabian's saddle. The others returned his greeting, but it was not a talkative crew. The lone exception was Xiùměi, a wrinkled Chinese dumpling of a woman with a grandmotherly face that utterly belied the tales that Max had heard of her burning British opium ships, assassinating rival warlords, and driving a particularly lawless clan of vampires from her native province. She rocked playfully in her saddle, her belly plump with age, and jested with her immediate neighbors, who could not help but smile.

Once Max had mounted up, the Red Branch followed Cooper into the thick woods along the school's southern border. There, they came upon an imposing gatehouse of white stone that was set into a wall some fifty feet high. Cooper called up to the guards—a pair of Mystics peering from a latticed window— and the Red Branch waited as Rowan's new gates were opened for the very first time. The gates swung inward, spilling bits of spoil and ivy and revealing the warding spells that David had engraved into every beam, band, and rivet of its exterior. With a groan, the gates continued their slow, grinding progress.

"What's out there?" Max whispered.

"Diyu?" Xiùmĕi chuckled, tapping Max's leg with a garlanded sword. "Acheron, maybe? My guess is trees."

Max smiled, but his heart beat faster as the gates opened. He felt a quickening surge of dread and, for just a moment, imagined that there was nothing beyond Rowan's gates—just a vast abyss that stretched on forever.

"I wish you were coming with me, young Hound," chuckled Xiùmĕi, patting Max's horse. "My sword arm is not as strong as once she was."

"We're only to observe and report," said Max, trying to comfort her.

"Tell that to the Enemy," she replied, loosening the razor-edged jiang in its scabbard.

Max saw that Xiùmĕi was right—beyond Rowan's threshold were no damned souls or proverbial lakes of fire, but merely a muted forest thickly carpeted with mist. The path from Rowan's campus came to an abrupt end once it reached the threshold of the gates. Beyond, all was wilderness.

This held true well past the moment their horses whinnied and nosed their way across the threshold and began the slow, clopping walk west toward Rowan Township. As Max's Arabian picked its way through the deep grass and flowered knolls, he sat up in the stirrups, straining for a glimpse of the clapboard church or the Grove, a cozy restaurant perched atop the hill that overlooked the town from the southeast.

But no such glimpses were to be had. The forest continued, uninterrupted, for as far as Max could see. The Red Branch rode slowly, tentatively, the horses' hooves carving wispy trails through the cool mist, which filled in behind them, leaving a white veil in their wake. But this was no haunted wood from fairy tales; squirrels leaped from branches, and birds issued a chorus of calls as the bundled crew picked its way among whatever paths allowed a passage through the bent, ancient trees.

After ten minutes, Max saw that Cooper had circled his Appaloosa around a small clearing clustered with violet and ivy. The Agent tugged at the reins and swung himself off the horse. Digging through the underbrush, he cocked his head and squinted at something before calling the others over.

"Anyone recognize this?" he asked, gesturing at a sharp gray shard of stone poking from the soil.

No one responded until a youngish man with auburn mutton-chops laughed and poked at the stone with a spike-topped ax.

"Why, that's the sword from the statue in the town commons!"

"Atta boy, Danny," said Cooper, scratching distractedly at his cap. "Don't bode well, sorry to say. Remember how tall this statue was? And the patisserie should have been"—the Agent gazed around and then turned on his heel to point decisively at a thick grove of ash trees—"there. We're smack in the middle of town, but it's been . . . swallowed."

Max's spirits sank. He had suspected this—dreaded this—but had nevertheless harbored a slim hope that Rowan's quarantine had just been a paranoid measure. He had hoped in vain.

"All right," said Cooper, remounting the Appaloosa. "Ben and Natasha will stay here and examine the site. The rest ride on as assigned. See you 'fore Samhain."

Beckoning to Max, Cooper spurred his horse on at a fearsome pace through the woods, weaving through the trees with a precision that Max—an excellent horseman in his own right—found difficult to match. Yet he kept up as they dipped and wove their way through the forest until the trees thinned and opened onto a meadow dotted with hazel and honeysuckle.

Glancing over his shoulder, Cooper caught his breath, which fogged in the air as he approximated the distance they had

traveled. Reaching into his pack, the Agent procured a thick
packet of tan parchment and unfolded it.

"God bless 'em," he muttered, scanning the document. "It
works—even at a full gallop."

Panting and patting his horse, Max leaned over and peered at
the edge of the parchment, which displayed a geographic record
of the territory they had covered, right down to the lightning-
split oak that stood alone in the clearing. Their progress had been
inked upon the Mystic scroll with all the art and science of a
master cartographer. Spurring his horse, Cooper set them on a
new course that veered to the southeast.

Like their wondrous map, the land unfolded before them—
mile after mile of rocky coastline and rolling forest bearing no trace
of human habitation. They rode in silence, each scouring a different horizon for evidence of man, monster, or the Enemy. From
what Max could tell, Rowan represented the only outpost of civilization in this corner of the world. It was a bleak, lonely thought.

For the next week, the duo rode on, and their map came to
resemble those of Cortés or Cabot. Massachusetts Bay yielded
nothing of note; there were no indications of Boston or of any
human habitation whatsoever. Examining the map, Cooper
steered them to the west, and for days Max played a game where
he sought to catch his shadow as the sun rose behind them and
turned the switchback grass to gold.

As the days passed, the air grew colder, and most mornings
found Max shivering as he washed his face with icy water and
prepared for the day's journey. Given Cooper's habitual silence,
Max entertained himself at night by trying to draw the many
creatures he had seen. He'd sketched birds and deer, squirrels, and
even a young black bear that had paused at their passing, nosing
the air before crashing off through the underbrush.

They traveled west up into mountains, through tall forests of spruce, and across streams so bitingly cold that the horses refused to drink. Making camp one evening on a mountainous slope, Max borrowed Cooper's bow to search for game to replace their stores, which were becoming tough. He walked along the mountainside, his eyes adjusting quickly to the deepening dusk, searching for suitable quarry.

Game was abundant, and Max found a choice target within the hour. A whitetail buck stood grazing upon hawthorn. Oblivious to its danger, the deer presented its profile and chewed its supper with a staid, quiet expression while Max notched an arrow and drew the bowstring to his ear. The arrow's flight was straight and true, striking the deer just above the heart and dropping it before it could take a second step.

Lowering his bow, Max crossed to where the buck had fallen and checked to ensure that it was dead. Removing the arrow, he set about field dressing the animal, removing its organs and cleaning the meat before he would carry what was needed back to camp. Max worked efficiently, taking a certain satisfaction from the idea that other animals and insects would use what he could not. Gazing west across the valley, Max saw the autumn trees blaze in a final flash of red and gold as the sun dipped below the opposing ridge and the landscape fell into twilight. Wiping his hands clean on the grass, Max shouldered the deer and turned to make the steep, slow walk back to camp.

But something blocked his path.

It was a human being. A boy.

He was roughly the same age as Max, with a tangle of dark brown hair. His shirt was ragged and his shoes were worn as if he'd been living in the wild for months or even years. Max's heart leaped at the discovery of this fellow human, and he fought hard against the temptation to whoop and embrace this wary stranger.

Easing the deer off his shoulder, Max held up both hands and bowed his head in greeting.

To his surprise, however, the boy did not respond. He merely stood, rooted to the spot and trembling, as though in shock. Only now did Max discern that the boy was gasping, struggling to catch his breath, while sweat ran swiftly down his mud-spattered face.

"I'm a friend," said Max calmly, showing his empty palms.

Thud, thud.

Max started at the ugly, nearly simultaneous sounds. From the boy's chest protruded two arrowheads, whose tips trickled with green witch-fire. The boy staggered, his eyes fixed upon Max; then he fell forward onto the slope, sliding down the dry leaves until his body curled into a limp ball at the base of a poplar tree.

An excited voice called from up the slope.

"Connla n'uhlun veh delyael morkün!"

Max froze.

This was the language of the demons.

Unsheathing his gladius, Max spoke a Word of Command and retreated a step as his illusion camouflaged him perfectly with his surroundings. He watched, gripping the short sword tightly as an imp hurried down the hillside to inspect the kill. Rolling the boy over, the imp hissed with satisfaction, revealing a pair of small, sharp incisors. It extinguished the eerie flames and extracted the arrows with a practiced hand.

Despite his revulsion, Max held still. The imp carried no bow. It had not fired the killing shots.

The hunters were still unseen.

Settling into a crouch, Max watched as stones rolled down the slope, loosened by whatever was now trodding heavily down the mountain. Something green bobbed uphill: an arrowhead wreathed in the same green flame as those that had killed the boy. As the flame came closer, Max saw its light reflected in three eyes—pale tiger's eyes—set within the face of a horned rakshasa. It was Lord Vyndra.

"Caia!" repeated the imp, pointing proudly at the slain boy.

The rakshasa stopped some twenty feet away, the third arrow still notched in the bowstring. A rumble sounded from its chest. It inhaled deeply, seeming to savor the night air and its kill. Its voice—resonant and long accustomed to command—spoke down to the imp. To Max's surprise, it spoke in English.

"Do you not see Death waiting for you, miyama?"

The imp swiveled its head and peered in shock at Max. Baring its teeth, the imp hissed and with a pop transformed itself into a snake that slithered swiftly beneath the fallen leaves toward its master. Max crouched lower.

"I am surprised to see you here," continued the rakshasa smoothly. Keeping his arrow notched, he turned to survey Max. "Were you hunting it, too?"

Max said nothing, but stayed silent in the shadows.

The rakshasa laughed. "Hide in spells or the shadows if you will, child of Rowan. It matters not. I see you."

Continuing down the hill, the rakshasa came to stand above the slain boy, turning the body over with its clawed foot. A dreadful purr sounded from its throat, and its eyes gleamed with some fire kindled deep within.

"He ran a long time, this one. Farther and faster than the others." Lord Vyndra glanced at the dressed carcass of the deer. "Does Rowan's Hound hunt for sport or food, miyama?" The demon stooped to sniff the deer's blood.

"I know not, master," hissed the imp, which now twined about the rakshasa's neck, its forked tongue flickering.

"Food," said Max, fighting the tremor in his voice as he

approached the demon. The rakshasa raised its bow when Max had come within a dozen feet. "What do you hunt for, demon?"

The demon did not reply, but instead pulled the bowstring taut.

"Put down that sword, child of Rowan. We do not seek a fight with thee."

"Ha!" said Max, unable to contain his scorn. "But you shoot a boy in the back!"

The rakshasa glanced down at the corpse, then at the deer, then at Max.

"You must see a difference. I do not."

"You're not supposed to be here," seethed Max, struggling to control his emotions. "The treaty, the edicts, all of it! This is Rowan's kingdom—you're not allowed to be here!"

At this the demon's three eyes narrowed to slits as it shook with laughter. With another pop, Vyndra's imp transformed back into its tiny, elfin shape and stood atop its master's shoulder.

"If the death of a stranger upsets humans so, how do they react to kin?" the demon mused. "I did not know that your kind was so sentimental. No wonder you fascinate Prusias so. Is it weregild you require?"

"What?" asked Max.

"Blood money," growled the demon. It nodded to the imp, which hopped down and held forth a small bag of coins.

"I don't want gold," said Max, glancing at the purse with disgust. "I want you to leave."

The demon seemed to consider this and cocked his head at the weapon in Max's hand.

"I am a guest in your kingdom," he acknowledged. "I will take my prize and go." With one great arm, the rakshasa scooped the boy's limp body and slung it over his shoulder.

"You're not taking him," said Max, his voice trembling. "You leave him here."

The demon turned and glared at Max, a hulking black silhouette in the darkening forest. Only his eyes shone through the dusk.

At length, the dead boy's body slid from the demon's shoulder and landed heavily upon the fallen leaves. From far off, a hunting horn sounded—a hideous, spectral braying that chilled the blood. The whole of the forest fell quiet, as if every creature in the broad valley took refuge within its nest or burrow.

"You may have Astaroth's favor, but be warned: Lord Vyndra has his limits."

The demon bared its teeth, withdrawing into the darkness with a contemptuous sneer. Max felt the surrounding air grow still before a sudden rush of scorching wind and fire rushed past him, flying off into the night with a wild, primal howl. Branches were snapped and needles were singed, but the forest seemed to breathe again. The demon had gone.

Max gazed down at the boy's corpse and wondered in anguish if the boy had believed him to be another hunter—a second demon—that had cornered him on the mountain. He recalled the boy's twitching panic, his confused indecision when Max had greeted him. Had that moment cost the boy any chance at escape?

The hike back to camp took Max most of the night. Not because the boy was heavy—he weighed little more than the deer—but because of the terrible hunting horns that periodically sounded across the valley, causing Max to halt and listen for long stretches. Even at a distance, the calls were terrifying.

As Max expected, the camp was empty—the fire was extinguished, its encircling stones cold and scattered. Peering at one of the moonlit stones, he made a hastily scratched "C" and knew the Agent would be back. Max sat cross-legged in the darkness, every sense attuned to his surroundings while the gladius lay unsheathed across his lap.

Shortly before dawn, Cooper returned.

The Agent came to stand by Max and stared down at the body of the boy.

"What happened?" he asked quietly.

Max told him the story.

"Vyndra's not the only one," he confirmed. "I left to scout. The valley's filled with hunting parties. You heard the horns?"

Max nodded.

"It ain't just demons out there," said Cooper. "I saw an ettin along that ridgeline." The Agent pointed to a jagged stretch of mountain whose peak was lost in the gray morning. "Two-headed giant. They're supposed to be extinct, but I think all kinds of things have woken up and are walking about."

Turning back to the body, the Agent inspected the wounds and frowned. "We'll bury him by that tree," he said, shaking his head. "And then we'll start back. We've learned enough for now."

"What have we learned?" asked Max, wearily.

"The cities and towns are gone," he replied. "And we're not alone out here."

The Agent lifted the boy and carried his body to the edge of the camp, where he began to dig a grave. Rising to his feet, Max fumbled in his pocket for the faded photograph of his mother. Max would bury the photograph with the boy. He knew his father would not want the boy to be left by himself on this lonely mountainside. As he walked over to the grave, Max spied Cooper's map lying open. The parchment was now richly detailed with mountains and hills, rivers, streams, and lakes. Cooper had scrawled a note upon their location. It contained only three words, but they sent a shiver down Max's spine.

Here Be Monsters

~ 9 ~

HONOR AND PRIVILEGE

The journey back to Rowan was long, with many river crossings and slow, arduous climbs through the mountain passes that walled the land's interior from the coast. The world may have changed, thought Max, but the seasons progressed as they always had. The brilliance of autumn was beginning to fade, surrendering its fiery plumage as great, whistling gusts from the north stripped the branches bare.

It was October 28, mere days from the Feast of Samhain, when Max glimpsed Rowan from afar. Max had never seen the new, rebuilt Rowan from such a perspective, and it reminded him somewhat of the gleaming castles that dotted the Sidh. The walls were a reassuring sight, a reminder that not all was darkness in the wild.

As they approached the city, Max was surprised to hear the hooves transition from turf to cobblestone. They were cantering along a lane that curved gently to the north and guided them toward Rowan's gates. The trees on either side had been felled, and now Max saw whiskered domovoi and humans in homespun clothes working in the woods, clearing brush and stacking firewood onto carts. Up ahead, the massive gates stood open, with many young children at play within their shadows.

Even Cooper smiled at the shouts and yells of the children zooming about, kicking balls, playing with hoops, and digging through piles of leaves. Among several adults, one familiar face stood out—Scott McDaniels sat patiently on an overturned bucket while a determined preschooler bunched his few hairs within a barrette.

"Max!" he cried, rising at once and inadvertently shooting the barrette off his head. "You're back! We've been worried."

Max grinned and swung off the horse, embracing his father and enduring the usual observations that he'd grown, looked tired, and "My goodness, was he growing a beard?" Eager to make his report, Cooper bade them farewell, and thus the two McDanielses were left to sit beneath the walls and watch the dozen preschoolers climb, dig, bawl, shout, and erupt with laughter.

"Are you ditching work?" asked Max.

"We have more help in the kitchens now," his father explained. "Most afternoons, I watch these little monsters. Now that they've opened up the gates, we've been heading out here. Nice to finally poke our noses out the door."

"Are you sure it's safe?" asked Max.

His father laughed. "There are sentries on the wall, and, besides, the whole forest's thick with woodcutters and surveyors cleaning things up and planning the new roads. Ten thousand people can't all live within Rowan's walls forever."

"But there are demons out there," said Max. "Other things, too, probably."

"Well, I don't know about 'other things,'" said Scott McDaniels, "but the demons don't seem altogether bad. By the way, you'll want to watch that term *demons* when you're inside. They don't care for it, preferring instead their clan names—imps, rakshasa, mazikin, and such. Sir Alistair passed out a chart, but it's hard to remember 'em all."

"Still sounds like you know a lot about them," said Max.

"Well, it's hard not to come across 'em in there. Gravenmuir's a busy place."

"Don't tell me you've been inside," said Max, appalled.

"Course I have," replied his father. "Most everyone's been in there at some point. Trade's been kicking up, and the ambassador's been hosting gatherings and salons in the evenings. Today's market's winding down, but I think some of the stalls are still open."

"Sounds like one big party," said Max grimly.

"Well," said his father, "given what everyone's been through and what everyone was expecting, you can't blame folks for breathing a sigh of relief and enjoying themselves."

"It's like everyone forgot what happened," Max mused. "How many millions of people died last year, Dad? Do you let that go because the demons now seem nice? Doesn't that seem wrong?"

"How many millions have died throughout mankind's wars?" retorted Mr. McDaniels. "War's an ugly thing no matter who's involved, Max. I'm for peace, and from what I can tell thus far, so are they. But enough of all that. I want to hear about your journey. You can tell me while we walk the little ones back. I've got your schoolbooks and assignments. The homework is really stacking up. . . ."

"No rest for the weary," Max groaned.

"Ah," said his father, clapping his arm. "It'll be good to be back in school. C'mon, let's grab these munchkins and head back in. They close the gates at nightfall and that's not so far off."

With two bickering exceptions, the children quickly fell in line and followed Mr. McDaniels, while Max led the Arabian back inside Rowan. While they walked, Max ruminated on his father's words and the idea that Gràvenmuir had become a part of daily life.

A sweeping glance of the central campus did not reveal any marked change. People bustling about on their way to evening classes or dinner or taking air on a stroll about the gardens. Gazing off toward the athletic fields, Max saw students playing Euclidean soccer—a traditional game complicated by the fact that the field might shift or change shape at random intervals. All seemed right with the world, until Max focused his attention upon Gràvenmuir.

The embassy was alight, the beautiful details of its black stone gleaming and streams of light issuing from every open door and window. Music could be heard from within, hypnotic, tantalizing chords of a belyaël. Within the embassy's fence, crowds of humans milled about, perusing tables and tents where merchants plied their wares. The combination of elements struck Max as strange—like a bazaar upon the steps of a dark cathedral.

Old Tom struck five o'clock, and Mr. McDaniels waved goodbye to the children, who continued on with the other adults.

"Well, what do you think?" asked his father. "Could be worse, eh?"

Max did not reply, but instead gazed upon building foundations and scaffolding beyond Old Tom and Maggie. "What's going on there?" he asked.

"More academic buildings," said his father proudly. "New

colleges. I'm thinking of taking a class or two. And that's not all—the new township's really taking shape in the Sanctuary."

"Is David doing all this construction?" asked Max.

"No," replied his father. "Which is why it's going slower than usual." Mr. McDaniels's energetic cheer faded, replaced with grim-faced angst. His voice lowered to a whisper. "Max, you should know that David's a hot topic these days—and not in a good way. People say he's not cooperating with Ms. Richter. And there are worse rumors, too."

"Like what?" asked Max.

His father glanced at a couple strolling nearby and lowered his voice. "That he's been secretly leaving school. They say he's been attacking demons . . . sinking merchant ships before they can reach Rowan Harbor. The ambassador insists David's been seen in Blys, but I don't see how that's possible. Blys is clear across the ocean, and Miss Boon says he hasn't missed a class since school began." Mr. McDaniels's face flushed, and he fidgeted uncomfortably. "The stories are ugly, Max. Disturbing. You'd never believe them of our little David, but he hasn't denied a thing. I hear Lord Prusias wants him arrested and is pressuring Richter. . . ."

"Have you talked to David?" Max asked. "He loves you."

"I tried," replied his father sadly. "Stopped by your room a couple of times, but he doesn't answer. The one time he opened the door, he just thanked me for the cookies I had brought him and closed it again. He doesn't look right, Max. I think it'd be best if you moved in with me."

In silence, the two led the Arabian back to the stables and then headed back to the Manse.

"It was a long trip," said Max. "I buried that photo of Mom. I left her with someone who needed her."

He told his father of the boy slain by a demon's arrow and

now lying in a mountain grave. Instead of the dining hall, the two took their supper in Mr. McDaniels's apartment. As they finished, Max spied a thick sheet of parchment. Holding it to the candlelight, he saw that it was a flyer, stamped with the golden seal of Prusias.

LAND, WEALTH, HONOR, AND PRIVILEGE!
The Great War is over, and opportunity awaits those wise enough to seize it!

Lord Prusias requires men and women of adventurous spirit and noble disposition to aid in the administration of his vast, expanding Kingdom of Blys. Suitable candidates shall be granted land, hereditary title, and a retinue befitting royalty in the grand tradition. Those candidates blessed with mehrùn—or magic, in your worthy tongue— are particularly desired, but all are encouraged to apply. We do humbly request submissions before the Feast of Samhain. Early applicants shall have first choice among the prized and lush estates.

Interested parties should see Mr. Cree, secretary to the high ambassador, and request an application forthwith!

"What's this nonsense?" asked Max.

"Oh," said his father, growing sheepish. "That. Well, it is what it says it is. An invitation to apply for a mini-kingdom or some such thing."

"And you've got it here as a joke," Max concluded. "I mean, you'd never consider . . ."

"Of course not," said his father with a snort. "Can you imagine Scott McDaniels tromping about with crown and scepter? Nope. Not me. Can't blame a fellow for indulging his imagination, though."

Max smiled and sighed, tossing the flyer aside. "Can you believe anyone would fall for something like this?"

"Yes, I can," said his father with a definitive nod. "I've seen lots of folks waving these sheets and asking for Mr. Cree."

"Well, they're fools," said Max bitterly. "Greedy, grasping fools. Ms. Richter or someone should stop them."

"By what right?" Mr. McDaniels chuckled. "We're not Ms. Richter's or Rowan's prisoners. People have a right to go where they will, Max. If it turns out to be dangerous or foolish, then so be it."

"Freedom of choice and all that," said Max.

"Amen," said his father, thumping the table. "Now go get some rest. You've got school tomorrow!"

By the time he set out for classes the next morning, Max felt as if he had been reborn. His hair was cut, his face was shaven, and for the first time in recent memory, he looked and felt like a real student. Hurrying down to the dining hall, he chatted with Rolf Luger, a fellow student, enjoying the heft of his books and even the horror stories regarding Third Year classes. According to Rolf, Miss Boon was tyrannical, Ms. Caswell assumed they were all crack mathematicians, and Mr. Vincenti's homework often necessitated all-nighters. At breakfast, the gleeful trio of Cynthia Gilley, Lucia Cavallo, and Sarah Amankwe joined them. The girls were as interested in Max's new look as they were in his travels.

"Too short, Max," Lucia said, inspecting his hair. "No soul, no style."

"Not at all," said Cynthia, wagging an authoritative spoon. "I like it short and preppy.

"What does Julie think?" asked Sarah with a teasing smile.

"Julie," said Max, tapping his fingers. "Well, I haven't actually seen her yet. I only got back last night and . . ."

The girls exchanged blank stares.

"Did I do something wrong?" he asked.

"Oh, Max," said Cynthia with sisterly affection. "We should really write these things down for you. Life isn't all dramatic leaps and swordplay."

"Is that what I do?" asked Max, thoroughly amused. "Dramatic leaps and swordplay?"

"Saved by the bell!" Cynthia crowed as Old Tom's chimes hurried them off to class.

Max headed toward the smithy as his first class was Devices, Mr. Vincenti's subject, which taught students how to make useful things. The room was a cramped space in which students crowded around low tables and benches. Mr. Vincenti stood by a forge at the front of the room, urging the students to take their seats. A pair of dvergar flanked him; one operated a bellows while the other worked at the hearth's perimeter to contain the hot fire. The hearth cast an orange glow on the dark walls, and heat issued forth in steady, oppressive waves. When everyone had arrived, Mr. Vincenti beckoned the class closer.

"I know it's hot, but squeeze in," he said. "Now, we've spent the last month learning that forging is one of the most basic skills a craftsman can have and getting you familiar with basic tools and their uses. At Rowan, there are no finer blacksmiths than the dvergar, whose very ancestors crafted weapons for gods. Today, we are very fortunate to welcome the brothers Aurvangr and Ginnarr, who have agreed to share some of their wisdom with us."

The dvergar ceased their activities and turned to face the class. Norse dwarves of the oldest and proudest lineage, the dvergar had long, braided beards, ash-colored skin, and milky eyes that looked blind from long years gazing into the fire. They spoke in hoarse, halting English, and Max listened with great interest.

"Our apologies, but humans are very poor workers of the metal," said Aurvangr. "The human uses his mind, but not his soul. The true smith does not merely shape metals. He is artist. The true smith calls to iron and makes it share its song."

Leaning forward, Ginnarr continued his brother's narrative. "There is only one language of Making, and this now is in Astaroth's keeping. . . ." At the mention of that name, the brothers made a simultaneous sign against evil. "The language of Making may belong to the Great Demon and his Book, but in Making there is music also. The clever smiths find its notes."

The dvergar reached for an ancient black hammer, its head worn to a gleaming nub.

"We help you find this music. But young smiths must first feel metal's sting, must sweat before the forge. Three swings to pay the smith's toll . . ."

By midafternoon, Max had said farewell to his classmates. They were off to study diplomacy, while Max would be teaching his course on combat. He climbed the steps to Maggie; however, as he arrived at the second floor, he stopped. Julie was there, lingering outside Max's classroom.

"There you are!" she exclaimed, giving a friendly wave.

"Hi," said Max, brushing past other students to embrace her.

"I'd heard you were back—look at you all cleaned up for school," she said. "Got your lesson plan all ready?"

"I, uh, thought I'd wing it," said Max. "You know . . . keep it spontaneous."

Julie raised an eyebrow, but stifled her comment and wished him luck.

Max found that room 222 was a large dojo packed with adults. Surveying the class, Max saw that the Red Branch was there, along with Ms. Richter, the senior faculty, several Mystics, and a score of Agents. They all wore exercise clothes and looked at him expectantly.

Beads of sweat broke out on Max's forehead. He slid his bag off his shoulder and placed it against the wall, then blinked stupidly at his pupils. It all seemed a bad dream.

"Hi," he said. "Sorry I'm late."

Silence.

"Um, welcome to Advanced Combat Training," he said. "I'm Max McDaniels and I'll be your . . . instructor. I guess we should begin with names."

"Gabrielle Richter, Director."

"William Cooper, Red Branch."

"Annika Kraken, Chair of Mystics."

The recitation continued while Max struggled in vain to brainstorm a suitable lesson. When the last student gave his name and rank, Max clapped his hands and rubbed them nervously.

"Right," he said. "Uh . . . does anyone here have any experience with combat?"

A pause was followed by slow, quizzical expressions as every hand rose.

"Of . . . of course," Max sputtered, growing red. "My mistake— stupid question. Moving on . . ."

He had the best intentions of moving on but discovered that he was simply standing mute, rubbing his arms as though he were cold. A throat cleared, and Max looked up to see Cooper raise his hand.

"Professor McDaniels?" he said without irony. "I believe you visited the Sidh last year."

"Yes," said Max, exhaling. "Yes, I did."

"And I've heard that you received training during your stay?"

"That's right," said Max.

"Well," said Cooper delicately, "I don't speak for the group, but I've seen my share of fighting, and I've studied about every combat technique there is. But I never learned anything in the Sidh. . . ."

"Right," said Max, immensely grateful for the prompt. "Of course. Where should we begin?"

"What are some of the specific techniques you learned?" asked Ms. Richter.

"There were lots," said Max. "T-ubullchless, 'the Apple Feat'; and ích n-erred, 'the Salmon Leap', and cless cletenach, or 'the Little-Dart Feat'—"

One of the Agents covered his mouth, stifling laughter.

"Do you have a question?" asked Max.

"No," replied the Agent. "It's just, I thought this class was for combat. Salmon and apples—sounds like cooking class."

"I see," said Max, perusing the room. He spied a weapons rack nearby and walked over to it. Taking up a scuffed training ball, he lobbed it in a high arc toward the far wall. As it flew, he grabbed eight small darts from a wooden case and loosed them in a blur. A second later, the ball fell to the ground looking like a sea urchin—each dart had found its target. "Cless cletenach," said Max. "Now . . . ích n-erred," he said. He took one running step before spanning the fifty-foot room in a single leap, retrieving the ball from the floor and testing its weight in one smooth motion. "And finally," he said, "t-ubullchless."

Max hurled the ball at a training dummy by the door. The ball exploded into its target, shattering the dummy's head and showering the class with scraps of stuffing.

The dojo was silent.

"I'm not much of a teacher," said Max, his fingers twitching. "But I've mastered these feats. If you have better things to do, don't let me waste your time."

Ms. Richter raised her hand.

"I can assure Agent Crowley that he does not have better things to do. Please continue."

By the end of class, Max was exhausted. He tried to assure himself that it had not been a total disaster. He might have fumbled for words now and again, but he was sure the next class would go more smoothly.

Wiping the sweat from his brow, Max scanned the quad for Julie. He had hoped they could have dinner and kicked himself for failing to mention it when he'd seen her earlier.

She was not lounging about the quad. Nor was she in the crowded dining hall. He planned to try the dormitories when he ran into her roommate on the stairs and learned that Julie had already taken her dinner and holed up to study for an exam.

"Am I in the doghouse?" Max asked.

"Maybe just a little," replied Camille.

He groaned.

Taking his own dinner to go, Max trudged up to the boys' dormitory wing. There would be other study sessions—at the moment, he needed to figure out a way back into Julie's good graces. Should he give her flowers? Too generic, he concluded. His father would say he should cook for her, but Max was hopeless in that arena.

By the time he had arrived at his room, he was back to flowers. Reaching for his key, he paused. Across the hallway, Connor Lynch's door was slightly ajar. There was a rustling inside and a muttered curse as something fell off a shelf. Poking his head inside, Max saw his friend tossing clothes into a large trunk.

"Hey," said Max.

Connor whirled at the sound of Max's voice. The Irish boy's eyes were red; his cheeks were tear-streaked. He rubbed a hasty sleeve across his face.

"Hey. Welcome home and all that."

"Thanks," said Max, coming inside and closing the door. "Didn't see you at classes today. What's going on? Are you sick?"

Connor shook his head with a rueful laugh. "I'm a dropout," he replied. "No more classes for me."

"What?" Max exclaimed. "You can't just drop out of school!"

"Already did."

Connor tossed Max a scroll bound with a red ribbon.

Max quickly unfurled it; his eyes devoured the contract, which was penned in glistening red ink.

October 28, Year 1
This contract indicates that Mr. Connor Braden Lynch, formerly of Rowan Academy, hereby renounces said Order and memberships in exchange for land and titles within the Kingdom of Blys. As such, he will swear fealty to Lord Prusias and depart from Rowan in two days' time.

Max raced through the additional details until he arrived at the final line.

As a pledge of good faith and a guarantee of loyalty, Baron Lynch does hereby pledge collateral as detailed in Appendix 1. This collateral shall be held, in trust, until the day of his death.

"Connor," Max breathed. "Exactly what collateral did you give them?"

Connor did not look at him. Instead, he turned and gazed at the dark meadow outside his window. The boy gave a helpless shrug and a bitter laugh.

"The only kind they take."

A WINDOW ON THE WORLD

Max held Connor's contract tenuously between his finger-tips. For a moment, neither boy said a word. Outside the window, shadows lengthened over the meadow.

"So they have your *soul*?" Max whispered.

"Not yet," sniffed Connor. "But they will. I surrender it when I swear fealty."

"Why would you do this?" asked Max. "Have you lost your mind?"

"Wish I had," said Connor, laughing ruefully. "I'm making good on Peter's advice."

Max recoiled at the name and handed the contract back to

Connor. That Peter Varga might have guided another loved one off into the unknown seemed too much to stomach. Any residual gratitude Max felt for Peter's past aid vanished in an instant.

"Peter Varga told you to sell your soul?" he asked. "For a bit of land?"

"In so many words," said Connor helplessly. "Peter said that moving to Blys would be my best chance to make amends."

"For what?" asked Max.

"For everything," said Connor, kicking halfheartedly at his roommate's chair. "It's all my fault. And there's such a thing as vengeance, Max. You know who babysat me when I was held captive during the Siege?"

"I do," replied Max. It had been Alex Muñoz, a former Rowan student who had become an inquisitor for the Enemy. When Alex had delivered his hostages in exchange for the Book of Thoth, he had appeared changed—as though his humanity had ebbed. Yet even before, Alex had been a born sadist; Max did not want to think about what he might have done to Connor.

"I'm going to kill him," said Connor with cold, quiet finality. "I will kill Alex Muñoz if it costs me my last breath and immortal soul."

A sharp knock sounded at the door.

"What?" Connor yelled.

"It's not just your room!" shouted a sullen, aggrieved voice.

Connor tore at his hair and gave Max a wild, incredulous look. "Don't they know I'm talking about my immortal soul and vengeance besides?"

Connor threw the last of his things in his trunk and secured the clasps as fists rained on the door with a mishmash of protests, threats, and curses. "Weenies to the end," Connor grumbled. He glanced at Max. "Can I crash at your place? It'll only be for a night or two."

"Of course," said Max. "We're not finished talking about this."

Dragging his trunk, Connor waddled to the door and opened it wide. His roommates stood there with balled fists, looking mutinous.

"It's all yours," announced Connor. "It's been a real pleasure roomin' with you gents these past few years. Every young man should get to bunk with Wanker, Pimple, and Stinky. Builds character. Fare thee well, boys. Good luck and God bless."

Wavering between anger and confusion, the three boys stood aside as Connor dragged his trunk across the hall to Max's door and waited patiently as Max muttered his apologies to the speechless trio and hurried across.

Connor leaned close as Max turned the key in the lock. "Is Davie at home?" he asked with a nervous titter. "Not that I believe the stories, but . . ."

"Relax," said Max, unlocking the door. "He's never here."

But Max was mistaken.

Walking across the threshold, the pair saw that David was indeed at home. In fact, Rowan's sorcerer was the centerpiece of a scene so surreal that Max and Connor merely craned their necks and gaped.

David Menlo was floating some thirty feet above the lower level. Compared to the dome, he appeared tiny, a mere doll whose arms were outstretched toward the curving glass. Beyond the dome was not the usual serenity of twinkling constellations, but a raging, churning cosmos.

"Hey now!" exclaimed Connor. "What's our boy doing?"

"No idea," Max whispered. "Shhh!"

The two boys crouched low and watched as David floated high above, a silhouette against the heavens. Max swore he could discern faint faces from among the stars—hooded, sinister figures whose contours and features could be gleaned from the patterns of lights and swirling nebulae. David made a gesture of dismissal, but the ghostly faces remained—an apparent obstacle to whatever he was attempting to do. Max heard David cry out, and the dome filled with a shimmering luminescence that crashed like a wave over the glass. By the time the radiance streamed away, the faces had disappeared.

So, too, had the view of the cosmos. Beyond a gauzy curtain of clouds, the dome now revealed a smooth gray sea. In the distance, Max spied a winking light, soon followed by what appeared to be masts and sails. As their viewpoint shifted, Max saw that it was a ship—a black vessel piled high with stamped crates. At the ship's prow, a witch held a burning staff aloft. Max guessed she was a weather worker, hired to beseech the wind and seas for a swift, safe passage.

But a greater weather worker had come.

As David stretched forth his arms, a black shadow fell upon the sea. The witch abruptly ceased her spellwork and looked toward the sky. Fascinated, Max watched her—a tiny figurine within some make-believe world—as she raised her burning staff toward the glass. Despite her desperate efforts, towering gray thunderclouds converged upon the ship like stampeding cattle. Peaceful seas turned to gray-green chop; frantic figures began to race about on deck, securing the cargo. The witch fell upon her knees and cast something—an offering of some kind—over the bow as the ship began to pitch upon wilding waves. Floating high above, David raised his fist and the dome suddenly blazed as lightning coursed from the blackening sky to shatter the mainmast. Silk sails came fluttering down like parade streamers.

Max watched, awed and horror-struck, as wave upon wave now slammed into the ship, battering it with a casual, feline cruelty. Lines snapped, sailors were whisked off deck and hurtled into the sea, and stacked cargo toppled after them like toy blocks.

With a measured, orchestral gesture, David seemed to gather the sea into his arms as though preparing for a hideous finale.

Upon the horizon, Max saw another swell of dark water—an innocuous band of slate, but he knew that it must be huge. As the wave cut across the dark sea on its silent, murderous course, its true scale became evident.

"My God," whispered Connor.

Max recoiled as the wave loomed, curled, and closed upon the tottering ship like a boxer's fist. The impact was inconceivable. The collision sent up a plume of spray, an explosion of water and mist that mercifully obscured the carnage beneath. When it had subsided, nothing remained of the trading ship—no spars or masts or figures upon the waves. It might never have existed.

Once again, the scene within the dome began to change. The roiling seascape gave way to night and finally to the familiar, peaceful constellations. As the dome reverted to its accustomed state, David sank slowly to the floor, racked by spasms of coughing. Settling into an armchair, he kindled a fire in the hearth and leaned heavily against the table. With his remaining hand, he fumbled for a handkerchief and pressed it against his mouth while his body was consumed by another coughing fit, which intensified until David pitched from the chair and collapsed.

"He's having a seizure or something," said Max. "Come on!"

Connor followed, pausing at the bottom stairs while Max stooped over his roommate and pried the blood-speckled hand-kerchief from his unresisting hand.

"Are you sure that's safe?" hissed Connor. "He—he might blow you up!"

At the moment, David did not seem capable of squashing an insect. He lay still, his lids fluttering while the eyes beneath swam about in rapid movements. The coughing had stopped, replaced by quick, shallow breaths that bordered on hyperventilation.

And then . . . the fit stopped.

David's eyes opened and he gazed up at Max. He blinked, coughed once more, and gently motioned for Max to help him into the chair. He registered Connor at a glance before returning his attention to Max.

"How long have you been here?"

While Max debated how to respond, Connor answered with his usual delicacy.

"Long enough to see you sink that bloody ship!" he exclaimed.

"Connor—" Max warned, but David waved him off.

"I'm sorry you had to see that," he said quietly. "You're probably wondering if all those terrible rumors are true. . . ."

There was an eerie calm in David's voice. Connor lost all color in his face and began backing up the stairs as though David might turn him into a toad.

"Of course I am!" Connor admitted. "Who wouldn't after what I just saw?"

"*Why* did you sink that ship?" asked Max.

"It was valuable." David shrugged. "That clipper was the first to hold cargo from all four of the kingdoms. Thus far, only goods from Blys have reached Rowan. Even Astaroth will hear of this little fiasco."

"So you're trying to provoke Astaroth?" asked Max.

A wan smile appeared on David's pale features.

"And you're doing it from *here*?" Max continued, growing angry. "From Rowan? Don't you think that's a bit reckless?"

"Is Max McDaniels going to lecture me on reckless behavior?"

Max glared at David, his fingers twitching with that terrible Old Magic that longed to take control.

"And since when did this room become a giant crystal ball?" Max asked, changing the subject with a sweep of his arm at the vast dome.

At this, David actually laughed. "Did you think it was just meant to be pretty?" David clucked his tongue and chuckled at the rhetorical question. "It's my base of operations, Max. My little window on the world."

"What were those faces beyond the glass?" asked Max.

David's smile abruptly faded. His face grew earnest. "Could you see them?" he whispered. "There are times I'm convinced that only I can see them. . . . Those were Prusias's very best magicians trying to find me. But they can't—not yet!"

"I don't like the idea of demons peeking through my window," said Max darkly.

"Don't worry," David assured him. "They can't see you here. The only chance they have is when I look out, and I'm very careful when I do."

"You're not being very careful if two people can just walk in here if they have the key," Max snapped. "What if I'd been Ms. Richter, David? I hear she's not so happy with you."

"Tonight was a special exception," replied David. "I needed to find that ship while it was still in Blyssian waters." His eyes wandered to the scroll clutched in Connor's hand. "Has someone been speaking to Mr. Cree?"

Connor appeared slightly nauseated by the question. Hanging his head like a scolded schoolboy, he nodded and handed the scroll to Max, who passed it along to David. After reading it, David placed it on the table with a weary sigh.

"So you're going to surrender your soul," he said quietly. "May I ask why? You like nice things, Connor, but I hardly think you're a fool."

"Maybe Varga's the fool," said Connor crossly. "Since summer, he's been on me to move to Blys. Says it's my best chance to make amends. Says it's my duty . . ." Connor trailed off, his cheeks flushing.

David pressed the issue. "Make amends for what?" he inquired coldly. "For stabbing me? For removing the mists that hid this school and laying us bare?"

"For . . . for last spring," answered Connor, looking away.

"Well," said Max, before every ugly detail could be rehashed. "It's clear we can't let Connor do this. I mean, we have to do something. Can we bargain with Mr. Cree?"

David shook his head and glanced wearily at the contract. "Mr. Cree is just a secretary, Max. He's not the owner of Connor's soul—just a dutiful notary. And I wouldn't be so quick to dismiss Peter Varga's recommendation. I know very little of prescience, but Varga's been right more often than not. Perhaps Connor should go to Blys. . . . Anyway, this contract cannot be broken. Connor will have to live up to it."

"I might be a lot of things," said Connor. "But I ain't a coward. If I have to, I can make a go of things in Blys. I've already said my goodbyes—the ones I could say, anyway. It's giving up my soul that's got me tied in knots."

David nodded his sympathies and was in the process of returning the scroll when he paused and gave it a second read. A low whistle escaped his lips.

"Maybe I can help," he murmured, tapping the document. "But it would be risky."

Connor sat up, his face brightening. "You mean I might not have to go?" he asked eagerly.

"No," said David. "You will have to go—that part of the contract is ironclad. The payment clause, however, is subject to interpretation. It requires you to surrender your soul upon swearing fealty to Prusias. Therein lies a possible loophole."

"What loophole?" asked Connor. "It seems straightforward to me."

"Tell me then, Connor, what's *your* soul?" asked David. "Is it the soul you were born with or the soul harbored within your body?"

"I'm hoping they're one and the same," muttered Connor, crossing himself.

"At the moment they are," said David. "But they don't have to be. What would you say if I offered to remove your soul and place it in something else . . . a vault for safekeeping?"

"Spiritual surgery?" asked Connor.

David nodded and revealed the pale scar on his chest. "A transplant. I'm very familiar with them."

"But a transplant requires a donor," said Max. "Where are you going to get another soul, David?"

"Not your concern," David replied coolly. "Suffice it to say, the donor will be willing."

"I don't like this, Connor," said Max. "It sounds a lot like possession, and you've had too much experience with that already. Do you want another Mr. Sikes crawling around in your head?"

"It is not possession," David corrected. "A human soul is a far cry from an invasive imp. The replacement soul will not guide your actions or corrupt you. Also consider that you'd have it for a short while. After all, Prusias will be taking it very soon."

"I guess that's true," said Connor. Standing abruptly, he paced before the fire. "Are you sure? I mean, are you positive that the donor would be willing? I don't want you knocking anyone on the head for their bleedin' soul."

"Like I said," replied David calmly, "the donor will be a willing participant. But you have to make a decision by morning."

"My God," said Connor, burying his face in his hands. He looked helplessly at Max. "And I thought I had a lot on my mind before! What should I do?"

"I can't answer that," said Max. "That's a decision only you can make."

"I need to run things through my mind once or twice," said Connor grimly. "Your bed's sounding awful good, Max. You can crash down here like a good lad, can't ya? I know you'd hate for me to spend my last few nights at Rowan on the floor."

"All yours," said Max, waving him away.

As Connor disappeared up the stairs, David shot Max a bemused glance.

"So, how are things, Professor McDaniels?" he asked.

Pulling off his shoes, Max plopped his feet on the table and stared into the fire. "Honestly, David, there are times when I think my head's going to explode."

"Hmmm," said David. "I thought the dvergar would interest you at least."

"They were the only saving grace," said Max. "When things settle down, I want to talk with them. They might be useful."

"Ah," said David, smiling. "Now we come to it."

"Well," said Max. "Maybe they could reforge Cúchulain's spear. . . ."

"Why?" asked David. "What's the use? The war is over, Max. Don't you know that we're supposed to sit here in our playpen enjoying a pleasant retirement?"

"I do," said Max. "But you seem to be fighting a war all on your own. Are you going after Prusias?"

"For humiliating my mother?" David asked. "No, I can't let personal feuds dictate my actions. I'm aiming higher."

"Astaroth?" Max hissed. "David, please tell me you're not going after Astaroth."

"'Going after'?" David inquired with a smile. "Max, this isn't some school-yard fight."

"So, what do you plan on doing?" Max asked. "I mean, you can't think that you're going to *destroy* Astaroth. Not even Bram managed that!"

"It would be tricky," David allowed with just a ghost of a smile. "Let's see . . . the Demon is immortal, nothing earthly can harm him, and he has the Book of Thoth. Should a legitimate threat arise, Astaroth could simply remove its truename from the lists and snuff the irritant out of existence. That is very real, utterly incalculable power."

David scratched at the pale stump where his right hand used to be.

"But it's an intriguing problem to turn over," he continued. "I suppose if one wished to destroy Astaroth, they'd have to devise a very special weapon. For the sake of example, let's say this weapon was a potion. . . ."

David reached for a clean beaker from a stand by his bookcase. He placed it on the table between them and considered it.

"Now, this potion's components and properties must meet two basic conditions. First and foremost, it must be lethal to demonkind. Second, the ingredients should be harvested from a world other than our own. These are difficult conditions to meet."

"I understand the first condition but not the second," said Max. "Why would it have to originate outside our world?"

"Because Astaroth has the Book of Thoth," David explained. "If the ingredient is an earthly one, its truename will be in that Book. If its truename is not in the Book, Astaroth has no power over it—he can't simply strike it out or change its essence. He becomes vulnerable."

"That's genius," said Max, simultaneously exhilarated by David's solution and anxious of its implications. "So those red flowers . . . they're from another world? You actually mean to destroy Astaroth?"

David said nothing; his expression remained inscrutable.

"Then at least tell me why you're so afraid for me to touch them," Max pleaded. "The demons talk like I'm one of them.

The dryads, the demons . . . they all say I 'shine.' What does that mean, David? What am I?"

David sighed and pushed back from the table. "Connor's situation with his contract requires a trip to the Archives," he said. "You can come along if you want. I'll share what I can, but I can't promise you'll like what you hear, Max."

Within the minute, the pair left the observatory, with Connor's unapologetic snores droning on behind them.

The hour was late, but the campus was hardly deserted. Lights issued from many windows in the academic buildings, and teachers and students alike still strolled along walkways. The sight of Max McDaniels and David Menlo together elicited many a curious stare, but David ignored these and pointed gleefully at Gràvenmuir. Even at a distance, Max could see figures hurrying from room to gilded room.

"I'd say they've heard about their missing ship," David said in a conspiratorial whisper. "Nothing travels faster than bad news. Isn't it wonderful?"

"Don't you worry they'll know it's you?" Max hissed. "You're the only one who could have done something like that!"

"Not necessarily," said David. "There are some truly powerful demons among the four kingdoms with their own agendas and factions and rivalries. They're like great big spiders sitting in different corners of a web. I can think of a dozen who might have had an interest in seeing that ship sink. So, is David Menlo jingling the web, or is it a rival spider?"

"That's a dangerous game."

"Maybe," David admitted. "But it's more fun being the revolutionary than the establishment."

With an air of subdued satisfaction, David hurried off toward Maggie, through which one accessed the Archives. Down the winding stairs they went, into the living heart of Rowan, where its oldest scrolls and greatest treasures were kept. Arriving at the bottom stair, Max halted at the shedu guardians. He cocked his head at the colossal figures, winged bulls with human heads.

"They look different," he said. "Older. Are these the same shedu?"

"No," David replied. "The other two were destroyed during the Siege—mauled to rubble. I had to borrow these from an Assyrian tomb."

Max had always felt nervous before shedu, as though he should appeal to their impassive faces in some way. As a member of the Red Branch, however, he had free rein of the Archives. The shedu remained still as Max and David hurried by.

The Archives were as Max remembered—enormous beyond reckoning, with endless stacks and corridors of books that nearly disappeared in the gloom as one's eyes traveled toward the vast cathedral ceiling. Seated at the many tables, Max saw scholars and teachers reading ancient manuscripts by lantern light. Nowhere at Rowan was Astaroth's elimination of modern electricity more apparent than in this enormous, sub-terranean space, in which candles and lanterns now flickered from the alcoves.

The pair arrived at David's private reading room. Encrusted coffee mugs were stacked three deep, along with chipped plates, mounds of books, and the occasional pool of spilled ink. David seemed perfectly at home, humming pleasantly while he lit several lamps and urged Max to take a seat.

"You know," he began, "I never wanted to pry too much into your time at Rodrubân, but we can't have this conversation unless I'm direct."

"Go ahead," said Max. "I always figured you knew, anyway."

David nodded. "I'll place my cards on the table then," he said.

"Scott McDaniels is not your father. And you are not Cúchulain, Max, but his kin. You and Cúchulain are brothers, though separated by great gulfs of time. You are both sons of Lugh the Long-Handed, High King of the Tuatha Dé Danann."

A jumble of emotions seeped into Max. He felt relief that David knew, that he could share his secret with someone else. But he also felt anxious that Scott McDaniels might learn the devastating truth, that Max was not his son. And he struggled with anger. He had been wrestling with his identity for years. Had David known the answers all along?

"If you knew all this," Max whispered, "why didn't you say anything sooner?"

"A person's past is their business," replied David. "I wasn't certain until you crossed the bridge at Rodrubân while I could not."

Max recalled the event. His irritation with David was replaced by something more celebratory.

"But this—this is great news!" Max exclaimed, smacking his hands together. "It means I'm not a demon!"

"Calm down," David urged. "It's not so cut and dry. Your family tree is a bit . . . complicated."

Max thought of his dreams, the great wolfhound and its recurring question: *What are you about? Answer quick or I'll gobble you up!*

"I want to know what I'm about," Max breathed. "Am I human?"

"No," said David. "Not fully human, anyway. Lugh is your father, and he is a god slumbering in the far-off Sidh. Should we call you a demigod? Would it make you feel better?"

"It's better than being a demon," Max spat.

"Are they so different?" asked David simply.

"What's that supposed to mean?" snapped Max, glowering at his roommate.

David placed his hand on a volume on Celtic myth and recited aloud.

> His longdrawn scream re-echoed like the screams of a hundred warriors; so it was that the demons and devils and goblins of the glen and fiends of the air cried out from that helmet, before him, above him, around him, whenever he went out to spill the blood of warriors and heroes. . . . The first warp-spasm seized Cúchulain, and made him into a monstrous thing, hideous and shapeless, unheard of. His shanks and his joints, every knuckle and angle and organ from head to foot, shook like a tree in the flood. . . . The hair stood up upon his scalp with rage. The hero-halo rose out of his brow. . . . From the dead centre of his skull a straight spout of black blood. . . . In that style, he drove out to find his enemies, and did.

"Is that not the description of a demon?" David asked mildly.

"Those stories are exaggerated," retorted Max. "Cúchulain was bloodthirsty. I'm not like that. I don't do those things."

"No," David reassured him. "You don't. But then again, you're burdened by a modern conscience. To Max McDaniels, killing is a necessary evil. But in Cúchulain's day, the path to glory was dyed in the blood of one's enemies. You're not cut from different cloth; you just live in different times."

Max brooded in silence, so David continued.

"Do you remember what happened last spring? When you faced the Enemy alone within the Sanctuary?"

"I don't want to remember," said Max. The episode seemed like a dream. Within the dark gorge, he had screamed. There had been light—a blinding light, brighter than the sun. Then he had fallen upon the Enemy, and they gave way before him. It was an elusive memory—numbing glimpses of wild, rampant violence. Vyes fleeing, scrabbling madly to climb out of the gorge and escape the predator within it. . . . Had Max become a monster?

"You can't have it both ways," David told him. "You can't seek truths and then pick and choose among them. If you want to know who and what you are, you must acknowledge the whole."

"I do," said Max quietly. "I'm no demon, David. I'm Lugh's son and Cúchulain's brother."

"And where does Lugh come from?" David asked.

"He's one of the Tuatha Dé Danann," Max replied. "For a time he was their king."

"But initially he was an outsider to the Tuatha Dé Danann," David corrected. "They made him king only after he led them into battle against the Fomorians and slew Balor."

"Who was Balor?" asked Max.

"The king of the Fomorians," answered David. "Balor was a giant, a monster so terrible that his single eye killed whatever it looked upon. At the Battle of Magh Tuireadh, Lugh put out the eye and slew him. In fact, the very expression 'evil eye' originates with Balor. Isn't it fascinating how these old tales make their way into the modern vernacular?"

"Gripping," said Max. "But, David, what does this have to do with me?"

"Well," said David delicately, "the details of Balor's death fulfilled an old prophecy. The prophecy foretold that Balor would die at the hands of his own grandson. . . ."

"Lugh is Balor's grandson?" Max exclaimed. "That would mean Lugh is part Fomorian . . . which would mean that I'm part Fomorian!"

"You say that like it's a bad thing," said David.

"I'm a monster," Max moaned. He remembered the grisly eye

he'd clutched in Cooper's room, and the gargantuan exhibit of a Fomorian he'd glimpsed in the Workshop's museum. "A monster."

"You're being dramatic," said David. "You just come from a very old line. When one goes back that far, bloodlines get muddled. Remember, Max: one man's god is another man's monster. . . ."

David returned to his work and Max understood that he had been dismissed. He made his way past the tables of Scholars, past the gleam of the Red Branch vault, and up the many stairs that led out of the Archives. The campus was dark and quiet; even Gràvenmuir's windows had been closed and curtained as though everyone and everything was fast asleep.

When he reached his room, he saw that a note had been taped to the door.

> *Camille said you'd been looking for me. Sorry I*
> *missed you. I know you've been busy and are probably*
> *stressed about the Shrope trial on Saturday. Hang in*
> *there! When it's all over, we can cut loose at the*
> *Samhain Feast.*
>
> *xoxo,*
> *Julie*

Max sighed. With everything that had been happening, he'd nearly forgotten about Mum and Bellagrog's trial. In two short days he'd have to sit on the witness stand and swear to tell the truth. He could only hope his testimony wouldn't lead to Mum's exile.

~ 11 ~

Ex Post Facto

On Saturday, Max was awoken not by Old Tom's chimes but by an insistent knocking at his door. Lying downstairs on his bedroll, he debated whether to answer. The Shrope trial was that afternoon, and he did not want the day to begin any earlier than necessary.

But the knocking continued. Tossing aside his pillow, he stalked upstairs and flung open the door.

Max discovered a domovoi waiting in the hallway. The little man was dressed soberly in a suit and tie, with gray hair that appeared to have been slicked back at birth. He stood next to a strongbox on a small dolly. Glancing at his clipboard, the domovoi cleared his throat and twirled one end of a waxed mustache.

"Agent McDaniels, I presume?"

"Yes," said Max, stretching his arms with a pointed yawn.

"I'm Mr. Thaler," replied the domovoi with a brisk, efficient air. "I am here to deliver your salary. It's been accruing while you've been away."

Mr. Thaler produced an ornate key and unlocked the strongbox. His legs trembled as he hefted up a large sack that fairly sloshed and clinked with bullion.

"That can't be right," said Max. "That's a lot more than four weeks' pay."

Mr. Thaler's lips tightened as though he'd been insulted. "It is correct to the milligram, Mr. McDaniels," he said stiffly. "Five ounces of gold per week as per your teaching agreement, plus twenty-five ounces per week as a member of the Red Branch." The domovoi's pompous manner cracked as the strain began to tell. "Dear me . . . perhaps I can deposit this inside and explain?"

Marching into Max's room, the domovoi slung the bag upon the central table and explained that Rowan's economy was now tied to gold.

"For one of your wealth, the gold may not be practical," Mr. Thaler considered, stroking his chin. "In fact, my colleagues and I would like to discuss several investment opportunities with you. There's considerable wealth to be made in merchant shipping, imports, or the more promising township businesses. Unlike our competitors, my bank has excellent contacts in all four kingdoms, including Zenuvia."

"What's Zenuvia?" asked Max.

"Lady Lilith's realm," Mr. Thaler explained. "The easternmost kingdom. A most promising economy, and the lady's advisers understand trade far better than Lord Rashaverak. He fails to grasp that one's partners must also make a profit."

"Your bank trades with demons?" Max asked. "You've met with Rashaverak?"

"Not directly," said the domovoi wistfully. "But his senior emissaries, certainly."

"Goodbye, Mr. Thaler," said Max, shaking his small hand and ushering him back up the stairs.

"Shall we set up a time to discuss the aforementioned opportunities?" inquired the domovoi.

"I don't think so," said Max. "I'm happy to keep it all under my bed."

This elicited a somewhat surprised glance from Mr. Thaler, but nothing more.

By the time Max had returned to the downstairs table, Connor was already stacking the coins into gleaming towers of gold and silver.

"Would ya look at that?" he said. "You're bleedin' rich! All this gold just for a month's salary?" He whistled. "In a year or two, you'll be sitting on a downright hoard."

"Eavesdropping, for shame," said Max, knocking down a tower of silver coins and shoveling them into Mr. Thaler's red velvet sack. "How are you feeling?"

"Better," Connor allowed, still gazing greedily at the coins. "But swapping your soul ain't no picnic. I feel like Sir Olaf sat on me."

The previous day, Connor had given his consent to David, who had removed his soul and exchanged it for another of unknown origins. Max had been banned from the observatory for the duration. Thus, he knew almost nothing of the process other than Connor's cryptic account that it had been the most terrifying ordeal of his sixteen years.

Given Connor's past experiences with the Enemy, this was a disturbing statement.

Max had never attended, much less participated in a trial before. An undeniable excitement permeated the orchard and the low hill known as Idunn Grove. The humid air practically buzzed with hushed conversation as lucky observers found seats and the unlucky formed crowded, jostling galleries.

As a witness, Max was seated in the front row, sandwiched between his father and Bob. Although the ogre was dressed in his best suit, he appeared gaunt and grim. Gumming his lips, he looked stoically at the table for the defense, where Mum was seated alongside the haglings and Bellagrog, who had elected to don an enormous barrister's wig for the occasion. From the plaintiff's table, Jesper Rasmussen was eyeing the absurd thing, but quickly looked away, once the haglings had taken notice and returned his stare from behind their leather muzzles.

Dressed in a judge's robes, Ms. Richter sat behind a dais that had been placed at the foot of a tree planted by Rowan's first class. A dozen jurors occupied a box to her left, selected from a pool of faculty and adult refugees. With a bang of her gavel, Ms. Richter began the proceedings and read from a prepared statement.

"This trial shall address allegations made by Mr. Jesper Rasmussen of the Frankfurt Workshop against the Shrope family, consisting of Bellagrog Shrope, Bea Shrope, and Bellagrog's children, who shall be known as Haglings One, Two, Four, Five, Six, and Seven."

Bellagrog cleared her throat and said, "If it pleases the court, you may strike Hagling Six from the proceedings, Your Honor."

"And where is Hagling Six?" asked Ms. Richter, peering over her glasses.

"Er, Hagling Six is in-dis-po-sé," replied Bellagrog, easing back in her chair and shrugging amiably.

"Indisposed, my beak," Hannah shrieked from the stands. "You ate her!"

"Order," said Ms. Richter, banging her gavel to stifle the subsequent chatter. "Hannah, must we remove you from these proceedings?"

Hannah said nothing, but merely shook her head and reclaimed her seat with a dissatisfied grimace.

Bellagrog stood and gestured angrily at the goose. "The defense moves to disqualify this jury on the grounds that they've heard damaging hearsay regarding hags and haglings."

"Excuse me?"

"Ex post facto, Your Honor," exclaimed Bellagrog, pounding the table.

"How does 'after the fact' apply here?" inquired Ms. Richter.

"Habeas corpus, then!"

"Bellagrog," said Ms. Richter, rubbing her eyes. "If your defense will consist of random legal terms presented in nonsensical fashion, the court will appoint an advocate for the Shropes."

Bellagrog scowled and settled back into her chair. "I talk for the Shropes."

"Very well," said Ms. Richter. "Then let's have the plaintiff's allegations."

Mr. Rasmussen's advocate—an imposing man in a gray suit—stood before the jury and pointedly glanced at his pocket watch. "Ladies and gentlemen of the jury," he said in a tone that suggested they were all old friends. "This trial is one of courtesy, not contentious deliberation. It should require little of your valuable time, for the facts of the case ring as clear as Old Tom's chimes. Five weeks ago, my client was abducted, assaulted, and on the verge of consumption by the defendants. We have motive, we have eyewitnesses, and we have the ignominious and well-documented history of hags. . . ."

"They're finished," Max whispered, gazing at Bellagrog and Mum, who appeared small and almost shrunken at the defendants' table. When the man had finished his statement, Max half expected applause. But he did not expect it from Bellagrog.

"Bravo, bravo!" said the hag, smacking her hands together. "Ain't you a pretty talker? That was a fine little story you just told. But that's what it is, ladies and gents, a story. Now, we all likes our stories, and I might not be such a slick talker as this prancing gent, but I'm here to tell the truth about a man what drank too much wine and fell into a wee bit of trouble. We got witnesses, too, so don't you all rush to judgment like you've been rushing to Mum's cooking the last forty years. . . ."

Bellagrog stepped aside so each juror could have a clear view of Mum, who was sprawled pitifully across the table. "That's right," she continued. "A hag what gave over forty years of service shouldn't be exiled just 'cause some drunk outsider gets the creeps from 'scary old hags.' Heck, I get the shivers every time I get a gander of his shiny bald melon, but you don't see me pressing charges!"

At this, several jurors actually stifled laughter. Max realized that Dr. Rasmussen might have a greater battle on his hands than he had anticipated.

When called to the stand, Jesper Rasmussen delivered his account in full. Every word was true, but Rasmussen spoke with such unmistakable arrogance and self-righteous indignation that several jurors actually frowned. Seeming to sense this, Bellagrog pounced during the cross-examination.

"You don't really like Rowan, do ya?" she inquired.

"Of course I do," Rasmussen retorted. "And I fail to see what that has to do with my abduction."

"Really?" said Bellagrog, consulting her notes. "Did you or did you not refer to Rowan as a 'magical petting zoo' in Ms. Richter's very own office?"

Dr. Rasmussen glared at her and gave a reluctant nod. "I may have said that . . . but I didn't mean it," he added pointedly to the jury. "I was upset."

"Do you always say things you don't mean when you're upset?" asked Bellagrog.

"No," said Rasmussen. "Again, I fail to see the relevance—"

But Bellagrog smelled blood in the water. She cut off the engineer with a cheerful shrug. "Let's move on, then," she said. "Let's talk about the Workshop, eh?"

Dr. Rasmussen pursed his lips but said nothing.

"Were you, until recently, the director of the Frankfurt Workshop?" inquired Bellagrog.

"Yes," said Dr. Rasmussen. "And I'm proud to say that I have been reinstated."

"Congratulations," drawled Bellagrog, rolling her eyes at the jury. "And as the head of this organization, can you testify whether or not it displays live creatures as museum exhibits?"

"Well, yes," said Dr. Rasmussen. "They're either humanely euthanized or placed into suspended animation. This is really a service of the first biological importance. For example, we might clone a specimen whose species is threatened by extinction."

"Oh, I see," said Bellagrog. "So you're doin' it for *them*, is ya? Does they come willin'?"

"Of course not," replied Rasmussen, glancing at his fingernails. "Even a flea possesses an instinct for self-preservation."

"Is you comparing hags to fleas?" asked Bellagrog.

"No," said Rasmussen quickly. "What I meant was—"

"Oh," interrupted Bellagrog. "So this is just another case where ya don't mean what ya say?"

"No!" shouted Rasmussen, smacking the podium in frustration.

"Temper, temper," cooed Bellagrog. She consulted her notes as though reading a transcript. "I believe you were telling the jury how ya kidnap or kill living creatures and display 'em against their will. . . ."

Once Dr. Rasmussen had been excused from the witness stand, Bellagrog strolled back to the defendants' table and idly sipped an iced tea while the haglings climbed up on Mum, clinging to her patchy gray suit like so many bats. Catching Max's eye, Bellagrog winked as though victory was just around the corner. While Bellagrog returned to her notes, Max arrived at a painful realization: With Rasmussen discredited, Max's testimony might well determine the verdict.

"Bellagrog's too crafty," whispered Mr. McDaniels. "Stick to simple answers or she'll twist you up in knots."

Overhearing this, Bob gazed down at the McDanielses and fixed Max with a sad blue eye. "Stick to the truth," he said. "The truth leads to justice."

Max nearly flinched as his name was called. Making his way to the witness stand, he became painfully aware that hundreds of observers had flocked to Idunn Grove and that even the Manse's slate roof and balconies were crowded with onlookers. Taking his seat, he saw Julie sitting in the front row with a press pass. She seemed to look through him; every aspect of her posture and expression suggested a professional reporter attending to her beat. As he was sworn in, Max took a deep, steadying breath.

"I know this can't be easy for you," said Rasmussen's attorney with a sympathetic smile. "You're very close to the hags, aren't you? I'd wager this trial has pulled you in two very different directions."

Max nodded, glancing at the defendants' table. Bellagrog was eyeing him curiously while Mum had nearly disappeared beneath the table, succumbing to either anxiety or the weight of her clinging, glaring nieces.

"Mr. McDaniels, you will have to speak up so the quills can transcribe your response."

"Yes," said Max, speaking into a magicked brass contraption that amplified his hoarse whisper.

"Which is why, ladies and gentlemen, this young man's testimony is all the more devastating to the defendants," the attorney continued with dramatic flourish, launching into a series of questions that painted the hags in a horrific light.

What was the purpose of the hags' Sniffing Ceremony? To ensure that they don't eat the students. Had Mum, in spite of this, attacked students in the past? Yes. Prior to the night in question, had Mr. McDaniels ever feared for Dr. Rasmussen's safety among the hags? Yes. Why was this? Because the Workshop had their cousin Gertie on display and they'd sworn revenge. Had the witness found Dr. Rasmussen in an enormous kettle far off campus? Yes. Did it appear the hags were going to eat him? Yes.

The next question, however, stumped Max.

"Had the hags been singing a song?" asked the attorney.

"Uh . . . yes?" said Max, wrinkling his nose at the memory.

"Do you remember its lyrics?" asked the lawyer coolly.

"Not really," said Max. "I was focused on trying to put out the fire and get Dr. Rasmussen out of the pot. I remember something about 'Rasmussen stew' and 'revenge is a dish that's best served hot.' It rhymed."

"Sounds like the hags were having fun," the attorney suggested with a knowing leer. "It sounds like a particularly cruel, premeditated crime."

"I guess." Max shrugged.

"No further questions," said the attorney, striding to his seat. "Incriminating testimony from the defense's dear friend. I think the court has heard all it needs to hear. . . ."

"Oh, I might have a question or two," interjected Bellagrog.

"By all means," said Ms. Richter. "Your witness."

Bellagrog adjusted her pants and swaggered toward Max like a prizefighter. She wagged a finger as though Max had been a very naughty boy.

"Those were some pretty nasty things you had to say about the Shropes, young man."

"I'm just reporting what I saw," said Max, slouched and miserable.

"Was you coached by the plaintiff?" inquired Bellagrog. "Did Dr. Rasmussen and his lawyer fella tell you what to say?"

"No . . . ," said Max hesitantly. Bellagrog spoke with such casual confidence that Max knew something—some haggish trick—was just around the bend.

"I see," she said. With a puzzled frown, she stroked her chin. "But then how could you possibly know what happened if you wasn't there?"

"What are you talking about?" Max snapped. "Of course I was there!"

"Oh, I'll concede that *a* Max McDaniels was there on the night in question, but how can we be sure it was *this* Max McDaniels?"

The plaintiff's attorney immediately objected while the crowd burst into excited chatter. Standing at the judge's bench, Ms. Richter cracked the gavel several times before anything resembling order was restored. She glared at Bellagrog, whose face remained open and innocent.

"The defense will clarify what it means and cease making a mockery of this court," said Ms. Richter.

"Will do, Your Honor, will do," Bellagrog promised, waddling back to her table and snatching up her papers. "I'll ask the witness if Max McDaniels visited the Frankfurt Workshop last year?"

"Yes," replied Max.

"And while Max McDaniels was in the Frankfurt Workshop, did he willingly surrender three drops of his blood to the Workshop in exchange for some fancy contraption?"

"Yes," said Max, somewhat defensively. "I had to in order to get Bram's Key."

"Of course Max did," said Bellagrog. "The Max McDaniels I know is a heroic, noble boy. Which is why we can't let a lying imposter like you sully his good name!"

"Explain yourself, Bellagrog," said Ms. Richter, before Rasmussen's attorney could object yet again.

Bellagrog grinned broadly, revealing two full rows of crocodile teeth. "The defense asserts that the Workshop has cloned the real Max McDaniels. The defense asserts that this witness is an imposter planted by the prosecution to further their case. The defense asserts that the testimony of this false, coached witness should be stricken from the record. And finally, the defense asserts that the real Max McDaniels must be in terrible danger and we should abandon this silly case to find Rowan's hero!"

Max sat, dumbfounded, while Dr. Rasmussen's attorney stood and issued a stunned objection.

"Whatchoo objectin' to?" thundered Bellagrog, wheeling on the man. "You said yourself that the Workshop kidnaps living things so you can clone 'em! How can you say that this is the same Max McDaniels from the night in question? Huh? Answer the question, ya blubbering man-thing!"

Dr. Rasmussen's attorney turned helplessly to his client. Jesper Rasmussen grimaced as though he'd chewed something profoundly unappetizing. His revulsion changed to a dark, murderous glare directed toward the crafty hag, who beamed expectantly. Whispering in his attorney's ear, he subsequently slouched and stared at his shoes.

His attorney stood and cleared his throat. "My client has informed me that this young man cannot be a clone of Max McDaniels, because he can attest that the McDaniels clones are all accounted for."

Even Bellagrog looked shocked.

The news spread through the vast audience like a tremor whose aftershocks were a sibilant hiss of disapproval. Max could not believe what he had heard—far off, in some Workshop laboratory, there were clones of him. He glanced across at Julie, but she was white-faced, frantically scribbling on her notepad. Every other reporter was doing the same.

"Your Honor," continued Bellagrog, "the defense moves to dismiss the case, as the plaintiff can't prove that this particular boy was ever present at the scene of the alleged crime! Bwahaha-haha!" she cackled, dancing a victory jig before Rasmussen's table.

"Order!" cried Ms. Richter, banging her gavel. "Order! The defense's motion is denied, but Mr. McDaniels's testimony shall be stricken from the record and the jury will disregard it. The witness is dismissed."

Bellagrog practically swooned with delight as Max left the stand. She did not seem to hear as Ms. Richter offered a few choice words to Dr. Rasmussen and his attorney before inform-ing them that she would now handle the questions. Only the mention of her name brought the hag from her dreamy-eyed reverie.

"Bellagrog Shrope, the court would like you to take the stand," said Ms. Richter, pointing the gavel at her.

"Oh," said Bellagrog, her smile fading. "As you like." She grunted as she squeezed into the witness stand, her bosom resting comfortably on the table.

Narrowing her eyes, Ms. Richter leaned down from the judge's bench and interrogated the hag. "Bellagrog Shrope, do you swear to tell the whole truth and nothing but the truth?"

"Sure thing."

"Did you swear a vendetta against Jesper Rasmussen?"

"Yes," said Bellagrog. "And rightfully so."

"Just answer yes or no, please. And did Bea Shrope, you, or your offspring abduct Mr. Rasmussen on the night in question?"

"Absolutely not," Bellagrog said, thumping the stand by way of exclamation.

"And did you intend to kill, cook, and eat Mr. Rasmussen?"

Bellagrog recoiled as though mortally offended. Reaching for a handkerchief, she blew her nose and fought back tears. "In that *precise* order?" she asked innocently, dabbing her eyes.

"In any order, Ms. Shrope," responded Ms. Richter.

"No," sniffled Bellagrog pathetically.

"So, Ms. Shrope, you assert that you and your family are utterly innocent in this affair?"

"I'd swear on me nan's tombskull."

"Thank you, Ms. Shrope. You are excused," said Ms. Richter dryly. "The court would now like to hear the testimony of Ms. Bea Shrope."

Mum glanced up from the defendants' table, bleary-eyed and beaten. "Really, Ms. Richter . . . do I have to? Can't we just leave it at Bel's word?"

"We are anxious to hear your account, Mum, and we need it for the record. Please take the witness stand."

With a sigh, Mum shuffled to the stand and was sworn in. On the witness chair, she looked like a withered bulb of garlic. Sipping gratefully from a glass of water, she managed a sad little smile, resigned to the question that would follow.

"Mum," began Ms. Richter, "are you innocent or guilty of the allegations made here today?"

Long seconds elapsed while Mum sat and stared at the glass of water.

"Answer the question, Bea," said Bellagrog, striking the match for her victory cigar.

Mum did not look at her sister, but instead gazed past Bellagrog at Bob, whose upright, attentive posture had not changed throughout the long afternoon. When their eyes met, the ogre's stern face softened and a single tear made a slow, steady descent down his cheek. He offered a slight, almost imperceptible nod of encouragement before the mask of stoicism returned. With trembling hands, Mum again sipped her water and spoke in a low, pitiable croak.

"I'm guilty. We're guilty on all charges."

Silence. Even as the words left Mum's lips, Max turned his eyes toward Bellagrog. For a moment, the enormous hag merely gaped while her match burned to her fingertips. Tossing her cigar aside, the hag gripped the table and seemed to swell like some nascent geological disaster.

Ms. Richter's voice was calm and compassionate. "Is this your final testimony, Mum? You are aware of what this could mean?"

"Yes, Director," said Mum heavily. "If Mum wants to be a reformed hag, she has to tell the truth. Even if it means she can't live here no more. We did everything Rasmussen said, and if ya gots to know, I'm not very sorry. He deserved it."

"Understood," said Ms. Richter. "Bellagrog, is there anything else the defense has to say? If not, the jury will adjourn to render a verdict."

For a moment, Max thought Bellagrog would conjure another argument, right her ship with the same wily ingenuity she had demonstrated throughout the afternoon. But the hag was speechless; her beady eyes bulged like boiled eggs as she glared at her sister in the witness stand. The pressure mounted until it finally burst in an eruption of froth and spittle.

"TRAITOR!" she thundered, stabbing an accusatory finger. "Yer violatin' the code! Yer violatin' Hag Law, and for what? A toothless ogre? Human laws what forbid vendetta?"

"Bellagrog!" exclaimed Ms. Richter. "You have been a wonderful hand in the kitchens and during reconstruction of the campus, but please stop while you have some dignity."

"Dignity?" roared Bellagrog. "I'll show ya dignity! Ain't no court o' fools proclaiming judgment on Bellagrog Shrope! My daughters and me will be on the next ship bound for Blys! Keep yer judgments and sanctimony. You can even keep your precious Mum, the bloody traitor. Oi! Come here, my pretties!"

Instantly obedient, the haglings clambered up onto Bellagrog. Oblivious to the haglings' weight, Bellagrog swept her documents into a floral handbag and stormed out of the proceedings, cleaving a path through the startled onlookers.

"See you at the party!" she bellowed, and disappeared into the throng.

Ms. Richter watched her go, impassive, then turned her attention to Mum, who clung to the defendants' table as thought it were a life raft.

"Would you like to bypass this verdict and join your sister on the next ship, Mum? Or would you like to hear the court's verdict, even though it might mean punishment or exile?"

Max could hear Mum's muffled sobs as she wept against the table.

"I wants to stay, Ms. Richter," she sobbed. "Mum can be good. Bob will help me."

"Very well," replied Ms. Richter. "The jury will adjourn and make its decision."

While Ms. Richter led the jury away, Bob sat next to Mum at the defendants' table. The ogre spoke softly to her, coaxing her head off the table, whereupon she blew her nose on his lapel.

"Why is she getting all the pity?" Rasmussen demanded. "Has everyone forgotten that I'm the victim here? She should be shipped off like the others."

"You keep your mouth shut, Rasmussen," warned Mr. McDaniels, half rising from his seat. "Max has saved your hide more than once, and you've got the nerve to clone him like he's some . . . some . . . I don't know what! What are you using them for? He's got a right to know!"

"I apologize for that," said Rasmussen awkwardly. "I never meant for something so sensitive to become public knowledge in such fashion." He looked at Max in direct appeal. "I'm grateful for your honest testimony, young man. You told the truth and I appreciate your loyalty."

"If you're so grateful, then why don't you turn over those clones?" asked Mr. McDaniels.

"I—I don't have that authority," stammered Dr. Rasmussen, looking surprisingly earnest. "If it were up to me, I would consider it, but my colleagues . . ." He made an apologetic face, shrugging as though such a thing were clearly out of the question.

"A weasel to the last," scoffed Mr. McDaniels. "So, is the Workshop building an army out of my son?"

Max grimaced as every reporter within earshot eagerly recorded the exchange, the volume of which was steadily increasing. Dr. Rasmussen's face darkened as he apparently swallowed an initial retort. Recovering his dry, arrogant footing, he merely replied that such a matter was classified and turned his back to them.

Despite his best efforts to focus on Mum and her impending verdict, Max was deeply shaken by Rasmussen's talk of clones. Could one clone a person with Max's heritage? Could Old Magic be replicated in a test tube?

But as the jurors returned to take their seats, all other thoughts fell away. Bob nudged Mum and the hag stood to face the jury. Blinking away her tears, she arranged her stringy hair into two scraggly halves and smoothed her topknot. Rasmussen leaned forward in an expectant frown as the jury foreman—a middle-aged Mystic—stood and read the verdict aloud.

"In the matter of Rasmussen versus Shrope, the jury finds the defendant, Bea Shrope, guilty of all charges levied against her, and hereby sentences her to exile."

There was a gasp. Mum clutched Bob's arm and shut her eyes.

"However," the foreman continued, "in light of the defendant's honesty, her genuine remorse, and the severe provocation preceding the crimes, the jury has elected to suspend the sentence and place Miss Shrope on probationary supervision for a period of five years."

With the exception of Hannah and Dr. Rasmussen, the crowd applauded the verdict. Max stood and cheered with the rest while Ms. Richter declared the proceedings closed. Mum, however, continued to stand at attention, maintaining a rigid, confused silence. As the jurors filed out of the box, the hag risked a glance at Bob.

"What does that mean?" she whispered.

"It means Mum can stay home," replied the ogre, stroking the hag's greasy head.

~ 12 ~

HAG LAW

By the early evening, it was time to prepare for the Samhain Feast, and Max's attention shifted to the pressing issue of his costume. At Rowan, the celebration was officially called the Samhain Feast in memory of Solas, but the residents actually called this stretch of the calendar whatever they liked: Halloween, All Saint's Day, Día de los Muertos, Dia de Finados, Feralia. Whatever the holiday, costumes were a common tradition to honor the dead, chase away evil spirits, and celebrate the harvest.

Like many of the older students, Max had not intended to wear a costume. However, while he was out, Julie had slipped a note beneath his door imploring him to do so, as it would be "tremendous fun!" Unfortunately, Max was a poor hand at improvisation and had already destroyed two perfectly good sheets before Connor informed him that a ghost was a pitiful effort. Dashing out to the township, Max was forced to compete with his fellow procrastinators for the dregs.

When he returned, the observatory was empty and Max was free to examine his costume in peace. Laying the items out on his bed, he realized that *costume* was too generous a term by far. It implied things that went together. As he gazed upon the array of mismatched pieces, he imagined there must be *some* combination that could pass for something cool. But whatever that might be, it eluded him. As Old Tom chimed seven o'clock, Max was officially late. He would simply have to make the best of it. Reaching for the largest piece, he wondered at its many buckles.

It was a regrettably long, brightly illuminated walk from the observatory to the Manse's foyer. On the way, Max passed numerous warlocks and witches and vampires and ghouls, who interrupted their conversations to stare at him.

While some were undoubtedly drawn to the plumed head-dress or the robber's mask, all eyes eventually gravitated to the enormous velveteen lobster tail that swayed and bobbed behind him. This tail was attached to a spindly-legged thorax, which Max had buckled to his midsection like a girdle. As he stalked down the hallway, he imagined the head and claws in the possession of the middle-aged man who'd simultaneously discovered the costume. The tug-of-war had been a draw, and thus Max was grimly determined to be the greatest half-lobster in Halloween history. Nodding to a gawking kid dressed as a pumpkin, he marched on.

Julie met him in the foyer. She was dressed in black with an eye patch and a black bandanna—a sort of pirate, if pirates wore pink lipstick. Max admired her restraint.

"Happy Halloween," she said, kissing his cheek. "Now, please take a turn so I can gaze upon the full majesty of your costume."

"It was the best I could—" Max began, but Julie held up a finger.

"Shhh," she said, her eyes twinkling. "You know, when I sent that last-minute request, I thought you might have time to throw together a tramp costume. Maybe a ghost. But a masked lobster priest? Max McDaniels, you've exceeded all my hopes and dreams."

Outside the Manse, Mystics had chased off the rain. The moonlit clouds gleamed like spun sugar, coaxed into a ghostly homage of Halloween shapes that drifted serenely above the campus. Beneath the clouds, thousands of flickering jack-o'-lanterns had been set to flight. Some made faces, some howled at passersby, and some merely wheeled about in slow arcs and lazy orbits.

"I'm sorry about what happened at the trial," Julie said. "That craziness with the Workshop. I tried to catch you after, but in all the commotion . . ."

"It's okay," Max said. "Really. With everything else that's going on, worrying about what the Workshop is up to feels like an indulgence." He cast a grim look at Gràvenmuir. Every door and window at the embassy was thrown open, providing glimpses into its crowded ballrooms and salons. Astaroth's seal had been stitched upon a huge white banner that fluttered high above the embassy roof. Max stared at its white silk whipping in the breeze—a final slap at Rowan, which carried on within its shadow.

"C'mon," said Julie, "tonight's about fun!"

She led him to a parquet dance floor near the gap between Old Tom and Maggie. Upon Maggie's steps, a dozen musicians were playing saxophones and clarinets, trombones and trumpets.

Max knew little about swing dancing, but Julie took to it right away. He tried to keep up, but it was not easy to follow the moves, much less maneuver around with a prosthetic lobster tail. Despite his best efforts, the tail swatted his neighbors aside, prompting him to spend as much time apologizing as dancing. For the most part, his fellow revelers laughed off the periodic knocks and swats. A conspicuous exception was a lobster-headed gentleman who seemed to think Max bumped him on purpose and promptly escorted his wife away.

While Max and Julie enjoyed themselves, no one had a better time than Mr. McDaniels. Sweat streamed from his round face as he danced with one, sometimes two partners at a time. For a big man, he was marvelously light on his feet, and took pains to teach Cynthia and Sarah how to do the more intricate steps. Eventually, however, he needed a break and scooted off the floor, where he mopped his brow and tapped his foot in time to the music. Catching sight of Max and Julie, he waved them over.

"Whew," he wheezed, fanning himself. "I didn't know you were a dancer, Max!"

"I'm not," replied Max, just as Mum rushed over to coax Mr. McDaniels back onto the dance floor, where the hag launched into an unsteady tango.

"Let's walk," said Julie, taking Max's arm. Clutching warm ciders, they wound through the partygoers to find a reasonably empty spot on the cliffs overlooking Rowan Harbor.

Max was amazed at how the docks and harbor had grown. Shipyards had been constructed along the southern coast, their docks extending well into a harbor that was now sheltered by a curving seawall. Lanterns winked from ships already moored within the harbor. There were a dozen or so vessels from the four demonic kingdoms, and half that number that belonged to Rowan's traders. Within the harbor's black calm, Max spied

Brigit's Vigil, a stony landmark rumored to be the very spot where Bram's grieving wife had waded out to sea. Once, it had been a lonely pillar of rock, the dominant feature along Rowan's coast. Now it was dwarfed by nearby loading docks and the customhouse, where traders supervised the unloading of cargo that had traveled from strange kingdoms, strange towns, and strange beings far away. Max watched a vye stagger down a ramp, bent beneath a stack of crates. The vyes were not permitted on campus, but dozens swarmed below upon the docks, wolfish shapes against the moonlit sea.

"Staying out of trouble?" asked a quiet voice.

Max turned to see Cooper and Miss Boon. Neither was in costume.

"What are you supposed to be?" asked Cooper, blinking at Max's outfit.

"Honestly, I have no idea," Max replied. "You?"

"A self-respecting man."

"Very funny," said Max as the Agent gave a dry, creaking laugh.

"William, look at that," said Miss Boon, directing his attention toward Gràvenmuir. Cooper stared grimly at the embassy and the piled trunks and boxes that littered its fenced grounds.

"Tonight's the night, I guess," he muttered. "Those sorry fools."

The sorry fools to whom Cooper referred were those residents and refugees who had accepted Prusias's offer of lands and title. Their worldly possessions were piled within Gràvenmuir's iron fence. Max had not told anyone of Connor's intention to leave. Gazing at all the baggage, he wondered if Connor's suitcase was stacked among them.

"How many are going?" asked Julie.

"Hundreds at last count," replied Miss Boon.

Just then, a terribly familiar call sounded from out on the ocean. The image of the dead boy flashed before Max's eyes.

The sound came from a demon's horn.

While the call differed slightly from the one Max had heard in the mountains, the common origins were unmistakable. Turning back to the ocean, his eyes scanned the docks and the shipping piers, and out over the black waters, where xebecs and barques pulled oars or raised sail to make room for the approaching monstrosity.

Prusias's galleon emerged from the night fog to split the waters of Rowan Harbor. Once more they heard the awful sound, a spectral horn that could waken the dead. Silk sails were lowered as the great ship coasted to a halt, dwarfing the surrounding vessels, which bobbed like toys within its shadow. The festivities on campus came to a halt as everyone hastened to line the cliffs and peer down at the newcomers.

As before, fireworks shot from bow chasers in brilliant arcs to illuminate the sky. More horns sounded, a chorus of earsplitting notes, as a veritable yacht was lowered into the water and rowed toward the beach. Prusias stood at the helm.

"Ladies and gentlemen," called a genteel voice from Gràvenmuir. "The time has come."

Max turned to see a thin imp dressed like an Elizabethan courtier addressing the crowds from behind the embassy's gated fence. Max guessed it must be the infamous Mr. Cree mentioned in the advertising flyers. In his gloved hands, the imp held a long, trailing scroll. Flanking him were the tall, eerie mummers that had originally arrived with Prusias but remained behind to serve as silent, ever-present sentinels at Gràvenmuir's gates. Max could not stand to look at them.

The campus fell utterly silent as those who had chosen royalty in Blys over hard work at Rowan congregated within the shadow of Gràvenmuir. There were hundreds of people, including whole families, who made their way through the crowds—some sheepish, some haughty, all carrying prized possessions not to be spared in the transition to a new life.

Max was hardly shocked to see Anna Lundgren among the assembled. The Fourth Year student had been one of Alex Muñoz's closest friends, a girl who had been cruel ever since Max had met her. Without so much as a glance at her parents, Anna and her friend Sasha hefted their bags and marched proudly through the gates.

Yuri Vilyak was there, too.

"Oh my God. Is that Connor?" exclaimed Julie.

The answer was Connor's telltale mop of chestnut curls weaving through the crowd. Max watched Connor's steady progress as though it were a dream. Dragging his duffel, the Irish boy nodded at Mr. Cree and took his place on the other side of the gate. Patting the coins in his pocket, Max ran down toward the gate before Connor had gone too far.

Calling Connor's name, Max tossed him the bag, which contained a handful of gold coins.

"What's this?" asked Connor, catching the bag and hefting it. "Charity?"

"An investment," said Max. "For a rainy day. Whatever. You can pay me back when you're a rich tycoon."

"Thanks." Connor paused a moment before cursing and making a frustrated swipe at the tears running freely down his cheek. "Best to let me be now, Max. This is hard enough as it is."

Max nodded and waved farewell.

By the time he had trudged back to Julie and the others, he had scanned the rest of the emigrants. Yuri Vilyak was no surprise—the former Director and deposed leader of the Red Branch had been disgraced and diminished since his mishandling of the Siege the previous year. But Sir Alistair Wesley was most unexpected. Max watched the white-haired etiquette instructor, dapper as ever, as he escorted his wife inside the gates and acknowledged Mr. Cree with a gracious bow.

Sir Alistair and Commander Vilyak were not the only high-profile members who had taken up with Blys. Max saw teachers, Mystics, and even an Agent he'd met from the Dublin field office scattered among the hundreds of minor scholars, trainees, and refugees who now waited for their new king.

Prusias appeared as before, with a burst of laughter that shattered the anticipatory silence as his dark, bearded face rose above the cliff steps. As before, lesser demons accompanied him, a motley entourage that trailed dutifully behind their lord.

Despite Prusias's festive air, Max noted that he now appeared girded for war. A corselet of dark mail hung from his massive form like a mantle of glistening scales. At his side hung a black broadsword, and gauntlets covered hands that were once replete with rings. He stopped well short of Gràvenmuir, his gleaming cat's eyes taking in the assembled hosts as he saluted in all directions.

"Fair Rowan, how I've missed thee," he announced in his operatic basso. Wetting his lips, he called across to his secretary. "Are they all here, Mr. Cree? Do we have all our lords and ladies?"

"We do, Your Excellency."

"Wonderful!" exclaimed Prusias. "Let them come forward and greet their new master. Let us sail to Blys, where their lands and titles await them. Give Lord Muñoz your lists so he may announce them—he has been so looking forward to this day."

Max gasped as a smaller figure stepped past a rakshasa to stand next to Prusias. Max had assumed it was a demon, but it was Alex Muñoz, a former Rowan student. When Max had last seen him, the boy had changed, but now he was almost unrecognizable.

Squinting, Max could still see hints of the old face—handsome features composed in some cruel contemplation—but that was all. The boy's tattooed skin was blue-gray, his eyes softly glowing as he bowed to Ms. Richter, revealing a pair of sharp, curling horns that jutted from his black hair. The Director did not acknowledge his bow but merely gazed at him with an expression of undisguised pity.

One by one, Alex announced the names and titles of those bound for Blys. Some went eagerly, kneeling before Prusias to kiss the proffered cane, but others lost their courage in the end. Max imagined that it was one thing to daydream about riches and titles, and quite another to meet the demon who promised them. Despite their apparent fears, most managed to present themselves with slow, hesitant steps.

But one newly minted viscount could not summon the necessary courage. He was an elderly scholar who, when his name was called, paused by Gràvenmuir's gates and protested that he'd been out of his mind when he'd sought out Mr. Cree and that there had been a mistake. He very much appreciated Lord Prusias's generosity, but he must decline. He could not go.

Prusias's demeanor changed. His smile faded; he looked impassive, bored, as though he'd seen a thousand such displays, heard a thousand such petitions. Once the man began to sob, Prusias shook his head and called to Mr. Cree.

"This will not do."

Mr. Cree nodded and turned to the tall, silent mummers.

To Max's horror, they began to move, turning slowly toward the gibbering scholar. The old man backed away, trembling, seeking refuge among the people behind him. With a sudden burst, the mummers bore down upon him. The scholar collapsed, clawing at the ground even as gloved and bandaged hands closed upon his wrists. While thousands watched, the sobbing scholar was pried from the earth and swiftly escorted down the steps to the red galleon and his new life.

"Why doesn't Ms. Richter do anything?" asked Julie, shaking with fear and anger.

"What's she to do?" hissed Miss Boon. "The idiot signed a contract!"

"Those poor people," muttered Julie, squeezing Max's hand. "We'll never see them again."

"Don't say that," said Max.

The procession continued. When it was Anna Lundgren's turn, Max's stomach churned as Alex embraced her. She beamed as she received Prusias's blessing and hurried eagerly down the stone steps. Connor was next, and a sickening possibility occurred to Max. Connor had sworn revenge against Alex, and he would pass very close to him when he took his oath. Would Connor do something rash?

But as Connor's name was called, Max's fears subsided. Walking past Alex, Connor did not even acknowledge his former captor. As he knelt before Prusias, his face was calm and proud. Prusias smiled, said something Max could not hear, and held forth his cane. Kissing the cane, Connor stood and bowed before hurrying off toward the cliff steps.

Once "Earl Vilyak" and "Marquis Wesley" and the rest had been named, Prusias glanced at his secretary. "Is that all, Mr. Cree?" he asked.

"Yes," replied the imp. "There's just the matter of some hags that have booked passage."

"Steerage, I trust," replied the demon with a gruff laugh.

Prusias departed with fair words—blessings to Rowan and a promise to visit in spring when the campus was in bloom. As the demon's entourage followed him, Bellagrog and the haglings remained near Gràvenmuir's gates. They huddled together until Mr. Cree rapped the fence with his scepter.

"Don't you dare make Lord Prusias wait," he hissed. "Be off!"

"Good riddance!" hollered Hannah.

Others promptly joined in, and Max could not help but pity Bellagrog as she finally trudged toward the cliff steps, lugging her bags while the haglings clung to her back. She sputtered and puffed, weathering the catcalls and abuse that were showered upon her from every quarter. It seemed that this was the golden opportunity for everyone Bel had bullied to safely return the favor. Insults and curses pummeled Bellagrog, who forged ahead with a murderous scowl.

As she reached the cliff steps, she turned as though intending to say a few last words. The jeers and catcalls died away. As Bellagrog opened her mouth, however, a single voice interrupted her. The crowd turned its attention to Mum, who swayed and crooned in blind, rapturous joy. "Only one hag left and it's me!" she sang. "The marvelous, beauteous Bea!"

Trailing off, Mum delivered a sudden karate chop at an imaginary foe and performed a great, twirling leap. It was only when Bob tapped her on the shoulder that the hag opened her eyes and realized her predicament. She turned and faced Bellagrog, who stood panting upon the top step.

Producing a handkerchief, Mum gave a tentative wave. "Safe travels, Bel—be sure to send a postcard!"

Mum laughed weakly, but her sister did not. Both suitcases dropped heavily to the ground.

"You had to push it, didn't ya?" Bellagrog seethed. "Couldn't keep yer mouth shut, could ya? And to think I was gonna let you stay put and raise these wee ones all on me own. . . ."

Mum began to tremble.

"Oh no," she muttered, shutting her eyes. "No, no, no, no . . ."

"Hag Law!" roared Bellagrog. "I'm invokin' it, so get your fat behind over here and lug these bags on the double! What am I doing sweatin' under me own brood? Go to your auntie, girls!"

The bundled haglings scurried off their mother and raced toward Mum, who groaned as they clambered up her party dress. Several people began to object, but Bellagrog brushed the protests aside, citing Hag Law as though it were a spell, an immutable custom beyond all question or resistance.

Mum staggered toward her sister, her hands clasped in supplication. "Please, Bel," she begged. "Be reasonable. I haven't packed! All my things are in my cupboard."

"Don't fret, dearie," growled Bellagrog. "I gots plenty of woolies. Get goin' now! Don't wants to keep the good lords and ladies waiting."

"But, Bel—!"

"HAG LAW, BEA!"

This final pronouncement was delivered with thunderous finality. Although her pace quickened, Mum's movements now had a mechanical stiffness, as though some unseen force were reeling her in against her will. Once Mum took up the luggage, Bellagrog chuckled triumphantly.

"Look out, world," she proclaimed. "Here come the Shropes!"

Clapping her hands, Bellagrog disappeared down the stairs. Mum followed, unable to manage a farewell glance at Bob or the school she loved.

~ 13 ~

WHERE THE CREEK NARROWS

The dark conclusion to the Samhain feast had shocked and saddened many at Rowan. All told, some six hundred souls boarded Prusias's galleon and sailed off into the east, lured by the promise of new lands and titles. This was not what shocked Max; he knew enough history to understand that some people would always grasp at land and titles. What shocked him was how quickly these people were forgotten.

Forgotten was, perhaps, too strong a term. These people had been loved; their family and friends missed them as one might expect. But Max knew something insidious was at work—a fading within the mind. Most people technically remembered the

departed, but the recollections were hazy, as though some fundamental bond had been severed or anesthetized. References seemed
more appropriate to a distant ancestor rather than one's immediate family. If asked, a person might fondly recall a friend or relative
who had once sailed off into the blue to make their fortune.

And that was where the stories stopped.

People didn't write once they'd left for Blys. Weeks had
passed and many trade ships had come and gone, but they never
carried any letters from Blys. Few who remained at Rowan
begrudged the silence. After all, Blys was where big things happened and its new nobles were understandably busy. Little Rowan
was a charming afterthought, a provincial outpost compared to
mighty Blys across the sea. It had *always* been that way. . . .

Max found this last sentiment particularly disturbing. The
Four Kingdoms of Blys, Jakarün, Zenuvia, and Dùn had not only
entered the lexicon, but had been woven into the fabric of daily
life. Many referred to them as though they had always existed.
Russia, Los Angeles, Egypt . . . countries and cities from the past
were lumped into a remote, exotic history that bordered on the
mythological. One might have been discussing Atlantis.

Memories weren't the only thing that continued to fade. It
seemed that each week, another modern innovation or techno-
logical insight had vanished. By now Max was accustomed to the
absence of television, telephones, electric lights, computers, and a
host of other contemporary conveniences. But the losses continued. By mid-November, most fishermen refused to sail beyond
sight of land for fear they'd be lost at sea. Antibiotics disappeared
from the medical stores so that a case of whooping cough or scarlet fever became life-threatening.

Despite the fading of memories and technologies, Rowan
managed to prosper like a great city of the Renaissance rather
than some Dark Ages backwater. The harvest had been full,

horse-drawn carts rolled smoothly along cobbled lanes, and there was as much milk and cream and butter as one could wish for. Money exchanged hands freely, and the shops were full of hand-crafted lanterns, quilts, and artworks. It was the rare wretch who had to beg for coppers or a woolen blanket.

At the moment, Max could have used a blanket. He walked briskly across the academic quad on a night that promised snow. The lamps had already been lit, illuminating trees whose bare branches formed a lattice against the deepening blue-gray sky. From out on the ocean, Max heard a bell—a ship was entering Rowan Harbor.

He walked east toward the sea, then curved to skirt the woods that led to the great gates. He glimpsed lights bobbing among the trees and heard his father's deep voice singing a ridiculous march.

"How was the spooky lantern walk?" asked Max as the group emerged into the clearing.

"Terrrrribly spooky," replied Mr. McDaniels, raising the lantern just beneath his face. "Shoulda joined us. The wood-cutters were roasting chestnuts off the main road, and we told some ghost stories."

Max smiled, waving to the bundled tykes who held their parents' hands and clutched their lanterns.

"Was it spooky, Tim?" he asked a shy little boy.

"A little," the boy replied quietly. "But not too spooky."

"Good," said Max. "Well, I could smell dinner already cooking in the Manse. Lamb stew, I think."

"Go on ahead," said his father, waving the group on. "Check the bulletin board for the next outing." Mr. McDaniels turned and cocked an eye at Max. "You gonna tell me what's wrong, or do I need to guess?"

"Nothing's wrong," said Max.

"Max," laughed his father. "You've never been one for hiding your emotions."

The two walked along the cliffs, slipping between Gràvenmuir and the white statue of Elias Bram. "It's just that I was sure I'd hear from Connor by now. Or Mum. But apparently none of the people who left for Blys have written. And no one seems all that bothered by it."

"Well, I wouldn't trouble your mind about Connor," said his father. "If anyone can take care of himself out there . . ."

"Do you find it harder to remember things, Dad?" asked Max. "Places like the Workshop or even important people?"

"Important people like your mother?" inquired Mr. McDaniels with a knowing smile.

"Yeah," said Max, looking out toward the sea. "I guess."

"Max," he said. "Rest assured, I will never forget your mother."

"You know," said Max cautiously, "we've never really talked about this, but you could start dating or something if you wanted to. I mean, I wouldn't be angry or anything."

"Are you giving me your permission?" his father asked, bemused.

"Yeah." Max shrugged. "I guess so."

Scott McDaniels laughed and looked affectionately at Max. "I didn't know I needed permission," he chuckled. "But it's nice to know I've got it. Besides, how do you know I haven't already been going out on dates? I might be a hot commodity!"

Max gave his dad a dubious glance.

"I'll tell ya what," said Mr. McDaniels. "When I stop dreaming about your mom, I'll start dating. Till then, she's still my sweetheart. Just last night I had the most amazing dream about her. . . ."

"Dad!" Max exclaimed. "I do not need to hear about it."

"No, no," laughed his father. "Nothing like that. This was

purely innocent. I was walking in my night thingies—pajamas—outside someplace. There were hills and a sky full of stars and a bright, magical moon. But something was behind me. I could hear it breathing, but I was too darned scared to turn around! So I just kept strolling along the road, trying to keep calm so as not to set off whatever was walking after me. Up ahead, I saw a house—a big house on a hill. I made straight for it. By the time I reached the door, Max, I swear that I could feel something's breath hot on my neck."

A chill inched down Max's spine. Mr. McDaniels's dream was eerily similar to his recurring nightmare of the monstrous wolfhound. It was the wolfhound that had followed his father; he was sure of it.

"What happened next?" he whispered.

"Well, I knocked and prayed to high heaven that someone would answer. Knocked again and still that awful panting just behind me. Knocked one more time, and who do you think opened the door?"

"Mom?"

"No fooling you," replied his father. "There she stood, pretty as the day I met her. Didn't say a word; just smiled and took me by the hand. And when her fingers touched mine, Max, I swear to you that I could feel it. I jumped like I'd been struck by lightning. Woke right up, of course, and just sat there in the dark wishing like hell I could fall back asleep and see her again. Isn't that something?"

"It is," said Max.

"Well," said his father, "when I stop having dreams like that, I'll start dating again."

"Fair enough," said Max, touched by his father's devotion.

Max's father looked past him then. "What's going on over there?" he asked.

Max turned and saw the tall, gangly mummers leading a small procession of demons across the lawn toward the harbor steps. By all indications, they were seeing someone off—undoubtedly a demon of high standing.

While the McDanielses watched, more figures came into view. There was Miss Awolowo and Ms. Kraken, both wearing shawls against the cold and conversing quietly with the Gràvenmuir ambassador, who stopped and waited for the final pair.

Max could not believe his eyes.

Ms. Richter, Rowan's Director, walked in step with the very demon that had shot the boy back in the fall. Every attitude and expression of Ms. Richter's was one of appeasement. Her hands were clasped, her face attentive as though seeking to agree, to comply. The rakshasa inclined its great tigerlike head, evidently pleased by the Director's latest utterance. Reaching the cliffs, they joined the rest of the company and proceeded down the steps.

"Who's that?" asked Mr. McDaniels, rubbing his arms against the chill.

"Someone who shouldn't be here," muttered Max. "Come on."

Max trotted up ahead of his father and gazed down at the piers, where a luxurious-looking yacht was moored at a dock piled high with baggage. Gray, lanky vyes were already loading the baggage aboard as Lord Vyndra and his escort reached the bottom and made their way across the icy beach.

Max did not bother to wait for his father. He dashed down the stone steps two at a time, and then ran toward the torch-lit pier.

While the vyes continued loading the ship, Lord Vyndra puffed upon a serpentine pipe. He faced the beach, looking both resplendent and bored while he listened to some final message or petition from the ambassador. Ms. Richter and the other Rowan representatives stood off to the side near the other demons and the mummers. As Max ran up the dock, Vyndra caught sight of him and blew a smoke ring into the brisk night.

"Best leash your Hound, Madam Director," he growled.

Ms. Richter turned just as the mummers stepped between Max and the group and crossed their tall halberds like a hideous mockery of the Vatican guards. The minor demons hurried behind them.

"Max, what are you doing here?" asked Ms. Richter calmly.

"Me?" asked Max, coming to a halt. "What's *he* doing here?"

"Lord Vyndra was visiting his embassy before his departure," replied Ms. Richter in a stiff, warning tone. "As he has every right to do."

"That demon has been here hunting humans," Max seethed. "I saw it with my own eyes! He murdered a boy right in front of me."

"Why didn't you report this?" asked Ms. Richter.

"Cooper made the report," said Max. "Ask him! He can verify it."

Ms. Richter pursed her lips and bowed her head by way of apology to Lord Vyndra, who merely stood by, puffing thoughtfully.

"Max, Agent Cooper reported nothing of the sort and is not here to verify your claim, as he sailed for Dùn this morning. Now, I must ask you kindly to leave."

Max gaped at Ms. Richter. "How can you side with him?" he exclaimed incredulously. "Look in his bags, Ms. Richter. I'll bet there are trophies in there, heads or skins or whatever else this monster took!"

"Max, please!" Ms. Richter snapped.

"Don't trouble yourself, Madam Director," interjected Lord Vyndra smoothly. The fierce, feline features were composed into an impassive sneer. "I am grateful for the extended stay within your lands, but this boy is delusional. Prusias may brook insults, but I do not. I will confess to taking a stag or two, but no skulls or skins of man. Search my baggage if you like," he said, gesturing for the vyes to unload the many trunks.

"That won't be necessary," said Ms. Richter.

"Are you insane?" Max shouted, utterly incredulous. "Search them!"

"No," replied Ms. Richter firmly. "That would be insulting to our guest. Now remove yourself or you will be placed under arrest and stand trial for insubordination. Is that understood?"

Max recoiled as though he'd been slapped.

"Nobody's arresting my son," sputtered Mr. McDaniels, coming up the dock.

"This does not concern you, Mr. McDaniels," said Ms. Richter. "Please take Max and go."

Lord Vyndra laughed. "Are you the Hound's father?" he asked with evident interest. "Can such a thing be?" Stepping between the two mummers, Vyndra leaned over the crossed halberds to gaze more closely at Scott McDaniels. The demon's presence was immensely powerful; Mr. McDaniels trembled like a baby bird held in thrall by a serpent. At length, the demon exhaled a cloud of sweet smoke and shook his head. "I think your wife has fooled you, my friend. You're not his father, just a well-fed cuckold."

"I'll kill you!" Max rushed toward Vyndra. Planting his foot, he leaped clear above the crossed halberds.

But Max did not fall upon Lord Vyndra as he had planned. Instead, his motion ceased altogether, as though time had stopped. His body was suspended in midair, his limbs cemented in place by a compressing force that nearly crushed the air from his lungs. He strained against it.

As he did so, a light began to shine from his brow, a radiance that blazed ever brighter as he struggled.

"Annika!" gasped Ms. Richter. "Ndidi, help!"

It was then that Max realized that it was not Vyndra but Ms. Richter who had acted against him. The energies required of the Director were so great that she had sunk to her knees, her arms shaking uncontrollably as they extended toward Max.

The whole harbor erupted in light as Max broke the spell.

He fell heavily to the dock. Scrambling to his feet, he recovered his balance and leaped again at Vyndra, who had not moved.

Again he was frozen in midair, this time by the combined efforts of the three powerful Mystics. He screamed again. Every window in the customhouse shattered. A wave of energy erupted from his body, warping the dock and nearly tipping all upon it into the icy sea. Mr. McDaniels was thrown backward. Still, Ms. Richter and the others maintained their unwavering focus.

"Go!" screamed Ms. Kraken. "We can't hold him any longer!"

The vyes hurled the last of the baggage onto the bobbing yacht. With a cold bow, Lord Vyndra stepped aboard his ship, followed by several attendants. Swiftly cutting the cables, the vyes thrust the yacht away from the dock with long poles so it could ease out into the cold swell. As though manned by a spectral crew, the sails were raised and the ship swung around to face the open sea.

All eyes were upon Max and the blinding radiance that surrounded him. His attention remained fixed upon the yacht as it sailed toward the harbor mouth and the dark ocean. Upon its deck stood Lord Vyndra, leaning upon the brass rail and smoking his pipe. He waved pleasantly to Max.

As Max stared, he noticed that the demon did not merely wave but was holding something aloft. The object gleamed round and white under the pale moon.

It was a human skull.

Max tried to yell, to signal the others to look, but now even his tongue and vocal cords had been paralyzed. His whole body was numb from the strain of spent muscles. Bolts of energy snaked from Ms. Richter, Ms. Awolowo, and Ms. Kraken's fingertips, reinforcing the sphere so that it grew stronger even as Max weakened.

"Ambassador, take your people and go," said Ms. Richter calmly.

Once the demons had returned over the beach and up the cliff steps, Mr. McDaniels spoke.

"You can let go of him now. I think it's safe."

But Ms. Richter and the others did not release Max. Not until Lord Vyndra's ship had gone and the light surrounding Max had faded did the women release their collective spell. It happened slowly, the sphere's energies unknotting and unraveling like a ball of thread until it dispelled entirely. Sinking slowly to the dock, Max lay in a panting heap while the surf churned and eddied beneath the icy dock.

Clearing her throat, Ms. Richter called out to the dumbfounded customs master. "Mr. Hagan, please send a missive to the healing ward and request some help. Annika may require medical attention. Ndidi, help me sit her up."

Max's strength slowly returned. Rolling onto his side, he took a deep breath and glowered at Ms. Richter, who now sat next to Ms. Kraken amid a spray of broken glass. The Director looked spent.

"Mr. McDaniels," she said. "If you're not hurt, please escort your son back to his room."

Max felt a pair of strong hands slide under his arms and lift him from the dock. Despite the weakness in his legs, Max managed to lean against his father and make the slow, shaky walk down the deck. There, he could see a crowd had gathered along the bluff. He scanned it for a friendly face and found none.

* * *

For the next two days, Max remained isolated in the observatory. There had been knocks and letters slid cautiously beneath the door. But he did not budge from his bed, not even for meals or to answer his father. Instead, he lay amid the warm sheets and watched the constellations turn slowly about the glassy dome. His emotions fluctuated wildly, swinging from anger to depression in sudden fits. He was furious with Ms. Richter—with all of Rowan's leadership—for kowtowing to the demons. Yet he felt guilty that he'd lost control.

He had not seen David, but he had been sleeping much of the time. Yawning, Max walked wearily about the observatory's deck and glanced down at the lower level. Although David was not present, there were signs he had been there. Papers and manuscripts were scattered about, and Max detected the faint smell of smoke from the fireplace. He pulled on his robe and went downstairs.

The table was a disaster, every inch piled high with books and papers. The nearest parchment had been brushed with a silvery substance that shone as though still wet. Curious, Max lit one of the thick candles and held the paper up to warm yellow light.

At first, the contents were indecipherable—a nonsensical array of words and letters, numbers and symbols. But as Max watched, patterns began to form. Words emerged, whole sentences as if he'd put on magic glasses. It soon became clear that the writings were Bram's and the parchment was from Bram's private papers.

January 11, 1633

Before his death, dear Kepler predicted this would happen. The day leaves me joyous and quaking. For three centuries, the high tower has been locked. Tomorrow evening, it is to be opened and I shall take up residence. The Elders have finally overcome their absurd misgivings as to my youth. Tomorrow, Elias Bram becomes only the fifth Gwydion Chair of Mystics.

Such a thing. Such an achievement for a man of twenty. I confess that I have petitioned for the title and that some would find it unbecoming, but the great take what is their due.

How shall Brigit react? With a witticism, no doubt, some feigned ignorance of the title. She delights in belittling my achievements with a charming indifference. But she cannot ignore this. Whatever Marley may say, I am winning the race for her affections. Within the year I shall speak with her father. No matter the bride price, I shall pay it.

Poor Marley. There is no truer friend, yet my fortunes must strike him a terrible blow. He will be happy for me, of course, but he cannot fail to realize what this means. He must lose his dearest companion and the woman he loves. Fate can be cruel. But the Gwydion Chair must put aside such concerns, for there are greater matters that demand his attention. . . .

Max turned the page over, but that was all. The journal's tone contrasted sharply with the sober, earnest accounts that Max had read from later years. This Bram seemed arrogant and ambitious, coldly insensitive to the heartbreak of his friend.

Max heard a sound from upstairs and put the paper down. The door opened, sending a shaft of hallway light into the dark observatory. Footsteps. A crinkling of paper.

"I come in peace!" called a warm English voice. "May I come down?"

"Sure," said Max, sitting up. Shoving aside a pile of books and papers, he attempted to make things semipresentable before Nigel had reached the bottom stair.

"Hmm," said Max's onetime recruiter. "It's a bit dark down here. Mind if I warm things up?"

"You said that when we met," replied Max. "'Cocoa and fire to soothe the soul' or something like that."

"Yes, well, you were a scaredy-pants and needed soothing," quipped Nigel, setting down a brown bag and a stack of papers. "Sorry to barge in, but your father gave me a key."

"Is Ms. Kraken okay?" asked Max anxiously.

"She's just fine," replied Nigel, frowning at a newspaper and slipping it to the back. "A bit overtaxed from all the excitement, but she's recovering."

Max nodded, feeling some of the tension drain from his shoulders. Nigel slid the brown bag toward him, and Max detected the buttery scent of popovers. They were still warm. He wolfed down two, grunting his appreciation.

"Etiquette's really smoothed out all the rough edges, hasn't it?" said Nigel, bemused.

"Hnnh enh Mnisses Bessow?" asked Max, taking another bite.

"I beg your pardon?"

Max swallowed, swatting a flake of crust from his chin. "How is Mrs. Bristow?"

"She's wonderful, thank you. Pregnancy has her in full bloom. I've never seen her more beautiful. How are you?"

"Fine," said Max.

"Hmmm," said Nigel. The man handed Max a stack of unopened letters. Sorting through them, Max counted four from Julie, two from Cynthia, one from Sarah, and one other whose handwriting he did not recognize.

"Do you mind if I take a look at this?" asked Max. "I don't know who it's from."

Nigel shook his head, and Max opened the envelope.

Dear Max,

This is a difficult letter to write. You've been a good friend to Julie and little Bill, and we appreciate that. But it is impossible to ignore the rumors and recent accounts in the newspapers. We love our children very much and want them to be safe. Thus, we respectfully ask that you cease all contact with them immediately. Of course, Julie is fighting us on this—she cares very much for you. If you really care for her, you will let her go and trust to the judgment of her family.

Thank you,
Robert and Linda Teller

"Good news?" asked Nigel with a hopeful smile.

"Not so much," said Max. "Julie's parents don't want me to see her anymore." He spoke in a monotone; the reality of the message had not seeped in. With Max's permission, Nigel read it for himself.

"Are you angry with them?" Nigel asked, once he'd finished the letter.

"No," Max sighed. "They're nice people. I know they're doing what they think is best. But I would never hurt Julie."

"I know that," said Nigel. "For whatever it's worth, I think they know that, too. From their letter, I don't think they're afraid that you would ever hurt her. I think they fear that you—by virtue of who you are—are a magnet for dangerous situations."

"That demon's lucky they stopped me," Max seethed. "I don't know what I would have done."

"Hmmm," said Nigel. "I think it's a good thing for all concerned that nothing untoward occurred. Rakshasa are exceedingly powerful, Max. You might have been badly hurt. And from what I hear, we need that particular rakshasa. . . ."

"Vyndra?" Max scoffed. "Why do we need him?"

"Lord Vyndra is very influential among his kind," replied Nigel. "And he has little love for Prusias. It's my understanding that Vyndra believes he should be the ruler of Blys. As you can imagine, this makes him exceedingly useful."

"He's a murderer," said Max. "I saw him hunt a human for sport."

"I never said he's a pleasant fellow. Merely valuable."

"I don't understand why we have to even deal with them," Max snapped. "This is supposed to be our land. It seems so cowardly to me, all this bowing and scraping."

"You would prefer that we simply duke it out, eh? Mano a daemona?" asked Nigel.

"Maybe."

The man smiled and crumpled the empty bag. "Max, as things currently stand, we wouldn't last a week," he said matter-of-factly.

Old Tom chimed three o'clock.

"I'm late as usual," Nigel sighed. "Max, I promised your

father I'd drag you outside to join the kiddies on their playdate. It snowed last night, my boy—everything's all white and sparkling. Striking, really. If you're game, I'll join you. It's been years since my last snowball fight. Tell me, do they throw terribly hard?"

"Nigel, they're five."

"Well, those little beasts can still pack a wallop."

Within minutes, Max had grabbed his coat, tied his boots, and hurried downstairs. He met Nigel in the foyer and pushed open the doors to see the quad white and twinkling.

This was Max's favorite kind of snow—clean and fluffy, with just enough moisture for packing. It clung in thick clumps to the tree branches, cloaked the fountain sculptures, and even caked the roof of Gràvenmuir, whose eaves hung thick with icicles. The quad was packed with students commiserating over finals. A carriage rolled past with a clop of hooves, dragging a makeshift plow that cleared the walk. Above the rooftops, starlings and gulls rose and fell on the air currents, crying out in shrill, sad voices.

"Are they in the Sanctuary?" asked Max.

"No," replied Nigel. "Outside somewhere. Your father said you'd know where—some creek or whatnot with a beaver dam."

They set out, making deep tracks in the smooth snow.

Rowan rarely bothered to close the great gates anymore. David's carvings upon the door and the myriad of spells now seemed a quaint design to welcome visitors who traveled the cobbled roads from the outlying farms and small settlements. Max and Nigel walked beneath the high stone arch, and Max expressed his frustrations with teaching.

"Everyone tries," he said. "Ms. Richter, the Agents . . . everyone gives it their best. But I don't know. They just can't do most of the feats. Even when they Amplify, there's just something missing. I can't quite pinpoint what's wrong, so we're trying to break things down into their component parts."

"Very sensible," said Nigel.

"Yeah, but something still gets lost in translation," said Max, stopping to read the new sign that had been erected where the road diverged. "Cooper can do one or two, but it's still not as effortless, as natural as it should be."

As Max led the way, they left the cobbles and veered onto a woodcutter's trail that curved through the forest and back toward the ocean. The day was growing overcast, the horizon a deepening gray that promised more flurries. As the sun subsided, the landscape took on a stark beauty of snow and shadow, black branches and green needles. The breeze grew colder, but not unpleasant. Far off, a bell rang from the harbor, its chime clear in the wintry air.

"Are you a wagering man, Max?" asked Nigel.

"Sure," said Max. "What's the wager?"

"That bell means a ship, as I daresay you know. Well, if the ship is a Blyssian xebec, I'll buy you a pound of Mr. Babel's finest chocolate. If it's a Zenuvian clipper, you buy Emily the same."

"Done!" said Max, shaking his hand. "Blyssian xebecs are twice as common as Zenuvian clippers. Ha! Someone made a sucker's bet!"

"Was it the someone who read this morning's shipping news?" inquired Nigel casually.

"Oh no," said Max, sliding between a pair of fir trees to reach a vantage point. He soon found one, a granite ledge that provided a panoramic view of Rowan's crenellated walls and a peep of Gràvenmuir's black spires. Far below, the harbor seemed tiny, a child's play set.

Sure enough, there was a ship. At first, they spied its lanterns—tiny pinpricks of light against the charcoal sea. The black hull was long and narrow, the tall masts built for an enormous spread of sail. Every line and curve suggested a ship built for carrying exotic cargo at speed—a Zenuvian clipper.

"Victory is sweet!" crowed Nigel. "I'll be sure to have Emily send a thank-you note. Incidentally, she prefers dark chocolate."

"Mr. Babel's," Max confirmed.

"Indeed," said Nigel. "We all need a bit of chocolate to fend off the chill, although apparently not that fellow. Who'd be sailing for pleasure in these conditions?"

"Where?" asked Max, gazing out at the ocean.

"Down there," said Nigel, pointing south at a hazy vessel that was bobbing within the shelter of a small cove. Waves crashed upon the nearby rocks, sending up a misting spray that obscured much of the ship. A swell finally pushed the boat higher, allowing them to see it clearly. Max caught sight of gleaming teak and a serpentlike prow. He'd seen that ship before.

It was Lord Vyndra's yacht.

"What's he still doing here?" Max muttered.

"Who?" asked Nigel pleasantly.

As though in answer, they heard the sound of the demon's horn. It came from the south—from land. The long, hoarse call froze the blood and sent birds fleeing from the trees.

"Do you have a weapon?" Max asked urgently.

Nigel's smile evaporated. "What? Of course not—Max, what's wrong?"

"Come on!" Max cried, running along the coast toward the sound. Nigel quickly fell behind, but Max could not stop to wait.

"Dad!" he yelled, scanning the woods ahead. No one answered. The daylight was starting to fade as Max hurdled a fallen tree and dashed along a snowy trail that wound toward the narrow creek where the children liked to play.

"Dad!"

No response—just the sighing of the wind and the percussive *thump-thump-thump* of his beating heart. Ahead, a snowman had been built. Two dark, uneven eyes peered from its white head.

Max ran past it, following the many footprints down the slope that terminated at the creek.

He could hear a sound up ahead—a child crying.

"Dad!"

And then he saw them.

The child sat in a pile of cold, wet leaves, while the snow-swollen creek ran over her boots. She was sobbing, her hand clutching Mr. McDaniels's coat as he lay slumped against a tangle of roots that poked from the creek bank.

"Oh no," Max gasped, lifting the girl free of the cold water and setting her on the blood-tinged snow. "Dad, can you hear me? Please tell me you can hear me."

There was a mild splash as his father's leg gave a sudden kick.

"It's going to be okay," Max whispered. "I'm here now."

Glancing down, he saw a tear in his father's sweater just below the breast. At first, Max thought it was just a tear in the fabric, until he saw the blood that seeped from it like syrup. Carefully, Max tore the hole wide and quickly unbuttoned the shirt beneath so he could examine the wound.

What he saw made him gasp.

His father held two arrows tightly in his hand—he must have made the hideous wound in his chest when he had wrenched them out.

The girl's crying became a scream of pitched hysteria. Max tried to block it out while he focused on what to do.

"Okay," he said, steadying himself. "Okay, okay . . . we're going to do this."

He felt his father's pulse—weak, but certainly present. He was cold, however . . . terribly, terribly cold. Max needed to keep him warm while he stopped the bleeding. Pulling off his coat and sweater, Max piled them upon his father, then wrapped his scarf around his own hands so that he could apply pressure to the wound. His father inhaled sharply, stiffening from the pain.

"I'm sorry," Max said. "I'm so sorry."

Mr. McDaniels let go of the arrows and fumbled blindly for Max's hand.

"You're going to be okay," Max insisted, seizing the hand and holding it fiercely. "The bleeding's already slowing. It'll stop soon. Everything's going to be just fine."

Max heard rapid footsteps along the creek. Nigel finally arrived, panting beside him. "Is he alive?" he gasped.

Max nodded.

"Where are the others?"

"I don't know," replied Max, trying to maintain steady pressure. "I only found her. I think the bleeding's stopped, but I can't carry him like this."

Raising his hand, Nigel shot a screaming flare of distress sparks into the sky. Their burst reflected in the dark creek, a bizarrely festive light. Nigel sent two more—emphatic bursts that trailed like a funnel cloud down to their location. Crouching, Nigel felt Scott McDaniels's pulse.

"I'm not getting much," he said, his face pale with worry.

"But it isn't bleeding anymore," Max insisted, peering beneath the scarf. "It's stopped."

Nigel's eyes darted down to the creek. Slowly, he dipped his hands into the water by Mr. McDaniels's side.

They came up red.

Max stopped breathing.

Clearing his throat, Nigel spoke with unnerving calm. "Max, I think there's another wound."

Gently rolling Mr. McDaniels onto his side, Nigel lifted up his shirt to examine his lower back. He went as white as a sheet.

Forgoing tourniquets altogether, Nigel immediately placed both hands directly against the injury.

"Do you know a spell?" asked Max, growing frantic.

"Not for anything like this."

Scott McDaniels's body shuddered. He had reached some tipping point. Leaning close, Max pressed his cheek against his father's. "Don't go," he whispered. "I'll be all alone. Please, please stay with me."

Max repeated the plea over and over. It became a kind of incantation. As long as Max said those words, his father could not go.

There was no little girl crying.

No Nigel.

No creek.

There was only his father's cold cheek against his warm one.

There were only the words that would keep him here.

~ 14 ~

FAREWELLS

The incantation failed.

The words had cheated him.

Two days later, Max sat alone at the foot of his father's bed. The room was so very quiet. The curtains were drawn to reveal a gray brooding sky.

Opening the armoire, Max checked his tie once again in the mirror. It was fine. His shoes were fine. The suit was, too. Scott McDaniels's clothes were arranged throughout the armoire, and Max stared at them. There were flannel shirts and dress shirts, charcoal trousers, and a basket of dark socks. One of the shirts had almost slipped from its hanger. Max fixed it and slowly closed the door. The armoire's faint scent of aftershave and cedar was a bitter reminder that his father had lived here, had inhabited this space.

Old Tom chimed three o'clock. There was a tentative knock and a deep, rumbling inquiry. Opening the door, Max nodded to Bob and the Bristows. Bob and Nigel wore black suits; Mrs. Bristow wore a gray dress that showed the round, promising lump of her unborn baby.

The walk to Rose Chapel was a silent dream, a blur of corridors, the sting of daylight, the resin scent of fir trees as they plodded through the damp chill. The chapel was located northwest of the Manse, past the last rows of the orchard. It was a humble, elegant building of white stone set within a clearing of spruce and ash and fir. Many mourners had already arrived, milling clusters of black suits and dresses like so many starlings. The priest arranged his notes and motioned for Bob, the Bristows, and Max to be seated in the front pew.

Max stared at the coffin.

Within it was his father's body, pale and suited. What a strange job, Max thought—to comb a corpse's hair and knot its tie. But it was just a vessel, he consoled himself, just flesh and blood, bones and teeth. Someone, some well-intended soul, had tried to beautify the deceased, but no makeup could mimic the life that had departed. Despite the effort at tranquil realism, the face looked off. It was a waxy counterfeit; it bore none of the spark or personality that had defined the man.

While the priest spoke, Max fixated upon his father's hands. There was much more of him present in his hands than in the waxy veneer of his face. There was his treasured wedding band and a class ring from a Boston university that no longer existed. Calluses and scars from his kitchen duties. The bent forefinger from a childhood basketball injury. The hands were folded upon his broad chest in a gesture suggestive of modesty or piety or both. It seemed a silly pose, such a meek and apologetic sign. His father had never carried himself that way. Max wondered if he would have approved. Is that how one was supposed to bid the world farewell, with crossed hands in a pine box?

Turning away from the coffin, Max half stood and peered past Bob's shoulders at the other mourners. Some dabbed at eyes and blew into handkerchiefs, while others sat in bowed, respectful silence. There were the Tellers, Julie's appalled and tear-streaked face staring into his own. There was Ms. Richter, flanked by Miss Awolowo and Ms. Kraken. The Director's expression was hard and thoughtful, her jawline sharp as scissors as she sat with her hands folded upon her black shawl.

David Menlo stood in the chapel doorway like a ghost, but this ghost had put on a suit. Even at a distance, Max could see tears shining on David's cheeks. He stood alone in the doorway and shook, sobbing silently as the priest read from an old Bible.

Max listened to the priest's consoling words, but they only made him angry. The Old Magic stirred from its deep slumber. Bob made a curious sound in his throat, twisting his old frame to gaze at Max with a watchful eye. The ogre must have sensed something, some subtle change in Max that the human mourners could not feel.

"We go outside now," he whispered.

Panting, Max nodded and felt the ogre's warm hand close over his own. There was a gentle pull on his arm, and he stumbled out of the chapel, ignoring the blur of faces and even David, who stepped aside to let them pass.

The cold air was a relief. Once outside, Max found that he was sweating profusely; he had soaked through his shirt and even the outer suit. Bob led him to a tree stump and lay his overcoat upon it so Max could sit and catch his breath. For several minutes,

Max merely hunched over and panted, his mind reeling with so many thoughts it was impossible to order them.

"When did you decide to leave?" he finally asked Bob, clutching the ogre's hand.

"Bob does not understand," replied the ogre.

"Your homeland," Max muttered. "What made you come to Rowan?"

"Hmmm," said Bob, rumbling in his throat as though the memory were buried deep within his history. In the gathering twilight, it began to snow—tiny, crystalline flakes that settled upon his bald, knobby head. "Long ago, in Russia, I hear of place where old creatures can go. During the Great War, I come here and learn to cook. It is what Bob was meant to do."

"Meant to do . . . ," muttered Max, musing on these words as the chapel's bell began to toll.

Mourners began to stream out of the doorway, holding hands and speaking quietly while the bell's clear note rang through the dark clearing.

Bob patted Max's hand. "Do you want to see your papa one more time?"

Max stood and gazed at the open church door. "No," he said. "He's gone, Bob. He's someplace else."

The ogre nodded and shifted his weight, flexing his fingers to drive off the cold.

"Bob will see to details," he said. "You go do what you must. Bob just asks one thing, *malyenki*."

"What's that?"

"Visit Bob one last time before you go," rumbled the ogre. "He misses his little Mum. He will miss his fierce Max, too."

"Who says I'm going anywhere?" Max protested.

The ogre merely smiled and shook his head.

"Before Bob was cook, Bob was ogre. Little ones not so hard to read. . . ."

Draping his overcoat over his shoulders, the stooped ogre lumbered back toward the chapel, stepping gingerly over the icy patches in the snow. As he did so, he waved absently at Julie, who stood upon the walkway some distance from her waiting family. Nodding politely to her parents, Max came and took her hand.

"Max, I'm so sorry," Julie whispered, once again on the verge of tears. "I've tried and tried to find you these past days—"

"I know," said Max. "I appreciate it, really. I needed to be alone."

"My parents said they wrote you a letter," she whispered, leaning into him. "Forget all about it—I don't care what they say. I want to be with you."

Max closed his eyes and felt them well with tears.

"Julie," called Mr. Teller, a note of concern in his voice. "We've got to go now—Bill's catching cold."

"Just a minute!" she pleaded, then lowered her voice. "We're going to be together no matter what my parents say."

"Julie," said Max. "Your parents are right. It's not good being with me—bad things happen to the people I care about."

"Nonsense!" she hissed, ignoring her father's second summons. She opened her mouth to speak when a gloved hand touched her lightly on the shoulder. Julie turned and Max looked up to see a woman dressed all in black, her face obscured by a hat and veil.

"I wanted to pay my respects," she said, her voice soft as smoke.

Brushing past Julie, the woman embraced Max and held him close. He felt the patterned press of lace against his cheek as the woman whispered through the veil. "Never forget you are the son of a king."

Releasing him, the woman departed, moving smoothly through the crowd until she disappeared from view.

"Who was that?" asked Julie.

"I—I don't know," Max stammered.

By now, Julie's father had lost patience and had stepped off the walk to reclaim his daughter. Condolences were muttered, apologies extended, and a protesting Julie was steered away.

It was better that way, Max thought. A prolonged goodbye would have been too painful, and it seemed there were endless people who wished to see him: Sarah, Cynthia, parents of class-mates, teachers who implored him not to worry about homework at a time like this. There was Miss Boon, alone now that Cooper was off on assignment. She hugged him close, as did Miss Awolowo and even old, cranky Ms. Kraken, who seemed to bear no grudge from recent events. Limping up, Ronin shook Max's hand and offered his condolences, as did Nolan, Monsieur Renard, and the other figures who had come to define Max's life at Rowan.

It was touching, this outpouring of affection, of sincere goodwill. But Max still felt very much alone in this place, upon this earth. And David was nowhere to be seen. The rest of the mourners departed until there was just one left, waiting patiently by the chapel door as the last bell died away.

Ms. Richter.

It was dark outside the chapel now, and the snow fell steadily. The Director walked toward Max, her shoes scraping softly on the cobbles.

"I'm so sorry, Max," she said, coming to a stop. "I wish there was something else I could say. Your father was a very good man. I can't imagine what it's like to lose him."

"Have you finished the investigation?" he asked pointedly.

"We both know there is no investigation," she said simply. "I believe every word of your statement."

Max felt conflicted. There was immense relief that Ms. Richter believed him, that his accusations and painful account had not fallen on deaf ears. But there was also a maddening frustration.

"If you believe me, then why won't you do something?" Max asked.

Taking his arm, Ms. Richter walked with him along the quiet paths of the snow-sprinkled forest. It was a moonless night and dark beyond reckoning when one strolled beyond the radiance of the occasional streetlamps. At the Director's summons, a pair of glowing orbs came into being and hovered just before them, lighting their way. It was a full minute before Ms. Richter answered his question.

"I wish I had an answer that would satisfy you," she said quietly. "We could demand justice and insist that Lord Vyndra return to stand trial. He would, of course, refuse, and I cannot imagine the ambassador would assist us in the matter of extradition. Demons do not operate on human time, Max. Even if they chose to humor our request for criminal proceedings, Vyndra might not deign to appear for centuries—long after I, Nigel, even you have passed."

"I don't care about criminal proceedings," said Max quietly. "I want revenge. I want to find Vyndra."

"I know you do," she said quietly. "It's the most natural response I can imagine. However, I must implore you to resist that urge, Max. It's very likely that Lord Vyndra wants you to seek him out and try your hand at revenge. Why else would he have made such an obvious, targeted attack? He wishes to bait you."

"Well, he's done it. And he's going to be very sorry."

"Max, Lord Vyndra is a monster. Don't let him turn you into one."

Max stopped and looked at the Director, genuinely puzzled.

"Aren't we monsters, too?" he asked. "What's happening to the rest of humanity while we hide behind our walls and gates and treaties? Doesn't our order exist to protect those who can't protect themselves? Isn't it our responsibility to hunt down monsters like Vyndra? Isn't that the whole point of studying mystics and combat and all the rest?"

Ms. Richter sighed. "Max, you've hit upon the dilemma that all leaders face. Should a leader cater to present wants or future needs? Shall I indulge your anger, your demands for justice, and declare war upon Vyndra or Prusias or the whole of demonkind on Earth? That might scratch a powerful itch, Max, but it would come at a terrible price for many. Do you remember Winston Churchill and the Second World War?"

Max nodded.

"Well," she continued, "early in the war, the British broke the Nazi's secret code. Thus there were times when they knew precisely when and where the Nazi warplanes would strike. Despite this knowledge, Churchill had to stand by and allow certain targets to be bombed. Can you imagine why he would do such a thing?"

"Sure," said Max. "If they always managed to defend the targets, the Nazis would have suspected that their code had been compromised."

"Precisely," said Ms. Richter. "Churchill had a critical choice before him. Should he act on his natural impulse to protect every target, or should he override this instinct to serve the greater good? Of course he chose the latter. Imagine the anger, the rage that some people must have harbored against him! Were they justified in feeling that way? Of course they were. But it doesn't mean Churchill was wrong. . . ."

"You're right," Max said. "Leaders do have to make hard choices. But I'm not a leader, Ms. Richter. I don't have to mind my behavior or wage a war in secret. I can make decisions for myself and do what I want to do—what I need to do."

"Not while you live here, Max," said Ms. Richter sadly. "If you live at Rowan, you must abide by our rules. I cannot allow you to indulge your anger and endanger everyone within this realm. If that's what you choose to do, then you must do it elsewhere."

"I understand that," said Max.

"But I would urge you to wait," added Ms. Richter. "Such a decision should never be made in haste or in grief. And even though you are of the Old Magic, you are still very young. There is much that we can teach you. There is still so very much for you to learn."

"In a perfect world, I would stay," replied Max quietly. "But this isn't a perfect world. You were born to lead this place and these people. I was born for other things."

A long silence fell between them, broken only by the low howl of the wind that bent the trees. When it became clear that Max had said all he intended, the Director smiled sadly at him.

"Where will you go?" she asked.

"I don't know," said Max.

"Well," said Ms. Richter, "wherever that may be, I wish you well. But always remember that you have a home here at Rowan, Max. You have a home and people who love you. . . ."

Like most of their kind, the brothers Aurvangr and Ginnarr preferred to live belowground, and thus Max knew he must be patient. The dvergar lived beneath their smithing shop and must have been fast asleep when Max rang the bell in the deep hours of the night. Standing outside the shop, Max gazed about the township and clutched his bundle to his chest. The streets were largely deserted, the windows dark.

Verging on despair, Max gave the bell a final, furious pull.

Inside, a light bobbed in the darkness—a flickering candle flame. The curtains were pulled, and a gnarled, curious face peered from behind the glass. Max stood by as Aurvangr unbolted the many locks and opened the door a sliver.

"I'm sorry to bother you," whispered Max. "But I have urgent business. Can I come inside and talk with you?"

"Did you bring gold?" asked the dvergar, cocking his head at Max's bundle.

"Yes," said Max.

Opening the door wide, Aurvangr stood aside to let Max enter. Stooping beneath the archway, Max saw the cold hearth and the great anvil on which the brothers plied their trade. The building was low, the roof supported by heavy beams that were carved with ancient runes and scrolling images of earth, sea, and sky. Max ducked beneath a hanging rack of pliers and tongs while Aurvangr shivered and pulled his nightcap squarely over his bristly ears. With a grunt, he shouldered the door shut and turned to fix Max with a curious gaze.

"A knock in the night means evil is afoot," sighed the dvergar. "What is it you want?"

"I want your boat," said Max simply. "I've seen you and your brother out sailing in the bay. I've seen that ship sail of itself, and I need such a thing."

"*Ormenheid* is not for sale." The dvergar shrugged.

From the back stairwell, Max heard the flapping of feet climbing the stairs. A voice called out from below.

"Who is that, Aurvangr?"

"It is the boy," replied the dvergar to his brother. "He wants our *Ormenheid*."

"Does he, now?" inquired Ginnarr with evident curiosity. "And where are your manners, brother? Bring him down and let us hear him."

Aurvangr frowned at his brother's hospitality. Grumbling, he motioned for Max to follow.

Following the dim light of the lantern, Max climbed down the steps, where tree roots poked through scrolling stonework. They passed small storerooms and pantries and a coal room before the stairs terminated at a cozy hollow some thirty or forty feet below the earth.

This ceiling was low—no more than five feet at its highest point—and Max was forced to sit on the floor, as none of the chairs could accommodate him. In the dim light of the lantern, he could see that the room had been excavated into an octagonal shape, with each angle braced by a sturdy beam that arced toward the center. These were carved with great care and seemed to tell a story—a tapestry of runes and glyphs etched in sturdy tree trunks. Three deep nooks, like alcoves, were set into the walls. One contained a little claw-foot bathtub and a pair of water pails. The other two alcoves housed wooden beds whose mattresses were of mounded straw, a sort of blanketed nest. Ginnarr promptly burrowed in the one nearest a cast-iron stove, his braided beard hanging like a bib over the red wool blanket. It was a snug-enough room, Max decided, but the air was mildly damp, and the smell revealed the brothers' affinity for ripe, moldy cheeses.

"Aurvangr was saying that you had a proposition for us," Ginnarr began.

"Er, yes," said Max. "I was interested in your boat, the *Ormenheid*."

"And your business required you to inquire in the middle of the night?" said Aurvangr.

"Yes," said Max. "I want to leave—leave Rowan. I want to do so tonight without all sorts of questions or prying or goodbyes."

"That is your business," said Ginnarr. "And your business is your own. Can you not book passage on a demon vessel? Why must you have *Ormenheid*?"

"I won't sail on a demon ship," said Max. "If you won't sell me your boat, I'll have to build or buy another. But I hope you'll consider my offer."

Reaching in his pack, Max removed a box of gems for which he'd exchanged his gold. It was a considerable amount of wealth, but the dvergar seemed unimpressed.

"My boy, you could not rent *Ormenheid* for that, much less buy it. Do you know what you are trying to purchase?"

"A ship that sails on its own."

The brothers glanced at one another and smiled.

"No, Hound. You are trying to buy an artifact of our people— a relic of our greatest achievements. Have you heard of *Skidbladnir*?"

"No," said Max. "I'm sorry to say I haven't."

"Long ago," Ginnarr began, "the trickster Loki had angered the gods through his deceits. He enlisted the aid of our people— the sons of Ivaldi—to craft gifts that would make amends for his evil deeds. Three great gifts we forged—golden hair for the goddess Sif, the spear Gungnir for Odin, and the ship *Skidbladnir* for Frey of the Vanir. The ship could sail swiftly with all of the gods upon it and cleave wave and wind alike, for all the elements were its home. And when *Skidbladnir* was not in use, it could shrink to fit a child's pocket. A wondrous thing, no?"

"Yes," said Max, trying to mask his impatience. "But I'm not trying to buy *Skidbladnir*. I want the *Ormenheid*."

"Ah," said Aurvangr, sipping his tea. "But *Ormenheid* was the model for *Skidbladnir*. It is the greatest treasure we still possess. If you offered one hundred times the wealth in that box, we could not sell it to you."

Max's heart sank. His mind raced as he considered what else

he might offer. He rummaged through his pack, sorting through his meager possessions.

"What is that?" asked Ginnarr, leaning forward.

From his pack, Max removed and unfolded a mail shirt. The supple armor had been a gift from the deceased Antonio de Lorca and was nigh impregnable.

"May we?" asked Aurvangr, peering greedily at it.

Max handed the shirt to the brothers, who held it between them and ran their leathery fingers over its smooth mesh.

"This is a pretty thing," said Ginnarr.

"There are runes here," observed Aurvangr, now peering through a jeweler's lens. "Runes and relics, brother."

The pair abruptly turned to Max as though they'd reached an unspoken agreement between them.

"We shall strike a bargain, eh?" said Aurvangr. "For the diamonds and this mail shirt we shall lend you *Ormenheid* for three years and teach you the words to master her. After three years, she must return to us."

"I don't know," said Max dubiously. "That shirt's a treasure of the Red Branch, and I might need it where I'm going. Besides, it seems an awful lot to pay for borrowing a little ship."

"Then you must bargain with the demons." Aurvangr shrugged.

"No," said Max, considering. "I won't bargain with them. You have a deal."

While Aurvangr prepared the contract, Ginnarr shuffled over to a bookshelf stuffed with odd papers and tiny portraits of their ancestors. From a small glass box, he removed what appeared to be a minute replica of a dragon-prowed Viking ship whose tiny oars and striped sail were rendered in exquisite detail.

Placing it in Max's hand, the dvergar patted it affectionately. "Here is little *Ormenheid*—the Gleaming Serpent," he said.

Max listened carefully while Ginnarr ran through the words that would command the vessel. The final word, cautioned the dvergar, must be spoken only when the ship had been set adrift in open water, for it would transform the toy into a full-sized ship of some sixty feet. Ginnarr inscribed this word on a slip of parchment, taking care to write the phonetics so Max would not mispronounce the Old Norse.

Once the contract had been signed in triplicate, the dvergar seemed intent on returning to their beds, but Max ventured one last request.

"I know it's late," he said, removing the final bundle from his pack. "But I also wanted to see what you might do with this."

Laying the cloth bundle upon the table, Max slowly unfolded it to reveal hundreds of razor-sharp shards of black metal and gray bone. To the layman's eye, the shards may have appeared as so many scraps. But these were the remains of Cúchulain's spear—the barbed *gae bolga*. Wounds inflicted with this weapon were always fatal. Max had shattered it within the Sidh but had salvaged every shard and splinter of the mythical relic.

A grim silence came over the dvergar, and they seemed to dismiss any thought of sleep. Bending over the table, they peered closely at the weapon's remains but were careful not to touch them. In a murmuring voice, Ginnarr spoke to the metal, teasing forth its history.

"This is the blade of the Morrígan," he croaked, staring at his brother. Both made a hasty sign and stepped away from the table. "We can do nothing with this. Nay, not even our forefathers would dare meddle with such a thing."

"What do you mean, 'the Morrígan'?" asked Max. "This belonged to Cúchulain."

"It may have belonged to Cúchulain," whispered Ginnarr, "but this is the weapon of a god—the Morrígan, who travels as wolf and raven among the dead and dying. She is the death-bringer, and these splinters hunger for it. Loathe should you be to set this thing to the fire and shape it anew. Scatter it to the four winds or bury it deep in hallowed ground. We will not touch it."

Max pressed the issue, but the dvergar were resolute. It was clear that continued overtures would only serve to frighten or anger them. Thanking them for the *Ormenheid*, Max rewrapped the bundle and stowed it carefully in his leather pack.

By the time he left the dvergar's shop, it was deep into the night and the time for a quiet departure was fleeting. Rowan Township was quiet as Max stole along the shadowy cobbles and plunged deeper into the Sanctuary in search of Nick. For nearly an hour he jogged along the wooded paths and climbed up into the hills calling for the lymrill by name.

By five o'clock, Max despaired of bidding Nick farewell and hurried back to the Manse. Entering his room, he was happy to find David absent. The hour was late, and Max had time for only one goodbye. Conscious of Astaroth's prohibitions, Max allowed himself no books but took one innocuous paper—a private note that he tucked into the warm traveling cloak now secured by his ivory brooch from the Sidh. With a final glance up at the twinkling skyscape, Max hefted his traveling pack, strapped the sharp gladius to his back, and took up the long walking stick with which he hoped to scale the far mountains of the world.

Bob was still awake when Max knocked lightly at his door. The ogre lived in a converted storage space off the kitchen cellars, a high-ceilinged room with windows cut along the eaves. Clutching a book against his huge nightshirt, Bob made a bow.

"I am glad you came," he rumbled. "I have something for you."

Upon a small bench, the ogre had placed a large basket of preserves, cured meats, and a tough, durable bread called hardtack.

"What will you do for water?" he asked.

"Find it when I can," said Max. "Use mystics when I can't. Water is the least of my worries."

The ogre nodded and accepted the bundle of letters and sacks of coins that Max asked him to distribute. It was strangely liberating as Max released them. Everything he now owned—or cared to own—was on his back. However, Bob insisted on making a quick inventory of Max's supplies, granting his approval only when satisfied with the stores of woolen undergarments and a harpoon that could be socketed to his walking stick.

"Please explain the things I can't," said Max, gazing about the room, trying to remember every last detail. "I'll miss you, Bob. You've been a good friend to me."

"And you to me," said Bob, stooping to look him in the eye. "Farewell, *malyenki*."

Minutes later, Max closed the Manse door quietly behind him. Skirting the main paths, he wound his way down toward the harbor, detouring slightly to run a hand along Old Tom's stonework.

Gràvenmuir was the last building he would pass. As always, the masked guards stood outside the gates, gangly and hideous. The more enterprising merchants were already setting up their stalls for the day, and despite the moonless night, Max kept to the hedges and shadows until he reached the stone stairs that led down to Rowan Harbor.

Each step seemed significant—a turning away from food and shelter, warmth and civilization. Another world lay beyond the harbor, and there were no guarantees that it held the answers, purpose, or vengeance Max so sorely craved. But he had to try. That was the thought that carried him along the rocky beach and away from the loading docks and private slips where prying eyes might follow him.

Clambering over rocks and sloshing through the ice-cold surf, Max walked a quarter mile before he deemed it safe to launch the *Ormenheid*. His teeth chattering, Max reached inside his cloak and set the tiny ship upon the black swell.

He leaned close and whispered to it. *"Skina, Ormenheid, skina."*

Stepping back, Max waited for something to happen. He had expected a shower of faerie lights or something similarly dramatic. For several seconds Max entertained the awful suspicion that he'd been the victim of a colossal joke and paid dearly for a child's toy while the real *Ormenheid* was moored elsewhere.

But he had not been deceived. The *Ormenheid* began to gleam, stretching sinuously through the water until it reached a length of some sixty feet. Its shape began to broaden, ribs emerging from the stiffening keel and curving up to form a shallow hull of over-lapping planks. Within a minute, the frame had assumed the characteristic shape of a Viking ship. As the mast rose and the sail unfurled, the great prow lengthened and formed the head of a dragon.

Resting his hand against the gunwale, Max marveled at the reassuring solidity of a vessel that had recently resided in his pocket. Tossing his walking stick and pack aboard, he lifted himself out of the chilly brine and gazed out at the first signs of the approaching dawn.

Changing quickly into dry clothes, Max arranged his bedroll toward the back of the ship, where the gunwales tapered. As he set out the last of the blankets, Max noticed a figure standing on the beach some twenty yards away.

It was David Menlo.

Max's roommate still wore his suit from Mr. McDaniels's funeral and his face still betrayed a ghostly pallor. As a fresh flurry of snow whipped about his shoulders, David merely stared at

Max with the same disquieting maturity he'd exhibited since he'd been a squeak of a boy.

"I came to say goodbye," said David, his voice carrying eerily over the wind and waves.

"How did you know I was here?" asked Max.

David merely shrugged. "Do you know where you'll go?" he asked.

"They're saying the Great God has returned," replied Max, smiling grimly.

"That they are."

"Well, then, I'm off to find him."

David offered a sardonic grin and a farewell wave that Max returned before setting the ship on its course.

"*Leita Blys,*" he commanded in a clear voice.

Long oars pulled through the surf, setting the ship into purposeful motion. A breeze filled the sail, and the ship eased out toward open sea.

Once he was away, Max retrieved a small spyglass and took a last glance at Rowan in his wake. There was David walking slowly along the gray beach toward the bright watch fires that lined the harbor's curving seawall. Raising the glass, Max glimpsed the statue of Elias Bram jutting above the cliffs, a tiny white figure set against the black sprawl of Gràvenmuir.

~ 15 ~

INTO THE BLUE

Max had been to sea before, but never alone. As the hours passed and all signs of land surrendered to a gray, impenetrable mist, the horrors of the sea and its immensity began to tell upon him. The breeze was cold and steady, the sky a spectral white that did little to distract from the gray, interminable expanse of wintry ocean.

He brooded on his father. He fixated upon death's terrible finality in that icy creek.

It was impossible not to brood in such a cold, wet seascape. He supposed he should be happy that there were no storms, no wild nor'easter to come screaming out of the treacherous black cloudbanks as in fishing tales and storybooks. But even the cry of the gulls had faded, and the swell was so smooth that the *Ormenheid*'s sharp prow cleaved the water as though it were fresh cream.

In the eerie silence, Max's thoughts turned to David Menlo.

David had always been odd, but his oddities were formerly marked by a cheerful, eccentric quality—the endearments of distracted genius. Of late, however, something darker had taken root. Max reflected upon David's obsessive secrecy, his attacks on Enemy ships, and his dangerous experiments. Individually, each was a cause for alarm, but collectively they suggested something far worse.

Max frowned.

History was littered with tales of brilliant men and women who had delved too deeply in arcane matters and were driven mad for their insolence. It was not for mortals to brave Olympus or stare too deeply into the abyss. . . .

As night fell, Max tried to banish these thoughts. He was comfortable enough in his warm nest of blankets, but the utter stillness of the sea disturbed him, and it would not do to compound its eeriness with dark musings. Well off in the distance—miles and miles across the sea—he saw the merest peep of light, a faint flickering against the dark. It was, no doubt, the prow lantern of a xebec or a particularly ambitious fisherman, and it comforted Max to know that he was not alone in this vast, darkening immensity.

But he did not risk a lantern of his own, and it was long hours before his nerves succumbed to sleep on the open, exposed deck of the *Ormenheid.*

As the days passed, Max fell into a sort of routine. At sunrise, he washed his face in cold water before starting a small fire in the shallow depression that served as a miniature hold. There, he strung and cooked his latest catch of the cod, which abounded in these waters.

Food was plentiful, but the ice posed a problem. When the temperature dropped, whole sheets of it formed on the *Ormenheid*'s gunwales and rigging, slowing the ship considerably. Max spent many afternoons patiently chipping it away, his breath forming great plumes of mist while the oars and sail urged the ship toward Blys.

He assumed they were headed in a straight line for Prusias's kingdom, but the farther he traveled, the less certain he became. There were strong currents in these waters that pushed the *Ormenheid* ever south. Whenever Max tried to alter the ship's course, however, the oars fell slack, as did the lines and rigging. After two occurrences, he concluded that the ship knew its business far better than he did and he ceased his meddling.

Leaving the sailing and navigation to the *Ormenheid*, Max occupied his time by huddling within his blankets and scanning the horizon for sight of a ship or icebergs. At night, it was much the same, although there were times when the sky was so wondrously clear, the stars so impossibly bright that he spent hours gazing up at them and listening to the whales singing their songs in the deep.

A week had passed when the weather began to change. Unlike the smooth swells of the previous days, rough waves now slapped against the *Ormenheid*, sending a freezing spray over the gunwales that soaked the clothes Max had strung out to dry. After an hour, Max despaired of drying his laundry and began the careful process of retrieving his clothes so that a sudden gale would not carry a beloved pair of underwear or comfortable socks out to sea.

As he stowed the cold, wet knots back in his pack, Max noticed something moving on the gunwale. A fat, hearty seabird had landed and was swinging its profile at Max as though deciding which of its cold, round eyes it should fix upon him.

Another bird settled nearby, squawking rudely at its neighbor. Then another.

Gazing up at the sail, Max saw dozens of gray and white birds alighting upon the spar while others dove and landed upon the deck in twos and threes until the ship was covered in them. Initially, Max found the scene comical, but soon he found that the battered-looking creatures were making a mess of his ship, fouling his deck, devouring his cod, and milling about in a dense jumble of feathers and beaks. Taking up his walking stick, Max did his best to shoo them away, but they merely flapped into the air, offered an aggrieved look, and settled defiantly back in their spots.

After ten exhausting minutes, Max gathered himself for one final effort. Whirling his stick about his head, he leaped and shouted and cursed and pleaded. To his delighted surprise, the birds collectively acquiesced and flew away in a great screeching mass. Feeling rather pleased, Max took a moment to savor his victory and ponder how best to scrub a magical ship that was awash in bird excrement.

The moment was brief.

As the wind howled, Max felt a dramatic drop in the air pressure. The sky was filled with birds—terns and gulls, skuas and cormorants all racing across the pale gray afternoon. Following the trail of birds, Max looked ahead and forgot all about cleaning the ship, finishing his drawing, or checking his stores.

He thought only about survival.

The horizon ahead was a vast, tattered spread of blackness. A shadow had fallen upon the ocean as though the heavens themselves sagged beneath the awful weight of the coming storm.

Max had never felt so small or helpless. There was no time to gape at the coming monstrosity. Running about, Max secured his belongings and lowered the sail to protect it from the grasping, greedy winds that threatened to rip it from the rigging. Pulling in the oars, he frantically tied them into long bundles and lashed them to iron rings set into the sturdy oak beams of the gunwale.

The only remaining cargo to secure was himself.

His breath sputtering in frozen gasps, Max wrapped a rope tightly around his wrist and tied a troll's hitch to another iron ring. Taking meager shelter behind the gunwale, he steadied his breath and waited.

Slowly, the *Ormenheid*'s bow began to rise as it climbed the first enormous wave. It was a smooth, gradual progression, but terribly unnerving as the rope tightened around Max's wrist and he found himself staring first at his boots, then at the stern, and finally at the gunmetal sea. Timbers strained as the ship climbed ever higher. When it finally crested, the ship raced down the wave's face in a gush of ice-cold seawater.

There was driving rain and sleet and the howl of unimaginable gales as the *Ormenheid* was buffeted about like a spinning top. Wave after wave bombarded the ship, oceanic haymakers of terrifying size. Whether by sheer luck or some marvelous magic woven into the vessel, the *Ormenheid* often managed to evade the full brunt and fury of the storm. It slid within troughs, righted itself, and generally presented a narrow profile to the waves, which were never able to land a decisive blow.

Max had never felt so close to death. He could not breathe— freezing rain and torrents of frothy seawater choked him whenever he gasped for air. Again and again his body was wrenched up from the deck, restrained only by his tether, and dashed against the hull or the gunwale's biting rings.

The noise was deafening—a screeching wail of wind and wave that was suddenly interrupted by a crack like a rifle shot. Max turned just in time to see an oar come loose and snap into several pieces of heavy, jagged wood. One or two pieces skittered harmlessly over the side, but another came rocketing toward him, skipping once on the deck before slamming into him like a freight train. There was a blinding flash, a dull ringing in his ears, and all became a warm, enveloping fog.

Gulls. He cursed their shrill calls, vaguely aware of their shadows flitting beyond his eyelids. His skull felt as though it were wedged within a vise. A dull pain threatened jagged fury when-ever he moved his head even a fraction. The sun was beating down upon his face—a far warmer sun than was usual for the north Atlantic. With a groan, Max cracked an eye and waited for it to focus.

He was lying on the *Ormenheid*'s deck, still lashed to the ship by his tether. Blood matted his hair and had pooled beneath his cheek so that it was almost glued to the deck's warm timbers.

Gritting his teeth, Max pushed himself up and climbed slowly to his feet. By the time he stood panting against the gun-wale, he was drenched in sweat. Despite the calm seas, he promptly threw up over the side and for several moments clung to the rail and tried to recollect what had happened.

Staggering about to inspect the ship, Max was shocked at how little damage the *Ormenheid* had actually taken. His packs were still lashed down, most of the oars remained, and the sail appeared whole. Bit by bit, he set about the task of sliding the oars back into their locks and hoisting the sail back up the sturdy mast, muttering, *"Leita Blys, Ormenheid,"* before he sank to his knees and fumbled about for water.

There was very little potable water left in his skins. His body was burning with a sickly fever, however, and he gulped down what remained. Bracing himself against the mast, he stood once more and got his bearings.

From the sun's position, he judged it was midafternoon. From the warm breeze, he figured he must have been adrift for hundreds of miles along a swift current that had brought him south and into warmer latitudes. There was no sight of land, just a rolling expanse of waves that might have been dunes but for their shimmer under the hazy sun.

To pass the time, he began to record his daily observations in his sketchbook. The storm had warped and waterlogged the book, buckling its pages and smearing the previous drawings, but Max dried it in the sun and flattened the pages into serviceable shape before he jotted down the weather, his ship's progress, and the animals he managed to observe.

And the animals were numerous: porpoises, whales, seabirds by the thousands, and fish of every size, shape, and variety. He sailed over great patches of kelp and spellbinding acres of phosphorescent plankton. There were rains and even swift black squalls, but nothing to approximate the terrors of the nor'easter he had experienced. The weather was warm enough that Max was able to dispatch with the heavy furs and blankets and spend his evenings in quiet contemplation by the small pool of witch-fire that he conjured for cooking and comfort.

Other than the storm, Max was surprised by the normalcy of the sea and sky, the general condition of the world beyond Rowan. He had always assumed that Astaroth would use the Book of Thoth to fundamentally reshape the world. Max had been braced for perpetual midnight, fire and brimstone, hell on Earth . . . not a tranquil sea and a mackerel sky.

Astaroth's impact might have been negligible, except for a sight Max witnessed some days later. It was late afternoon and dusk was falling quickly when he heard a splash from starboard. Abandoning the fire, Max peered over the side and saw a seal suddenly leap from the water.

He had already seen dozens of seals on his voyage, but this specimen was particularly fat and its skin was as red and shiny as a tomato. Leaning out over the gunwale for a better look, he spied a crimson blur streaking alongside the ship. Rising, it broke the surface once again, and he was able to get a proper look.

It was not a seal.

The creature had a seal's plump, tubular shape and flipper-like appendages, but its face was decidedly toadlike, with large yellow eyes and a thin, drooping mouth. It dove smoothly into the water and wriggled in the manner of an enormous tadpole. As Max followed the submerged creature's progress, he heard strange, tittering calls that were similar to a loon's.

Some quarter mile ahead, Max saw a series of black rocks jutting from the ocean. Peering through his spyglass, he saw that the rocks were littered with hundreds, perhaps thousands, of the strange red creatures issuing their strange call or sliding down into the foamy sea. Upon closer inspection, he learned that the leaping specimen alongside the *Ormenheid* was hardly representative. In fact, no two creatures upon the rocks were identical beyond the plump sack of their bodies, the vivid redness of their skin, and the hyenalike titters that issued from their pumping throats. Some faces were toadlike, but others were birdlike, or bovine, while some bore a chillingly human physiognomy. These peculiarities were not limited to their faces. Some creatures had two fins, others four, while still others displayed vestigial limbs akin to a crab's that sprouted feebly from their stomachs and backs. Max had never seen more hideous, jumbled forms of life.

While the *Ormenheid* sailed on, Max settled in and watched the strange red creature that was shadowing his ship so closely. Despite its grotesque appearance, there was an efficient elegance to the creature's movements, and the powerful flippers that doomed it to a clumsy existence on land were a fluid marvel in the water. Max grinned as he watched the red torpedo repeatedly dive down, dart ahead, and grow larger as it rose again to the surface.

This time, however, something rose with it. A dark shape whose size quickly dwarfed the rising red creature until it seemed a mere bull's-eye within an ever-expanding shadow.

Max jumped back from the rail as the red creature burst from the water, pursued by a shark that was easily half the length of the ship. There was a spray of splinters as the shark shattered several oars and breached clear of the water, allowing Max to see the roll of its awful bulk and a dead black eye that stared into his own. For a single, terrifying moment, Max feared that the shark's momentum would carry it over the gunwale and onto the deck, but instead the monster fell back to the sea with its prey clamped tightly within its jaws. The *Ormenheid*'s hull gave a dreadful shudder as the shark's tail slapped its side and churned the waters into red foam.

Scrambling to his feet, Max seized up the harpoon and raced to the back of the ship in the event that the monster decided to pursue the boat. But the shark stayed behind to lurk in the waters where the attack had taken place, its huge fin turning lazy circles amid the screaming throng of scavenging birds.

As the days progressed, Max found the breezes growing unseasonably warm. He had been to sea only three weeks, but it seemed an age. He had given up trying to approximate the *Ormenheid*'s position in so vast an ocean. He trusted to the ship's magic, the invisible forces that pulled its oars, adjusted its lines, and fixed the rudder toward Blys. While the strange seal-creatures compelled him to examine closely anything he caught, food had been reasonably plentiful, and he'd discovered that the simple act of enchanting a hook so that it glowed was an irresistible enticement to many a fish at nightfall.

* * *

And finally, land. It appeared one afternoon, a mere sliver of black that broke the monotony of the gray, flat horizon. Max leaped up at the sight of it and leaned out over the prow, fearful that it was a mirage, a teasing trick of the mind.

But it was no mirage. Within hours, the *Ormenheid* was sculling through a shaded waterway between two cliffs of dark rock. Max gazed up, hopeful for signs of life, but he saw nothing more than stone and the tangled trees that clung to its footholds.

Days passed until the *Ormenheid* suddenly veered to port, steering for a small beach that was sufficiently sheltered from dangerous rocks and surf to make a landing. Cutting a diagonal across the waves, the ship rose and fell, sliding ever closer to the dark sand until its shallow hull at last ground to a halt.

For several moments, Max merely sat in the boat and watched the first stars peek from the indigo sky. The evening was cool, the waves melodic as they broke gently on the beach and spilled over the sand. As he gazed along the landscape, the shallow cliffs and stands of dark trees, he saw no hint of habitation. He had arrived in Blys to find it as quiet and peaceful as a poem.

Following months at sea, the sensation of solid ground was pleasing and strange. There was no roll to the earth, no sudden movements to jostle or buck the unwary. Taking up his pack, he made another inventory of his possessions and girded the gladius to his back. With an apologetic glance at the mauled *Ormenheid,* Max spoke the word that would make it as small as a matchbox and then plucked it from the wet sand to stow it safely in his pocket. Smiling grimly at his bedraggled, beggarly appearance, Max took up his walking stick and began the slow trudge from the beach up to the rocky spit of land that jutted from the broader coast. It was a fine night for walking, and Max's weariness soon drained away. He felt as strange and wild as anything he might meet.

* * *

He walked for days and never saw a soul. The land had recently emerged from winter, shaking off snow to reveal a mix of muddy hills and bare trees. But the palette was not all gray and ocher, for periodically Max traversed vast carpets of knee-high blue flowers that stretched across the landscape like a Van Gogh. When darkness fell, Max often heard the deep, lowing calls of animals, and remembered Bob's advice to seek small, secure places at night.

It was an entire week before he saw the witch.

At first glance, Max thought it was a bird, but the shape grew larger until he saw the trailing tatters of cloak, the lump of a woman soaring above on a twisted staff of yew. It would do no good to conceal himself; he was walking along a ridgeline in the morning sun, and there was no place to hide. Besides, Max was anxious to speak with another human.

Sure enough, the witch had seen him, for she altered her course and began to circle back, skimming low over the hills until she hovered a stone's throw away. With a reedy laugh, she wagged a thin finger at him and spoke in Italian.

"What have we here?" she cackled, a malicious gleam in her eye. "A fugitive, perhaps?"

"I'm no fugitive," said Max coldly.

Dismounting from the staff, she peered suspiciously at him. "Who are you then?" she croaked. "You do not speak like a native."

"A traveler."

She laughed and spat on the cold ground. "Travelers don't come here," she said. "You are in Blys. I thought you were some slave from that accursed place, but you . . . you are something else, I think. Show me your mark," she ordered grimly, gesturing at his hand.

Curious that the witch would know of such a thing, Max

revealed the Red Branch tattoo upon his wrist. She stared at it for a full ten seconds.

"Gods above," she whispered, backing away. "Are you really him?"

Max frowned and pulled his sleeve low. "What did you expect to see, witch?" he asked, ignoring her question.

"The marks of Prusias and the local brayma," she explained. "You are on demon lands—all humans must wear such a mark. Forgive me, blessed child, but anyone will know you by your mark."

"What is a brayma?" Max asked.

"The local lord," she replied, gazing about the hills as though she expected his or her arrival. "Oh, you mustn't travel openly without their permission, young Hound! They will come for you."

"Let me see *your* mark," said Max, glancing at her dark hands, which were riddled with tiny, hieroglyphic tattoos and mystic writing.

"The witches bear no demon brands," she replied, pushing back her sleeves to the elbow. "Our home is in Aamon's realm, and he brands us not."

"Lucky you," said Max. "If your home is in Aamon's kingdom, what are you doing here?"

"I am a weather worker," she replied. "Contracted to a ship in Blys that is weighing anchor for Zenuvia. They are expecting me."

"Not so fast," said Max, seizing her broomstick as she sought to climb upon it. She grimaced, revealing small teeth filed to points. "Where are Lord Vyndra's lands?"

"I know not," she whined, weakly tugging at her broom. "I think far to the north, but I make no promises. Please let me go—we will be seen up here!"

"You said there are humans nearby," said Max, maintaining his hold on the broomstick. "You thought I was some kind of slave. Where are they? Who's keeping them?"

"You don't want to go there," she warned. "No, no, almost anywhere else."

"Why?" Max asked. "What's wrong?"

"I can't say," the witch hissed, her teeth nearly chattering with some nameless fear. "Aamon would roast me alive! He always knows if one's been talking. The stories . . . the stories!"

"We're going to make a bargain," said Max calmly. "I'm going to let you go and make the winds blow for the demon ships. In exchange, you're going to tell me of this place where humans live and then forget you ever saw me."

"I can't," she panted. "It's for your own sake. Go far, far away from this place!"

But Max would not relent, and at last the witch told him to continue northeast until he arrived at the ruins of a road—an ancient Roman road that had survived the Fading. There were humans nearby, she insisted, and Max could find them if he followed the road and kept clear of the goblin tribes that inhabited the region. When Max asked whether it was the goblins that threatened the humans, the frightened witch merely shook her head, insisting that she'd done as their bargain required, and sped off to the west.

Max tightened his pack and trotted down from the ridgeline. A dense forest of birch trees lay ahead, and Max chose to camouflage himself among them as he trekked across the cold ground in search of the rumored road.

After several hours he found it—though half choked with weeds, it was an undeniable avenue of dusty stone that threaded through the hills. Max walked upon its worn stones, stopping occasionally to peer at crumbling milestones that had been built when Caesars ruled the land.

The road was not all that had survived the wars and Fading. Occasionally Max saw houses, deserted stone structures whose roofs had collapsed. In one of these, Max had discovered evidence of a long-abandoned goblin camp—scattered bones and hideous graffiti that had been scrawled upon the wall. But he saw no sign of humans.

As the shadows lengthened and daylight began to fade, Max started to despair. Despite the witch's warnings, he was anxious to find the humans soon. The idea of a warm fire and conversation—real conversation—sounded better than all the world's treasures.

The gibbous moon was high above when Max finally heard a welcome sound. It was the unmistakable shutting of a door, and the sound came from just beyond a low hill some fifty feet off the road. Jogging ahead, Max climbed the hill's crest and practically gulped the smell of wood smoke and the aroma of roasting vegetables. There was a large farmhouse, the moon illuminating its smooth stone walls and the slope of its thatched roof. From a chimney trickled white smoke that rose until it caught the breeze that carried it past Max's nose. Through the small, shuttered windows Max could see glimmers of golden light that made him almost skitter down the hill in his eagerness for company.

But the witch had warned him that something was amiss among the humans, and Max paused to scan the surrounding territory. Within the broad clearing, there was an animal pen stocked with sheep and goats, a black patch that must have been a vegetable garden, and several dark storehouses. Past the vegetable patch was an old stone well, its uneven rim a jagged ellipse beneath the pale moon. Something small was crossing the yard, its progress slow and unsteady. Gripping the gladius in his hand, Max slunk down the hill, sly as a fox, and quickly crept upon the figure from behind.

It was a little girl.

She was no older than six, dressed in a woolen jacket and a skirt that was too long for her short legs. She clutched a bundle of firewood, her breath misting the chilly air as she made for the farmhouse.

Quickly sheathing the gladius, Max knelt down to her height and called softly in Italian. "Hello there," he said.

The child dropped the firewood and froze.

"Shhh," Max said, coming round so she could see him. "It's okay. I'm a friend."

"Are you the m-monster?" she whispered.

"No," said Max. "I'm not a monster—I'm a friend."

"Friend?" inquired the girl with a dubious tone.

Max nodded and collected the fallen firewood. "My name is Max," he said calmly. "What's yours?"

"Mina," breathed the tiny girl.

"Is this your house, Mina?" Max asked gently.

Before she could reply, the farmhouse door opened. Its light framed a large man in the doorway. He spoke rapidly, his voice sharp with reproach.

"I told you to hurry, Mina!"

From the darkness, Max called out his apologies and insisted that it was his fault. At the sound of Max's voice, the man started and stared out into the clearing. Conjuring an orb of soft blue light, Max illuminated the area where he stood with Mina, who went absolutely rigid.

"*Demon!*" the man cried, slamming the door and triggering a chorus of young screams and the frantic barking of a dog.

Taking Mina's hand, Max hurried toward the house, whose lights had abruptly gone dark. There was the grating of something heavy being drawn across the door. Whispers from within the house—furious shushing and the sharp sound of broken pottery. Mindful that his knock might bring a pitchfork, Max rapped once and stepped back to speak in a slow, soothing voice.

"I'm sorry. I didn't mean to frighten you."

There was no answer, but Max could hear the man breathing heavily just on the other side of the door. Mina still held Max's hand, but there was no life within it. She clutched his fingers as though she were already resigned to some hideous fate.

"I understand," Max called through the door. "It's dark and you're frightened. I'm leaving Mina here. We can talk in the morning."

Patting Mina's cheek, Max left her on the doorstep with the firewood and retreated some fifty feet to a pile of straw just outside the animal pen. On the other side of the fence, a drowsy goat blinked curiously at him before drifting back to sleep. As Max spread his bedroll on the mattress of hay, he heard Mina pleading with the man—presumably her father—who had yet to open the door.

Max strained to hear and decipher the words. *No, he didn't hurt me. He's still here.* Something about going to sleep and Mina's growing impatience due to the cold. At this, the door cracked a handbreadth. Max saw an arm shoot out, grabbing Mina by her collar and snatching her inside. With a solid thump, the heavy door slammed shut once again.

The farmhouse lights went out, leaving it dark beneath the bright moonlight that conveyed a soft glow to the hills and distant mountains. Despite the rude welcome, Max felt a rush of delight. Inside that house were people! They were frightened, of course, but the daylight would ease their fears and allow a warmer welcome. As he snuggled down deeper into the hay and blankets, he breathed the cold night air and tried to get a wink of sleep.

Daylight arrived with a rooster crow. He imagined the sound must have been a rooster—did hens bother making such a terrible noise? There was a contented clucking behind him, the prolonged *baahh* of a lamb, and Max opened his eyes to see a young boy still in his nightshirt tossing grain to a yard full of strutting fowl. Nearby, a pair of girls milked a goat that chewed upon a handful of branches, looking bored. Propping up on his elbows, Max almost leaned into a long spear that trembled as it was leveled at his face.

"Who are you?" demanded a gruff voice. "What are you doing here?"

Gazing past the spearhead, Max looked upon a large man approaching sixty, holding a spear so rusted that it looked more likely to break than cause any real damage. The man was missing several teeth and squinted at Max as though his vision was poor.

Holding up his hands, Max spoke slowly. "My name is Max and I come in peace."

"You're no demon?" asked the man, trembling as sweat ran down his broad forehead.

"No," Max insisted, climbing cautiously to his feet.

While they spoke, some dozen grimy children continued to go about their chores, offering only quiet, curious glances at the strange interview. Given Max's imperfect Italian, it was a halting conversation, but several things soon became clear. The first was that the man was not the father of the children present—he was merely their caretaker. Max gathered the farm must be a sort of orphanage or commune. When asked about the children's parents, the man merely plucked at his gray whiskers.

"Dead," he muttered, fixing Max with a pair of small, hard eyes. Scratching at a crown of graying thatch, the man made Max understand that he was not welcome to stay. There were too many mouths to feed already. The man chuckled grimly as he said this, spreading his hands as if to say, *We are both men. We understand each other, no?*

Max saw three brands upon the man's right palm. The largest, located just beneath the fingers, was Astaroth's sigil.

Below that, in the center, was Prusias's, and finally, beneath that, a smaller circle. Within it was some design, but Max could not make it out. He pointed at it, but the man scowled and abruptly closed his hands.

Anxious to change the subject, Max asked after food.

The man glanced at the sheathed gladius; suspicious eyes wandered over Max's face. The man seemed to be weighing a variety of possibilities. At length, he grinned—an insincere grimace that stopped well short of his eyes. Of course, he said. There was food inside. They would be happy to feed Max, but he must be on his way before nightfall. Hard times. Hard times. The young man understood. Of course he did.

While they walked toward the farmhouse, Max noted that none of the children were talking. They ranged in age from mere toddlers to a youth approaching his teens. He said hello to one— a girl of perhaps nine—but she only pursed her lips and nodded under the stern eye of the guardian. Something was profoundly wrong here, and Max eyed the grinning man with darkening suspicion.

Max's first impression of the farmhouse was one of unimaginable squalor. Despite its high ceiling, the great room was dark and dreary, its walls charred and oily from a fireplace that was clearly blocked. The stench was unbearable—a fetid reek of human waste. Max gagged, glancing to see if he'd caused offense, but the man merely tossed the ancient spear into a corner where a spotted mutt lay gnawing on an old shoe from a pile of many.

"Is he gone, Pietro?" came a woman's voice. "We have chosen."

"Be quiet!" replied the man sternly. "We have an honored guest."

He laughed as he said this, then clapped Max on the shoulder and led him around a wall, where two women sat at a large table set near a stone hearth. The first looked to be the same age as the man, a stout, weather-beaten woman with a hard face. Her expression remained stoic as she appraised Max. She offered nothing, no hint of a smile or even a nod of acknowledgment. Her hands were folded on the table near a piece of rose quartz that glinted in the thin light streaming from a slit of a window in the northern wall.

"This is the choice?" asked Pietro heavily.

The woman turned to her younger companion, who merely nodded and continued nursing the infant at her breast. A tense silence ensued. Pietro sighed and led Max past the table, where there was a half-barrel of some filmy, fermenting alcohol. It smelled toxic. Dipping a wooden goblet into it, the man promptly drained it before offering it to Max, who declined and turned instead to the younger woman.

"What is her name?" he asked, smiling at the baby. Heavy, unblinking blue eyes rose to meet his own. The mother could not have been older than twenty. Her wan features offered nothing more than a blank, hostile stare.

"Take your food and go," she said.

"The moon, Pietro . . . ," hissed the older woman, looking past Max at the man, who had continued drinking.

"You think I don't know?" snapped Pietro, hurling the goblet into the barrel. The women stiffened. Wine sloshed over the barrel's rim, running down its sides to soak the straw-strewn floor. With a grunt, Pietro tossed a rag toward the older woman and motioned for her to clean the mess. She went about it immediately, but with the same limp resignation with which Mina had held Max's hand.

"There's no need for that," said Max sharply.

The man glowered at Max, his red face trembling with impotent rage. Pietro was broad in the chest, had perhaps been a man of consequence, but those days were long past. Bloodshot, calculating eyes broadcast the man's thoughts as if they had been spoken aloud: Here was a tall, well-armed youth who must be cajoled, not conquered. The man swallowed his rage and bustled toward a back pantry that had been converted into a disgusting smokehouse, where rank haunches of meat hung from the rafters. With a grunt, the man shoved a piece of dried lamb at him.

"Later," said Max, reverting to English. "I want to speak to the children."

"Eh?" asked the man, as though pretending not to understand.

Max abandoned any pretense of civility. Towering over Pietro, Max jabbed a finger in the man's soft belly and repeated himself. The man closed his eyes, trembling in anticipation of a blow that never came.

Looking into Max's hard face, his foul breath came in short, gasping sputters. "I am not the monster here!"

Pietro's face was now covered with droplets of sweat that ran into his blinking eyes. Max glanced again at the hanging meat, the rusted cleaver that lay across a crude chopping block. His eyes spied another small shoe lying in the dark corner by a broken stool. There had been many small shoes by the door; far too many to account for the dozen orphans he'd seen.

Max stared at Pietro's round belly, the jigsaw teeth chewing nervously on red-stained lips. Horrific thoughts began to flit through Max's mind.

"What are you doing here, Pietro?" he asked quietly.

With a defiant stare, Pietro cursed and spat at Max's feet. Seizing his wrist, Max dragged him roughly through the house, past the bewildered women, and out the front door. Marching him across the yard, Max threw the struggling man into the hay pile. The children abruptly stopped their chores and stared at Pietro, who merely lay panting in the morning sun.

"Is this man hurting you?" asked Max, rounding to address the group.

The children said nothing, but instead turned their attention to the two women who had followed and stood watching from the doorway. The young mother clutched her baby and screamed at Max to go away and leave them alone. She said he should go away, dig his grave in the hills for all she cared, but he must go away at once—couldn't he see that he was hurting poor Pietro?

It was nonsense and Max wasn't having any of it. He had heard of such gruesome things in wartime but had never witnessed it for himself.

Spotting Mina among the group, Max called softly to her. "Mina," he said, continuing only when her eyes shifted from Pietro to him. "Is this man hurting you or the other children? You can tell me, Mina. . . ."

"No," she whispered, her eyes shifting back to the old man.

At this, Pietro covered his face with his hands and devolved into silent sobs.

"Then what's the matter here?" Max asked, bewildered. "What's wrong with you people?"

Instead of answering, several of the older children helped Pietro to his feet and led the sobbing man back into the house. The rest returned to their chores, leaving Max to gaze about in stupefied silence. Regardless of what Mina had said, Max knew something was off. The witch had been frightened of this place; the children's eerie calm and quiet resignation suggested some terrible, numbing trauma.

Storming back into the house, Max chased the dog away and counted the shoes in the pile. There were sixty-seven shoes but only fourteen children present. Pietro was now slumped against the table, where the older woman tried to console him. Cradling her wailing infant with one arm, the younger woman set about throwing bread, dried olives, and a round of salted meat into an old flour sack. This she threw at Max's feet.

"Who are you to judge us?" she asked with teary rage. "You are a beggar—just a filthy beggar!"

"Who do these belong to?" asked Max quietly, gesturing at the shoes.

"Other children," she muttered, looking away. "Other children who got sick and died."

"Where are their graves?" asked Max, gesturing out toward the yard. "I want to see them."

"Who are you to meddle with the dead!" she hissed. "Go to hell!"

"I think I'm already there," Max muttered, brushing past her to inspect the rest of the house.

The ground floor was large, some forty feet to a side with a high, beamed ceiling that sloped down to meet a balcony that overlooked the great room from the second floor. Beneath the nauseating grime and filth that caked the walls, Max could make out faded frescoes. Long ago, this must have been a prosperous farm, but age and disrepair had driven it into a state of horrific squalor. Rat holes were evident throughout, and as he made his way through the unimaginable reek of the upper rooms, only one item served as evidence that humans and not animals lived here—a child's rag doll propped carefully against a stained pillow.

But none of the rooms had bones or other evidence of cannibalism. He had been expecting a charnel house, but all he found was bedding and broken furniture. This held true for the root cellar and the storehouses.

But Max could not shed a nagging uneasiness that preyed upon his mind. The children were too quiet, too mechanical in their movements as they went about their chores. The three adults had borne Max's investigation with sullen resignation.

They sat assembled about the table muttering quietly to one another while the younger woman soothed her baby and Pietro rapped the bit of quartz against the table in sour meditation.

It was midafternoon when Max was satisfied that he'd thoroughly searched the house and surrounding area. It was cool, but he was sweating from his exertions, having thumped walls, crept into crawl spaces, and prodded through piles of filth that sent him retching into corners on more than one occasion. The place should be condemned, he decided, but it was not a house of horrors.

Given his filthy state, he needed to bathe and eyed the ancient well past the vegetable patch with something approaching desperation. To his dismay, however, he found no bucket or chain—just a crumbling pile of large stones that ringed a black hole some four feet across. A shift in the wind brought a faint, foul odor from its depths and Max recoiled. He turned to see Mina standing behind him.

With her same blank expression, she informed him that the well was dry, but the others would fetch him fresh water. Taking his hand, Mina led him back toward the house, where Pietro stood in the doorway holding Max's sack of food. In no uncertain terms, Max was told that he was welcome to bathe, welcome to the food, and then welcome to leave. These instructions were delivered in a slurred jumble as Pietro wobbled within the door-way. The man was blind drunk, his eyes bloodshot from alcohol and weeping. Gesturing weakly for Mina, he held her against him and repeated his demand that Max leave before nightfall.

On the side of the house, there was a trough filled with water the children had brought from a lake Max could see through a gap in the poplars that lined the old road.

"Ignis," he muttered, spreading his fingers and heating the one remaining pail. Mixing the hot with the cold, he did his best to scrub the dirt and filth that he'd accumulated in his grisly search. Bringing the remaining water to a boil, he stropped and shaved using his father's old straight razor. It was an imperfect job, but he felt both refreshed and infinitely cleaner as he let the chill breeze dry his face and skin. Tying his filthy clothes into a bundle for later washing, he changed into his spare clothes for the long miles ahead.

The sun had already set and the moon was rising when Max finished packing his gear. The family—or what passed for one—was all gathered on the farmhouse stoop as Max said farewell. The children stared dully ahead while Max apologized for any offense he may have caused. He had meant no harm. This elicited a disbelieving grunt from Pietro, but no more. The women said nothing but stared at Max with a restrained, simmering hatred that he found deeply unsettling. When Max asked if there were other humans nearby, Pietro grew furious and gestured at a darkening sky whose luminescent moon was framed by heavy storm clouds.

"It is late and the children are hungry," said Pietro, each word punctuated by flecks of spittle. "Go and leave us—we have nothing more to give you."

"Thank you for the food," said Max, bowing.

And with that, he hoisted his pack and set out for the road, keeping to its fringes as the moon rose higher over the rolling countryside. For the moment, it was a storybook night, one of those magical evenings where the clouds had a crowding volup-tuousness, their soft contours set aglow by the full moon.

But the wind was rising, a bitter gale that swept across the landscape, bringing the smell of rain from the far-off mountains. Crowding out the moon, the clouds closed over its shining face and cast the land in shadow. Max had not been walking twenty minutes before a cold rain began to fall.

What began as a drizzle soon turned into a downpour. Hurrying beneath the branches of an evergreen, Max crossed his arms for warmth and considered what to do. He could camp here, certainly, but it was bound to be a miserable evening. Comfort on such a night would necessitate a sizable fire, and the witch's talk of goblin tribes made him uneasy about drawing any attention to himself in the wilderness. Glancing back at the road, he considered the farmhouse. He had not walked very far; he could go back and bed down in one of the unused storehouses. They were hardly luxurious, but they had a roof, and a roof in the rain counted for much. Pietro and the others would not even know he'd returned.

Dashing back through the rain, Max kept to the canopy of branches that provided imperfect shelter from what was progressing into a sizable storm. Thunder rumbled overhead and the wind howled, but no lightning strafed the sky to light Max's path. Instead, he conjured a pale blue light orb and relied upon it as he leaped over gullies and carved a shortcut across the slippery meadows and cold, packed earth. As the moon poked through the racing clouds overhead, Max glimpsed the silhouette of the farmhouse upon the hill.

Extinguishing the orb, Max hurried ahead, anxious not to disturb the occupants who might refuse him shelter. Giving the house a wide berth, he made for the nearest shed and slipped inside with nary a sound. He grinned in the darkness—here were four strong walls and a roof to conquer the elements. It was a small victory, but a victory nonetheless. Slinging off his pack, he set to kindling a fire, careful to channel its smoke out a slat that faced the countryside.

This accomplished, he leaned back against the ancient stone and listened to the wind howl while rain pounded on the roof. As he closed his eyes, however, Max heard other noises, too. Above the rain, he could hear screams—terrible, bleating screams of the animals in their pen. Something had driven them into a panic. As Max peered out the doorway, he saw the motley herd bolt from one end of the fenced enclosure to the other. Scanning about, Max squinted for some sign of a predator—a wolf or jackal that would elicit such a fearful reaction. However, given the gloom and the rain, he saw nothing.

Poking his head out of the shed, he turned toward the farmhouse to see if Pietro or one of the older children had heard the disturbance and had come to investigate. But every door and window was closed to the storm, so that not even a peep of light escaped. The lambs bleated louder—a pitched, frantic screaming—and now Max stood from his crouch to get a better vantage on the yard.

All the animals had fled to the southern end, except for one small lamb that remained in the center. There was still no sign of a predator, but something had clearly frightened the animals, which were frantically attempting to escape the pen. Fastening the harpoon head to his walking stick, Max went out into the storm.

Crossing the clearing, he trotted toward the stockyard, scanning the dark night for the shine of a predator's eyes. Hopping over the fence, he tried to soothe the animals, but they continued to bleat and scream as though they were being eaten alive. Exasperated, Max walked to the center of the yard where the one lamb remained separated from the others and lay in the cold, wet mud.

As he drew nearer, however, details began to emerge on the small white form. He was looking at a child, a little girl hunched into the fetal position. Hurrying over, Max saw that it was Mina.

Her eyes stared ahead, unseeing, as she sucked her thumb and took slow, steady breaths. How or why she lay in the freezing mud Max could not guess, but the child would die of exposure if he didn't do something quickly. Tearing off his coat, Max wrapped her within it and hefted her out of the mud. She made no noise as he did so—not a murmur of protest or thanks—but merely clung to him, a trusting bundle of ice-cold flesh.

"It's going to be okay," Max whispered in her ear while the animals continued to scream. "We'll get you someplace warm...."

Mina began to tremble and clutched him with a sudden ferocity. Holding her close, Max turned in the direction she had been staring.

Thirty yards away stood the old stone well.

Something was crawling from it.

~ 16 ~

HORRORS IN THE WELL

As Max watched the thing crawl from the well and spill onto the wet earth, he was grateful for the darkness. The sky seemed alive. Clouds roiled and raced across the moon, whose light fell upon the sickening shape, which began to creep down toward the yard.

The creature's advance was so bizarre, so hideous, that Max stood rooted to the spot as its forelimbs dug into the soil, pulling its body forward. If it had legs, they were merely dragged behind the creature as though some accident had damaged them beyond repair. At times its progress was no faster than a crawling infant, but periodically it would shoot forward to cover ten or even twenty feet with a crocodile's swiftness. The monster was roughly man-shaped, but its limbs and joints hinged in odd directions, to create a horrifying silhouette as it slid down the rain-soaked grass toward the animal pen.

Mina had gone perfectly rigid and clung to Max with every ounce of strength she could muster.

"We're getting out of here," Max whispered. "Don't look at it."

Backing away, Max reached the fence just as the monster had arrived at the enclosure's opposite end. Scrambling over the fence, it fell heavily onto the earth, but promptly righted itself in a fitful race to reach the spot where Mina had been lying.

"Stay quiet," Max whispered, swinging his legs over the top rail. "Shhh . . ."

Once out of the pen, Max backed slowly toward the farmhouse, his eyes fixed on the monster as it prowled about the center of the stockyard. It did not exhibit any interest in the animals, which were left to panic and bleat in the far corners. It focused solely on the spot where it had expected to find a human.

And then the monster screamed.

It was a terrible sound, one that mingled human chords with something altogether alien. It was so sudden and jarring that Max almost dropped the child to clamp his hands over his ears. The scream was too much for poor Mina. Whether compelled by some insidious lure in the monster's call or driven by mere terror, Mina responded in kind.

Again and again the child screamed, a bloodcurdling cry that cut the monster's wails short.

The nearest lambs bolted for the opposite end as a blur hurtled past them to crash against the uppermost rail. For a moment, Max caught the moonlight's gleam on a single white eye that stared at him with an awful, unexpected intelligence.

Racing to the house, Max rained frantic blows upon the front door.

But no one answered.

Perhaps they were simply too frightened, but Max feared there was a sinister complicity at work. He guessed that Mina had been left in that pen as some sort of offering, a sacrifice to the dark shape that now slid over the rail and crawled toward the house.

They could run, of course. The monster was no match for Max's speed, and he could whisk Mina far away from the danger at hand. But here was a houseful of people, and whether Pietro and the women had made some devilish bargain, he imagined the children were innocent. He could not leave anyone—not even a criminal—at the mercy of this thing.

It was coming now, closing the distance between the pen and the farmhouse. Gathering himself, Max sprang onto the lower portion of the gabled roof, still clutching Mina to him. The tiles were slick with rain, and he nearly slipped before his fingers caught a lip of tile over the ridge. From this vantage, he could see the monster clearly and realized, to his horror, that it was not dragging a pair of broken legs.

It had no legs at all.

Instead of legs, a dozen writhing tentacles extended from a humanlike torso whose back was matted with long hairs. It was the tentacles at its base that periodically propelled it forward at lurching intervals.

These tentacles propelled it now out of view, onto the front porch. Once Max clambered up the roof, holding Mina tightly, he slid down the opposite side and toward a shuttered window. While he pounded against the shutters, the creature screamed again and Max heard a dull thud from far below. No one answered at the window. Setting Mina down, Max kicked furiously at the shutters, shattering them into pieces and exposing the dark space within.

Crawling inside with Mina, he felt something stab into his leg.

Reaching blindly about the room, he felt an arm—Pietro's—and seized it, dashing the man against the wall. Pietro groaned and fell into a woozy heap as Max reached down to inspect a small wound in his thigh. It was superficial, probably a kitchen knife, and in his current state, it barely registered. Conjuring a glowsphere, Max saw them all—Pietro, the women, and the remaining children—huddled in a fearful clump against the far wall. They recoiled at the light and were evidently shocked at seeing Max once again. But this paled in comparison to the abject horror they exhibited upon seeing Mina.

"Abomination!" cried the old woman. "The child is accursed—she has brought the devil to our door!"

"Shhh!" Max hissed as another resounding thump sounded from downstairs. "Come and help me," he said. "It's trying to get in."

No one moved. He had no time to argue. They might elect to stay behind, but he could not leave Mina with them for fear that they would hurt her in some mad effort to placate the thing outside. Lifting the child up once again, Max limped toward the open door and made for downstairs.

The great room was dark and eerily still. Max scooted Mina under the heavy table and whispered for her to be quiet, to remain silent no matter what happened—even if the creature called for her. Overcoming her terror, the girl nodded obediently and curled into a ball. Once she was safely stowed, Max crept to the center of the room and listened for any sign of the creature.

For a full minute there was nothing, just the sound of rain gushing from the gutters. But then Max heard a muted giggling, a terrible sound as though the monster could not contain its delight at this unexpected game of hide-and-seek. There was a sliding noise along the eastern wall followed by a probing thump against a shuttered window that was far too small to admit the monster. As Max's eyes adjusted to the darkness, he turned about the room, following the monster's movements as it circled the house. Now and again, it emitted an earsplitting scream, an awful summons to the little girl curled beneath the table.

"Shhh," hissed Max, holding his finger to his lips.

Mina nodded, her face furious with concentration as the scream subsided into giggles. There was rattling at the back shutters, almost playful. And then, to Max's infinite revulsion, the monster began to talk. At first, Max thought that it was nonsense, garbled sounds and gulps that happened to approximate words. But there was a definite pattern to them, distinct syllables and intonation, as though the monster were trying to mimic human speech. Was it saying Pietro's name?

The thumping at the door resumed. The door had been crudely reinforced, mismatched planks hammered into place along with a heavy beam that served as a drawbar. But the door was beginning to give. Max heard a crack and saw rivulets of powder spill from the hinges as they were pried slowly from the wall. Throughout, the monster screamed and giggled, occasionally making a hideous gurgle that sounded like "Pietro."

As Max watched the door shudder, his limbs trembled. Frightful energies began to build within him, as though his body were a conduit for the very storm that raged outside.

Several furious blows suddenly hammered upon the door. It groaned inward, permitting a pale arm to shoot within the gap and fumble madly at the crossbeam.

Max threw himself against the door, pinning the arm against the jamb and twisting it violently about. There was a howl of pain, a furious thumping as the creature sought to free itself. Leaning against the door, Max gained a firmer hold on the monster's wrist and elbow. Terrible strength lurked in that limb, and Max strained to maintain his grip while the monster thrashed about. To his horror, he discovered there were feelers on the monster's sinewy forearm, snakelike tentacles with needle teeth that fastened onto Max's flesh like hungry lamprey.

For the better part of a minute, the two engaged in a grisly tug-of-war. Max's arm ran red with blood, but the creature screamed with pain from the iron grip of its assailant. Again and again, Max threw his weight against the door, crushing the creature's arm within the narrow opening.

As the monster weakened, Max grew stronger. The Old Magic that crested within him was terrifying, electric surges of energy that rocketed through every vein and capillary. With furious determination, he slammed the door and wrenched the monster's arm backward. There was a pitiable howl as the limb was twisted from its socket. A chilling voice spoke through the door, its gurgling words now perfectly comprehensible.

"Mercy," it wheezed. "I will leave."

Max leaned forward so that he came face to face with the monster.

The gap in the doorway was narrow, a mere six inches, but he could make out several features in the darkness. The first was an eye. As round and protuberant as that of a horse, it stared wide in an expression of astonishment or horror. The face was roughly manlike but looked as though it had been skinned and the skull grotesquely lengthened. That such an abomination should now be talking to him was almost too much to bear. Even as it pleaded, its tentacles continued to gnaw at Max's arm.

"Mercy?" Max scoffed. "Do you ever show mercy?"

The creature screamed and tried to slip away, but Max held

fast. Using all his strength, he gave the arm a terrible, twisting wrench. There was a crack followed by a pulpy squelch as the arm tore clear away at the elbow. Max fell backward, clutching the grisly trophy as the monster gave an ear-splitting howl. The door fell inward, framing the monster's awful silhouette against the night.

As Max clambered to his feet, the monster wheeled away. It raced across the clearing toward the muddy slope that led toward the well. Max dashed after, prying the mouths from his wounds and flinging the severed arm aside. While the monster moved frantically toward its lair, Max hobbled to the storehouse, where he had left his sword. A moment later, he had the gladius in hand.

Just before Max reached the well, the monster disappeared within, its tentacles slipping over the side like a snake plunging into its hole. Max halted abruptly at the dark opening and caught his breath. He had been taught never to blindly pursue anything into its burrow. Staring down into the black aperture, Max could hear nothing above the rain, no slapping of tentacles or gasps from the injured creature. It was as if the monster had simply dropped from the walls and fallen into an abyss.

But this monster was flesh and blood. It was no wrathful spirit that might disappear into the void. There was a bottom to this well and some lair where this monster sought refuge. Max would not give it refuge; he would press his advantage and finish the fight once and for all.

Wrapping the gladius's strap about his wrist, Max conjured a glowsphere and sent it down into the well. It descended some ten or fifteen feet before it flickered and then disappeared altogether. The darkness almost seemed a tangible thing, a cauldron of ink that permitted no light whatsoever.

But Max had other senses. He would not turn back; he would

not allow the monster to escape and nurse its wounds only to terrorize the farmhouse another night. This was why he had labored and trained in the Sidh. Rowan might abandon the people outside its walls, but Max would not. Max would pursue these horrors to the deep places of the world, and no pool of darkness—natural or not—would stop him.

But as he climbed down into the well and sank into that consuming blackness, his certainty wavered. Clinging to the curving wall, he inhaled a fetid reek and endured the eager scuttle of unseen spiders over his bleeding arm. There were air currents from below, nauseating drafts that rose and fell as though the well itself were aspirating. His chief fear was that the monster did not reside at the well's bottom but had tunneled out a lair at some point along its length. If this was the case, it could wait for him to pass and strike when he was exceedingly vulnerable.

As he descended even farther, another chilling thought occurred to him. He had been assuming that the monster was solitary. But what if there was a mate or even offspring that resided in these awful depths? He envisioned a nest of the creatures, a writhing mound of tentacles and arms and lidless eyes.

Even before Max reached the tunnel, he felt its presence. The reek was now almost unbearable, an overpowering smell of damp earth and decomposition.

At last Max's probing foot met an empty space along the wall of the well. Using his toe to feel around the perimeter, Max slid hand over hand until he had inched several feet to his right. Holding his breath, he descended several more feet until his senses told him that he was positioned next to the opening.

For several minutes, Max waited in the blackness, straining to hear anything of the monster's breathing or motions. But silence prevailed. He could try the Solas spell—a sudden blinding flash of light. He'd never known the measure to fail, but it was risky. This blackness was an unearthly dark. If the spell failed, Max would not have blinded the creature or even illuminated his surroundings, but merely revealed his position.

Given the darkness, illusions were useless, and Max was hopeless at other enchantments. As he weighed his dwindling options, he found himself hoping that the monster would do something hasty—launch an attack, anything to end this excruciating stalemate.

Long minutes passed before Max decided to crawl within the opening. He felt about the edges and determined that the hole was four or five feet in diameter.

He was confident the monster had come this way. The tunnel was cold and damp, but occasionally Max's left hand slid across a warm slick—droplets of blood that marked the creature's retreat. His right hand held the gladius, and he used its sharp point to probe the darkness ahead. But it met only air, so Max inched ahead, blind as a mole.

After some twenty yards, the gladius struck hard rock. Feeling about, Max realized that the tunnel had diverged. This posed a serious dilemma. If one tunnel had become two, then two could become four. The whole area might be a labyrinth of tunnels that harbored one monster or many. Within such impenetrable darkness, Max might become hopelessly lost—he might crawl about forever until weariness, hunger, or the monster overtook him.

It was no good, he decided. The tide had turned and there were too many factors in his opponent's favor. Better to live and fight another day. From what he could guess, the monster had one food source—the farmhouse—and Max would wait until it emerged again. Backing away from the fork, Max retraced his steps, crawling backward lest the thing catch him unawares.

As Max retreated, he became aware of a grating noise, the

unmistakable sound of sliding stone. The sweat on Max's brow grew icy. This was no good. He had to get out of this place. Abandoning any effort at stealth, Max ceased his backing shuffle and turned around so he could crawl swiftly back toward the well. He no longer cared if he struck his head or tumbled down the well's remaining depths—anything was better than remaining in this tunnel whose walls seemed to shrink and smother him.

The grating sound filled Max's ears. No trick of acoustics could mask the origins now; the noise was coming from just ahead. Max's sword struck a huge block of stone as it was being pushed across the tunnel's opening. Frantic, he felt for the remaining gap. It was a mere two feet and dwindling. Max hesitated—he might be crushed if he tried to wriggle through. . . .

Boom.

Max winced as the tunnel opening was sealed. The sound reverberated all around him, a note of paralyzing finality that soon left him in a sickening silence. Exhaling, Max felt blindly about for the block's edges. Its seal against the tunnel's opening was tight in most places, but all along the bottom there was a slender gap. Digging his fingers underneath, Max just managed to touch something made of wood—a rod or series of rods that served as rollers to move the barrier. Max strained to push or pull the block out of the way, but it was no use. The stone weighed many tons, and some remote mechanism had secured it into place.

Leaning his back against it, Max stared into the blackness and tried to collect his thoughts. His worst fears had come true—he was entombed. For a second, he found himself wishing for David Menlo. He knew it was a wistful and childish sentiment. David could not come and make it all better—David was not here. Nor was Cooper or Bob or Ms. Richter or Hazel Boon or anyone who could help him. Max was alone. Only he could solve this problem.

And he must do it soon.

Max understood that his constitution was capable of enduring great extremes of heat and cold or even pain and injury. But when it came to such a consuming atmosphere, such a press of surrounding stone, his sanity was as susceptible as any.

"Keep your wits about you," he whispered.

Crouching in the darkness, Max considered a variety of factors.

The first was the monster itself. It was badly injured but not incapacitated, for it remained healthy enough to flee and had mustered the strength to operate whatever mechanism closed the door.

The mere fact that there was such a door was profoundly disturbing. To move such a mass required intelligence and a sophistication of engineering. Whatever had built these tunnels possessed not only the capacity to delve through rock, but also the foresight and skill to devise a barrier capable of barring intruders or trapping prey. Either it had an accomplice of greater intelligence, or the monster possessed a considerable intellect of its own.

An intelligent creature, Max reasoned, would not seek an open fight against a demonstrably stronger opponent. Such an opponent would be more likely to lurk nearby until its prey wounded itself in some trap or was weakened from a lack of food, water, or will. It was unlikely to attack directly unless an advantageous situation presented itself.

It was also likely that an intelligent creature would have an alternate means of escape. Max guessed there must be other exits somewhere in the tunnels. At the very least, there must be a lever or contraption that had moved or secured the stone behind him. An alternate exit might be very far away, but the mechanism that had moved the stone was likely to be close by. Where there was a will, there was a way, and Max resolved that no lack of spirit would make him a meal or a prisoner.

While he was determined to search for the mechanism, he still did not know whether the monster was alone or if other hellish things were waiting in the darkness. Aboveground, the monster had displayed a gloating cruelty when it believed it was in control. Now that Max was bottled up like a fly, could it be goaded into doing the same?

"Hello!" he cried into the darkness.

The word shot off, echoing throughout the unseen tunnels.

"Can you hear me?" Max called.

Silence.

"Do you think I care about that stone?" Max shouted. "Do you think I care about the darkness? None of it matters! I'm coming for you all the same. . . ."

This did elicit a reaction.

The sound was obscured initially by the fading echo of Max's words. But it grew louder. It was a deep, steady giggling that filled the tunnels and seeped into Max's soul. The laughter was terrifying, but it also served its purpose. Although he could not pinpoint its precise location, Max had still learned that the monster was relatively close and that it was most likely alone.

Steeling himself, Max began the slow, cautious journey down the tunnel. The blackness yawned before him like the universe. When he reached the spot where the tunnel branched off, he ran his hand over the stone. Like Theseus in the Minotaur's labyrinth, Max would leave a trail so he could retrace his steps. Taking his pocketknife, Max carved an *X* in the soft limestone. Despite his anxiety, he exercised patience and retraced the grooves, ensuring the mark would be obvious if he crossed it again.

On and on he went, creeping along the tunnels like a sewer rat, groping blindly in the darkness and listening for any sign of the monster. It was impossible to gauge time—he might have been worming his way for days.

And then Max's sword struck something soft. He stopped and considered the space before him. There was water, rhythmic dripping into a nearby pool. The acoustics suggested a cavern, some sizable hollow. Fumbling about, Max searched for anything he might throw to better approximate the space. When his hands slid into cold, rank water, he eased forward, pushing his fingers through grainy silt until he discovered some pebbles among the sludge.

There was something oddly familiar about their shapes. Turning one over in his hand, Max thumbed a pronged end that tapered to a smooth, flat edge. Feeling about the silt once again, Max discovered dozens more and recoiled from the pool.

The objects were not pebbles. They were teeth.

Breathing deep, he tried to overcome his horror with the comfort that he had discovered something important. The cavern must be the monster's lair or feeding place. Listening carefully, Max concluded that he was alone.

From his initial throws, he learned that the cavern was indeed a very large space and that not all of it was submerged. Several tosses suggested that there was a rim of dry rock that ran along the perimeter, while the *plunk* from a high toss indicated that the ceiling was high and the water became considerably deeper. Standing, Max threw a handful of teeth directly ahead.

He expected to hear them striking rock and water, but one of the teeth made a sharp *ping* that resonated throughout the chamber. It had struck something metallic. With several more tosses, Max divined that there were a variety of objects situated upon some sort of island in the pool.

Max had to investigate such a curious development, but it would necessitate crossing the dank water. Gripping his sword tightly, Max edged into the pool, feeling with his toes for any sudden drop-off. The water grew progressively deeper until it reached Max's chin. Straining to keep his head above the surface, Max slid his feet through a sickening layer of slime. After twenty or thirty feet, the floor gradually rose and he clambered onto the island.

Groping ahead, Max made a most unexpected discovery.

It was a filing cabinet. At least it felt like one—a metal box some three feet tall with a number of thin, flat drawers. Easing past it, Max felt the edges of a large table and a wooden chair. Running his hands over the table's surface, Max encountered paper and pens a pad of some kind. Lifting the pad, he felt it knock against something. There was an audible wobbling just before the object slipped off the table.

Max jumped at the sound of breaking glass.

Seconds later, he heard a scream.

The rending cry echoed throughout the chamber, pouring in from all directions as though this space were the nerve center of many tunnels. The ground trembled slightly. Crouching low, Max held his sword and stared out into the blackness.

As he waited, shapes and glimmers began to emerge. It was not a mere matter of his eyes adjusting to his surroundings. The cavern was actually growing lighter, as though the unnatural darkness had been dispelled. Max quickly conjured another glowsphere.

After hours in the dark, the glowsphere's sudden light almost blinded him. Shielding his eyes, Max squinted at his surroundings and glimpsed for the first time the cavern's smooth walls and the many fish that swam about in the deep pool.

Again, Max heard a scream . . . a curdling cry considerably closer than the first.

Wheeling about, he counted nine gaping holes spaced about

the circular chamber—nine black corridors that fed into this central hub.

The monster was coming; that much was certain. But from which tunnel?

With nine openings to watch, Max turned in a slow circle. From the corner of his eye, he spied movement in the pool. Several fish suddenly darted away as something huge spilled forth from a submerged tunnel.

Even as Max turned, the monster shot out of the water and rolled atop Max, forcing him back into the pool's shallows.

Recovering from the initial shock, Max realized he was in a terrible position. He was pinned beneath the monster's horrific weight, its thick tentacles coiling about Max's legs. Max's head was submerged, water already filling his lungs as he struggled wildly for breath. Above him, the monster was giggling madly, its remaining hand fastened around Max's throat.

Through the water's murky haze, Max glimpsed an alien face bearing down upon him. Its one great eye glistened and its teeth shone like porcelain shards as it snapped forward. Instinctively, Max recoiled and gasped for air only to feel more water gush into his lungs. Spots swam before his eyes. There was a pounding in his ears. Surf . . . drums . . . the monster's screams.

He tried to buck the monster off, but it was to no avail. Its tentacles were wrapped doubly and triply around his lower body. Frantic, Max reached out and seized the monster's injured arm. Feeling blindly for the dreadful stump, he clamped his hand around it and squeezed with all his might. With a shriek of pain, the monster released Max's throat and sought to pry his hand away from its awful wound.

This was the only window Max needed.

Bolting upright, Max gasped a mouthful of air and swung the

gladius at the great head looming above him. There was a sickly sound, a stiffening of the creature's body, and a heavy splash some ten feet away. The monster's headless body toppled, its tentacles slackening so that Max could scramble up and away from the twitching corpse.

He lay on the cold stone, coughing the repellent water out of his lungs and stomach. Once he could breathe, he crouched and listened to hear if anything else lived in the tunnels and was coming to investigate. But there was just the slow drip from the roof and the looping glimmers of fish in the dark water.

When he had recovered more fully, Max conjured new glow-opheres and sent them to various points about the cavern. It was a grim place, and he did not linger long on the many skulls that grinned from the water's depths.

Glancing at the monster's grotesque body, Max saw that the tentacles had ceased their slow writhing. Looking away, Max went to the table hoping to discover something that would help him find his way out of the accursed place, but he found no obvious key or clue among the strange assortment.

On the ground he found a most unexpected item: a sketched portrait in a frame and covered now with cracked glass. In the drawing, Max saw a woman sitting with a young girl on a bench in the country. The girl was the image of her mother, both fair-haired with dark, cheerful eyes. Setting this down on the table, Max opened a silver humidor to find a handful of ruined cigars and a gold wedding ring wrapped in a silk handkerchief.

Searching the cabinet, Max found a score of architectural plans—beautifully drawn exteriors and blueprints for banks, office buildings, and luxurious homes. None of the drawings approximated anything like the well or its tunnels, but Max still found himself lingering over the drawings. Several stood out conspicuously from the rest—crude, childlike scribbles of towers and squat ovals bordered by tiny, cramped writing that made no appreciable sense.

Why would such a monster have these things? Surely it was not plunder acquired from its poor farmhouse victims. And why had everything been arranged so carefully? Max recalled the monster's sudden scream when the portrait's glass frame had shattered.

A horrific thought took shape in Max's mind.

Had this monster once been *human*?

It was too terrible an idea to contemplate in such a setting. Emptying the cabinet, Max quickly rolled up the various drawings and papers before sending a glowsphere bobbing toward the tunnel from which he'd entered. With the aid of its light, he made quick work of retracing his steps and exploring other tunnels he had bypassed. Within the hour, Max discovered the lever.

When it moved the block, his heart nearly leaped for joy.

~ 17 ~

PRINCESS MINA
AND THE GOBLINS

By the time Max emerged from the well's depths, the storm had long since disappeared. There was a nip in the air, but that air was clean and most welcome after his ordeal far below the earth. It was early morning, the specter of the full moon still visible in a dawn sky of pale peach. The farmhouse was still shuttered, but smoke was issuing from its squat chimney. Glancing at the waterlogged pen, Max saw that the sheep and goats had resumed their placid demeanor.

In the daylight, Max examined his wounds more closely. His neck was horribly stiff, and both his forearms were ringed with ugly sores, but already these seemed to be healing. There was no trace of the wound from Pietro's knife. Although Max was exhausted, what he really desired was a bath so that he could remove every trace of the nauseating tunnels and the cavern's rank pool. That would come; first he needed to check on Mina.

Something had been propped behind the broken door so that it could be secured into place. Max had to knock and call several times before he finally heard an angry hiss and the sound of furniture being dragged away. Wobbling on its remaining hinge, the door nearly fell in before Max caught it and looked upon the tired, anxious face of the young mother.

"Good morning," he said.

"The—the monster?" she gasped, looking past him.

"The monster is dead."

The woman put a trembling hand to her mouth and leaned heavily against the table. Motioning Max to enter, she turned and went to the bottom of the stairs, where she spoke too rapidly for him to follow the Italian. Walking inside, Max recoiled again at the greasy, soot-filled space.

"What is your name?" he asked, opening some nearby shutters to let in some fresh air.

"Isabella," replied the woman, looking worried. "Pietro is drunk . . . sleeping. He can't talk to you."

"I don't need to see him," said Max, putting his sword and the salvaged papers on the table. "I need to see the children, Isabella. Right now."

Nodding, Isabella went upstairs and soon returned with them in tow. To Max's relief, he saw Mina among them, still wrapped in his woolen coat. None of the young ones met his gaze, but they obediently gathered around the fireplace while he pulled up a stool. The old woman also appeared, venturing halfway down the stairs to stare at him with black, calculating eyes.

While the children stood like zombies, Max explained that the monster was dead and that it could no longer hurt them. They barely reacted to the news, merely staring at Max. Max glanced at the oldest, a boy who looked to be in his early teens.

"What's your name?"

The boy slumped as though forced to endure a lecture or scolding.

"You won't get an answer from him," said Isabella mildly. "He hasn't spoken since he arrived. His name is Mario."

"Mario," said Max, shaking the limp, unresisting hand. "I'm Max. Can any of you share your names with me? I'm here to help you."

A girl, perhaps eleven years old, looked at him with a pair of brilliant green eyes. "Is it really dead?" she whispered. "Are you sure?"

Max nodded.

"But how could you have killed such a monster?" asked Isabella.

Max shrugged and did his best to explain that he was trained for such things and had fought many battles. It was his job to protect people, and thus he needed to know why these children were here and living this way.

"Mind your own business!" hissed the old woman from the stairs.

"I will not," replied Max calmly, turning to face her. "Are you responsible for sacrificing children to that monster?"

"There was nothing we could do!" she replied with an indignant scowl. "The vyes arrived one day and drove something into the well. Goblin carts came later with prisoners—children from the camps. We were told to leave one in the pen every full moon or the monster would come for us instead."

"Why didn't you simply leave?" asked Max. "Take the children and go elsewhere?"

The woman said nothing, merely shaking her head as though no answer would satisfy such an unreasonable inquisitor.

"The goblins control this valley," explained Isabella. "Every few months, they bring more children and supplies."

The old woman hissed at the younger woman, who coolly returned her stare.

Max stood and walked toward the crone, his anger quickening. "So, I'm to understand that you left children outside for a monster because you were too frightened to leave and you wanted the goblins to bring you things?"

"The goblins said we would be cursed if we left the monster untended," said Isabella. "They said it was a demon and that we were bound to its care. They marked us with the well. . . ." Holding up her palm, she showed Max the same tattoos borne by Pietro— the seal of Astaroth followed by those of Prusias and the well. "The goblin said that the monster could always find us by this mark, that we could never escape."

"None of that justifies what you've done," muttered Max, disgusted with the whole business. He stared hard at Isabella, who faltered and looked away. "Are Pietro and this woman your parents?"

"No," she said. "My husband was killed during the war. I fled the city and found this place. Ana and Pietro took me in, helped me birth my daughter. You mustn't be too angry with them. Pietro wept whenever a stone was picked."

Max remembered back to the piece of quartz lying on the table.

"No," he snapped. "That wasn't a stone—that was a child.

They weren't picking stones, Isabella. They were picking children to be left outside."

"We are not soldiers like you!" spat Ana from the stairs. "And these are not our children! They were dropped on the doorstep. We had no choice."

"Well," said Max, "you have lots of choices now—you're free to go any direction you choose."

"What do you mean?" asked Ana.

"You will pack and leave," said Max. "You cannot stay here anymore. This is the children's home."

At this announcement, Ana's chin jutted forward, revealing a row of yellowed teeth. "Nonsense!" she hissed. "This is our house—we found it!"

"No," said Max. "This *was* your house. It belongs to the children now—they've more than paid for it. You can either live down in the well or you can travel elsewhere. You have until midday to decide."

"But there are goblins," objected Ana. "Hobgoblins! We are defenseless!"

"Not defenseless," said Max, walking over to the ancient spear that lay near the dozing spaniel. Picking it up, he thumbed its point and leaned it against the doorjamb. "This is more of a defense than you gave Mina. And if it's just hobgoblins out in the wild, you'll stand a chance."

"It's murder," spat Ana.

"No," Max replied. "It's exile."

"Are Gianna and I to go, too?" asked Isabella.

Glancing at her baby, Max shook his head. "I'm not sending a nursing mother away."

With that, Max climbed the stairs and searched the rooms until he found Pietro sprawled in a snoring heap on a filthy mat. There was a bucket of water nearby, and Max dumped it onto the sleeping man, who promptly sputtered and peered drunkenly at him. Questions ensued, confused, mumbling inquiries that Max simply ignored as he helped Pietro to his feet and led him downstairs to where Ana was hunched near the doorway like a gargoyle.

While the children watched, Max explained the situation to the older man. Angry protests followed, with Pietro and Ana damning Max to eternity—how dare he drive them out into the wild! Had he no heart? At this, Max merely pointed to the pile of discarded shoes and began raiding the pantries and larders.

When he had packed some food, Max tossed the satchels at Ana's feet and placed the spear in Pietro's hand.

"I'd go west," he advised. "I came from that direction and met no trouble. There are many springs, and the walking is not too hard. You are never to come here again or speak of this place. If you do, I'll put a curse on you myself."

As Max said these last words, he held forth his hands so that bluish witch-fire sprang from each. The flames danced across his fingers before rising into the air and splitting into several crackling bolts that ringed and orbited the bewildered pair.

"*Daemona!*" shrieked Pietro, clutching at his wife.

"Call me what you like," said Max, leaning close and catching the sparks, which raced back to his hand. "But remember the curse, Pietro. Not a word about this place, these children, or me."

It was a mere bluff, of course. Max didn't know how to invoke anything as complex as a true curse. He doubted the goblins did either, but their threat had been sufficient to frighten Pietro and Ana so Max guessed a bit of pyrotechnics would be more than sufficient to ensure the couple's silence. The last thing he wanted was for anyone to broadcast his whereabouts in Blys.

"Goodbye and good luck," said Max, ushering them firmly out the door.

After a heated debate, the couple did not go west. Instead, they chose to travel northeast. They made a beggarly spectacle as they departed, Ana waddling beneath her mound of belongings and Pietro leaning on the old spear and prodding the dog. Had their crimes been less atrocious, Max might have been moved to let them stay. But they were murderers, he reminded himself, just as guilty and pitiable as the monster in the well.

"They will be all right," said Isabella, bouncing her baby, who was cooing at her. "I think they're off to Nix and Valya."

"Who are they?" Max asked.

"Another couple who lives across the valley. They visit sometimes, bring the children presents."

"Aren't *they* afraid of the goblins?" asked Max, curious.

"They must be," replied Isabella, "but they've lived in the valley a long time and seem to know its ways." If the departure of Pietro and Ana had upset Isabella, she masked it well.

Once he had bathed his wounded limbs, Max ate and began to work. The children were still wary of him and merely watched as he set to lugging Pietro's fermenting tub out of the house and dumping the rancid contents down the far slope. While the older boys and girls set about their chores, Max rummaged through the farmhouse and gathered what he needed.

He managed to scavenge some hundred nails, an old hammer, a saw, and a broom that was languishing within a crawl space. There were several unused buckets, some lye, and even a pot of red paint gathering dust upon a shelf. Of most immediate value was the shovel that Max discovered leaning against the house's side. It was a rickety old thing but serviceable.

Throughout the day, Max made dozens of trips in and out of the house. With his shovel and a wobbly wheelbarrow, he carted away mounds of rotting hay, filthy laundry, and unconscionable mounds of waste. This he piled downwind from the house, whose windows stood open so that sunlight and cool air could rush into corners that had been moldering too long.

As the sun set, Max ignited the heaps of trash and watched the flames and smoke rise high into the spring twilight. The stars were beginning to twinkle, and the rich purples of the deepening sky reminded him of the long hikes he used to take with Nick when Nick had been a very young lymrill. He missed his charge dearly—not only for his snorting company, but also for his undeniable skills. The lymrill would have made short work of the rodents that no doubt infested the farmhouse.

When the piles finally burned to ash, Max walked wearily to the house, where firelight flickered from the windows. Far off, he heard a wolf's mournful howl. It rose with the moon and trailed off to silence somewhere out in the dark valley.

Inside Isabella was making a stew using a freshly butchered lamb and some root vegetables that had escaped the rot of the wet cellar. Supper was held in relative silence. Max had decided to let the children adjust to the new circumstances in their own way. As the plates were cleared, he shuttered the windows and set the door back into place. At Max's insistence, the filthy blankets had been gathered from upstairs and spread onto the floor before the fireplace. Everyone would sleep downstairs; the upstairs remained uninhabitable. Kicking off his boots, Max drowsed upon a chair and watched the golden firelight dance upon the walls while the children curled up on their blankets and drifted off to sleep.

As far as Max was concerned, it would be days—weeks, perhaps—until he could get the house in order and make his way north. That was his plan, as far as he had one. Somewhere to the north lay Vyndra's lands, and Max was determined to find him.

* * *

The ensuing days were much the same. While the children went about their chores in the fields or animal pen, Max worked to make the house habitable. When all the trash had been removed and burned and the blankets washed and hung to dry, he set to scrubbing away the layers of dirt that had come to cover the walls, floor, and even the ceiling. It was wearisome work but quickly yielded appreciable results as soot gave way to clean stone, dark wood, and faded yellow paint.

As Max worked, he noticed that some of the younger children had taken to watching him. They stood in the doorway or lingered on the porch, thrusting tousled heads indoors as he repaired furniture, scrubbed baseboards, and scoured the kitchen until its tiles gleamed.

It was Claudia—a stout, inquisitive girl—who was the first to work alongside Max. She never said a word but simply picked up a nearby rag and helped him clean the fireplace and surrounding mantel. Marco soon joined them, followed by a mischievous boy named Paolo. Within the hour, eight of the children had ventured indoors and were scrubbing the walls alongside him.

Isabella watched this development with some amusement, but she said nothing as she looked after Gianna and supervised the work outside. Max's disdain for her was evident; he had spared her exile only because of her baby and the fact that the children would need a caretaker after he had gone. Isabella seemed to sense this and was polite but reserved as she prepared meals from grain and whatever eggs the six hens produced.

At twilight, Max would wash his face and hands and hike far out over the hills, getting a better sense of the landscape and whether additional dangers lurked nearby.

It was stunning scenery, and as Max whipped the old estate into shape, he could envision what must have been a prosperous farm and influential family. But Max realized that, despite his efforts, those days were ancient history, and it would take much more than rags, water, mops, and brooms to restore the place to a thriving, secure home that could support these children.

Security was his primary concern. The monster from the well was dead, but he wondered if its presence had kept other things away. For now, all was quiet in the valley, but certain details continued to trouble him.

He discussed them with Isabella the following morning as she roasted old coffee beans in the fireplace. To date, Max had addressed Isabella only when absolutely necessary, and when he spoke, the children abruptly ceased in their chores to listen.

"The coffee," said Max, gesturing at the burlap sack. "The tea and sugar. Those don't grow here, Isabella. Where did you get them?"

"Nix and Valya brought them," she explained, a tinge of caution in her voice. "On their visit before Yuletide."

"Yuletide?" said Max, looking sharply at her and blowing on his tea. "Do you remember Yuletide, Isabella? Do you remember life before the demons? Before Astaroth?"

But Isabella would not answer this. She merely gazed at the fire, tossing the beans about in a long-handled metal basket thrust over the coals. Her mouth was grim, and Max perceived a growing sorrow in her eyes. Turning to the children, Max asked them to work outside so he could converse with Isabella alone. They obeyed, even Christopher, the most willful among them. When they had gone, Isabella removed the basket from the flames and went to check on her daughter.

"The past is too painful," she said, adjusting the baby's swaddle.

"Your past is your business," said Max gently. "But there are others who visit this place—this Nix and Valya, for one. And you've mentioned goblins. I'm asking because I want to ensure that the children will be safe with you after I'm gone."

Isabella's shoulders stiffened. "Gone?" she exclaimed, turning to him. "But where are you going?"

"There will be a day when I leave this place," said Max quietly. "I have business of my own."

"Oh, but you can't!" Isabella protested, plucking at her baby's blanket. "You are an angel sent to protect us! I prayed and prayed for deliverance from the evil and here you came!"

"I'm not an angel," said Max. "I'm just a boy from across the sea."

"But you perform miracles," she declared.

"Listen," said Max. "I can't stay here forever. I will help with the spring planting and finishing up the house, but the most important thing I can do is deal with the goblins. They will come here again, Isabella, with more prisoners for the monster. But that monster is dead. The goblins will eventually learn this. Do you think they will simply leave you be?"

"So what will you do?" she asked.

"Have a talk with them," he said, eyeing the sword that hung upon the wall.

"But we need the goblins," Isabella blurted. "They bring grain and livestock. We will die without them!"

Pacing about, Max mused upon this dilemma while Isabella began to methodically mix grains and milk for Gianna's breakfast. At last he had an idea.

"When do the goblins visit here?" he asked.

"Every other month," replied Isabella. "Around the quarter moon—they do not want to be near when the monster is active. They will be coming soon."

Max nodded and stood up to stretch.

"What will you do?" she asked again nervously.

"Nothing to endanger you or cut off your supplies," he said, putting on his boots and thrusting his hand out a window to gauge the chill. "Don't mention this conversation to the children."

But the children were particularly perceptive. If they had displayed a tendency to cluster around him before, they shadowed him with the same watchful diligence as Hannah's goslings. They seemed to sense that Max might be leaving, and wished to keep him in their sight.

The children were not merely perceptive; they were resilient. Within days of the monster's death and Pietro's departure, Max heard them whispering to one another, studying him when they thought he was oblivious. Now they offered shy smiles at his approach, and the round lump of a six-year-old they called Porcellino had even taken to showing Max his muscle.

"Very impressive," said Max, stooping to pinch the small, soft arm while its owner's face blazed red with strain. "You're going to be big and strong!"

Porcellino beamed while the others crowded around and followed suit, jostling one another aside to show Max their biceps or clamor for him to see the blackberry bushes or the stream where Claudia had caught a trout. When Max fashioned a crude soccer ball from old stuffing and shoe leather, any lingering reservations evaporated. Under Paolo's precocious leadership, innumerable games and contests were hatched. Kicking games, throwing games, rolling games . . . Max was amazed at the ingenuity behind each and the enthusiasm that followed. Within days, Max's ball was destroyed, and Isabella stayed up late one evening to craft another, sturdier version with triple stitching.

The only child who remained quiet and aloof was Mina. This was understandable. Of all the children, she alone had been left in the pen and had seen the monster, had heard it calling to her.

She worked alongside the others but still exhibited many of the dull, mechanical qualities that had marked the children when Max first met them. As the weather warmed, it broke his heart to see her linger indoors while all the rest played outside. Max took to bringing her with him on his chores, particularly those that would entice the little thing to get outdoors and soak up a little sunshine.

And there were endless chores to do. In addition to repairing the main house and storage sheds, there remained the daily business of tending the livestock, preparing the fields for spring planting, gathering firewood, and innumerable other tasks whose difficulty was compounded by few tools of poor quality. During the rebuilding of Rowan, Max had learned a fair bit of carpentry and masonry and now he bemoaned the lack of a good hammer or plane or even nails that were straight and free of rust.

But they managed to make do with what they had, and as the sun set on a beautiful spring day, Max put the door back upon its hinges and applied the last dab of red paint. Isabella and the children gathered round to see this final touch, a cheerful splash of color upon the entrance of a large house whose rooms were swept and scrubbed. Clean water filled the barrels, fresh rushes lined the floor, and a cantankerous old goat was on the menu. Behind the proud assembly, the mountains loomed purple and the clouds drifted past like wisps of pipe smoke.

That night as the children sprawled on their blankets, Max told them a story. While the fire crackled, he paced about the great room, sharing the tale of a little girl who had fallen under an evil spell and forgotten who she was. Determined, she wandered the world to learn her identity. The girl was brave beyond measure and sought out all the forest's creatures—the frogs and snakes and even the black bear deep in his den. But none could answer her, and so she sailed across the sea and spoke to the fish and the whales and the sleepy turtles that blinked from their hard green shells. But none could answer her questions. Undaunted, she strode off into the hills and climbed the snowy mountains until at last she stood at the highest peak and shivered in the cold. No animals lived at such a fearsome height, and the girl despaired that there was no one left to help her. But just at that moment, she noticed the stars twinkling in the night sky and stretched her hands toward their loveliness.

As Max told his tale, he conjured colorful images of creatures, from a bloated bullfrog to a great whale spouting a spectrum of lights from its blowhole. The children lay spellbound, every mouth agape. By the time the girl stood upon the mountaintop, little stars floated just above their heads, twinkling against the ceiling's stout rafters.

With her hands outstretched, the girl asked the stars if they could answer her questions. Who was she? What was her name? As she waited in the cold, the stars seemed to come closer, as though they were as curious about this little girl as she was of them. Lower and lower they came until it seemed they were swarming all around her.

The children shrieked with delight as the sparkling lights descended lower like inquisitive pixies, zooming about the room and pausing periodically at each eager face. When they arrived at Mina, however, the lights lingered and began to orbit around her head like a crown.

Because the girl was brave and had climbed such fearsome heights, the stars would help her. The girl was royalty, they said, a beautiful princess who was wise and beloved by her people. They missed her terribly. Could she not guess her name?

At this, Mina's impassive face gave way to a hesitant smile. "Is her name Mina?" she whispered. "Princess Mina?"

"That's right," said Max. "Princess Mina's people missed her and needed her and have been searching for her all this time. Is she ready to go home?"

Isabella put down her needlework, and the children ceased their squirming. All eyes focused on Mina, who was nestled in the far corner. She glanced up at the stars orbiting her head and then across at Max, who repeated the question.

Was the little princess ready to go home?

Mina nodded, and her crown's stars burst into tiny lights that zoomed about the room before rocketing up the chimney like a comet's tail. It was a fitting finale, and the other children clapped and scooted aside to make a place for her in the center. Grinning shyly, Mina gathered up her blankets and joined them.

While Mina laughed and joked with the others, Max settled back into his chair and mused upon the show's finale. It had been a truly dazzling conclusion to the tale, one that had required an accomplished Mystic's talent and control. There was only one problem.

The Mystic had not been Max.

He pondered this in silence while the children fell asleep. When the room had been silent for some time, Isabella motioned for Max to follow her upstairs.

"That was a very good thing you did," she said. "I did not think Mina would smile again. You did not know her, but she had so much life before that terrible night. It makes me happy to see her smile."

"It's nothing," said Max, feeling awkward under Isabella's close gaze.

"How old are you?" she asked, setting down her lantern.

The simple question stumped him. His birthday was the fifteenth of March, and he imagined it had recently passed without his noticing. By a conventional calendar, Max should have been fifteen, but he had spent many days in the Sidh, where time ebbed and flowed in mysterious ways. He could not be certain.

"Sixteen," he guessed. "Maybe seventeen? It's hard to say."

Isabella nodded at this, then unlatched the shutters to peer out the window at the windy evening.

"Do you still think I'm such an evil person?" she asked.

"I never did," replied Max. "I thought you made an evil choice."

"Sometimes every choice is bad," she said.

Max thought back to past conversations with Ms. Richter and Nigel. They were good people. What sacrifices might Ms. Richter make on behalf of Rowan, or Nigel on behalf of his unborn child? Had Mrs. Bristow already given birth? Max wondered at this and at many things. In his heart, he knew that Isabella was a good person. Max was not a parent; he could not imagine the choices he might have made in her position.

"I'm not angry at you, Isabella," he said wearily. "There's no point to it."

"Thank you," she murmured. "Before, I did not care so much. But now I do."

An awkward silence ensued and Max fidgeted. He did not know where this was going or why Isabella needed to have this conversation so far from the sleeping children.

"The goblins will come," she said hastily. "It has been nearly two months and the moon is right. They will visit tonight or tomorrow."

"Then I need to get ready," said Max, relieved. "Where do they usually come from?"

"There," Isabella said, thrusting her arm out the window. Max's gaze followed her outstretched finger to the dark road that ran toward the mountains.

"How many?" Max asked.

"I don't know," said Isabella. "Pietro would go out and speak with them. I tried to spy, but I was too frightened to get very close."

Max nodded and began piecing together his plan.

"What will you do?" Isabella asked cautiously.

"Go out and wait for them," he said simply.

"Please be careful," she said, clutching his sleeve. "If they know the monster is dead . . . I've heard terrible stories of the goblins! Th-they'll make you a prisoner and take you away!"

"Goblins are dumb, Isabella," said Max, "but they're not that dumb. . . ."

As the moon rose higher in the spring night, Max waited in the boughs of a sycamore whose budding branches overhung a bend in the road. There was wind in the valley. It rustled the leaves but not oo loudly that Max would be unable to hear the sound of wheels. As he watched the bats skim and dart in search of food, he tried to recall everything he knew about goblins and their ilk.

Goblins in all their forms were miserable creatures—cruel, tyrannical, and bullying whenever they could manage the upper hand. The dryads hated them and would not live in groves near a goblin den. These dens were usually underground or in deep mountains where clans formed a loose confederacy under the absolute rule of a chieftain, who was often chosen by virtue of his size. In many ways, the all-male goblins and all-female hags shared a common culture, and Max wondered if the two species were not distant kindred. Unlike hags, however, there was considerable variety in goblin size and appearance. While some of the smaller hobgoblins might stand a mere three feet, a true goblin chief might look a grown man in the eye and exceed three hundred pounds. With his rope and his sharp sword, Max was prepared for either.

Goblins were active traders and were liable to have considerable news of other creatures—or even demons—that resided in the surrounding area. Based on the farmhouse's basic supplies and livestock, these goblins were both wealthy and active. They would know of any trade routes and might even have a map to share if Max could be persuasive.

It was very late when he finally heard the clopping of hooves. Blinking the sleep away, he peered into the darkness as a team of mules and a wagon pulled into view, followed by a small herd of sheep. Atop the wagon sat five squatty goblins, the largest snapping the reins and barking at the mules. Their eyes shone through the darkness, tiny pinpricks of light that peered from beneath the wide brims of their oversized hats.

When the cart had nearly reached the sycamore, Max dropped from the branches and stepped into the road.

"Misch-misch!" hissed the driver, pulling hard on the reins. The other goblins sat up to peer at Max, who stood calmly in the road.

"Hrunta, e nugluk a brimboshi? Ilbrya shulka nuv klunkle," hiccupped the smallest goblin.

His comrades laughed at this, but the driver scowled and leaned over to snatch away the speaker's flask.

"Where is Pietro?" croaked the driver, removing his hat to scratch his head.

"Pietro is gone," Max replied. "I'm in charge now."

"Did you hear that?" exclaimed the goblin, turning to his companions. "He said he's in charge! Tell us, maggot, what exactly are you in charge of?"

"I'm in charge of this farm," Max explained. "And that lake and this valley and the mountains beyond. I would rule the sky, too, but that is beyond my reach."

"He must be a drunk like Pietro," chuckled the goblin, his

eyes glittering. "Enough with this drivel—we are already late. Unload the cart and be gone before we peel your skin for sport!"

"Yes, sir," said Max, snapping off a salute. Trotting around to the back of the cart, he found three children bound there, along with several crates. Untying their bonds, Max asked if they were able to walk. The eldest—a girl of eleven or twelve—nodded, and Max told her to herd the flock up to the farmhouse and knock on the door. She should call for Isabella and then ask Mario and Claudia for help with the animals. Could she manage that? She could. The younger children, siblings judging by their similar appearance, then helped Max unload the crates before following the girl up the hill.

"That's the spirit!" laughed the driver, waving his whip at Max. "Put 'em to work before they go down the well!"

Max shrugged. "Actually, they need to carry the things because I need to speak with you. Your delivery's incomplete."

"What's he talking about, Hrunta?" hissed one of the goblins to the driver.

"We brought the usual," Hrunta grumbled, "and I don't like your tone."

"My tone is the very least of your worries."

At this insolence, Hrunta raised the whip and cracked it down at Max like a thunderbolt. But the goblin was far too slow. Sidestepping the blow, Max caught the whip, wrapping it twice around his hand and promptly wrenching Hrunta from the driver's seat. The goblin landed with a crumpling thump on the road, his legs kicking in the air like an upturned beetle. His companions merely gaped, stunned.

At Rowan, every student receives a book, a compendium detailing the habits and behaviors of known enemies. Even a First Year knew that goblins hate to be turned upside down—it could induce a panic so severe that they abandoned all resistance.

It was the only way to handle them humanely. Quick as a flash, Max tied the whip around Hrunta's ankle and threw the loose end over a stout sycamore branch. A second later, Max hoisted up the puffing, protesting goblin so that he dangled upside down like an enormous, leather-clad pear.

"Kill him!" barked the outraged goblin, flailing his stubby arms at his fear-stricken comrades.

Max turned as one of the goblins lobbed a dagger. In his haste, however, the young goblin had neglected to remove the sheath, and it thudded weakly against Max's shoulder.

"What's your name?" said Max, casually addressing the guilty party, whose spindly arm remained frozen in the act.

"Eh . . . Skeedle, my lord."

"Do you think that was wise, Skeedle?"

"No." The mortified creature blinked. "No, I don't."

"Come here," said Max, beckoning the goblin forward.

"Do I have to?" moaned Skeedle, showing five sharp teeth in a grimace that displayed his revulsion.

"Yes," said Max, measuring out a length of rope. "I'm afraid so."

A minute later the juvenile goblin dangled upside down alongside his commander, who cursed and swatted at him in vain. As Max secured the rope's hitch, he heard the *clink-clink-clink* of iron-soled shoes as the remaining goblins fled the scene.

Max was acquainted with goblins, having encountered some in Germany the previous year. But those had been wilder, and not so quick to flee at the first sign of real trouble. The present company was of a more genteel variety—similarly cruel but more articulate and uncommonly fat and soft from feasting. Max almost pitied the fleeing trio as he ran them down and bound them to one another in a wriggling bunch that was soon hoisted up into the tree.

"Now," said Max, pacing before the suspended, sputtering

creatures. "I'd hate for this to take any longer than necessary. After all, I've seen wolves prowling about the valley. . . ."

The goblins made a whining noise in their throats and glanced at one another in an escalating panic. Goblins lived in mortal fear of wolves, which were known to hunt them with a savage enthusiasm.

"What do you want?" pleaded Hrunta.

"I'm going to ask questions," said Max calmly. "And I want the truth. When I ask the question, you'll all respond together. If one of you fails to answer, he stays up in the tree. If you're the last to answer, you stay up in the tree. If one of you provides a different answer than the others, he stays up in the tree. See how this works? The answers must be quick and truthful or I will know. . . ."

The goblins cursed and thrashed about feebly before finally agreeing to Max's proposal. For the next hour, Max peppered them with questions about their clan, their home, and the valley. He learned that they were of the Broadbrim clan, that their chieftain was the venerable Plümpka, and that the Broadbrims had driven off all the other goblins within the region. The exiled goblin clans—the Sourbogs, Blackbacks, and Greenteeth—had all taken refuge over the mountain. As Max guessed, there were no dryads nearby. But there were lutins, satyrs, and fauns in the southern glades and even a vicious troll in the northern passes where the goblins refused to hunt. The goblins knew of vyes that lived at the base of the mountains, but if an honest-to-goodness demon had claimed title over the region, it had yet to bother with the Broadbrims.

Max turned his questions toward other humans. To his disappointment, the goblins universally denied that there were any free humans living in the vicinity. Max recalled Isabella's mention of two people named Nix and Valya, but he decided to keep those names to himself.

"No free humans," Max clarified. "How many humans have the Broadbrims enslaved?"

"None!" protested Skeedle. "They're already slaves when we get them. The traders bring them from the great city! We just deliver them here according to the contract."

"Contract with whom?" asked Max.

"We don't know," replied Hrunta. "That's Plümpka's business."

"Well, then," said Max. "Where's the 'great city'?"

"South," they squealed. "A fortnight's journey south!"

"Is that where you get all your trade goods?"

"No," they answered, and Max soon learned there were other markets and settlements. According to Skeedle (who was the most forthcoming), there was a trading post two days to the north and a fairly sizable village of various creatures due east over the mountains.

Max listened carefully to these and other details regarding who and what lived in the vicinity. When a wolf howled from down by the lake, the goblins broke into a chattering sweat.

"Now," said Max, stooping to shine the goblins' lantern in Hrunta's eye. "That wolf sounds hungry and I want to wrap this up. Where's the entrance to the Broadbrim caverns?"

Silence.

"Oh dear," said Max, pausing to let the goblins hear the answering howls throughout the valley. "I think they know you're here. . . . I'll ask one more time. Where's the main entrance to your home?"

"Between the red stones of the highest peak!" shrieked Skeedle, despite Hrunta's glaring admonition. "It's true! It's true!"

"And the password?" asked Max. "I know there will be a password to move the guardstones. . . ."

"We can't tell you that," Hrunta insisted. "Plümpka'd eat us whole!"

"He doesn't have to know." Max shrugged. "And it's that or the wolves, so let's have it on the count of three. One . . . two . . ."

"Bitka-lübka-boo!"

The goblins spat the password out in unison just as several pairs of eyes loped into view. The mules snorted and stamped the ground, their flanks shivering as three gray timber wolves set their tongues a-wagging and began to growl.

"Back!" Max yelled, hurling a bolt of bright blue witch-fire that sent the wolves retreating into the dark forest. He turned to the goblins, which were now gibbering and pleading with Max to release them. One by one, Max untied the goblins and lowered them gently to the ground. They rolled to their feet, eyeing the nearby trees for any sign of the wolves.

"Now," said Max, shepherding them back to their cart. "Just so we understand each other. I know where you live. I know the password. I know your leader's name and the clans you've displaced. If you try to get sneaky or betray me, I can promise you that the Broadbrims will be visited by the Sourbogs, Blackbacks, Greenteeth, and maybe even that troll in the northern passes. . . ."

"Not the troll!" exclaimed Skeedle. "It's the wildest thing in the valley!"

"No, Skeedle," said Max, lifting the little goblin up into the cart. "I am."

~ 18 ~

NIX AND VALYA

It was late May, and Max was whistling one afternoon as he trudged up the steep path that led from the lake to the farm-house. Porcellino tried to accompany him, but his efforts resulted in little more than a breezy hooting.

Claudia stopped and turned to him. "You're spitting on them," she growled. "You're spitting all over my fish!"

"Put them in the basket," replied Porcellino, unconcerned. "You only have them out to brag."

"I like to see their colors in the sun," declared Claudia, appraising the four shimmering trout. "You're only jealous because you didn't catch any."

"I caught lots of fish," the boy maintained, crouching to tie his shoe. "But I'm not greedy like you, so I just put them back. I caught a huge one just before we left."

"Then why is there still bait on your hook?" demanded Claudia.

"I like to be ready for next time."

Claudia scoffed loudly and Max told her to stop. She should focus on her magnificent catch, Porcellino should practice his whistling, and Max should enjoy a respite from their incessant bickering.

Pollen drifted on the warm breeze, and the forest was abuzz with chirping birds and squirrels that chased one another from tree to tree. As they walked, Max thought of Julie and his friends at Rowan. Final exams would be coming soon. The libraries would be full, the coffeehouses and cafes of Rowan Township bustling with students frantic over runic symbols or elemental conjurations. . . . He thought of the kitchens and Bob cooking without the company of Mr. McDaniels or the hags. But this made him sad, so Max instead tried to picture Nick and Circe, aged YaYa, and even Sir Olaf ordering poor Frigga and Helga about. Rowan seemed a lifetime ago.

Max's life at the farm was relatively quiet and insular. Ever since they'd met Max, the goblins now made two deliveries each month, and five more children had come to live at the farmhouse. Their prosperity and growing numbers had Max considering expansion. The main house boasted eight bedrooms, but even these were getting crowded now that there were so many children, along with Max, Isabella, and little Gianna, who was teething and often testy.

Nearing the farmhouse, they heard a myriad of familiar sounds. There were the sheep, of course, but since the goblins' last visit these had been joined by three milk cows and a surly bull. The latter was lowing from the pasture, its amorous call joining a pair of hammers that rapped away on the farmhouse roof—no doubt Mario and Paolo repairing the leaky tiles above the northwest bedroom. But then Max heard a sound he did not expect.

It was a man's laughter.

Hurrying over the crest, Max looked across the road and saw a wagon parked alongside the new fencing that protected the grapevines. Two black mares were tied to the fence eating oats from Mina's hand. She waved to Max as he emerged from the woods with Porcellino and Claudia in tow.

Max heard the laughter again; it came from the other side of the farmhouse. He laid his fishing rod by the watering trough and walked around to the porch, where he found Isabella conversing with two strangers, a man and a woman.

"Ai!" exclaimed the woman as Gianna snatched her hair and tried to eat it. The woman laughed and tucked white braids back beneath her kerchief, leaving the baby to chew on her own pink fist.

"Rub some olive oil on her gums," suggested a robust, rangy man who appeared to be in his seventies. "She won't be so grumpy." His eyes flashed to Max, who had stopped short to observe them. "You must be Max!" he exclaimed.

"Hello," said Max, nodding politely to the pair.

"What a pleasure," said the woman, returning Gianna to her mother. "Isabella's told us all about you."

"Has she?" Max replied, his smile fixed.

"Says you're a blessing," chuckled the man. "And looking around, I'd say she was right. Never thought we'd see this place looking so good."

The old man radiated good health and vitality as he extended a strong, calloused hand.

"I'm Nix," he said, winking a cheerful blue eye from beneath a heavy gray brow. "And this is my wife, Valya."

The roly-poly woman offered a hearty grin and shook Max's hand with the same warm assertiveness as her husband.

"We live across the valley," he explained. "We're overdue for a visit but had to tend to Pietro and Ana when they showed up at our door."

Valya made a face.

"How are they?" asked Max.

"Couldn't say," said Nix, easing back into his chair. "They moved on a few months ago. They didn't want to stay after the troll lumbered by our cottage one night."

"You live by the troll?" Max asked, his interest piqued.

Valya nodded. "Right within its shadow. It's never bothered us before, but lately it's been coming down from its mountain. When the passes melted, Pietro and Ana continued east."

"Their choice, of course," said Nix. "But we weren't too sorry to see the back of them, were we? Never approved of what went on here," he said, reaching for one of the olives that Isabella had set out on a wooden tray.

"If you didn't approve," said Max stiffly, "then you might have done something."

"We tried," said Valya, coating her finger with olive oil and swabbing it around Gianna's gums. "But we're no match for such a monster. We encouraged Pietro to leave . . . brought the little ones treats when we could."

"Brought some more today," chuckled Nix, gesturing at a stack of crates, "but they seem a little paltry compared to what you've been squeezing out of the Broadbrims. Just look at this place . . . fresh paint and cows, new tools, and even chocolate— chocolate, for all love!"

"Isabella showed me the spinning wheel," whispered Valya,

leaning forward with an eager, conspiratorial air. "The enchanted one that works all by itself . . . where does a girl lay her hands on one of those? My poor hands get so cramped."

"Hmmm," said Max, glaring at Isabella. "Sounds like someone's been sharing all our little secrets. Maybe we should keep one or two."

"Oh, nothing to quarrel over," chuckled Valya, rubbing her eyes as the breeze brought more pollen. "We're all friends here. Isabella said you were a brave boy, but she didn't mention how handsome you were!"

"For heaven's sake, Valya, don't embarrass him," said Nix. "Besides, I'm sitting right here."

"Oh, be still!" she snipped. "I'm exercising the privilege of my age. Old ladies can comment on whatever they like in perfect safety. And if I want to say that this young man is the most beautiful creature I've ever seen, then I will. You think I've forgotten about that tramp Sophia?"

"She was an actress!" Nix moaned, rubbing his temples. "I never even met her! I only saw her in a film fifty years ago, for the love of God. . . ."

"It's the same thing!" insisted Valya, pursing her lips.

"You remember movies?" asked Max with interest.

But Nix merely blinked and smiled at Max as though he did not hear the question. Max repeated it, but the couple simply continued bickering until the conversation drifted back to pleasant small talk.

"So," said Valya, patting Isabella's knee, "the goblins have been bringing you food and tools, but what about toys, eh? I bet the little ones could use some toys."

"I suppose so," said Isabella. "But you've already been so kind."

"Nonsense!" said Nix, slapping his knee. "Giving gifts is what we like to do. Now, I think we could maybe trade for some toys out at the Crossroads. They might be made for other folk—little fauns or satyrs—but the kids will like them all the same."

"If you don't mind me asking," Max said, "how . . . er . . . how do you move about so easily? You don't seem to be afraid of the goblins."

"What do nasty goblins or an old troll want with us?" chuckled Valya. "We leave them alone and they do likewise. Live and let live."

"Now, Max," said Nix, peering at him with a shrewd eye. "I hope I don't insult you when I say you don't speak our language like a native. Isabella said you arrived one day from across the great sea. Can such a thing be true?"

Max was taken aback by the question and did not reply.

"You talk too much," Valya hissed, frowning at her husband.

"No," said Max, crossing the porch. "Isabella does. Please excuse me."

Walking inside, he cursed Isabella's foolishness. He knew she meant no harm, but it was clear that Nix and Valya traveled all over the valley and interacted with other people or even creatures. The last thing Max needed was for word to get out that the farmhouse was prospering under the protection of a mysterious human from across the sea. That could raise questions and attract curious parties—perhaps even a brayma—to make inquiries. Max kicked a stool, which clattered across the floor. He glanced about the great room. The magic spinning wheel was at work in the corner, transforming carded wool to fine thread. Fresh paint covered the walls, and the pantries were filled with salted pork, fruit preserves, even honey that the Broadbrims had sealed in glazed earthen jars. Outside, there was the frame of a new barn, stacks of fresh lumber, and a pasture filled with livestock. The household's newfound wealth was rather conspicuous.

Perhaps Max had been the fool.

Climbing the stairs, Max walked down the long hall toward his bedroom. It was the smallest of the eight, a nook tucked just beneath the rafters, with one narrow window that looked upon the green hills and the road that stretched south.

He laid his possessions upon the small sleeping mat: his battered pack, the walking stick, the gladius, and his personal effects, which included his father's razor and the ivory brooch from Scathach. Within the pack were the shards of the *gae bolga* wrapped in white linen. Beneath the linen bundle, Max retrieved the battered pages of his journal.

There was a knock. Isabella stood in the doorway, looking anxious.

"I know I have done something wrong," she said. "I am sorry—please don't be angry with me."

"Where are they?" asked Max.

"Valya is holding Gianna, and Nix is kicking the ball with the children."

"You must trust them," Max observed.

"I do," she said. "They are very good people. They are sorry if they caused offense."

Max nodded. "Try to understand, Isabella," he explained. "I have lots of enemies who might be wondering where I've gone. Those enemies know that I come from across the sea. If people start talking about this place . . . start talking about a boy who killed the monster, those enemies could come looking for me. They would find this place and everyone here, and they are far worse than goblins."

"I will tell them to say nothing," she said. "I'm sure they will understand. They are very smart people—professors before the war, I think. They usually spend the night when they visit, but I'm sure they will go if you want them to."

"No," said Max, feeling guilty and inhospitable. "I'll speak with them after supper while you put the children to bed. They can stay in my room."

Isabella nodded before glancing at the brooch. "Did a woman give you that?" she asked.

"Yes."

With Max's permission, she examined the brooch and cooed over its artistry before gazing at an open journal entry.

"Can you read those marks?"

"Of course," said Max. "I wrote them."

"Would you teach me?" she asked. "I knew them once and often dream of them . . . but the dreams fade and I cannot remember. I would like to learn them again."

Max thought of Astaroth's edicts.

"I can't," he sighed. "If anyone knew you could write . . . It's not worth the danger, Isabella."

"I'd better get supper ready," she said stiffly.

An hour later the great room was filled with chattering children and adults clustering around several tables. The goblins had brought real tablecloths, whale oil for the lanterns, and even salt and pepper sprinkled sparingly in little bowls.

Max sat at the head of the main table and managed polite conversation with Nix and Valya when they were not besieged by the children who had met the couple on previous visits. When Claudia had served the pair two fish from her catch, Nix turned to Max.

"You've been a godsend to this place," he said, buttering his bread. "Please accept our apologies for the misunderstanding earlier—we meant no offense."

"Of course not," said Max, focusing on his plate. "We'll talk after supper."

That opportunity did not come until late in the evening. The combination of visitors and presents stimulated the children beyond all reasoning. They sped about the great room, climbing over furniture, unwrapping treats, and generally creating chaos until an exasperated Isabella herded them upstairs. They departed in a thump of footsteps and aggrieved protests until Max was finally left alone with the elderly couple.

He urged the pair to keep their seats while he cleared the dishes. "I hope you understand my concerns," he said. "It would not do for others to hear about this place, our arrangement with the goblins, or me. . . ."

"We'll be discretion itself," Nix promised.

Valya nodded her agreement before sneezing into her napkin.

"Do you have a cold?" asked Max, stacking the dishes in a tub of soapy water.

"It's the pollen," she griped, pawing at her eyes. "It's always dreadful this time of year."

"How long have you been living in the valley?" Max inquired.

"Oh," chuckled Nix, "a long time . . . longer than we'd like to admit."

"Are those the Alps I see to the north?" asked Max.

"No," replied Nix, selecting a cookie. "The Apennines. Americans often make that mistake."

Max glanced sharply at the man. "You remember America," he observed. "And you remember movies, too. How unusual."

"Like I said," sniffled Valya, glaring at her husband, "you talk too much!"

"It's all right, dear," said Nix gravely, his eyes never leaving Max's. "Something tells me that this friendship will require trust more than delicacy."

"Isabella said you were professors," said Max. "Where did you teach?"

"Siena," replied Nix. "I taught mathematics and Valya taught medicine."

"How is it that you two remember things before the Fading?" asked Max. "How is it that you can live in this valley as though nothing has happened? Something's wrong. . . . Something doesn't make sense."

"The children say you can make pictures and lights appear in the air," said Valya. "They say you make fire from your hands. They say you are a magician."

Nix sneezed into his sleeve, then pushed a guttering candle away from his reddening eyes.

"Of a fashion," said Max quietly, concluding that a denial was pointless.

"Well, we are magicians, too." Nix smiled. "Of a fashion . . ."

At a flick of the man's fingers, the candles were extinguished before suddenly bursting back into flame.

Nix chuckled. "Alas, that is nearly the limit of our little tricks," he said. "We failed the tests. . . ."

"The Potentials tests?" asked Max, his heart quickening. "You were . . . Potentials?"

"Are you a student from Rowan?" asked Valya. "We suspected as much. Long have we wished to visit that school, but it was not to be."

"Is it as beautiful as they say?" inquired Nix.

"Yes," said Max, smiling at his memories. "It's a very special place. But . . . why did you fail?"

"Oh," said Valya, shrugging, "the tests were very discriminating. We each failed the last."

Max remembered when Nigel had administered the tests long ago in Chicago. The last one had been a test of character, of courage. Were Nix and Valya cowards?

Nix sneezed again, scratching at his eyes, which were growing red and inflamed. "It's getting late." He sniffed, glancing at his wife.

"Go up, dear," she said. "You always get so sleepy after a big meal, and I've got my knitting."

Bidding the pair good night, Nix trudged up the stairs. When he'd gone, Valya reached for her bag and produced a lump of yarn that she was knitting into a pair of socks for Mario, whom they'd known the longest.

"He grows like a weed," she sighed. "Can't have his toes sticking out for all to see, can we?"

"You know," said Max, stacking cups, "Mario asked me the funniest question the other day. Stumped me, but I'm sure a professor could answer it."

"I'll give it my best," she chuckled, her needles clacking away.

"Well," Max began. "There's this farmer who owns a fox, a chicken, and a bag of grain. He needs to transport all three across a river using his boat, but he can only bring one at a time."

"Oh?" asked Valya, glancing up with polite interest.

"But there's a problem," Max continued. "Without the farmer to supervise them, the chicken will eat the grain and the fox will eat the chicken."

"Of course," chimed Valya. "That's their nature."

"Indeed," said Max. "So the question is . . . how can the farmer transport all three safely across the river if he can only bring one at a time?"

"Well, that's simple," replied Valya. "If he just takes the grain across . . . no . . . no . . . the fox will eat the chicken. Hmm . . . He should bring the fox across! No . . . then the chicken will just eat the grain."

As Valya wrestled with the riddle, Max watched her closely. The knitting needles were laid aside, and the ball of yarn fell to the ground, unraveling as it rolled. Chewing at her lip, Valya rocked back and forth, her voice growing agitated.

"But he can take only one!" she snarled to herself, recounting the riddle's conditions. Max stood by the table, watching her fingernails scratch and claw at the table. Pausing at a place setting by the stairs, Max casually slipped a knife into his hand.

"Valya," he said, but the woman did not respond. Snapping his fingers, Max called louder.

She glanced up, her eyes red and suspicious as she rocked back and forth.

"Do you really think I don't know what you are?" asked Max, his voice deadly quiet.

The blood drained from Valya's face; her breaths quickened to rapid gulps.

"And do you really think I don't know Nix is right behind me?"

As Max finished the sentence, he turned to see a gray snarling face looming over him. Baring its teeth, the vye went to seize him by the shoulders, but Max twisted out of its grasp, wrenching its arm behind its back even as he kicked its legs out from under it. In the blink of an eye, the stunned vye was pinned facedown upon the floor with Max atop it.

"Don't hurt him!" pleaded Valya, nearly toppling out of her chair. "Please!"

"Don't you move," Max hissed, his knife at the vye's throat. "You move and that's the end. Do you understand me?"

The vye wheezed beneath Max's grip, a hoarse whine sounding in its throat as the blade pressed against it. Nix's fur was pewter-colored, his ice-blue eyes rolling back to look at Max even as the bearded, blackening snout wrinkled back to speak. The voice was chillingly human, that of the grandfatherly professor who'd been playing with the children.

"We understand perfectly," he panted. "Dear boy, it is you who does not."

"What's to understand?" asked Max, seething. "A pair of vyes so cowardly that they have to bribe and charm their prey?"

"No," said Valya, her voice taut with fear. "That's not it at all. . . . You must let us explain."

"We love the children," said Nix gently. "We would never hurt them."

"It's true," said Valya. "Please don't judge us just because we're different. If we had wanted to hurt the children, we could have done so long ago."

"But you're vyes," said Max, glaring at Valya. "Vyes came to my house. Vyes attacked Rowan. Vyes are the ones who brought back Astaroth!"

Valya crossed herself.

"Please," she hissed. "Please, don't call evil things lest they answer."

"A vye concerned about evil?" Max sneered, tightening his grip on Nix. "Vyes are evil. I know all about your kind."

"Your knowledge comes from Rowan," coughed Nix. "And Rowan has never understood 'our kind,' as you so eloquently put it. My boy, please let me up. We mean no harm to you or anyone else."

"If you meant no harm," said Max, "then why did you change shape? Why did you try to sneak up behind me?"

"The reason is not as sinister as you might suppose," explained the vye. "I changed shape because human form is painful. I had already transformed in my room and came downstairs because I heard Valya getting agitated. It was clear enough what you were doing. I merely wanted to make you stop torturing my poor wife and restrain you until we could explain."

"Why should I believe you?" asked Max. "Why shouldn't I end your life right here?"

"Because you don't strike me as a murderer."

"Please let my husband up," said Valya softly. "You're hurting him."

The sorrow and sincerity in this last sentence gave Max pause. Nix's body was no longer tense; his breathing came slow and shallow while his eyes stared ahead. The vye seemed utterly resigned to whatever fate Max decided to impose.

Slowly, Max released his grip on the vye's tangled ruff and eased off its back. Nix glanced cautiously at him and the knife Max held before climbing slowly to his feet and padding around the table to join his wife. Even as Max watched, the vye shrunk, its wolfish features receding until it was only the old man looking tired and worn in his nightshirt.

"Thank you," said Nix, exhaling as Valya anxiously mopped sweat from his brow.

For several moments, no one spoke, and the great room was awash in silence and shadows while the candles guttered. Max watched Nix and Valya closely, his eyes darting between the pair as they looked at one another and shared an unspoken moment.

"Okay," said Max, pointing with the knife. "You wanted to explain, so here's your opportunity."

"Where to begin?" asked Valya, giving a rueful smile. "It is no easy thing being a vye. Imagine being hunted your entire life, being forced to hide your identity lest Rowan Agents track you down."

"I lost four siblings to Rowan," mused Nix, counting on his fingers.

"My entire family was hunted down twenty years ago," said Valya. "When they gathered to celebrate my uncle's birthday, they were ambushed in the forest."

"Do you wonder why we hide?" asked Nix. "Do you wonder why we masquerade as humans and cloak our true nature?"

"Rowan wouldn't hunt vyes if vyes didn't commit evil acts," Max snapped.

"Ah," said Valya. "Would vyes commit evil acts if humans

didn't hunt them? No—please don't argue, but listen for just a moment."

Max eased back in his seat and bit back his retort while Valya continued.

"There are many vyes who prey upon humans and who have joined forces with the Enemy. There are vyes who infiltrated governments and corporations and helped bring about the return of the Demon. But vyes were not born of evil, my dear. There is nothing intrinsically evil about us."

"Right," Max scoffed. "Vyes are just 'misunderstood.' I get it."

"I'm curious," said Nix thoughtfully. "What do you actually know about our history?"

"Everything," said Max, reciting from Rowan's compendiums. "Carnivorous shape-shifters who live secretly among humans. Vyes can hypnotize victims with their voices, but riddles can distract them and trigger an obsessive-compulsive response. Typically larger than werewolves but considerably more diverse in their appearance. Can control their transformations, which are independent of the lunar cycle. Highly light-sensitive. Intelligent opponents who often mate for life and work in pairs—"

"Just as we suspected," said Valya, turning to her husband. "Rowan teaches them nothing more than the means to identify and kill us."

"Vyes tried to abduct me before I met anyone from Rowan," said Max darkly.

"Alas, many have turned evil," Nix acknowledged. "We won't pretend otherwise. But vyes are not evil by nature any more than humans or wolves or bears. Humans have always lashed out at what they fear, and they have feared vyes from the very beginning."

"What is that beginning?" asked Max. "And why haven't I heard it before?"

"You haven't heard it, Max, because it's been suppressed and woven into a mythology all its own," said Nix. "But the roots of vyes originate close to this very valley. They are tied to the very founding of Rome."

"What could vyes possibly have to do with Rome?" asked Max, looking dubiously at the pair.

"Well," said Valya. "As you may have learned, the city is named after a man. This man was named Romulus, and he and his brother Remus were left to die in the wilderness. But they were saved by a wolf, who cared for them so that they might live. Now, this wolf was no ordinary wolf, but an elder spirit in wolf shape, and some of her essence was passed to these children whom she reared."

"As they came of age," continued Nix, "Romulus desired to rule over men and sought to suppress the wild, animal aspect of his being. But Remus shared none of his brother's ambitions or shame and spent his days within the forest. The historians say that Romulus slew his brother to claim uncontested rule over the city that would bear his name, but this is not what occurred. The truth is that Romulus worried that Remus would betray their secret and reveal to all their dual nature. Fearing that they would be shunned or even hunted, Romulus planned to murder his brother and ensure the secret would be kept. But Romulus could not bring himself to strike the blow and instead sent his brother into exile. And thus, Remus wandered north and largely faded from history."

"We like to think he traveled past this very spot," said Valya, squeezing Nix's hand.

"Well, we can't say definitively, but it is likely," said Nix. "We do know, however, that Remus met an Etruscan witch and the two lived the rest of their lives together, eventually migrating north to Gaul and Germania. Their offspring were the first vyes, and these direct descendants were gifted with both the wild spirit of their father and the magic essence of their mother. They were also gifted in the mystic arts, just like those who would study at the ancient schools, but vyes were prohibited from attending."

"Why?" asked Max.

"Because the humans were afraid of them," replied Valya. "It was the same when Nix and I were given the Potentials tests."

"What a travesty," Nix sighed, shaking his head. "One morning I saw something most unexpected—a golden light that flickered and danced just out of reach. I ran after it to no avail, but soon received a letter from America and a far-off school called Rowan. A Recruiter arrived the next day while my parents were working in the fields. I completed the first two tests, but the third frightened me so badly that I blundered into my true shape."

"What did the Recruiter do?" asked Max.

"Packed up her suitcase and left." Nix shrugged, grimacing. "She was surprised, of course, but not nearly so shocked as my parents when they learned what had happened. We had to bundle up our things and flee before the Agents came hunting for us. We escaped for the moment, but they eventually caught up to my family. I was studying at university when it happened."

"But that's terrible," said Max, fidgeting. "I mean, had they done anything wrong?"

"They were guilty of being vyes," explained Nix.

"I'm so sorry," Max murmured. "I—I had no idea that things like this happened . . . that Rowan could be responsible for such things."

"It's a good thing you left Rowan before you became an Agent, too," said Valya. "There's still hope for you."

"But I'm already an Agent," said Max, reddening. "Or at least I was."

"You?" laughed Nix. "Beg my pardon, but aren't you a little too young to be an Agent?"

"No," said Max. "I took an oath. I'm even in the Red Branch."

The pair shuddered at the name, before Valya abruptly chuckled and patted her husband's arm.

"He's teasing us, love. It's a joke."

"No," said Max, standing to pull back his sleeve and display the tattoo on his wrist. "I really am in the Red Branch."

The two old vyes merely stared at him, their jaws slack with horror.

"You mean that you're . . . Max *McDaniels*?" Valya asked incredulously.

Max nodded.

"B-but that's impossible!" sputtered Nix. "Max McDaniels is a monster! He's not a boy!"

"The Hound drinks the blood of his victims," muttered Valya, looking pale.

"He's a demon," added Nix. "A demon in human form . . ."

"Where did you hear that nonsense?" Max asked.

"What do you mean, where did we hear it?" asked Valya, perplexed. "Every vye's heard of him! He's become a bogeyman to keep young vyes in line."

"Go to sleep or Max McDaniels will get you!" said Nix, intoning it as though it was a proverb.

"You're joking," said Max, equally amused and appalled. "But I'm nothing like that."

"Exactly!" exclaimed Nix. "The real Max McDaniels is ten feet tall—"

"And when he roars, the mountains shake," chimed Valya decisively.

"You're just a rascal with a cruel sense of humor," Nix sighed.

But as Max stood looking at them, their watery eyes repeatedly strayed to the red tattoo upon his wrist—the upraised hand and loop of cord that symbolized Rowan's elite.

"It really would be just our luck," Valya sniffled dejectedly, hugging her shawl.

"I told you something was wrong," muttered her husband. "Goblins don't just bring people magic spinning wheels!"

"And now I'm going to die," Valya moaned, peering at the machine's polished magnificence. "Die before I even get a chance to use it."

"What are you talking about?" asked Max.

"Well, you're going to kill us," Nix concluded matter-of-factly.

"And festoon the walls with our insides," added Valya. "That's your trademark!"

"You're not serious," said Max, searching their faces.

Holding hands, they nodded in sober earnest.

"I'm not going to hurt you," he laughed. "I was going to apologize—to ask your forgiveness for the suffering that Rowan's caused you. If what you say is true, there have been terrible misunderstandings and injustices. It isn't right."

"So . . . you're not going to kill us?" whispered Valya, grimacing.

"No," said Max, waving off the idea. "I was going to make you tea. Transform into whatever shape you prefer. You're my guests."

"Is he serious, Valya?"

"I believe he is."

"Just think of it, dear," exclaimed Nix, adjusting his nightshirt so it covered his pale shins. "Max McDaniels is making us tea."

"With two lumps," Valya requested. "If he doesn't mind . . ."

* * *

Max and the vyes talked long into the night. To his surprise, he found their company to be a tremendous comfort. The pair listened well and offered measured, thoughtful responses to his many questions about vyes, their personal histories, and the Kingdom of Blys.

This last subject was the focus of his attention, but Max was disappointed to learn that Nix and Valya's knowledge was hemmed by the Alps and the Apennines. Of the lands beyond the mountains, they knew relatively little and could only say that Blys was divided into ten duchies that were ruled by demons of great stature or lineage. Prusias might have been king, but it seemed his kingdom comprised a somewhat fractious confederacy, where alliances shifted like the sand.

Nix and Valya offered names of counties and baronies and their respective rulers, but it was nothing more than random snippets they'd overheard from the goblins or others on the emerging trade roads. Nothing systemic emerged, nothing so useful as a map of the kingdom or a list of the grand duchies and their rulers. Max had done some good since he'd arrived in Blys, but he was no closer to vengeance, and the point rankled whenever he weighed his father's razor.

"You have mentioned this Vyndra several times," said Valya, looking at him thoughtfully. "And there is hatred in your voice. Has this demon wronged you?"

"He killed my dad," said Max, his voice as taut as piano wire.

"Ah," said Nix. "And thus you mean to seek out the demon and have your vengeance, eh?"

Max nodded and the vyes became very grave.

"Max," said Nix delicately. "That is a fool's errand. You're sticking your neck in the noose."

"Maybe," replied Max quietly. "But it's my neck to risk."

"Would Mina agree?" asked Valya. "Would Isabella? They depend on you now."

"I won't leave until things are situated," said Max, "but that day is coming."

"The world is changed," said Nix, pouring Valya more tea. "In this world, Max, we are all orphans. We have all lost someone. You have lost your father. But these children . . . haven't they lost everything?"

Max looked away under the vye's contemplative gaze.

"Rowan murdered our families," continued Nix softly. "They took nearly everything from us. Should we surrender more of ourselves to the tragedy? Should anger and rage dominate the rest of our lives? Is that the wise course?"

"I admire that you can let go of such things," said Max, thrusting his hands in his pockets and peering out an eastern window. "But I can't do that, Nix. It's just not in me."

"Then consider the practical matters," said Valya, sitting forward to wag a plump finger. "The demons are not of this earth. They are immortal, and—forgive my directness—no boy is going to simply walk up and strike down a spirit such as this. If this Vyndra lusts for Prusias's crown, then he must be very great. One of the dukes, perhaps. He is fire and death and pestilence. He will slay you as surely as the sun will rise."

Max gazed at the shadowed landscape and the sliver of light that hinted at the dawn. "I'm not asking for companions," he said, turning to them. "Just information."

Valya's wolfish face was quiet and composed, hardly the frightful mask of feral cunning he'd always associated with her kind. She plucked at her necklace and studied its small charm of hammered gold.

"He has put his faith in us, Nix," she sighed. "We must do likewise."

"That we must, Valya."

With this, the vyes climbed wearily up the stairs to claim an hour or two of sleep before the household stirred.

They stayed at the farmhouse for another two days. When the children were not pestering them for games or treats or wild tales, the vyes sat at the table and lent their experience to the many calculations that had been challenging Max and Isabella.

They calculated the number of mouths to feed, egg production, planting cycles, harvest yields, and food storage. Throughout, Max noticed that the vyes always included themselves in the projected headcount, claiming the need to "be conservative" in their estimates. He never commented on this, but secretly Max hoped that the vyes would move in permanently and look after Isabella and the children.

When it was time for the vyes to leave, Max loaded their wagon while they said their goodbyes to the children and cooed to Gianna. Climbing up into the driver's seat, Valya promised Max they would do their best to gather information and return in a month or two. Clucking his tongue, Nix shook the reins and the horses began a snorting trot down the old road.

· 19 ·

SKEEDLE AND THE TROLL

In late June, Max composed a letter to Julie Teller. She would be finishing her final exams, and he imagined her sitting at a desk in Maggie, scribbling feverishly under an instructor's watchful eye. He smiled at the image.

Max had no real intention of sending the letter. For one thing, there was no one to carry it to Rowan. For another, he was not certain if Julie would even want to read it, given his sudden exodus. Regardless, it felt good to get down his thoughts and share his experiences with a friend, even if it was only on paper.

Max was describing the farmhouse, when he finally noticed Mina.

She had perched silently on the stool beside him, her chin tucked to her knees while her dark brown eyes followed the letters and words that flowed from Max's quill.

"You sneaky thing," said Max, blowing the ink dry. "How long have you been there?"

She shrugged and climbed from the stool to settle on his lap. Peering closely at the journal, she thumbed back to its first page.

"What's that?" she asked, pointing at a drawing.

"That's Nick," said Max. "He was my very own lymrill."

"He looks mean," she mused, tapping the curving claws and bristling tail.

"No," said Max. "But like you, he's a fierce little beast. If Nick were here, he'd hunt every rat in the valley and we'd have no more problems in the storehouse."

"And what's that?" asked Mina, flipping to another page.

"That's Old Tom. It's a great tall building with a clock in its tower. Every hour it makes a funny sound to tell us what time it is."

Mina grinned and pointed to a drawing of a black lioness with a broken horn.

"That's YaYa," said Max. "She's bigger than Nix's wagon, but very wise and gentle."

"What about him?"

"That's Bob," said Max. "He's as tall as the climbing tree."

"Is he a monster?" she asked.

"Well," said Max, considering. "He's an ogre. But a very nice one."

"And what about them?" asked Mina, turning to a page depicting Mum and Bellagrog.

"Oh," said Max, studying the pair. "Well, they're hags. . . ."

"Are they nice?"

"Not so much."

Max quickly turned the page lest the leering faces give the girl nightmares, but Mina stubbornly flipped it back.

"I'm not scared of them," she said. "I think they're funny."

And as Mina uttered these words, the drawings began to move. Max gaped as Mum's image turned cartwheels while Bellagrog cavorted about and stuck out her tongue. It was like watching a cartoon.

"Mina," Max breathed. "Are you doing that?"

She gave a hesitant grin and nodded.

"And did you make the lights shoot out the chimney?" Max asked.

"Wasn't it pretty?" she whispered, looking up at him.

Max nodded and was going to ask another question, when Claudia finished the dishes and came rushing over to see what they were doing. Instantly, the hags reverted to their original poses.

"What is that?" asked Claudia, climbing onto the armrest and reaching for the journal.

"Nothing much," said Max. "Just some words and pictures I made."

He glanced at Mina, but the girl had resumed her quiet, unassuming demeanor.

"Ooh!" exclaimed Claudia, wriggling closer to see a sketch of a shedu.

Soon other children had gathered round, and Max was forced to hold up the journal so all could see the pictures he'd drawn of the selkies and the Highland hares shelving books in Bacon Library. Max answered many questions about the various creatures, but the children were most interested in Rowan itself and the very concept of a school. Was there really a place where young people learned how to write and draw like Max had done?

"There is," said Max, "but it is far away across the sea."

Even if the school was far away, Max could still teach them! Claudia made this pronouncement with the same fearless zeal that characterized her forays into fishing and farming and everything else. The announcement brought a cheer that utterly drowned Max's protests. Isabella merely smiled and continued to feed Gianna from a bowl of cherries.

The room was in such a tumult that Max barely heard the soft knocking. At first, he thought it might be squirrels on the roof, but then he heard it again.

"Shhh!" he hissed, bolting up to seize his sword from above the fireplace.

The room became dead quiet as Max drew the blade from its scabbard and strode toward the door. The knocking had ceased. Motioning Isabella and the children toward the stairs, Max tightened his grip on the sword and leaned close to the door.

"Who is it?" he asked. "And what do you want?"

"Beg pardon, master, but it's your Skeedle!"

"Are you alone?"

"Yes," shivered the goblin. "Oh, please open up—there might be wolves about!"

Lifting the crossbeam, Max opened the door to see the little goblin standing on the porch, holding his enormous hat between his twiddling fingers. Peering past Max, the goblin smiled nervously at the children and Isabella, who huddled by the stairs.

"Er, good evening," he began, rocking on his heels. "I'm sorry to come knocking, but I didn't know where else to go. . . ."

"What is it?" asked Max sternly. "Be quick."

"Well," said Skeedle, "Hrunta said I'm to make all the deliveries from now on. . . ."

"So?" asked Max.

"Alone," Skeedle whimpered, his lower lip aquiver.

"Well," said Max. "You know the way well enough. What's the problem?"

"The t-troll!" Skeedle cried. "He's come down from his mountain and he's eaten half our flock. He'll eat me too if he sees me all by myself. He lurks by the road now, still as a stone!"

"Why didn't he eat you tonight?" asked Max.

"I left before sundown," he squeaked. "Lashed the mules to a lather, poor things."

"So, what do you want me to do?" Max asked.

"Well," murmured Skeedle, fiddling with his hat. "You said you were the wildest thing in the valley, and I was hoping you could talk reason to it."

"Talk reason to a troll!" Max almost laughed, but caught himself when he realized that the goblin was in earnest. "Why can't your clan help you, Skeedle?" he asked gently. "If the Broad-brims could scare off the Greenteeth, I'm sure they can manage a troll."

"Hrunta says it's my rite of passage," explained the goblin hopelessly. "Now I'm supposed to challenge it. But he never had to challenge anything so big and hungry as a troll!"

"What did Hrunta challenge?" asked Max.

"A badger."

"Well, that doesn't seem fair."

"It isn't."

Max studied the dejected, sniffling goblin. He was a tiny, potbellied thing, absurd with his oversized hat and iron-soled shoes. Skeedle was still young, uncommonly curious, and not yet hardened into the cruel habits of his elders.

"Can you get me back here by sunset tomorrow?" inquired Max.

Once Skeedle nodded, Max knelt down to shake his clammy hand.

"Then I'm your man."

The goblin burst into grateful tears.

True to his word, Skeedle returned Max by sunset the next day. As the wagon came to a halt, Max heard the farmhouse door fly open and bang shut as a jumble of excited voices came racing down to the road. Skeedle greeted the children happily and hopped down from the driver's seat to tie up the mules.

"Did you find the troll?" said a breathless voice belonging to Claudia.

"Oh yes," replied Skeedle.

"And did you talk reason to him?" asked Porcellino.

"We sure did," the goblin crowed. "We talked all the reason that troll could handle!"

"Where's Max?" asked Paolo, sounding dubious. "Why didn't he come back with you?"

"Oh, he's just resting up in the back," replied Skeedle.

The children's faces appeared within Max's view, framed against the deepening sky. They stared at him in anxious silence until Claudia poked his arm.

"Are you dead?" she asked.

"Nope."

"What happened to your sword?" wondered Paolo, holding up its crumpled remains.

"The troll smashed it."

"Did he smash you, too?"

"Does it look like he did?"

Their heads nodded in unison.

Max groaned and gingerly felt his face. One eye was swollen shut and he was almost certain his nose was broken. Every muscle ached, and his knee made a funny clicking noise whenever he shifted his legs.

"Hey," said Porcellino. "This is a different wagon!"

"The troll ate the other one!" explained Skeedle, with something like real delight. "This one's only borrowed. Help me get Max in the house and I'll tell you all about it!"

Minutes later, Max hobbled through the front door. Isabella shrieked at the sight of him, practically launching the evening meal into orbit. Recovering herself, she helped ease Max into his favorite chair.

"Are you all right?" she asked.

Max nodded and gratefully accepted a damp cloth to hold over his eye.

"What happened?" she breathed.

"I was just about to tell the tale," said Skeedle. "Make yourself comfortable!"

Taken aback, Isabella merely stood aside as the audacious goblin hopped onto the bench and then the tabletop so he could address the assembled group. Removing his hat, he cleared his throat and lowered his voice as though telling a ghost story.

"The trouble didn't start until we were high up in the mountains. We were getting close to a tricky bend where you have to slow your wagon or you'll drive right over the edge. Well, that's where that crafty old troll was waiting. Now . . . who here can tell me something about trolls?"

Despite his injuries, Max smiled as the children bombarded the goblin with whatever tidbits they'd heard about trolls—how they had great big horns and glassy green eyes and beards that were made of vines and moss.

"That's right," said Skeedle. "And they like to sit on their mountaintops, chewing on dark thoughts or reciting old poems."

Pacing about the table, the goblin lowered his voice and offered a grumbling impersonation:

> *They call me Troll,*
> *Gnawer of the Moon,*
> *Giant of the Gale-blasts,*
> *Curse of the rain-hall . . .*

The children howled with laughter, and Max had to admit that the little goblin was an engaging storyteller. Yet despite Skeedle's dramatic gifts, Max found his eyelids growing heavy. As he dozed, he caught only bits and pieces of Skeedle's account.

". . . I thought the troll would listen to Max, but I was wrong! When it punched him, I did the sensible thing and ran far away to form a plan. . . .

". . . so Max's sword was broken and the troll was chasing him all over the place, tearing trees up by their roots and making so much noise I could hardly concentrate on my plan. . . .

". . . When Max tricked him over the cliff, my plan was finally ready so I went down to finish the job. 'You going to find another mountain, Troll?' I shouted. Well, he didn't want to answer, so I had to slap him around a little bit. . . ."

A climactic burst of applause woke Max. He opened his eyes just in time to see Skeedle take a gracious bow. Beaming at his audience, he placed his hat back atop his head and gazed longingly at the kitchen.

"Storytelling sure makes a goblin hungry," he reflected.

"Would you like to stay for supper?" asked Isabella, masking her smile.

"I'd be delighted!"

* * *

The troll might have crumpled Max's sword and broken his nose, but the encounter had its rewards. Not only was Skeedle's clan status elevated tremendously, but the troll's absence also enabled the Broadbrims to utilize better trade routes. As a result, the farmhouse enjoyed more frequent deliveries of better goods.

Within two months, the farmhouse boasted ten cows, and several blocks of enchanted ice that transformed a section of the cellar into a working refrigerator. At night, the children could eat actual ice cream while Max taught them the alphabet and how to write their names.

The farm was thriving, but Max was growing impatient. As the summer harvest came and went, he would often take his spyglass and climb atop the roof, scouring the roads and hills for any sign of Nix and Valya. The vyes had promised him information, but it had been three long months since they'd departed. Leaning against the chimney, Max watched yet another sunset and resolved to leave by the first frost.

By early October, the apples were finally ripe, and Max herded the children outside to pick the fruit before the rain arrived. While they worked, the children recited the alphabet or challenged one another to spell the word for something within view. *Fence, tree, mountain, cloud* . . . the words were assembled in singsong fashion, from little Mina all the way to Mario.

It was Porcellino who first spied the wagon.

Max assumed it must be Skeedle. Trotting down the slope, he crossed the animal paddock, pushing past the sheep and goats until he could get a clear view of the road.

To his great surprise, he saw that it was Nix and Valya's wagon.

And to his great delight, he deduced their intent to stay.

The wagon was piled high with the vyes' belongings—chairs

and paintings, a grandfather clock, and a wardrobe. Four black horses pulled the heavy wagon, while a flock of sheep followed obediently in its wake. As the horses pulled alongside the fence, Nix raised his hat in greeting.

Within the hour, they'd unloaded the cart and stabled the horses before the rain finally swept in from the north. It pelted the soil, sending the children racing toward the house, swinging their buckets and catching the drops on their tongues. Whooping, Claudia and Paolo quickly drove the flock into the paddock, and soon the entire household had taken shelter inside, clamoring about the great room while Max started a fire.

The children might have been delighted at Nix and Valya's visit, but Isabella seemed less so. Throughout dinner, she smiled as the children showed off their drawings or alphabets or elementary sentences, but her expression was distant and distracted. When Claudia asked why Nix and Valya had brought so many things with them, Isabella glanced sharply at the pair. Chuckling, Valya made room so Claudia could squeeze in next to her.

"We're getting old." She shrugged. "Too old to be living off on our own anymore or chopping our own firewood. And besides, we miss you little beasts."

Claudia grinned at this and began playing with the vye's necklace, whose charms gleamed in the firelight.

"Where will you sleep?" asked Paolo, understandably anxious, as he'd been moved twice to accommodate new arrivals.

"They'll sleep in my room," said Max.

Something in his tone commanded instant attention. Forks and knives were lowered, and the younger children gathered round from the side tables. Max had been preparing this speech for some time, but now that the moment had arrived, he found it difficult to begin.

"Um, this isn't easy for me," he said, glancing around. "But there's something I have to tell you. You see, I originally came to this land because I had an important job to do. But when I found this place and met all of you, I wanted to stay and help. . . ." Max paused and took a sip of water. "But now that the farm's doing so well, it's time I left to do that job."

The great room was utterly still until Isabella finally spoke. "How long will you be gone?" she asked quietly.

"Probably for a long time."

There was a general outcry among the older children. The younger ones looked anxious and confused.

"We'll go with you," offered Claudia. "We can help."

"Not with this," said Max. "You can help me by listening to Isabella, Valya, and Nix. They are in charge and I want you to be good for them."

The children nodded, but all of the energy had been leeched from the room.

"When will you leave?" asked Isabella, staring pensively into the fire.

"Within a day or two," said Max. "It's a long journey. You should all be fine. The harvest is in, and the goblins will leave you be."

"But what about our lessons?" complained Porcellino.

"Nix and Valya can teach you better than I," said Max. "And Skeedle will bring you more ink and paper if you need it. I expect you all reading and writing by the time I return."

"When will that be?" asked Mina, tugging at his sleeve.

"I don't know," Max replied. "By next spring, I hope, but I can't make any promises. No crying or moping. Diego, pick five helpers to clean up while I help Nix and Valya get settled."

Upstairs, the vyes set their suitcases down and rubbed at their reddening eyes.

"You really should tell them," said Max, closing the door. "I think they would understand. You'll be miserable in human form all the time."

Nix smiled appreciatively at the suggestion but shook his head.

"Another day," he said. "They have enough on their plates with you leaving. Don't worry about us—there are medicines and remedies that can help."

"And we can always transform at night," added Valya.

"Well, I appreciate what you're doing," said Max quietly. "Moving in. Looking after them."

Nix waved him off, reaching inside his satchel for a large, folded sheet. "Here's your map," he said, unfolding it and smoothing it on the bed. Gazing down, Max surveyed a map whose general outline comprised what had been Europe and North Africa. But while the map's basic contours were familiar, its many boundaries and labels were not.

"So that's the Kingdom of Blys," Max breathed, peering closer at the parchment.

"Correct," said Nix. "We've had to travel far and consult with many an unsavory character to patch this together, so treat it like gold."

"Your Vyndra is indeed one of the dukes," murmured Valya, pointing to a section of the map that comprised the majority of Germany, Denmark, and the Netherlands. "We heard lots about him at the Crossroads and beyond—a tyrant, jealous of King Prusias's throne. Some think he's in league with King Aamon. There's not yet open war, but the duke is suspected in two attempts on Prusias's life. The vyes we spoke to claim he is terrible, Max. Even those who served the Enemy . . ."

"Well," Max muttered. "I never thought it would be easy."

"Do you have a plan?" asked Nix, concerned. "Surely you don't mean to walk to Azur and challenge its ruler. There are now but two passes through these mountains," he said, pointing to the former Alps and Carpathians, "and they are closely watched. You don't want to travel east and loop back, as that will take you to Holbrymn."

Max found the name, a large region encompassing what used to be the Ukraine and Georgia.

"What's the matter with Holbrymn?" he asked.

"That's Yuga's realm," said Valya. "Nothing lives there—Yuga has eaten it all."

"The demon takes no form." Nix shivered. "The vyes say she is a whirlwind, a moaning storm that has stripped the land bare and devoured all life within it. Not even other demons will travel there."

Thinking of the *Ormenheid*, Max traced his finger west through the Mediterranean, north past the Bay of Biscay, and along the coast of a duchy called Harine until he arrived at Azur.

"I can sail," he said. "The weather shouldn't prove too rough compared to what I've already been through."

"True," said Nix. "But from what we hear, the strait is now guarded. Nothing gets in or out without passing by Mad'raast—another duke and a close ally of Prusias. You will never sail through without inspection."

Max grew increasingly frustrated and began scouring the map for spots along the coast, rivers, and lowlands that might provide an easier path than scaling the mountains or slipping through some toll or checkpoint. For each solution he identified, the vyes proposed a counterargument.

"You're just trying to keep me here," Max snapped.

"No," said Valya. "We're trying to prepare you for the realities."

"Let's assume you can even reach Azur," said Nix. "How will you defeat him? You have no weapon that could harm such a demon!"

"I do have a weapon," Max insisted. "I just need to get it fixed."

"Well, we know a blacksmith at the Crossroads," said Nix. "And there are dvergar in the mountains between here and Azur. You might ask them if you go that way."

Max shook his head. "I've already asked dvergar. They won't touch it."

"Then I don't know what to say," sighed Nix, sitting on the small chair.

The vyes sat patiently while Max tapped the map with his pencil and probed mountain ranges and coastlines for possible routes toward Azur.

"I'll try the strait," he concluded, glancing at the narrow opening. "I'll travel fastest by sea, and at least the strait will be the only barrier. Mad'raast is probably more concerned about what comes in than what gets out. Maybe I can slip through and sail north."

"So, let's be optimists," mused Nix. "Let's say all goes according to plan. What then?"

Max had no ready answer. His mind had been so consumed with abstract thoughts of vengeance or concrete realities of the farmhouse that he had not yet plotted his life beyond the moment of retribution. He doubted he would be welcome back at Rowan. He might seek out Connor, but he did not know where to find his friend's tiny barony. Of course, he could live quietly at the farmhouse, but this struck him as an irresponsible use of his gifts and training. Max had already tamed or slain the greatest threats in the valley; Nix and Valya could look after the farm and care for the growing household.

"I don't know," he admitted. "I'll have to cross that bridge—" Max paused at a sudden commotion, quick footsteps coming down the hall. There was a sharp knock and Mario's anxious voice from beyond the door.

"Max, come quick. Skeedle's here!"

Puzzled, Max hurried downstairs to find the goblin pacing anxiously on the doorstep.

"Don't tell me there's another troll," Max chuckled.

Wiping sweat from his brow, Skeedle shook his head and beckoned frantically for Max to follow him outside onto the porch.

"I didn't want to frighten the others," he whispered, "but trouble is coming, my lord. Trouble of the worst kind!"

"What are you talking about?" inquired Max, his smile fading.

"He knows the monster is dead!" exclaimed the goblin. "The monster that lived in the well!"

"Who knows?" asked Max.

"And he knows about the troll!" hissed Skeedle. "The *real* story . . ."

"Who are you talking about?" asked Max.

"He knows it was you!" shrieked the goblin, tugging at his hat brim. "You have to run!"

"WHO KNOWS?" yelled Max, taking hold of Skeedle's shoulders.

But the little goblin was incapable of answering. Fear had totally overwhelmed his senses, and he was reduced to hoarse, unintelligible gasps. Max repeated the question, but Skeedle merely sobbed and shut his eyes. A crowd gathered behind Max as Isabella and the children hurried over to see what the disturbance was about.

"Skeedle," said Max, softening his voice. "Please talk to me. Who knows I'm here?"

But the goblin had fainted.

Instead, another voice answered, in tones as rich and warm as pooling blood. "I do," it laughed. "And I bid you welcome to my kingdom!"

~ 20 ~

BLYS

Prusias emerged from a hawthorn's shadow like a barbarian king plucked out of time. His black hair looked leonine, and his black beard fell in ragged plaits across his broad chest. Seven feet he stood, but it was not his shocking height or girth that drew attention; it was the demon's eyes, which flashed in the light from the open doorway.

The demon appeared elated, his dark, rough-hewn face stretching to an exultant grin as he staggered forward on his cane, one arm held wide as though to embrace them all.

"Max," he cried. "Come down and greet your old friend Prusias."

A shiver raced down Max's spine as he digested the demon's glazed eyes, the compulsive licking of lips. Every limb trembled as though Prusias sought to restrain some horrific impulse.

"Don't move," Max murmured to the fear-stricken children standing about him on the porch. Steeling himself, Max walked slowly down the steps and onto the paved walk where Prusias was waiting. As soon as he came within arm's reach, the demon cackled and snatched Max to his chest.

Even through his corselet of black mail and silk robe, Prusias was blistering hot. He laughed with sincere pleasure, appraising Max like a delighted relative. But throughout the demon's jesting chatter and salutations, Max focused on one horrifying realization.

There was blood on his breath.

There was blood on the demon's boots, too. And more smeared the gloves that gripped Max's shoulder with such terrible strength. It was still red, still wet, as though Prusias had cut a murderous swath through the valley.

"Please don't hurt them," Max murmured, numb with fear. "They haven't done anything."

"Well, now," replied the demon with a dreamy smile. "That all depends on you. Are you going to invite me in or must I loiter outside like a beggar?"

"Of course not," blurted Max. "We would be honored if you would grace our home."

The demon leaned upon Max and his cane, his heavy boots crunching through the fallen leaves and up toward the house.

"My compliments to the lady," said Prusias, bowing to Isabella and holding forth a diamond necklace in his bloody fingers. She took it in her trembling hand, her eyes never leaving the exultant grin of the giver. "I daresay these adorable children don't all belong to you!" he laughed, glancing at the small figures backed against the walls.

With just the tiniest shake of her head, Isabella stood aside as the demon stepped over the inert goblin and ducked beneath the doorway. Lifting Skeedle, Max followed the demon inside and watched as Prusias hobbled toward the rocking chair by the fire. Easing into it, he laid his cane across his lap and looked about as though expecting the evening's entertainment to emerge from offstage.

His eyes fell upon Gianna's crib.

"May I see the baby?" he asked, beckoning greedily.

Isabella glanced at Max, who overcame every instinct and nodded. Scooping her daughter from her crib, Isabella crossed the room and handed the sleeping baby to the demon. Upon settling against his chest, Gianna stirred and began to cry.

"Shhh," cooed Prusias, his darkly handsome face hovering inches from the baby's. Removing his glove, he held out a finger, which Gianna dutifully clutched. The bawling subsided to sobs and then bewildered silence as she stared up at the grinning demon.

"May you never want," he murmured, kissing his fingers and touching them lightly to her forehead. While Prusias rocked the silent child, his eager eyes traveled about the room. They fell upon the enchanted spinning wheel, dutifully spinning fleece into yarn.

"A gift from the goblins," he observed, his eyes continuing to wander. They lingered on a harp and the blocks of paper bound with glue. Stacked upon the paper was a mug stuffed with pens and an ink bottle that had leaked upon the topmost sheet. "What have we here?" inquired the demon amiably.

"Nothing," said Max quickly. "The children like to draw."

Leaning over, the demon reached down and plucked a sheaf of papers from a stack on the floor. Sweat trickled down Max's neck as the demon perused sheet after sheet of alphabets and writing exercises.

Prusias intoned the commandment that Max had heard one year earlier. "Edict three: It is forbidden to teach reading, writing, or history to humans beyond Rowan's borders. Do you remember the penalty for violating this edict, young Max?"

"I do," Max muttered, closing his eyes. "And I beg that you will not invoke it. I beg you to be merciful and wise as a king should."

"Ho-ho!" the demon exclaimed, bouncing Gianna on his great knee. "How desperation makes you courteous. You know, Max, these aren't my rules but our lord's. And if he requires the execution of every man, woman, and child within a hundred leagues, what am I to do?" Prusias laughed and offered an apologetic shrug.

"This is your kingdom," said Max, scraping every reserve of calm. "You could ignore those pages or pardon them or forget you ever came here."

The demon chewed on this a moment, a wry twinkle in his hooded eyes. "Well," he purred. "I suppose one good turn would deserve another, and perhaps there is something you could do for me. Yes, yes, I think that would answer."

"What?" asked Max, both relieved and wary of any favor a demon might require.

"We'll talk on the road," muttered Prusias, rising to settle Gianna back in her crib. "You have a charming daughter," he remarked to Isabella. "She'll do very well."

Blinking suddenly, the demon shooed Max along as though he were late for school. "Pack your things," he muttered. "I wish to reach the palace by dawn."

Max hurried up the stairs, where he found Nix and Valya crouched upon the upper landing. Putting a finger to his lips, Max motioned for them to follow him down the hall to his room.

"I only have a minute," he hissed, emptying his pack upon

the bed. "Don't interrupt, and do exactly as I say. I need you to send the map, this little ship, and these metal shards to William Cooper at Rowan. Smuggle them or something, but make sure he gets them along with a note explaining what happened. Okay?"

Nix nodded and quickly slid the items beneath the bed. Valya helped Max pack everything else. Tying his bag's straps, Max stood and quickly embraced the pair before hurrying back down the hall.

Prusias was waiting by the door, tapping his cane and smiling pleasantly at his terrified hosts. The children stood ramrod straight, their eyes trained upon the demon's shadow, which writhed unnaturally upon the wall. Putting on his coat, Max turned to the many faces that now looked to him.

"Goodbye," he said. "Be good and look after Skeedle."

And with that, Max followed Prusias out into the night.

"This is a happy chance," chuckled Prusias, looping an arm around Max's shoulder and leading him toward the road. "Here I am scouring the lands for warriors and I stumble upon Max McDaniels hiding in my very kingdom! I blush at my good fortune. . . ."

Stepping onto the road, the demon took up his cane and rapped it impatiently upon the cobbles. There was an explosion of light, a plume of sparks, and cascading witch-fire that made Max start and shield his eyes. When he opened them, he looked upon a carriage, a gleaming black Berlin stamped with Prusias's royal seal. Four horses pulled the carriage, but they were not of flesh and blood, but billowing flame and smoke—spirits of fire forced into an earthly, animal shape.

A glass window slid open, revealing a small, anxious face.

"My lord!" sputtered a red-skinned imp, opening the door. "I thought you wished to travel inconspic—"

"Change of plans," muttered Prusias. "Mr. Bonn, say hello to Max McDaniels. He'll be accompanying us home."

"Oh!" exclaimed the imp. He bowed to Max before giving Prusias a knowing grin.

"Don't sit there smirking," scolded Prusias. "Max is our guest. Take his bag and let's be on our way."

In an instant, the apologetic imp had stowed Max's bag and helped him inside the Berlin, whose rich, spacious interior far exceeded its external dimensions. Sliding in after Max, Prusias sighed and reached for a handkerchief. Easing back, the demon mopped his brow and beard, grunting at the dried blood that he wiped from his mouth.

"How embarrassing," he chuckled, tossing it across to Mr. Bonn. The demon rapped against the carriage door with his cane, and the fiery horses bolted into motion.

For the first few minutes, Max sat in tense silence, watching flames race past the glass window as the carriage rocketed smoothly down the road. Prusias slouched low in his seat, his taloned fingers plucking at his mail sleeve while he poured a glass of whiskey from a crystal decanter. He offered it to Max, who quietly declined. With a shrug, Prusias leaned back and took a sip.

"That was bad business about your father," he rumbled. "Bad business indeed. Vyndra goes too far."

Max stared at the demon as he swirled and sipped his drink.

"So you admit Vyndra murdered him," said Max coldly.

"Admit?" remarked Prusias. "Of course I admit it. I feel responsible!"

"What does it have to do with you?"

"Vyndra wants my throne," said Prusias with a rogue's grin. "My beautiful city is infested with his spies and assassins. The nobles expect a civil war and are naturally trying to predict and align with the victor. Should Vyndra defeat someone of your reputation, it would weigh in his favor."

While Prusias poured himself another drink, Mr. Bonn cleared his throat and opened a leather case stuffed with official-looking papers and certificates.

"My king," said the imp. "While you've been away, matters of state have been piling up."

"Let's hear them, then," growled Prusias, rubbing his eyes. "And mind our guest, Mr. Bonn."

For the next hour, Max gazed out the carriage window at the purple blur of countryside. Now and again, yellow flames licked the glass and played about the edges of the pane, while Prusias replied to various petitions with a begrudging yes or an emphatic no.

When the imp reached for another stack, Prusias waved him off. Sitting up, the demon slid the glass window open so the night air could come rushing in.

"I remember when this road was made," muttered Prusias. "I've traveled it so many times, but I never tire of it."

"If you find it so enchanting, why are you tearing it all down?" asked Max bitterly.

"I'm not," the demon retorted. "In the capital, you'll still find many of the old things. I've just given them their proper scale."

"Why do you hate mankind so much?" Max demanded.

"If you believe that, you don't understand me," said Prusias. "I love mankind. Love everything about them. The passion, the energy, the emotions, the desperation to do something, to be something before death claims them in a few short years. Mankind is a fireworks show. There are days I wish I'd been born human."

Max scoffed.

"It's true," agreed Mr. Bonn. "I've heard him say it many a time."

"Immortality's overrated," purred Prusias. "It robs one of all urgency! Most mortals fail to understand that death's imminence is really a gift. Humans may fear me, Max, but I know them and love them. They will find no stronger ally among daemona. . . ."

Prusias's voice trailed off as the carriage came to a jarring halt. Mr. Bonn blanched under his master's glance and practically leaped out of the carriage to see what was amiss.

"What's the matter, Mr. Bonn?" Prusias growled. "Why are we delayed?"

The imp's frightened face appeared at the door.

"Those flowers again, m' lord," said the imp. "They're . . . everywhere!"

Prusias cursed and reached into an inlaid box for a silk kerchief. Pressing it tightly to his face, he snatched up his cane and slid his infernal bulk across the seat. Poking his head out after the demon, Max saw the spectral horses rearing uneasily, their manes tossing flecks of fire. Ahead, the road descended toward an ancient bridge, a crumbling span that arced across a gurgling stream. David's red flowers—thousands of them—fanned out from the banks, sloping up the hillside until they twined about the overpass, choking it like a noxious garland.

"What are those?" asked Max, feigning ignorance.

"Nothing," coughed Prusias. "A pestilential weed."

With a sweep of his cane, the demon destroyed the flowers in an immolation of golden flames. The twining stalks swayed in the heat, each petal hissing as the heat forced its poisonous sap to burst forth as from a blister. Prusias watched the bridge burn in silence, removing the kerchief only when the flowers and their vines were reduced to a smoldering lattice. There was a frightful gleam in the demon's luminous eyes when he returned to the carriage, and Max backed quickly inside and against the far seat.

At Prusias's command, the carriage lurched into motion once again, and the demon's mood gradually improved. He seemed almost childlike, sitting forward and glancing occasionally out the window as the sky brightened toward dawn.

"Have you visited the great city, Max?" asked Prusias. "Skulked about its borders or braved an inner ward since living in my lands?"

"No."

"Come here." The demon beckoned, motioning for the imp to move. "You can see it better from Mr. Bonn's seat."

Sitting in the imp's place, Max gazed out the window to see a morning sky of pale gold. The sun rose behind a series of hills, driving off the night mists and illuminating a city whose walls and buildings sprawled about the hills and valleys, stretching forth along the Tiber like a growing garden.

"Could you stop the carriage?" Max whispered, pressing at the glass. Cackling with delight, the demon accommodated him, and Max slid out to stand on the worn road and gaze upon a city that transcended his imagination.

In the morning light, the entire city seemed a sculpture, a smooth array of strange volumes and shadows, grand shapes that melted into one another at surprising junctions to form complex geometries or bizarre, organic shapes reminiscent of sea life. Throughout this mad jumble, however, Max could see unmistakable elements of human architecture—Chinese pavilions, Islamic minarets, Egyptian obelisks, massive domes and cupolas whose scale dwarfed their human antecedents. These and countless other buildings were piled upon one another, partially obscured by a smoglike haze.

The palace itself was of unimaginable scale. It was as if the

Palatine Hill had been raised up into a mountain, where terraced slopes and buildings all converged upon the massive palace that crowned the peak. A gargantuan pyramid served as the base of the palace, its shape blending gradually into something akin to an enormous replica of the Coliseum. From this second stage rose yet another structure whose inspiration must have been Notre Dame Cathedral. But this version of the Gothic masterpiece had been stretched, its verticality exaggerated beyond that of the original so that its tallest spires rose to unfathomable heights.

"And you thought we'd tear everything down!" laughed Prusias, delighted. "Come now, before they get news of us."

Max wondered at this remark, but it soon became clear. "They" were the countless human refugees who lived outside the city in sprawling tent communities and corrugated metal camps that littered what had been the Field of Mars and the Tiber's western banks.

Men, women, and children came running, thousands of them, in states of ragged squalor. They lined the roadway, pushing and jostling one another, crying out at the carriage that now raced along the road, scattering the stragglers. Faces passed in a blur, young and old, each marked with a singular desperation.

"Fortune!" they screamed, each straining to be heard above his neighbor. "FORTUNE!"

"Why are they yelling that?" asked Max, deeply disturbed by the spectacle.

"They wish a boon," sighed Prusias, drumming his knuckles on the window. "Pick one."

"Excuse me?" asked Max, blinking as the carriage raced on, leaving hundreds in its wake.

"Pick one," repeated Prusias.

"Her, I guess," said Max, pointing at an elderly woman in a black wrap.

The Berlin screeched to a halt, the flaming horses bucking wildly. The crowd surged forward, kept back only by the flames that licked the carriage's side. A crazed, frantic hope was stamped on each eager face as Prusias slid open the window.

"You there," he murmured lazily. "Not the brat, the woman behind."

A youth scowled and stood aside as a wrinkled crone hobbled forward, her hands clasped in supplication.

"Fortune!" she wheezed, a pitiable rapture on her unblinking face.

"Fortune is granted," cooed Prusias, showing his small teeth and patting the woman's hand. "Ease your worries, Grandmother. Mr. Bonn shall take your name, and you shall enter Blys this very day."

While the imp handled the details, the passed-over youth muttered something under his breath. Prusias's face darkened and he thrust his great head out the window.

"Stop that boy," he barked, gesturing angrily at several men. The youth was dragged before the carriage, his face pale but defiant.

"What did you say?" asked Prusias mildly.

"Nothing," replied the boy.

"Is that so?" wondered the demon. "I could have sworn I heard a hint of protest. Could this be?"

"No," said the boy, all defiance draining from him.

"Are you saying that I'm lying?" asked Prusias.

"No," said the youth, looking away.

"Are you saying that I'm mistaken?" Prusias inquired dreamily.

"No," whispered the boy, now trembling like a leaf.

The demon raised an eyebrow and glanced sideways at his assistant. "Mr. Bonn, at sundown, you will release ten vyes from my dungeons and let them prey among the human camps."

"NO!" yelled the boy.

"Make it twenty," said Prusias with a shrug.

"But—!"

"Fifty." The demon smiled. "The vyes may do as they will, but this boy is not to be harmed."

"Yes, m' lord," replied Mr. Bonn as smoothly as if he were jotting down a shopping list.

"Do you see?" asked the demon, wagging a clawed finger at the stricken youth. "Defiance and ingratitude reap no reward in my kingdom. Remember this lesson and perhaps one day Fortune shall be yours. . . ."

The window was closed and the carriage clattered on. Prusias settled down once again into his seat and yawned before making further observations about the city—various quarters and districts that Max might explore with proper escort. When the demon digressed into observations about his chef's latest dishes, Max broke in.

"So, you're just going to let vyes hunt among the people who are huddled at your gates?" he asked.

"Does that violate your delicate sensibilities?" inquired the demon, amused.

"It's barbaric," said Max. "Those people need you."

"And I need them," Prusias acknowledged. "But on my terms, Max. Always on my terms."

"What will happen to that woman?" asked Max, swallowing his outrage.

"She will enter Blys and live in the Garden District," Prusias explained. "She will enjoy a life of ease and plenty."

"So she's won the lottery," said Max. "All these people languishing in filth, praying for the 'Great Prusias' to stop and make their fortune."

"But that's what I do," laughed the demon. "Who suggested

that Cleopatra smuggle herself in a carpet? Who told Alexander to sever that knot? Who helped Drake ambush the Spanish? I've been making fortunes for eons, Max."

Max wanted to hurt the demon; he wanted to inflict pain upon Prusias as the demon had done throughout the centuries. It was a wild, sadistic impulse—a sudden, unblinking surge of emotion. Alas, words were his only weapons.

"I know why you walk with a cane," Max blurted, staring at Prusias's lame leg. "Bram broke you like a stick across his knee. He sent you fleeing out the window."

The demon's smile evaporated.

An unholy fire kindled behind Prusias's eyes, and for a moment, Max feared that he had made a terrible error. The demon gazed at Max from across the carriage.

But at length, Prusias shrugged. "Bram was a powerful Sorcerer," he acknowledged. "Good company, too, until he over-reached."

"What are you talking about?" said Max.

"I assume you learned of my injury at Rowan," mused Prusias. "Perhaps from Bram's very own account?"

"Yes," said Max, remembering the chilling excerpts he'd read of Prusias in the *Conjurer's Codex.*

"What did it say, I wonder?" said Prusias, a malevolent smile playing about his lips.

"It said that you possessed his servant," said Max. "That you meant to kill him until he discovered and broke you!"

"Is that his version?" exclaimed the demon. "That is telling! I'll have you know, Max, that I was there at Bram's bidding that evening. He needed my help, and in the midst of our conversation, his young servant entered and witnessed his master trafficking in forbidden arts. Your noble Bram brought madness upon the boy and cast me from the circle before curious parties could arrive. Remember him however you like, but Bram was the most ardent student of black magic I've ever met."

Max opened his mouth and shut it again. The demon sighed.

"It hurts to learn your heroes have a wart or two," Prusias observed wryly.

They rode on in silence, Max gazing out at the uneven shantytowns and lean-tos.

"Please don't loose vyes on the camps," he whispered. "Leave those people alone."

"That's why I love humans!" crowed Prusias, smacking his knee. "Whenever I focus on their faults, some noble impulse rears its head and shames me." The demon glanced keenly at him, as though weighing the moment. "Do you know what my favorite game is?" he asked.

"No," said Max.

"Quid pro quo," said the demon, playfully emphasizing each syllable with a tap of his cane. "You do for me, I do for you. For example, tonight will begin a series of games—spectacles for the populace. Since you refused to partake in the médim, you will partake in these. If you perform well, I shall be inclined to grant favors to the humans. If you perform poorly . . ." Prusias shrugged and grimaced to reveal his tiny, perfect teeth. "But you won't perform poorly," the demon concluded. "We shall have to disguise you, of course. Mr. Bonn shall see to all the details."

"I won't fight for you," snapped Max.

"You're not fighting for me," observed the demon smoothly. "You're fighting for them. . . ."

They were nearing the Tiber now and the broad bridge ramp that spanned the river. The ramp rose toward a towering stone disk upon which was carved the face of a bearded man whose mouth served as the main gate. There was something in the mindless eyes and hollow expression that Max found disturbing.

"The Mouth of Truth," remarked Prusias. "I was so taken with the original that I had it enlarged."

Through his window, Max gaped up at the stone face, its blank eyes staring ahead while its mouth stood open to receive them. Passing within the mouth, the Berlin entered a tunnel whose only light came from the fiery horses.

When they emerged on the other side of the wall, Max saw that the ramp had diverged. One causeway continued to the outer ring of the city—the Market District, Mr. Bonn pointed out. The second, however, continued to rise above the city, winding above the conical rooftops and chimneys toward the second series of walls. Max sat in silence, peering below at crowds of humans, hags, goblins, and vyes streaming about the squares and marketplaces in what might have been a Renaissance fair.

"There are humans here," said Max, astonished. "Lots of them."

"Certainly," replied Prusias. "Servants and craftsmen and artists, of course. I do love artists. My great city is a melting pot."

Max did not reply, but simply stared out the window at the gardens and gables below. He could feel Prusias's eyes boring into him, but the demon seemed content to ride in silence as the carriage swept along the royal road that arced above the city and passed beneath a rune-covered arch as heralds trumpeted the king's return.

When the carriage stopped, Prusias cleared his throat. "No one is to know you're here," said the demon pointedly. "Mr. Bonn will see to your accommodations and disguise. Your compliance and enthusiasm for the games will ensure the safety of the farmhouse and the human habitants of the city. Is that understood?"

The demon leaned forward so that his dark face hovered inches away from Max's. "We can help each other," Prusias whispered. "Become my champion and I'll help you get your revenge. Become champion and I will give you the means to slay Vyndra."

"And if I don't become champion?" asked Max.

"A pine box of your very own."

Soon the carriage came to a halt before a Mediterranean villa of pale stone. An iron gate loomed in front, and many cypress trees shielded the house. Mr. Bonn and Max stepped quickly to the street, and the carriage proceeded. Producing a key, Mr. Bonn unlocked the gates and led Max inside a garden of scented flowers and shade palms.

This same key unlocked a metal-plated door that bore many warding runes and glyphs. The carvings issued a faint greenish glow that lent a spectral quality to the stone, glass, and wood. Six attendants seemed to glide across the tiled foyer to stand at attention.

"The malakhim shall see to your needs and escort you from the grounds when you are summoned," said Mr. Bonn, handing the key to the nearest robed figure, who took it in a black-gloved hand. "You are not to leave this house without them. The consequences to the farmhouse and the refugees would be most severe."

When Mr. Bonn left, closing the door behind him, Max turned and faced the black-robed figures.

"Malakhim," he said, sounding out the word. "Is that what I should call you, or do you have names?"

None of the figures answered, but stood in a silent line of obsidian death masks.

"Which room is mine?" Max asked.

A gesture from one led him to believe that he was free to choose. When his additional questions failed to yield any answers, Max left the foyer and explored the mansion. The malakhim followed, their footsteps silent upon the tiles and rugs as Max crossed from a sitting room into a ballroom and a small library. The mansion and its gardens were as rich and luxurious as anything Max might wish. The cushions were soft, the artworks beautiful, the fountains soothing as the sun traced its arc across the sky.

It was late afternoon when one of the malakhim brought figs and olives on silver dishes. As it set down the tray, Max noticed something unusual. At first glance, he had assumed the malakhim were identical. Their masks were all a shining black with beautiful, almost genderless features. Looking closer, however, he noticed that this one's features were marred with slight cracks and deformities about its nose and mouth, It looked as if some great work had been vandalized.

He then discerned each of the malakhim's masks was marked by a unique deformity. One had a great gash at the mouth; another's eye socket was broken and cracked; six shrines of ruined beauty. A memory came to Max, and he found their name dancing on his tongue.

"Malakhim," he breathed, gazing at them. "But aren't the malakhim angels?"

The figures nodded.

"What are angels doing serving Prusias?" asked Max. "Why are angels in a demon's city?"

But the figures simply turned away.

The sun was setting as Max finished his supper, and shadows settled across the mansion. Standing on the terrace, he leaned out over the rhododendrons and orchids and lemon trees that perfumed the evening air. From out in the city, great gongs sounded. Bats were fluttering around the rooftops, and the air shimmered with spirits of air and fire, smoke and shadow. He was living in Blys, a city of demons, and it disturbed him to admit how beautiful he found it.

His thoughts were shattered by the sound of a distant horn—a discordant note that wrenched him from his reverie. He had heard such sounds on the mountainside and on the day of his father's death. Hurrying to his pack, Max took out his spyglass and trained its lens far out toward the western gate. There was activity there—a retreating surge of torchlight and dust as though the humans had stampeded from the walls like spooked cattle.

It was a full minute before he saw the vyes.

· 21 ·

THE RED DEATH

Breakfast consisted of a small, sweet fruit that Max had never seen before. Its flesh was pink like a grapefruit but had the firm texture of an apple. He sniffed it. Satisfied, he took a bite and chewed thoughtfully while the malakhim laid out a pair of dark breeches and a shirt.

"So, what am I to do?" asked Max, pacing about the mansion's great room. All six of the malakhim were assembled. Their impassive features and ongoing silence were oppressive. Max would have thought them specters but for the fact that they opened doors, their steps made footfalls, and the curtains swayed at their passing.

His question hung in the air, languishing without a response until a bell sounded. Two of the malakhim slipped out of the room and returned a minute later with Mr. Bonn.

The imp was dressed in finery of the court—a bright yellow jerkin and curling blue shoes that would have suggested something of the jester if not for the grave expression on his face. He bowed to Max and inquired after his well-being.

"I'm fine," said Max. "But I didn't have to sleep in the camps."

"Beg pardon?"

"The vyes," said Max. "Prusias sent them hunting among the refugees."

"Of course he did," replied the imp. "A ruler must make good on his threats."

"I thought he was going to grant the humans favors," said Max.

"Ah," said Mr. Bonn. "You'll have every opportunity to earn those favors. In fact, that is why I'm here. You've been added to the arena lists, and I am here to ensure you give a satisfactory performance."

"To ensure my victory?" asked Max suspiciously.

"Whether you are victorious is unimportant." The imp sniffed. "We celebrate the grand gesture. It is not sufficient to merely dispatch an opponent. Combatants must *entertain*, Master McDaniels. They must reveal the artistry in their souls. The médim should have taught you this. We will discuss this further, but our immediate concern is your disguise. Your identity cannot be known. We must therefore mask not only your face but also your shine."

"What does that mean?" asked Max. "I've heard that before."

"Daemona do not just perceive flesh and blood as humans do," said Mr. Bonn, "but also essences and auras. I don't know what you are, master, but you shine very brightly, and we must hide it lest you are recognized."

The imp motioned for one of the malakhim to bring forth a horned helmet of red steel. Its interior was lined with soft leather, but as Max pulled it on, it cinched uncomfortably tight against his skull, clinging to him like an octopus. The face of the helm was open, but Mr. Bonn soon produced a fearsome-looking faceplate.

The mask appeared almost Asian in origin, its painted features depicting some foreboding spirit—a tengu or oni. Like the helmet, it was also red, with the exception of Astaroth's seal, which was traced in fine white lines upon the forehead. There were no openings, no cuttings that would allow the wearer to see or breathe. Max pushed the mask and its repellent seal away in disgust.

"The king insists," grunted the imp. "I urge you not to disobey."

Max recollected the punishment Prusias had inflicted on the camps, and the vulnerable farmhouse mere miles away. Frowning, he snatched the mask from Mr. Bonn.

Max felt it come to life. It stirred in his hands, tugging toward the helmet as though by magnetic attraction. Twisting from his grasp, the mask attached itself to his face and plunged Max into darkness.

Max panicked as the air inside disappeared. Gasping, he lurched forward and caught himself against one of the malakhim, who eased him down upon a nearby divan.

"Just relax," urged the imp. "You will be able to see and breathe momentarily."

Max ignored him and wrenched at the mask with both hands.

"Only Prusias or I can remove it," explained Mr. Bonn calmly. "We cannot have you revealing your identity in a fit of pique or spite. When you are in the arena, this is how you must appear."

Max listened to his heart pounding in his chest. Gradually, he became aware that he was breathing, that air was somehow filtering through the mask.

Mr. Bonn was directing the malakhim to lay out a suit of light armor comprised of ornate red plates sewn to an underlying garment of black leather. "You will wear this suit and that helmet when you are in the arena and any time you are outside of this house. This armor will cloak your aura but offers little in the way of real protection. It will not stop sword, spear, or tooth."

"Lucky me," said Max.

The imp stepped back and folded his arms expectantly. Taking up the suit, Max slipped it on. Like the helmet, it adhered to his body like a second skin. Every inch of his person was covered, from his horned head down to his steel-tipped boots. Like nanomail, the suit was exceedingly light, but the helmet's weight still felt unaccustomed and alien.

"Excellent!" exclaimed the imp, walking around Max to observe him from every angle. "No face and no aura. Bragha Rùn will be just another combatant courting fame in the arena."

"Who's Bragha Rùn?" asked Max.

"You are," replied the imp. "That shall be your name in the arena. You should be honored. Lord Prusias chose it himself and it is a most fortuitous title."

"What does it mean?" asked Max.

"The Red Death."

Max walked to a large mirror by the door.

A demon was reflected in its surface, a nefarious thing with curling horns and a cruel, pitiless face. Upon his forehead, Astaroth's thin white seal shone like a brand, a mark of property.

"Your first match is this evening," said Mr. Bonn, coming over to remove the mask. It slid from the helmet, air rushing in as the seal was broken. The imp tossed the mask on the bed, where it stared emptily at the ceiling.

"And how am I supposed to *entertain*?" asked Max.

"You will demonstrate your daring and skill by refusing to attack your opponent until he has struck at you one hundred times," replied the imp. "If you earn the right to retaliate, you must end the contest with a single blow. This will mark you as an artist in the arena and spark your reputation."

"That's ridiculous," Max scoffed. "That's not remotely fair."

"Quid pro quo," recited the imp. "If you entertain the spectators, Prusias will grant the humans favors. If you fail, he will punish them."

And with that, the imp departed.

For the remainder of the day, Max wandered about the house. He eventually settled in the library. Most of the titles were written in the demons' spidery runes, but some were in Latin and Greek and even English. Max's eyes settled on one thick tome written by an imp named Calumny. The title consisted of two words: *On Humans.*

The reading fascinated him. Calumny was just an imp—no Spirit Perilous or fearsome rakshasa—but he had served many humans throughout the ages and had cataloged his observations. He might have been an anthropologist, as his remarks betrayed a belief that humans were animals defined by their inability to suppress their basest wants or to learn from history.

Innumerable case studies were cited. Despite the imp's irrepressible disdain and delight in misfortune, Max also detected a certain fondness for his subject, especially children. Calumny found children to be more transparent and honest than adults. If they wanted something, they simply took it and did away with clever rationalizations.

Max brooded upon Calumny's writings until he dozed off.

* * *

When Max awoke, the room was dark. Calumny's book had slid from his lap and lay facedown upon the tiles. By the doorway, a pair of lamps had been lit, and one of the malakhim stood like a tall, grim totem.

"What time is it?" Max asked, shaking himself awake.

In answer, the malakhim merely held up the blood red mask.

Within the hour, Max was bumping along in a carriage that wound its way down the tree-lined streets of his neighbors' mansions to the broader avenues that swept up toward the palace. Max felt absently at the mask that hid his face, plucked at the red, overlapping plates that encased his body. The malakhim sat on either side of him, their hands clasped complacently on their black robes. Max did not feel present; he felt he was observing his own life from a remote, hazy vantage.

This state of dreamlike languor continued even as the carriage was pulled up toward the looming palace, whose walls and spires were aglow with torches and spectral lights. The air vibrated with the throb of drums and hypnotic belyaël notes as carriages and palanquins surged toward the great gates for the evening's entertainment.

With a shout, the cloaked and hooded driver cracked his whip, urging the flaming horses off the main avenue and through a broad portico whose attendants stood aside to let them pass. The festive lights and noise grew distant as they galloped on a slow curve around to the far side of the monstrous palace.

Turning, Max saw the lights of the human camps winking far below on the Field of Mars. This was for them, he reminded himself.

Cooper would have scoffed at such sentimentality and demanded Max's focus. It had been months since Max had trained, much less fought. Flexing his fingers, he looked dubiously at his hands encased in their red-taloned gauntlets. He could not help but wonder if he was little more than a storied weapon whose edge had dulled. Shutting his eyes, he remembered back to his lessons within the Sidh. He recalled Scathach's voice from atop the towers whose battlements served as their training: "A true warrior does not see an opponent or even many opponents; he sees patterns. Combat is a dance. It is your dance. It is a dance of blood and death and glory. You make the pattern; you lead the dance."

Max blinked and sat up as the carriage came to a halt. An ogre came round the carriage and peered inside. One of the malakhim handed the grimacing creature a letter, and the ogre stepped aside as a pair of iron-plated doors creaked open on their massive hinges. With a snort, the spectral horses pulled the carriage into the palace.

Max soon glimpsed faint torchlight dancing on walls of rough-hewn stone. A sour, dank smell of mold and livestock flooded his nose. The tunnel led down into the bowels of the palace.

These gloomy tunnels, his strange costume, and his forbidding task preyed on Max's mind until the anticipation nearly became unbearable. Finally, he heard a familiar sound—the unmistakable ring of a hammer striking an anvil. The walls brightened, burnished to a red glow by the open fires and oppressive heat of a smithy.

Max was surprised to see the figure of Mr. Bonn standing patiently outside the carriage. The imp's diminutive size and festive outfit seemed garishly out of place against the hellish backdrop of gnarled dvergar and vyes hammering steel and plunging their works into quenching tubs that sent up squealing plumes of steam into the air. Consulting his timepiece, the imp shook his head and opened the door.

"You're late," he said, glaring at the malakhim. "Now we must rush. Young master, come along with me."

Max slid out of the carriage and, glancing around at his surroundings, saw that the dvergar had stopped working at their bellows and anvils to stare at him. Mr. Bonn quickly led Max toward the nearest smith, an ancient specimen wearing a worn and tattered apron.

"Sudri," said the imp, addressing the wizened thing. "This is the new entrant I spoke of: Bragha Rùn. Is his weapon ready?"

The dvergar nodded and turned to a barrel that contained a dozen swords of various shapes and sizes. From these, Sudri selected a slim longsword with a red blade and handed it carefully to the imp. Mr. Bonn thumbed its edge.

"It's sharp," he observed. "Are you sure it will meet our needs?"

"Aye," muttered the dvergar, mopping his brow. "She's sharp but brittle. That sword will shatter on the first hard blow."

"Did you hear that?" inquired Mr. Bonn, turning his brilliant eyes upon Max. "One blow is all this sword can manage before it is no more. If the time comes, you must strike true."

Max took the sword, testing its weight in his hand. It was a beautiful weapon, its hilt gilded and its pommel winking with rubies. It seemed pointless to put such artistry into a thing designed to break, but the dvergar were a strange, obsessive folk. Perhaps they could not bear to craft a thing of low worth.

Flanked by the malakhim, Max followed Mr. Bonn under a massive archway. Here the walls were smoother, the air less foul. Max imagined they must be within some outer reach of the pyramid. Turning down a corridor, Mr. Bonn led Max to a most unexpected sight.

It was a Workshop elevator pod.

The pod rested in a tubular column, a silvery egg floating

weightlessly within. Max had ridden in such pods before; they were the primary conveyance of the Frankfurt Workshop. His mind reeled with questions. Hadn't Astaroth done away with technologies such as this?

The imp chuckled. "A luxury, I must admit. Insufferable boors, but those Workshop people do serve a purpose. Lord Prusias delights in their toys. After you."

Once Max stepped inside, the doors closed noiselessly behind them and the pod began to ascend, accelerating until it reached a nauseating speed.

"You understand the challenge before you?" Mr. Bonn inquired.

Max nodded.

"Excellent. My lord instructs me to tell you that if you meet his expectations, he will grant one hundred humans entrance to Blys and deliver food and supplies to those remaining outside."

With marvelous fluidity, the pod slowed to a stop and hovered before a large, dark room whose rich trappings were lit by shallow bowls of phosphoroil. Beyond was a broad corridor.

A pair of ogres stood flanking a portcullis that had been lowered to prevent entry into the arena. Through the bars, Max gaped at the arena's size. It was several football fields across, surrounded by row upon row of seats and private boxes that rose up and up toward the twisting replica of Notre Dame, whose spires stretched toward the moon. There must have been a hundred thousand beings packed into the Coliseum. The faces were a blur. But it was the noise, like the purr of an engine, that dominated Max's senses. There was electricity in the air, a tangible buzz of anticipation.

Across the arena, a portcullis was raised and something ducked beneath the archway to step into the arena. Max leaned heavily against the bars and stared at his opponent.

It was a vye, but unlike any that Max had ever seen.

For one, it was far larger—as tall as an ogre and covered with sleek white fur. Far more peculiar, however, was the fact that the vye had two heads.

"That is Straavh," whispered Mr. Bonn, "the offspring of both ettin and vye. He hails from the far north, and he is brutal, young master. When my lord's emissaries sought him in his homeland, they say that bones littered the whole of the forest. Human bones."

Max turned to the imp.

"Know that the humans will pay a terrible price if you fail," muttered the imp, blanching.

Max stared grimly through the bars at Straavh, who now trotted toward the center of the arena, smashing the side of his battle-ax against his shield and entreating the crowd. Coming to a halt, the monster stood panting, his two heads glaring at Max's portcullis, which now ground into motion.

"Good luck," whispered the imp.

Max could not reply. His heart was racing; his face was sweltering from his breath, which came in hot, shallow gasps within his helmet. From somewhere, Max heard an announcer call the name "Bragha Rùn." There was a hush, as though the crowd was expecting the announcer to divulge the gladiator's exploits and history and perhaps inform the wagering. But no tales were told. The announcer merely repeated the name, and disappointed spectators hissed catcalls and threw coins at the oddsmakers.

Despite the arena's gargantuan scale, Max tried to keep his focus upon his opponent. Steeling himself, he walked toward the creature, who gazed down at him with haughty interest. They stood mere paces apart, Max coming only to the monster's waist. Upon closer inspection, Max saw that Straavh's two heads were not identical; the right was broader and almost boarlike in its visage, while the left was decidedly more wolfish. The pale fur about his muzzle was flecked with blood. Black gums peeled back to reveal a row of yellowed teeth.

A drum sounded. Three concussive beats and Straavh turned to face a royal box from which the golden seal of Prusias was stitched upon a purple banner. The king himself sat in the box's center, surrounded by imps and courtesans. Prusias nodded, and Max, echoing Straavh's example, dropped to one knee and bowed.

The drum sounded again, and the hushed crowd resumed its roar.

The match had begun.

Immediately, Straavh attacked with a vicious, sweeping stroke that Max sidestepped at the last instant. His reactions were slightly slower than he was accustomed to, and it was with a grim, resigned humor that he began his count.

One.

Straavh pressed his attack. Again and again the ax whistled down—merciless strokes intended to hammer or cleave as the monster sought closer quarters in which he might simply seize his quarry and dash him against the arena's red sands.

As the fight progressed, however, Max found his old skills returning. His opponent's every detail became clear: the dilated pupils, the foaming jaws, and Straavh's clumsy habit of over-lunging. . . .

Straavh's fortieth blow was a particularly violent stroke that sent Max sprawling behind one of the many marble pillars that were spread about the arena like triptychs. For a moment, Max retreated behind the pillar as Straavh advanced. The crowd jeered with pure disgust. Food and garbage rained down into the arena. A quick glance showed Prusias sitting impassively in his seat, stroking his beard.

This would not do, Max concluded. They would think him a mere coward. He would have to take more chances; he would have to lead the dance without yet going on the attack. He must be a matador and grin at Death even as it came to claim him.

Max stepped into open space. Straavh paused, cocking each head as his opponent saluted once with his flimsy sword and promptly tossed it aside. The monster's ice-blue eyes narrowed, and his conclusion was plainly evident in his evil sneer: His opponent was a coward and was begging for a quick death.

Straavh intended to oblige him. Raising his ax high, the monster took three running steps and aimed a decapitating blow.

The stroke missed badly. Its momentum caused Straavh to stumble and almost lose his balance. The creature wheeled around only to find that Max had been standing right behind him.

Even without a weapon in hand, Max dominated the fight from that moment forward. He advanced upon Straavh, circling and darting, taking unconscionable risks before slipping just out of reach. The crowd was laughing now, jeering at Straavh and applauding the bold, foolhardy newcomer. Max ignored the many cries; he focused instead on counting.

Eighty-one . . . eighty-two . . .

Desperation grew on Straavh's faces. His swings became increasingly wild and clumsy. Max made new patterns, pushing the monster backward without ever raising his hand to strike in kind. Straavh's hundredth stroke was a defensive swipe, a pitiful attempt to keep Max at bay. Halting abruptly, Max permitted the ax's lethal edge to come within a millimeter of his chin. The blow whistled past to the crowd's delight. Nobles stood to watch as Straavh staggered back against the arena wall.

Turning his back upon his opponent, Max walked to the arena's center with all the arrogance he could summon. His pace was slow, almost casual. Not once did he look back to see how Straavh would respond to the insult.

The crowd's response was immediate.

The cheering reached a frenzied pitch. If Straavh charged, Max would never be able to hear the approaching footsteps. But he refused to turn. Everything hinged upon bravado, the bold and fearless gesture. Marching toward his discarded sword, Max focused on the crowd. They would tell him all he needed to know.

One imp in particular caught Max's eye. Its master sat in one of the royal boxes, a bloated demon with a fanged, toadlike face. The imp, however, was a timid-looking creature and appeared to be a most reluctant spectator. Max watched it intently as he approached his sword.

Suddenly, the imp's eyes widened. With a spasm of sudden fear, it clutched the railing and turned away.

It was time.

In one seamless movement, Max seized up the sword, turned, and stabbed.

The blade met Straavh's shield, cleaving it in two and shattering even as its point pierced the monster's heart. Staggering forward, Straavh slammed against the cross-guard. The monster's two heads gazed down at Max with an appalled expression before it collapsed upon the sand.

As the crowd roared, Max stared at the body. His sword arm stung, but he felt utterly and electrically alive. But that excitement was tempered by guilt and even sadness. He had toyed with his opponent, utilizing his superiority to humiliate and destroy a foe for the purpose of delighting a crowd.

Max was dully aware of the announcer's voice rising above the clamor of the crowd. He heard the name once again: *Bragha Rùn!*

The crowd began to chant the name. The howling cries chilled his blood but stirred the Old Magic within him. Coins and flowers and other trinkets were tossed in the ring. Turning on his heel, Max walked purposefully out of the arena, ignoring the spectators' cries and pleas for his attention.

Mr. Bonn did not speak until they were safely in the carriage. When he did, his face was suffused with pleasure.

"Prusias was right," he cooed. "You're a natural."

Max's second match was scheduled for the following week. By then, Prusias's heralds and bards had spread word of "Bragha Rùn" to every corner of the kingdom. When Max met Prusias's challenge and dispatched of his foe in record time, vendors were able to charge exorbitant sums for the privilege of witnessing Bragha Rùn in the arena. Gamblers rushed to wager on this promising newcomer. Petitions rolled in to meet Bragha Rùn, to have him attend various affairs of state and private functions. These were universally denied, further fueling the air of mystery that enveloped this silent, artful killer. As Max's victories accumulated, his fame grew by leaps and bounds. Within two months, Bragha Rùn had become one of the most popular and intriguing topics in the kingdom.

But Max was not the only topic. There were reports of border skirmishes with Aamon's kingdom, and merchants complained incessantly of attacks on their trade. Whole fleets had been lost on the ocean with no survivors to tell the tales. And then there were those strange red flowers, popping up in old churchyards and along important trade routes.

One morning, Max was wondering about these very things when Mr. Bonn interrupted his thoughts with a question.

"Is something troubling you?"

"Excuse me?" asked Max, picking at a platter of food. The

imp had been savoring a cheroot, whose sweet smoke he conscientiously directed out the window. Putting it out, the imp came to sit by Max and followed his gaze out over the city.

"You're so quiet today," Mr. Bonn observed. "I'd come to enjoy our morning talks."

"I'm thinking about tonight's match," Max lied.

"Ah," replied the imp, selecting an olive. "Well, you know I'm forbidden to reveal the opponent. You'll find out soon enough."

"That doesn't matter." Max shrugged. "There are only three possibilities: Lord Rùk, the grylmhoch, or the other one—Myrmidon, is it?"

"Correct," replied the imp,

"Have you seen all the matches?" asked Max.

"I have."

"Whom would you rather face?"

"None of them," he quipped.

"I want Rùk," Max mused aloud. "If I'm ever to have a chance at Vyndra, it makes sense to fight one of his kind. Are rakshasa really so terrible?"

"Yes," said Mr. Bonn soberly. "They have eaten many souls."

"What do you mean, they *eat* souls?" asked Max, chilled by the very concept.

"Of course they eat souls," said Mr. Bonn. "All greater daemona eat souls—it's their primary sustenance. And don't look so outraged—it's no different than humans consuming meat or drink."

"But Prusias eats food," Max recalled. "He eats enough for ten."

"That's simply for pleasure," chuckled the imp. "An indulgence of the senses. Bread and wine do nothing to sustain a greater demon, much less allow it to evolve. A rakshasa could never have achieved its lofty state unless it had consumed thousands of souls. Most have been through *koukerros* dozens of times."

"What's *koukerros*?" asked Max, sounding out the word.

Mr. Bonn considered the question.

"When a demon has amassed enough life force—souls, typically—to evolve into a higher order of being, that sublime moment of change is called *koukerros*."

"So will you be a rakshasa someday?" asked Max.

"Not likely," said Mr. Bonn sadly. "*Koukerros* is reserved for greater demons. An imp cannot achieve it by himself and must be granted the initial honor by a high-ranking demon. This honor is very rare, as the senior demon must surrender a portion of their essence in the process. Few masters are willing to make such a sacrifice, and thus most of my kind remain locked in their state forever."

"Being an imp sounds kind of hopeless," said Max.

"Not entirely," said Mr. Bonn. "Some masters *do* grant *koukerros* to a favored servant. And then there is Patient Yuga. Every imp knows that happy tale."

"Would you tell me the story?" asked Max.

The imp nudged the plate of food toward Max. As he did so, something caught his eye and he pointed out the window.

"What manner of bird is that?"

Glancing outside, Max nearly choked on a grape.

It was David Menlo's bird. More precisely, it was one of two brilliant blue and yellow specimens that David had created beneath Brugh na Boinne when they had recovered the Book of Thoth. Amid the treasures of the Sidh, David had opened the book and spoken words of Making, fashioning the truenames that brought the delicate creatures into being. Max stared at it.

"Is it Old or New?" continued the imp.

"I couldn't say," said Max, glancing to see if the imp had registered his initial shock.

"Well, it is a pretty thing," Mr. Bonn concluded dreamily, tossing it a pinch of bread. Cocking its plumed head, the bird flew off with the blurry speed of a hummingbird.

"You were going to tell me of Yuga," said Max quickly.

"Yes," said Mr. Bonn, reaching for another cheroot. "Forgive me. As the tale goes, there had never been a more capable, steadfast imp than Yuga. She served her master for eons without reprieve. They say that at the beginning of each new century, her master promised to grant her *koukerros* when the century ended. But her master had no intention of honoring his pledge. When the time came, he invariably found fault where there was none and punished her for her impudence. Yuga's master was very powerful, but too blind to perceive her growing hatred and much too proud to fear her. And so Yuga, in secret, consorted with his enemies and struck a bargain—she would deliver her master into their hands if they would grant her *koukerros*. They agreed and the conspiracy began."

Max saw a gleam of pride flash in the imp's eyes and perceived the faintest trace of a smile.

"But Yuga's lasting fame stems from what happened next. Clever as she was, she convinced her master's enemies to grant her *koukerros* before she would lead them to him. In their eagerness, they acquiesced and the little imp became a demon true. What they did not know, however, was that Yuga had already sown seeds of treachery among them. She had convinced each conspirator that the others planned betrayal and intended to gorge alone upon her master. No sooner had they slain her master than they turned upon one another. The heavens shook, and when the battle was finished, four great daemona lay dying. As they were now too weak to resist her, Patient Yuga emerged from hiding to feed. So ravenous was her appetite, so potent her feast, that she soon became very great herself. And thus the story of Yuga teaches every imp that a bit of patience can be rewarded and that even a lowly servant may someday eclipse his master."

This last line ended on a happy, hopeful note. Visibly content, Mr. Bonn exhaled a masterful smoke ring and sent it scudding toward the gardens.

Crack!

The windows slammed shut.

Startled, Max and Mr. Bonn turned to see Prusias standing in the doorway, accompanied by all six of the black-robed malakhim. The king was smiling, but Max knew this was a grin to fear.

"Are we holding court, Mr. Bonn?" inquired the king, leaning forward on his cane.

The imp slid dejectedly from his seat and bowed low. "A thousand apologies, my lord. Your Bonn forgot his place."

Prusias stepped farther into the room, which darkened as though the sun had slipped behind a cloud. The king's smile remained fixed.

"Were we telling tales of Yuga?"

"Yes, my king. The young master was curious about *koukerros.*"

"And you thought that a story about a treacherous imp was the best means of educating him?"

"It was an unwise selection, my king."

Prusias's smile widened until it stretched taut across his broad, dark face. Mr. Bonn was trembling so uncontrollably that his teacup was rattling in its saucer.

"Perhaps, Mr. Bonn, you will allow me to worry about Max's education."

"Of course, my lord."

"Thank you, Mr. Bonn," said Prusias. "You may leave us."

"I am at my lord's service."

It was a pitiable sight. Still trembling, the imp bowed to Max and then to his master before walking stiffly out the door. Max saw Prusias glance at the malakhim. Some unspoken command passed between them, and they slipped out of the room.

~ 22 ~

A GREAT RED DRAGON

M r. Bonn did not accompany Max to the Coliseum that
evening. Max's only company was the malakhim. Max wondered
what the arena would have in store for him. Gazing out the
window, he reflected on how dangerous the matches had become.
He could no longer take his victories for granted.

Blys was already ablaze, every district from the ghettos to the
minor palaces awash with light and crowds, dense clusters of
revelers eager to partake in the atmosphere surrounding the
tournament's concluding matches. Max glimpsed a banner several
stories tall on which his likeness—or rather, Bragha Rùn's

mask—had been printed. The sight of Astaroth's seal upon his forehead nearly made him sick.

Just a little longer.

Easing round a bend, the carriage began the final climb to the back of the palace and the competitors' entrance. Once inside the gate, the malakhim escorted Max to where the dvergar were waiting in the smithy. Max approached them, expecting Sudri or his subordinates to hand him the weapon he was to use, as had become the custom.

This time, however, the dvergar indicated by word and gesture that Max was free to choose from among the dozen or so arranged before him. They spanned almost every class—a heavy bardiche, a flanged mace, and even a two-handed word as tall as he was.

Why these weapons?

Max doubted they had been selected at random. Examining them more closely, he saw that they were coated with a bluish metal he'd not seen before. It was used sparingly and only on edges and points. Max gathered that the material must be exceedingly rare and highly valued. He imagined his opponent's defenses must be very difficult to pierce.

Max lingered at a weapon that was a hybrid of sword and spear. It was tall and heavy, with a leaf-shaped blade some three feet long. It would do.

After riding up in the Workshop pod, he found an unfamiliar teal-skinned imp waiting for him. The officious creature did not bother introducing himself, but led Max swiftly down the hall to the empty waiting room. Bowing, the imp took his leave, and Max was left alone in the dark room, with its bloodstained pelts and bizarre, unearthly artworks. Several minutes passed before Max heard the announcer's voice. She spoke in the demons' language; the only parts Max understood were his name and the roar that followed.

Inch by inch, the portcullis was raised.

Max felt the familiar twitching in his fingers.

Taking up his spear, Max McDaniels emerged from the doorway's shadows and walked one more time into that arena where he had come to expect so much light, noise, and pain.

This was the only time he'd been summoned first into the arena. The experience was profoundly different. In the past, Max's opponents were already waiting and had provided him with an initial focal point. But now he stood alone in that vast space before the eyes and expectations of a hundred thousand spectators. He had never felt so isolated. A nervous dread hollowed his stomach as he stared at the opposite portcullis. Was Death lurking behind those bars?

Max shook off these thoughts, determined not to betray any doubts or weakness by stance or gesture. Gripping the spear, he stood as tall and proud as the image of Cúchulain he'd glimpsed in the tapestry so long ago. If this was to be his end, he'd meet it with both eyes open.

The announcer's voice droned on. Over the crowd, Max strained to hear the name of his opponent, sifting the words for anything approximating *Rùk* or *Myrmidon*. But he heard nothing of the sort. Instead, a curious migration began—a surge of spectators who abruptly abandoned the lower rows of seats and crowded into the aisles of the upper tiers.

Despite the activity in the stands, Max kept his focus on the far portcullis. It did not move. Instead, an entire section of the neighboring wall slid aside, exposing a vast black opening. Staring deep within, Max saw tiny winking lights that almost resembled the constellations in his bedroom at Rowan. But these lights were growing rapidly, as though on an approaching train.

When the grylmhoch rushed into the arena, Max knew that its origins were fundamentally from *someplace else,* some distant star or universe or hell.

The first comparison he made was to an enormous spider, for the monster had a cluster of many eyes amid the center of what passed for a face. Below these eyes were snapping mouths that appeared and disappeared spontaneously, as though the creature's bubbling, glabrous flesh created them at random.

Max realized it was pointless to compare this creature to anything terrestrial. Nothing in the monster's form remained a constant. Not even its *phase* appeared fixed, for there were moments when its dreadful bulk abruptly flickered and became translucent, as if some natural law rebelled against its presence in this world.

Within the grylmhoch's spherical eyes, there was no spark of animal intelligence. Its dozens of eyes stared unblinking about the arena.

While its appalling size and pale, squidlike coloration had the power to shock, it was the monster's movements that evoked true horror. The grylmhoch did not walk so much as slide about the arena floor, pushing aside cresting dunes of sand as it advanced using some slimelike substance that it secreted from its spreading underbelly. It had a host of legs and arms along with flipperlike appendages, tentacles, and pseudopods, but these seemed wholly inadequate for propelling such a mass. It seemed better suited to the ocean or even space.

Max involuntarily retreated a step and glanced at his weapon. How could a *spear* possibly hurt such a thing?

One by one, the pivoting eyes came to focus upon him. A scream issued from one of the grylmhoch's mouths—it was the scream of an afrit, a spirit of fire. Max had heard that sound once before when an afrit had escaped the Frankfurt Workshop's biological museum.

Why was the grylmhoch screaming like an afrit?

The answer soon became obvious.

As the creature slid toward Max, another mouth protruded and made a wholly different sound, the ferocious roar of some unknown creature. The roar transitioned to a weird, subsonic hum followed by a repulsive chittering.

The monster was mimicking sounds it had heard. Were they some mindless echoes of past victims or some bizarre attempt at communication? Max shuddered as a woman's hysterical voice issued from the abomination.

"Send someone right away! My husband has done something terrible."

The crowd cheered wildly as Max stood his ground, failing to realize that he did so from complete shock. The monster loomed over him, bigger than a house. As Max stood, transfixed, the grylmhoch formed a fleshy pseudopod and extended it slowly like a probe. The appendage halted some four or five feet away from Max's face, its skin boiling and bubbling with pustules. To Max's horror, these pustules formed a mouth—a squashy circle of puckered flesh that yawned wider as razor teeth pushed through its pale pink gums.

Revolted, Max overcame his shock and swung the weapon.

As the blade met the grylmhoch's flesh, Max felt an electric jolt that raced up his arm. The edge sliced cleanly through the pseudopod, cutting it in half. The severed portion thudded onto the sand, its mouth snapping blindly about, while the remaining stump withdrew slowly into the monster's body.

Max backed quickly away from the severed, snapping mouth at his feet. Its flesh began to bubble once again. Dumbstruck with horror, Max gaped as the flesh reshaped itself into a man-sized version of the grylmhoch. With a squeal, it rushed at Max, who leaped aside just as its full-sized parent sent several more pseudopods toward him.

The crowd yelled as one of these pseudopods seized Max in midair. Its still-forming mouth clamped onto his left wrist. Its hold was surprisingly soft, until Max felt a sudden, enormous suction. In an instant, his arm was enveloped up to the shoulder by squelching, pulpy flesh that reeled him steadily toward the tooth-lined abyss that was forming in the monster's midsection.

In his free hand, Max gripped the spear. With terrified desperation, he cleaved it down upon the pod that had engulfed his other arm. There was no time for precision; he could only hope that he would not cut himself.

He experienced another electric jolt, followed by a sensation of falling. Crashing to the arena floor, Max found that he still possessed both his arms but one remained encased in the grylmhoch's pulpy, living flesh. He tore frantically at the rubbery tissue, peeling off squirming chunks and flinging them away from him.

With chilling patience, the grylmhoch hunted Max from one end of the arena to the other. Like the troll, it pursued him with a mindless determination. But unlike the troll, the grylmhoch did not seem to tire. It moved no faster than a jog, except that it could maintain this pace indefinitely. Throughout its patient pursuit, it never ceased making alien cries or frantic pleas in a host of languages.

And yet Max could not focus solely on this carnivorous mountain, for he had lopped away four more pseudopods, which had also formed into miniature offspring and joined the others in pursuing him about the arena.

The smaller the offspring, the faster it moved. Whenever Max was able to evade the gargantuan parent and race to the arena's opposite end, its spawn was already in swift pursuit. Forced to defend himself, Max invariably cleaved the things into ever-smaller pieces, which swarmed like ravenous jellyfish while the methodical grylmhoch bore down once again.

The crowd delighted in his anguish. He had never heard the arena so loud. Coins and flowers rained down upon the arena floor as Max ran, panting, toward the other end. His helmet was insufferably claustrophobic. His lungs felt scorched. Desperate to catch his breath, Max sagged against the bars of the portcullis. He had not rested for more than a second or two before he heard an eager squeal.

Turning, he saw the smallest and swiftest of the things catching up to him. Too weary to muster a full swing, Max transfixed it on the spear and let the heavy blade's weight bear the flailing thing to the ground. Again, he felt a mild shock as the weapon delivered its electric charge. Instead of simply removing the spear as before, Max allowed it to deliver multiple jolts. A hideous smell filled Max's nose, akin to burning hair.

The spawn stopped moving entirely.

There was no time to marvel, for the others were soon upon him. Using his weapon's handle as a bludgeon, Max knocked the creatures back, stunning them until he could destroy each with a fatal dose of electricity. Within five furious minutes, their still forms littered the arena.

But despite this momentary triumph, the grylmhoch remained.

And as exhausted as he was, Max found that the colossal thing was now gaining on him. Despite Max's previous blows, the creature appeared utterly unharmed. No scars or stumps marred its pale, fleshy whole. Eyes and mouths continued to form at random as it slid across the arena, pursuing Max while it methodically enveloped and devoured its lifeless offspring.

It could seemingly do this forever; Max could not.

Staggering to the arena's center, Max turned and tried to gather his wits. In the stands, many of the spectators rose to their feet as though anticipating a climactic finish. The Coliseum hushed as though the crowd held its collective breath. Over the past two months, they had seen Bragha Rùn cleave shields and shatter swords, but his unique appeal lay in the possibility that he might do something that the crowd had never seen before. These moments were as unpredictable as they were dramatic, an explosion of raw rage and power that utterly overwhelmed an opponent and often brought the match to a sudden, spectacular finish.

Behind his mask, a grim smile spread across Max's sweat-drenched face. He knew what they were hoping for, but it was not to be.

Sorry, folks. No more rabbits in the hat. I'm all tapped out.

Max would have given anything to tear off the mask and fling it away. If this was to be his end, he wanted to see the stars and breathe the night air without its unwholesome filter.

Max wanted the crowd to know who had been behind the mask.

Taking up the spear, he resolved to make a final charge. He took five running steps before planting his foot to spring. He felt that wonderful, momentary weightlessness as his body soared ever higher. The grylmhoch's many eyes followed his trajectory. Mouths formed, great yawning maws that could have swallowed a bulldozer. Carrying just past them, Max plunged the spearhead into a glossy eye some eight feet across.

The point slid smoothly through the pupil.

And Max's world exploded.

In a spasm of pain, the grylmhoch flung him halfway across the arena. Crashing upon the hard-packed sand, Max felt several ribs crack. There was a ringing in his ears, but he could still register the wild screaming of the crowd.

Rolling onto his side, Max recovered his wits slowly. Despite his blurry vision, he perceived that the grylmhoch was advancing with the steadiness of an ocean liner. Still dazed, Max reached distractedly for his spear.

But it was gone.

Squinting, Max spied the spear still protruding from where the enormous eye had been. That eye had been withdrawn, apparently churned back into whatever alien matter constituted the creature's essence. Now there was merely a bubbling expanse of vascular white tissue that puckered about the weapon's shaft. A moment later, the spear was absorbed into the grylmhoch's body like a splinter.

For a moment, Max simply watched it come closer. He could not fight such a thing. While Max was battered and disarmed, the monster did not even appear tired, much less wounded. An ugly temptation reared its head.

Lie still. Lie still and it will soon be over. . . .

But something in Max smothered that thought. It came from someplace deep—Max could not decide if it was the Old Magic or something else, something profoundly human. Digging his fingers into the sand, Max pushed himself up.

The crowd roared as Max regained his feet. He backed unsteadily away from the monster until he found himself pinned against one of the arena's high, enclosing walls. But even as the grylmhoch was closing in on him, Max suddenly noticed something peculiar about the crowd.

At the match's beginning, the majority of spectators had abandoned the lowest rows of seats as soon as they'd learned that Bragha Rùn would face the grylmhoch. It was a sensible decision— why would anyone stay within reach of so huge and mindless a thing? But in one of the lower sections, the spectators remained. He could see them across the arena, occupying the first rows of seats just beneath the royal box.

Why hadn't they bothered to move?

There must be some reason why they felt safe despite their proximity to the monster. . . .

But that monster now loomed above Max. Its writhing white mass was framed against the ink-black sky and the twisting spirals of the cathedral far above. A pair of pseudopods whipped toward Max. Exhausted, he could barely duck as they smashed into the wall behind him. Scrambling to his feet, it was all he could do to run.

He staggered toward the royal section, his heart and lungs ablaze as he whittled away his final reserves of energy. He could hear the grylmhoch's squelching, droning pursuit but refused to turn around. Instead, he kept his attention riveted on Prusias, the surrounding nobles, and the spectators shrieking beneath them.

And then he saw it.

The object was hanging some twenty feet up the wall face, its dull appearance inconspicuous against the rich hues of Prusias's banner. It was a stone seal some two feet in diameter that had been etched with a crude sign shaped vaguely like a star. Max had never seen it before. Did it exert some influence over the monster?

Too exhausted to jump, he would have to climb and scrabble to reach it. Gasping, he sank his fingertips into the soft mortar, determined to reach the stone.

As Max climbed, the grylmhoch continued to close. All too soon, its shadow began to envelop him. Frantic, Max tried to redouble his efforts, but he simply lacked the energy. He would never reach the stone in time.

But then something curious happened.

The grylmhoch appeared to have stopped.

Glancing over his shoulder, Max confirmed it. The monster had halted some fifty feet away as though it had reached some invisible barrier. Its roiling eyes were still intent upon him, but it would come no closer. Instead, it bubbled and screamed, its appendages searching for some other way to reach its quarry.

As the thing lingered at this apparent threshold, its physical state flickered with a greater intensity. Max could now see through the monster, glimpsing hazy patches of the arena beyond. Gritting his teeth, he resumed his slow, painful progress toward the dull, greenish stone.

The seal's crude star was worn and weathered, suggesting that it had been carved eons ago. Unhooking it from its iron chain, Max took a deep breath and dropped down to the ground.

Max landed on the sand and his legs nearly buckled, but he propped himself against the wall. The grylmhoch abruptly ceased its gibbering speech and sprawled upon the arena floor like some beached abomination. Staggering toward it, Max hoisted the tablet aloft so that the strange, star-shaped sign faced the flickering monster.

The flickering intensified to a blur as Max approached.

When Max had arrived within an arm's reach of the quivering creature, the stone grew unbearably hot and issued a pulse of white light.

In a blink, the grylmhoch was gone, banished to some alternate world or plane of existence.

Dropping the heavy stone, Max collapsed onto the sand.

He awoke upon a table in a dim, candlelit room. Moaning softly, he felt about with his fingers and struck some sort of ceramic bowl. An herb-scented liquid sloshed over its side, wetting his arm. Some gentle hand sponged the liquid away before guiding his arm back to his side. Glancing up, Max expected to see one of

Rowan's kindly moomenhovens, but instead he saw the cracked, sorrowful masks of the malakhim hovering over him.

"What . . . ?"

Memories of the grylmhoch, of his broken ribs came flooding back. In a daze, he sat up and scooted his legs off the table, knocking several bowls and metal instruments to the floor.

Was he on an operating table?

Clutching his side, Max felt his naked skin and half expected to find a gaping wound. But there was no wound; no pain, either. Confused, he stared at the silent malakhim, who were dutifully cleaning up the mess he had made.

"Am I dead?"

He spoke the question aloud, his voice hoarse and low.

To his surprise, someone answered.

"No, my boy. You're very much alive."

Turning, Max saw Prusias sitting in a deep chair at the far end of the room. The demon's eyes were mere slits as he casually sipped champagne.

"How do you feel?" he asked.

"I feel . . . fine," said Max in quiet astonishment. Looking down at his torso, he saw no bruising, no blue-black wreckage of his ribs. There was only smooth skin and the faintest trace of a thin scar along his left side. "Is that from me?" he asked, gesturing at a small pile of bloodstained towels.

"It is," said Prusias. "Touch and go at first, but you are resilient."

"Where are we?" asked Max, gazing about the room.

"The Coliseum," Prusias replied. "The malakhim were afraid to move you."

"How long have I been here?"

"Almost two days."

"And the grylmhoch?" asked Max.

"Gone," Prusias chuckled. "To the relief of all, I think . . ."

"Where did it go?"

"Back to Astaroth," said Prusias with a charming shrug. "Back to Astaroth" had become a popular expression in Blys, another snippet of propaganda suggesting that the Demon was the divine singularity. In the grylmhoch's case, however, the phrase seemed a literal possibility. As Prusias sipped his champagne, his eyes twinkled. "How did you realize the Sign could help you?"

Max told him, and the demon thumped his cane upon the floor.

"Good!" he exclaimed. "You cost me a fortune, but I can hardly begrudge it."

"Why did I cost you a fortune?" asked Max.

"I bet against you," said Prusias, grinning like the Cheshire cat.

"I thought you wanted me to win," observed Max coldly.

"Of course I do!" laughed the demon. "But that doesn't enter into it—not against a grylmhoch! Your draw was the unlucky one. Lord Rùk and Myrmidon had an easier time of it."

"Who won?" asked Max.

"Alas," said Prusias, "Lord Rùk has also gone back to Astaroth. . . ."

"So I'm to fight Myrmidon for the championship?" asked Max.

"That depends on two things," said Prusias. "Whether you feel up to it and whether the committee elects to disqualify you."

"Disqualify?" Max exclaimed. "Why would I be disqualified?"

"Some claim that you broke the rules," said Prusias. "Your critics have submitted a petition, contesting that you did not actually defeat the grylmhoch. They maintain that you merely found a clever means to flee from your opponent before it finished you."

"What do you think?" Max demanded, his face flushing angrily.

"You should not care so much what I think," said Prusias easily. "You do your critics too much honor, Max. It's an easy thing to sit off to the side and point." Raising his glass, the demon recited in his stentorian voice: '*It is not the critic who counts; not the man who points out how the strong man stumbles, or where the doer of deeds could have done them better. The credit belongs to the man who is actually in the arena, whose face is marred by dust and sweat and blood. . . .*' Do you know who said that?"

"No."

"An American president by the name of Teddy Roosevelt," said the demon. "Energetic fellow . . . consulted me on Panama. Never openly acknowledged what I was, but I think he knew."

"Why are you telling me this?" asked Max quietly.

"Because you're not a timid soul, and I won't have you act like one," said Prusias, rising from his seat. The malakhim stepped aside as the great demon approached the table. "You've faced many a worthy foe in the arena and yet you quail at *critics*? My boy, they aren't fit to say your name."

"So how will the committee rule?" asked Max.

"That might depend on you," said Prusias, cocking an eyebrow. "Do you *want* to fight this last match?"

"I don't do what I want," said Max bitterly. "I do what I have to. If I don't fight, what will you do about Vyndra?"

Prusias shrugged. "Nothing," he said simply. "I'd do nothing to help you. Why would I?" He almost chuckled at the thought. "My assistance with Vyndra is contingent on your becoming my champion. I've never said otherwise."

Max reflected angrily on the matches he'd fought. "But I've already—"

"Earned rewards for which you've been paid," interrupted Prusias sharply.

Closing his eyes, the demon paced slowly around the room, his voice rising. "In payment for your victories, I have given one thousand people sanctuary within the city walls, supplied the human camps, and forbidden the vyes to prey upon them. I have placed those who live at your farmhouse under my own protection. And yet you cry injustice!"

The demon fell silent but continued pacing. Upon the wall, his huge shadow writhed and twisted about, resembling a nest of flailing serpents.

Max's eyes flicked from the shadow back to its owner. There were times when the demon's appearance and jovial manner almost tempted Max to think of him as human—or at least *mostly* human.

But he was not human, Max reminded himself sternly. Prusias was something else entirely. And as Max stared again at that terrible shadow, a passage flashed like fire in his mind: "And behold, a great red dragon!"

He could not remember when he'd first heard those words, but they triggered a deep, nebulous fear. For this dragon was not some storybook lizard that dined on maidens, but an ancient evil. One that devoured nations.

Gradually, the shadow's movements grew less wild. When Prusias finally opened his eyes, his tone was genial once again.

"I'd say quid pro quo has been the basis for a rather successful partnership. Without it, our relationship depends on mere charity. I don't do charity, Max—it's not my style. So, let's keep things simple: You help me, and I'll help you."

Max considered these words. He was so close to getting what he wanted, so close to gaining a chance at revenge while helping others in the process. It was just one more match. He had already fought so many.

"Do you think the committee will disqualify me?" he asked.

At this, the demon actually laughed.

"Max," he chided. "Don't you fret. I *am* the committee."

"Okay then," said Max. "I'll do it."

"Excellent!" exclaimed Prusias. "That's all settled then. We'll announce that the championship match will be held two weeks from today—Mr. Bonn can see to all the details. In the meantime, let's get you something to eat. You'll need all your strength if you're to tackle Myrmidon!"

~ 23 ~

MYRMIDON

Two weeks later, Max stood gazing out the uppermost window in his silent mansion. A cold spell had descended upon Blys, bringing a torrent of snow and wild gusts that came screaming past the window. Max pressed his forehead against the cold glass. The streets below were teeming with activity. Despite the inclement weather, the city's residents were gathering in district plazas or along the broad avenues to celebrate the great tournament, which would conclude that evening.

There was a knock at the door and Max turned to see Mr. Bonn. The imp was holding Bragha Rùn's helmet.

"Aren't you early?" asked Max.

"The streets are icy," replied the imp. "And there will be even larger crowds than usual."

"What are the latest odds?"

"Three to two," Mr. Bonn reported briskly. "You're still favored, but the odds are dropping due to rumors you're injured. A vast sum was wagered on Myrmidon just this morning."

"Did you place a bet?" asked Max with a wry smile.

"I'm not allowed." The imp shrugged. "I have inside information."

"How *would* you wager, Mr. Bonn?"

Crossing the room, the imp gazed up at Max with a solemn expression. His small face still bore evidence of his punishment, but the welts were healing. Raising the fearsome helmet, he offered it to Max.

"Despite my station, you've always treated me with kindness and respect," said Mr. Bonn. "If I could, I'd bet on you."

"Even against the grylmhoch?"

"Yes, sir."

Taking up the helmet, Max sighed. "Mr. Bonn, you're a loyal friend, but you'd make a terrible gambler."

The malakhim were already waiting outside with the carriage. By the time they had arrived atop the mountain and its uppermost palaces, the hills below seemed alive. All of the avenues blazed with lighted carriages and torches streaming toward the palace as though lava flowed uphill.

On the evenings when he fought, Max had grown accustomed to hearing his name shouted in the streets or from the gabled rooftops. But tonight, the thousands of revelers called another name, chanting it with a wild, maniacal enthusiasm.

"Astaroth! Astaroth! Astaroth!"

The Demon's seal was not merely etched on Max's helmet,

but stamped upon a thousand banners and pennants that fluttered from the city spires. It had been almost two years since Max had surrendered the Book of Thoth, two years since he had seen the Demon in person. Would he see him tonight?

The carriage slowed to a halt, and Max saw that they had reached the smithy. Tonight there were no dvergar or forges or weapon racks. This would be the final match, and it appeared that the dvergar had packed up their equipment. The only furniture remaining in that vast, empty space was a worktable bathed in a lantern's golden light.

Upon that table lay a spear. Not a huge, heavy weapon such as Max had used against the grylmhoch, but a shorter variety with a sharp, leaf-shaped blade. Taking it up, Max turned and bid Mr. Bonn farewell.

"D-don't you want me to ride up with you?" asked the imp.

Max shook his head.

The imp seemed to understand why and simply bowed. "It has been my honor."

After leaving the pod, Max counted the steps to the arena's threshold, timed them to the steady beating of his heart. At this moment, that heart was all he wanted to hear—it would be his drum, his cadence when he stepped into the arena.

Still, it was hard to ignore the crowd. Their cries echoed in the vast hallway and sent dust raining down in little streams. Clutching the spear, Max arrived before the portcullis and stared at its black bars like a caged animal. He wanted them to rise and release him one last time.

When the announcer finally said his name, there came that wild, intoxicating roar.

The portcullis rose and Max stalked into the arena.

His opponent was already waiting at its center.

Myrmidon was equipped in the classical fashion as a Roman murmillo and wore a high-crested helmet of bluish steel whose dense visor obscured his face. Upon that helmet was the white seal of Astaroth and thirteen slashes that Max took to represent his victories during the tournament. While his entire body was covered with black cloth, only the gladiator's left side was armored with scalloped plates of the same bluish steel as his helmet. Upon his left arm, Myrmidon bore a shield—a curving, rectangular scutum. Within the glove of his right hand, he gripped a traditional gladius.

Max embarked immediately upon the grim calculus that had become second nature: His spear offered more range; Myrmidon had better armor, but the gladiator's right side was vulnerable to a counterattack; his foe tended to rock forward, indicating an aggressive nature. . . .

Only one variable came as a surprise: Myrmidon was the smaller of the two.

Max found this strangely unnerving. In every previous battle, he had been the smaller combatant—often by hundreds or even thousands of pounds. Scathach had taught him to embrace such imbalances; he could simply impose another pattern, one that favored him.

Physically, a larger opponent could perhaps overpower him, but Max had always been quicker. Furthermore, a smaller combatant could often intimidate a larger one. When faced with a smaller, yet undaunted opponent, the larger party often seemed to hesitate, as though wondering, *What terrible trick does this little thing have up its sleeve?*

These doubts could play havoc with the mind, and Max chafed at the very idea he might fall victim to the same misgivings. Even so, it was impossible not to wonder how this gladiator had advanced so far in a tournament riddled with so many fearsome and experienced foes. He stared at Myrmidon, reconsidering every detail of his adversary's weapon, armor, and stance.

Myrmidon stared right back.

Max pried his eyes away, as custom dictated that the combatants face the royal box. There was Prusias, the king, standing to issue some sort of tribute or benediction. Max was not listening.

There were no vyes in the stands, no hags or cheering goblins. The tournament's finals were for the elite, and only nobles, wealthy merchants, and visiting dignitaries were in attendance.

Among these visiting dignitaries, Max spied a delegation of witches. All were robed in black and bore the dense tribal tattoos that had made such an impression upon him when he'd first met one. At their center, Max glimpsed Dame Mala, the matriarch of her clan.

The Workshop was also present. Their representatives were seated in a neighboring box, Dr. Rasmussen's hairless head shining conspicuously under the glaring lights. The humorless engineers seemed out of place amid the crowd's commotion. They might have been attending a laboratory experiment.

Despite the event's prominence and the extraordinary demand for tickets, one section remained nearly empty. It was the grandest of the royal boxes, an array of large and luxurious seats that Prusias normally claimed for his personal use.

On this occasion, however, it had been reserved for another.

Gazing up, Max saw that Astaroth's banner had been hung from its railing. And this was not the common standard of red silk bearing Astaroth's white seal. Such things were ubiquitous. The colors on this banner had been reversed and displayed a red seal upon a white background.

Only Astaroth employed this design.

Max searched for the Demon himself. But Astaroth was not

present—at least not in any visible form. Instead, a lone figure sat in the midst of the otherwise empty box. The figure was small and unobtrusive, and Max's temper flared upon seeing him.

For it was none other than Mr. Sikes, the cruel and clever imp who had played such a pivotal role in Astaroth's rise to power. He sat perfectly composed, immaculate in his tailored suit, while he surveyed the arena with polite expectation. Max fought a sudden urge to attack him on the spot.

The ceremonial aspects of the match were reaching their conclusion. As was the custom, Max raised his spear in response to Prusias's salute. In his peripheral vision, he saw his adversary do likewise, and a sudden, horrific thought occurred to him.

Was Myrmidon merely Astaroth in disguise?

The idea seemed a very real and terrifying possibility. After all, Mr. Sikes was here as a spectator, but his master was nowhere to be found. Furthermore, the Demon was roughly Myrmidon's height and build. And finally, Astaroth's participation would certainly explain how such an ostensibly unimposing gladiator had reached the championship match. . . .

Staring at his opponent, Max suddenly and savagely *wanted* it to be Astaroth. The Demon was the source of all their problems. Without Astaroth, humans would not have to languish in fear and servitude while demons transformed the world into their own hellish fiefdoms.

The Old Magic was now surging, howling, straining within him.

When the last drum sounded, it burst.

With a speed and brutality yet unseen, Max hurled himself against his foe. His spear crashed against Myrmidon's shield. His opponent retreated a step, but the shield remained whole.

Even though it had been blocked, the impact of this opening salvo rang like a thunderbolt and sparked the crowd into an excited buzz. It had been an uncharacteristically furious opening assault from the famous gladiator.

Again and again, Max hammered at his opponent in a blitz of expert thrusts, jabs, and slashes that effectively transformed his single weapon into many. Neither gladiator seemed interested in choreographing a dramatic entertainment. No tactics were employed for their decorative effect as was common in the arena. In this match, every attack and defense had been stripped of artistic flourish and distilled down to its brutal core.

Max's helmet was a furnace. Sweat poured down his face, stinging his eyes as he pressed the offensive at a relentless pace. The metallic clash of spear striking against shield and sword intensified until it rivaled a machine gun's staccato. Skilled as this opponent was, Max was steadily registering his patterns. Momentarily, he would expose his unarmored side, and there would be an opening. It would appear for only an instant, but then—

With freakish speed and control, Max shifted his weight and spun about on his heel and prepared to drive the spear beneath his adversary's outstretched arm.

Myrmidon's unprotected heart was just inches away.

With a roar, Max unleashed the measured stroke that had finished Straavh. As before, the feat required him to focus every iota of strength and will upon the lethal point of his weapon. When it struck, it would end the fight.

But with a dexterity and swiftness that shocked even Max, his opponent leaped backward and put enough distance between himself and the razor point that he caught it again upon his shield.

The blow did not destroy Myrmidon, but the impact sent him hurtling backward over the sand, and he crashed into the arena wall. The collision was enormous, bringing even the most jaded observers to their feet. Coins and flowers came raining down into the arena, along with calls for Bragha Rùn to finish him.

Max could have done so, for Myrmidon lay in a crumpled heap against the wall. But he would not pounce upon a fallen adversary—not even if this were the Demon himself trying his hand in the arena.

Long seconds passed before Myrmidon began to stir, but stir he did.

Rising with grim determination, the gladiator merely glanced at Max as though to assess whether he would attack immediately. Satisfied that Max would wait, Myrmidon examined his battered shield. Enchanted or not, the thing had absorbed such a pounding that it had been effectively destroyed.

With admirable aplomb, the gladiator merely tossed the shield aside. Turning again to face Max, Myrmidon offered a brief salute and advanced.

Without his shield, Myrmidon altered strategies and now went on the attack. For the first time in the match, Max was confronted with his own vulnerabilities. Faceless behind the imposing helmet, Myrmidon displayed a newfound ferocity. His utter fearlessness was unnerving, and with his short gladius, he exhibited a knack for slipping within the defenses of his taller, stronger opponent. Max evaded a lethal thrust by only the slimmest of margins.

In the Sidh, Scathach had often asserted that a warrior's confidence, his faith, was much more vital than his life's blood. In battle, spilling a foe's blood meant progress, but shattering his faith meant victory. And as Max redoubled his attack, he studied his opponent carefully for any clue that his faith and confidence were waning.

But as they circled one another, Myrmidon's carriage remained proud, his movements poised and predatory. There was no sign of fatigue, no telltale shuffle or dip of the head.

There was no victory here. Not yet.

An opportunity at last arose when Myrmidon appeared to slip upon the loose sand. Pouncing on this rare opening, Max struck his opponent two hard blows across the helmet with the butt of his spear before whipping the blade around to finish him.

Too late did Max realize his error. In a flash, Myrmidon had shifted the gladius to his other hand. As Max lunged forward, he impaled himself upon its point even as Myrmidon twisted away from the spear so that it merely grazed his neck.

This was first blood, and the crowd leaped to their feet.

Staggering backward off the sword, Max reached down and pressed his hand against the wound. The gladius had pierced his armor's thin metal plates and inflicted real damage. The initial pain had been sharp, but what followed was a dull, aching throb. Glancing down, Max saw that his hand was drenched with blood.

During this time, Myrmidon had backed away out of reach. He appeared to be examining his own wound—a long, shallow slice across the neck—but Max knew he was really studying his opponent and assessing the harm he had caused.

It was no doubt an ugly wound, but Max exhaled with relief. Nothing vital had been pierced, and his remarkable constitution would soon stop the bleeding and seal the wound. Myrmidon would have to strike a mortal blow to win this match.

But then Max felt something odd.

As expected, his wound had gone numb, but it was still bleeding. Pressing his hand against it, he felt an uncharacteristic pumping of fresh blood against his fingertips. His knees buckled, and Max staggered drunkenly to his right.

He did not fall, but the crowd reacted as though the match

had reached its tipping point. There was a roar, shouts of joy, bloodlust, and dismay. Glancing up, Max saw Myrmidon running at him with his sword raised. He meant to end the match with one dramatic stroke, as Max himself had done so many times.

Instead of retreating, Max took a sudden step forward. The maneuver surprised Myrmidon, and Max was able to seize hold of his adversary's sword arm. Dropping his spear, Max struck Myrmidon full in his face, crumpling the left side of his helmet. Momentarily stunning his opponent, Max wrenched him clear off the ground and held his foe at arm's length.

But Myrmidon still possessed his weapon. Even while he was being throttled, he managed to twist his right arm free and slash at Max. The blade cut across his shoulder, and while the wound was superficial, Max did not want to risk a more targeted attack at such close quarters. He hurled Myrmidon away with all his strength.

His opponent smashed into a stone monolith with such force that it cracked. The angle of impact was so awkward that Max was sure he must have broken his neck. By all rights, his opponent should have been sprawled in a lifeless heap.

But he was not.

Surely this was Astaroth.

He almost laughed with disbelief, for the Demon was stirring once again.

Max had almost forgotten that his spear was not in his hand but lying at his feet. Bending down to seize it, he noticed something disturbing.

His wound had still not stopped bleeding. If anything, his exertions had made it worse. A sickly coldness was now spreading throughout his torso. Propping himself against the spear, he stared in disbelief at this seemingly invincible opponent.

Advancing like a juggernaut, Myrmidon closed the distance

and slashed at Max's throat. Max parried the attack, but his movements were now mechanical and sluggish; they had none of his normal strength or fluidity. Unable to press his opponent back, Max gave way even as Myrmidon forced the blade ever closer to Max's vulnerable neck. With Max's attention focused on the weapon, Myrmidon suddenly kicked his legs out from under him.

Max fell, crashing onto the sand and doubling over as pain flared from the wound in his stomach. He expected the gladius to come screaming home, but it did not. Glancing up, Max saw that Myrmidon was staring down at him, his helmet framed by the stars. But he did not strike. With cold disdain, the gladiator stepped over Max, took up a position some ten yards away, and turned his back.

The gesture was infuriating, but in his condition, there was little Max could do. His blood was pooling beneath him. The wound simply would not clot. Nausea spread throughout his limbs, and Max came to a grim conclusion.

Myrmidon's blade was poisoned.

There was a method to the Demon's madness. Not only did his scornful gesture delight his audience, it also allowed the poison more time to have its effect.

Beneath the ghostly moon, Myrmidon's breath came in misty plumes as he held up his arm and accepted the crowd's adulation. As Max lay bleeding on the sand, he gazed at the royal box. Prusias had risen to watch the imminent conclusion, but his expression appeared grave and he did not clap or cheer. Mr. Bonn looked positively ashen. But the rest of the crowd was ecstatic; Max had never seen Dr. Rasmussen or his colleagues so animated. He'd despised the Workshop, and it was a bitter pill that his defeat should give them pleasure.

But there was one among these seats who had not risen with all the rest. The figure was seated near the witches, and for a moment, Max thought she was one of them. But her robe was gray, not black. Leaning forward, she removed the hood that had hidden her face.

It was Scathach.

Max perceived the maiden with such clarity that she might have been an arm's length away. Scathach's was an unearthly beauty, an ivory face framed by long raven hair. Her gray eyes were gazing at him with such love and anguish that Max nearly bowed his head in shame.

There was no doubt she knew who he was.

He would not allow her to see him in a coffin bed of blood and dust. He would not yield to treachery, or poison, or even Astaroth himself.

When Max stood, the crowd cheered as though to topple Jericho. Turning on his heel, Myrmidon merely stared at Max.

Max's entire body shook and trembled as though the poison were exercising its final, fatal influence. To the spectators' delight, Myrmidon acknowledged his adversary's spirit and applauded with the flat of his sword. There was an unmistakable solemnity to the gesture—a farewell to a worthy adversary. When the gladiator ceased his ovation, the crowd quieted to a tense, anticipatory silence.

But even as Myrmidon advanced to deliver the killing stroke, he seemed to realize his error.

Max had not been trembling from weakness.

The Old Magic burst forth with such terrible pride and rage that it threatened to engulf him. It eclipsed everything; there was no wound, no poison, no pain. They were gone, simply consumed by the wildfire within him.

What remained was only a demon in a gladiator's clothing.

The match was over in an instant.

Myrmidon slumped against the monolith. His sword had

been shattered, his body impaled with such inconceivable force that it was now pinned to the very pillar. In shock, he gently touched the spear as though trying to grasp what had happened. His fingertips traveled slowly up the spear until they reached the still-trembling hands of the victor.

Initially, Max thought his enemy meant to pry his hands away from the spear, but he was mistaken. Myrmidon merely wished to touch him, to fold his hands over Max's and hold them there. The act was so unexpected and so gentle that Max did not know how to respond and simply stood by.

The moment was strangely beautiful, but it could not last.

Slowly, Myrmidon's head dipped forward as though in prayer.

His hands slipped away from Max's, and with a final breath, he died.

The Coliseum almost erupted in a riot. Ecstatic spectators streamed down from their seats and into the arena to celebrate.

But Max was only dimly aware of the commotion.

His attention remained fixed upon his fallen foe. While hundreds of malakhim kept the crowds at bay, Max knelt to remove Myrmidon's helmet.

He needed to confirm what he now suspected.

Lifting the helmet away, Max looked upon his clone.

Myrmidon appeared to be a younger, slighter version of himself—Max as he looked at fourteen or fifteen. The Workshop clone's face was eerily peaceful. Wavy black hair swept across a forehead that still glistened with cooling sweat. There was an ugly bruise on the left cheekbone, but that was the only blemish upon a pale, handsome face whose youth had been tempered by hard experience. Myrmidon might have been young, but he'd met his end with open eyes.

Those eyes were dark and fierce and brimmed with a secret

wisdom that only death conveys. Numb with sorrow, Max closed their lids and silently said goodbye to a twin he'd never met.

Rising, he looked briefly about for Scathach. When she was not to be found, Max turned and marched straight out of the arena. His anger and disdain were so apparent that the crowds immediately parted to let him through. As he disappeared inside the tunnel, they let out a great, appreciative roar.

The Red Death was above praise and glory.

He lived only for the arena.

Was he not a worthy champion?

~ 24 ~

WHISPERS IN THE DARK

The news of Bragha Rùn's spectacular victory spread quickly throughout the capital. The kingdom's champion had not only won in impressive fashion, but it was rumored that Myrmidon had been none other than Max McDaniels, the infamous Hound of Rowan. This gossip was met with healthy skepticism, until several vyes who had collected the gladiator's body had confirmed it. These same vyes had taken part in the Siege of Rowan and witnessed the historic moment when the boy had surrendered the Book to Astaroth. By dispatching this villain, Bragha Rùn had avenged many of their fallen comrades. The Hound had

been slain, and the kingdom now boasted a worthy champion—
a great victory, indeed.

This match had electrified the city, particularly the poorer
districts that spread out along the Tiber's banks. There, great fires
engulfed clusters of dwellings. Max watched the plumes of
smoke from his bedroom while Mr. Bonn recounted the rumors
and gossip from the street.

"Why are they burning their own homes?" asked Max quietly.

"Oh, much of it's mere revelry," replied Mr. Bonn. "They'll
start building again, I daresay. But some of the fires are offerings
to *you*—or perhaps I should say that they're offerings to Bragha
Rùn. The vyes hope to gain your favor and perhaps even entice an
appearance."

Max shook his head in grim disbelief. Even from the lofty
height of his mansion, he could hear the shouts and calls from far
below. The match had ended hours ago, but the chants continued
with the same unsettling devotion.

"Why doesn't Prusias stop them?" Max wondered, watching
a distant minaret topple as it was finally consumed in flames.

"Oh, he would never stop such a thing," Mr. Bonn observed.
"He's no doubt in their midst, encouraging their zeal and
showering the crowds with gold. The king believes one must
keep the masses focused on wealth, war, and games lest they grow
discontent. People will endure a tyrant, so long as they believe
he's one of them. Prusias loves a good riot."

"It sounds like he has it all figured out," Max muttered.

"He is a fearsome enemy, master," said Mr. Bonn with a cautious, appealing note. "It does not do to oppose him. I know the
true identity of Myrmidon has upset you, but I beg you will not
do anything unwise. You do not know Prusias like I know him."

"But don't you see?" said Max. "He'll never let me leave. I'm supposed to be dead—there are a hundred thousand witnesses who saw my clone die in that arena. So what's his plan?"

"I won't pretend to know the king's mind on all matters," replied the imp. "But I believe he thinks highly of you and the possibilities you offer."

"Too valuable to kill," Max concluded with a bitter laugh. "So, I'm to be kept here unless he wants to trot out Bragha Rùn for a public appearance."

"There are worse fates, my lord," said the imp.

"Indeed there are, Mr. Bonn!" exclaimed Prusias, stamping snow from his boots. "Things almost got away from us there at the arena, but what a match! I'll confess I thought you were done for, but you were only playing possum, weren't you?"

The king wagged a finger as though Max were a delightfully wicked boy.

"I wasn't playing at anything," replied Max coldly.

"Ah, you're upset," observed Prusias with a sigh. "I suppose it was inevitable. No picnic to see your likeness in such a regrettable state."

"'Regrettable state'?" Max exclaimed. "My 'likeness'? Myrmidon wasn't just another opponent—he was me!"

"Nonsense," Prusias snapped, settling into an armchair. He glanced at the fireplace, whose logs promptly burst into flame. "You might as well weep over fingernail clippings. Your grief is either feigned or you're vainer than I'd supposed. Frankly, if anyone should be upset, it's me. Myrmidon cost me a fortune. . . ."

The king frowned at this unhappy thought, fumbling about for a cigar and grunting at Max to occupy the other chair.

"So I'm to be Bragha Rùn forever," concluded Max. "Max McDaniels is dead."

"Alas, so he is," chuckled Prusias. "The great Hound of Rowan . . . may he rest in peace, et cetera, et cetera."

"I'm surprised at you," said Max.

"Eh?" said Prusias, fixing him with a bright blue eye. "What do you mean?"

"I'm a dirty little secret," Max laughed. "Everyone thinks the Hound of Rowan is dead, but he's really stowed away in a lonely mansion on a hill. How would your rivals react to the truth?"

Instead of growing angry, the king's expression turned melancholy. With a grimace, he heaved himself out of his chair and paced about the room, his shadow growing strange once again.

When Mr. Bonn saw this, his manner became exceedingly meek and unobtrusive, as though he wished to simply shrink out of existence. Max was frightened but determined not to let it show.

"You know," reflected Prusias, "that clone did what he was told. He destroyed whatever he was told to destroy without debate. In this world, one is either useful or useless. And that clone was useful."

Max remained quiet. It was hard to imagine a younger version of himself stealing about Blys to do the evil bidding of the king.

"Myrmidon's skill in that regard got me thinking about you," said Prusias. "While he was very good and didn't balk at a little knife work, he didn't have your special dash and spark. You see, I think there's something very great in you, Max. And I don't believe the Workshop can duplicate it—not even if they could separate you into little jars and look at those little jars with their wonderful machines."

Prusias grinned maliciously.

"Well," he continued, "I have enemies. Lots of them. Among my enemies, there are some who bore me, others who divert me, and still others who can even amuse me. But very few can threaten me. However, I've recently learned that one *does* threaten me. Even more than I had supposed."

"King Aamon," Max guessed aloud.

"Precisely," acknowledged Prusias. He turned toward his imp. "You see, Mr. Bonn? I told you he would understand our problem and want to help."

"I never said that," said Max.

"Oh, but you will," laughed Prusias. "It's really best for everyone if you do."

Max kept a wary eye on Prusias's shadow. During conversations such as these, it was so easy and tempting to forget one's danger. *This is not a man,* Max reminded himself sternly. *You are in a locked room with a great red dragon.*

And he wants something from you.

"I'd do it myself, of course, but Astaroth has forbidden me from taking a direct hand in matters. A sensible rule, but it does complicate things. Now, let's look at the details, shall we? An associate of mine has taken the liberty of mapping out Aamon's castle." With a smile and a theatrical flick of the wrist, Prusias unfurled a parchment. "There are sentries, of course," he said. "But we've scouted their positions, and I believe you should be able to eliminate them. . . ."

Max merely stared at the map, uncomprehending. It was like planning an operation with Cooper—but he was taking orders from a demon.

What on earth was happening to him?

Prusias was oblivious to Max's rising concerns, instead pointing out various traps, possible means of entry, and the underground chapel where Aamon was known to retire.

"The malakhim will travel with you as far as the border," said Prusias. "At that point, one of them will give you a relic—a weapon that even Aamon has reason to fear—and you will go on alone. You are not to be captured."

"Why not give me the relic now?" asked Max coldly.

"Not while you're close to my person," Prusias growled, his shadow flaring behind them like a cobra's hood. "Do this for me and the rewards will be beyond your wildest imagination."

"You know," said Max carefully, "you already promised me something: a cleared path to Vyndra. You promised me a chance to avenge my father's death."

"And you'll have it!" proclaimed Prusias. "But Vyndra must wait."

"It seems you want a second service before you've paid for the first," said Max. "As you said yourself, a productive partnership is based on quid pro quo rather than charity. I've fulfilled my part of the bargain, but you have yet to pay."

The king blinked. "Max . . . I thought we understood one another," mused Prusias with a wry little smile. "Do you expect me to choke on my words? Does a youth presume to lecture me?"

Glancing at Mr. Bonn, Max could see he was petrified. The imp's eyes effectively screamed at Max to desist, to retreat, to rock the dragon back to sleep. But Prusias's own eyes had widened into feral blue orbs; his small teeth sank into his lower lip and sent blood streaming down into his beard. He stalked around the room, huge and dangerous. Max did not dare move.

"You want to negotiate with me?" rasped the demon. "Let's have at it, then. What will you give me to spare your farmhouse friends for one more night? Make me an offer, you miserable little thing, or I'll show you such a scene of carnage that you'll never sleep again!"

With a furious jab of his cane, Prusias shifted his attention to the imp.

"Mr. Bonn, take this down: I want *every* vye in the opium dens and the jails and the dungeons loosed upon the camps tonight. *Every single one, Mr. Bonn!*"

"Please," Max whispered, but the demon wheeled upon him and held up a finger for silence. Max could not even look at the demon's face. He could only stare at the trailing shadow whose vague, threatening shapes resolved themselves into that of a horned beast with many heads and coils. When Prusias next spoke, his deep voice trembled.

"Do you now see just how generous I've been?"

"Yes," said Max.

"So you'll do what I ask?"

"No."

The pacing stopped. The huge, barbaric head and tangled mane of black hair swiveled at Max. "Say that again," Prusias whispered. "I'm begging you. Say no to me just one more time. . . ."

Max had never been more frightened. Swallowing, he battled to make the words come forth.

"No," he repeated, meeting the demon's gaze. "I'm not going to do as you ask. I'm not going to be enslaved or turned into a monster because you threaten to hurt the people I care about. That's a game that never ends. There will always be some terrible thing you want me to do, and there will always be someone I care about."

With a savage blow, Prusias backhanded Max with his great fist. The impact sent Max careening into a bookshelf. With a horrific, primal howl, Prusias fell upon Max and seized hold of his throat. The demon's mouth was frothing, his pupils dilated so much they filled his wild eyes to the brim. Trembling, the demon heaved Max off the ground with such force that Max thought his spine would snap. He was slammed against the wall and pinned so that his feet dangled several feet from the floor.

"Mr. Bonn!" Prusias roared. "Remove this thing from my sight before I swallow him whole!"

Max's throat felt like it was caught in a red-hot clamp, a vise whose screws were tightening by the second. He was already losing consciousness as the malakhim closed upon him, their masks eerily calm and beautiful as they bound his wrists with a slender cord.

When Max regained consciousness, he was steeped in a darkness so black that it was disorienting. He discovered that he was still bound by the same cord, an enchanted fetter that suppressed any instinct for escape or resistance. He felt pain on his neck where the demon had seized him, but Max could not even lift his hands to touch the wound. All he could manage was a slight wriggling, and from these pitiful motions he gathered that he was slumped upon some sort of raised stone bench.

There was no breeze. The air smelled as though he was deep underground, but he could not be certain. He tried to smother the terrifying notion that he was back in the farmhouse well, abandoned within its pitch-black tunnels. Lying silently in the dark, Max felt that he was losing any and all ties to reality.

But drifting as he was, Max became vaguely aware of an irksome clicking. Something was creeping down from some perch or nook above him. Straining his ears, Max heard one cautious step followed by another in an unmistakable clicking of talons on stone.

When Max heard it hiss, he knew what it was: a baka—a leathery, batlike creature that was used to torment captives. Max had seen them before. To know that such a thing was creeping toward him and that he was unable to stop its advance was excruciating.

The creature sniffed and made a peculiar gurgling sound before its talons gripped his shoulders and it deposited its sickening weight upon him. Max slid farther down the wall, his eyes staring ahead into the blackness. Nuzzling its face against his neck, the baka began to whisper, and neither Max's mind nor his memories remained his to control.

He is in a car. Even half-asleep, Max knows they have turned onto his street. There is a familiar purr to the engine as his father eases off the accelerator and lets the car simply coast. When they turn into the driveway, the suspension gives its customary bounce and Max knows they are home.

He is now awake and alert, but Max keeps his eyes shut and pretends to be asleep. For in a moment, his door will open and he'll feel his mother's arms scoot beneath him, cradling his body as she carries him to the house. . . .

His father is hunched over the dining room table. He's talking to the policemen, and Max wants to go sit by him, but a pretty policewoman takes him by the hand. She kneels beside him and offers a very uncomfortable smile.

"Max, did your parents ever fight? Did you ever see your dad yell at your mommy? Did you ever see him hit her? . . ."

The police are gone; the house is quiet. The mail for Bryn McDaniels is stacked in a hopeful pile. There is a knock at the door. His father is doing dishes and asks Max to answer. He peers out the window. A vye stands upon the doorstep holding a suitcase. Max is afraid but cannot help himself. He opens the door. . . .

Max stands in a creek holding his father's body. He sees a wound they have not closed. Nigel is kneeling next to him weeping as though his father is already dead, but he is not. If only they can close the wound . . .

Max felt an ache. The ache was real and it was in his head—his eyes. The pain came from a light. Yet he yearned for the light to come closer—anything to drive away the dark.

Max shut his eyes as water trickled down his throat.

"That's all I can give you," said a voice.

A face came slowly into focus. It belonged to Mr. Bonn. The imp appeared grave; his eyes wandered over Max's face and body as though what he saw disturbed him. The baka remained where it was, but the whispers had stopped.

"Where am I?" Max croaked.

"Prusias's dungeons," murmured the imp.

"How long have I been here?" Max croaked.

"Please, master," murmured the imp. "I'm not allowed to answer any questions; I'm only permitted to ask one. Will you do as Prusias commands and swear everlasting fealty to him? For if you agree to do so, all shall be forgiven and your torment will end this very minute."

"I won't," whispered Max, shaking his head ever so slightly.

Anguish spread across the imp's face and he glanced over his shoulder.

"*Please* reconsider," he begged. "We both know the king's temper. Such an offer might never come again."

Max tried to swallow, but he couldn't. Squinting at the imp, he merely smiled.

"Turn off that light, Mr. Bonn. Can't you see I was sleeping?"

Mr. Bonn nodded sadly. As the imp departed, so did his light. And just beyond that lantern's shimmering wake, Max could see the darkness waiting to seep back in like a floodwater to swallow up his world.

And when it did, the whispers returned.

It was impossible to gauge time. Max was familiar with nightmares; he'd experienced many. But these nightmares led one into the other, then looped back around again.

But Max still preferred the baka's whispers and the nightmares to those brief moments of real or imagined lucidity. During these moments, an amber glow of unknown origin illuminated his prison and allowed him to look upon its corners and the bars that separated him from the vast blackness beyond.

When the amber light faded, there was only the blackness, the baka's whisper, and the nightmares that followed.

The night smells of spring, of wet grass and thistle, of possibilities. The great house stands upon the low hill. It is not far off. Max tosses his ball far ahead and runs to catch it like the great Norse wolf that chases the moon, and it's within his reach and he can snatch it, for this moon has not yet seen his face and it doesn't know its danger. But something else is waiting, a great wolfhound, and Max is caught like a silly boy without an answer to his name, for the wolfhound yawns, and from its throat comes a question—What are you about? Answer quick, or I'll gobble you up! And the moon strikes the ground and rolls away to play with him some other time. . . .

The dream ceased, but nothing replaced it. With anticipatory dread, Max stretched his eyes and gazed about to see if the amber light had returned.

It had not, but something else *was* coming.

Max could see it through the bars of his cell, drifting toward him in the dark. He couldn't be certain of anything—whether he was awake or asleep, whether his eyes were open or shut, whether he was alive or dead. But he didn't worry about such things; he simply marveled that his dream had come true. The moon *had* fallen to earth, and it had come to play with him. . . .

The moon grew larger and ever more luminous, rolling toward him until it appeared to hover just outside his cell. There was a pricking at Max's shoulder, a painful pinch as the baka suddenly tensed and scrambled away. Something had come to replace it.

That something fluttered through the bars, its graceful form silhouetted against the bright, beautiful moon. It landed on the tip of his nose, a gypsy moth whose soft antennae tickled his face. Max stared at it, amazed, until the moon spoke to him in its ancient, honeyed tenor.

"O God, I could be bounded in a nutshell and count myself a king of infinite space, were it not that I have bad dreams."

The door opened and the moon entered his little cell, and as the bobbing white shape came closer, Max discovered that it was not the moon that had come to play.

It was Astaroth.

The gypsy moth took flight and flew back toward the moon before shimmering back into its true form, the imp, Mr. Sikes.

As Astaroth approached, Max was overwhelmed by the force his presence exerted. Like the moon, Astaroth seemed to exude his own gravitational pull.

While Astaroth's presence had assumed divine proportions, he still looked the same. There was the same sardonic, genderless beauty stamped upon his luminous white face. His hair was smooth and shining black and streamed past his shoulders while he gazed about the little cell with a look of mild interest. The only thing that had changed was the Demon's attire, for instead of luminous white, he now wore robes that were of such unyielding black that they seemed woven of the void.

The Demon sighed. "Max," he chided. "I give you a brand-new world to explore and you end up here? Such a shame. What could you have done to upset Prusias so?"

Max tried to answer but could not. Words failed him.

"Speak," said Astaroth mildly. "I have missed your voice."

As though a bulb had been dimmed, the Demon's aura diminished so that conscious thought and free will returned. Max took several long, slow breaths.

"I won't serve him," he whispered. "He wants me to kill Aamon and I won't."

"Yes," said Astaroth, amused. "I'd thought as much. You're a prideful thing, and Prusias is as impulsive and transparent as a child. He and Aamon have never gotten along. I suppose a war is inevitable."

"Won't you stop it?" asked Max.

"Of course not," Astaroth replied. "These things must play out."

With a sigh, the Demon sat next to Max upon the stone bench. For several moments, the two merely sat together, like old friends waiting for a bus.

"Why are you here?" asked Max wearily.

"I want to talk about David Menlo," replied Astaroth. "I want to know what he's doing."

"I thought you knew everything," said Max.

"Oh, not *really*," Astaroth chuckled. "I often do, of course, but I have to tip my cap to your young friend. Search as I might, I can never quite find him. He flits just beyond my sight like a hummingbird and plays his little games."

"What little game*s*?"

Astaroth grinned and leaned a playful shoulder into Max. "That's what you're going to tell me," he whispered. "We both know about his bothersome assaults upon the merchant trade. It's a clever little diversion—target the ones who will complain the loudest—but we both know that's not what he's *really* doing."

The Demon looked at him expectantly.

"I don't know what he's doing," said Max. "Even before I left Rowan, David didn't share much with me. Everything he does is a big secret."

"Humor me," said Astaroth. "I want you to tell me everything you know."

Max refused, to the Demon's great delight.

"Such pride!" He clapped. "Such stubbornness—no wonder Prusias threw you down here. But I am not Prusias, and you cannot possibly refuse me, little Hound."

When Astaroth stood, his overwhelming presence had returned and left Max spellbound. The Demon's indomitable will seized upon Max's mind like an octopus, prying his memories open and invading every sacred secret. The Demon delighted in every shame, and even though he could have read that mind for himself, Astaroth forced Max to speak David's secrets aloud.

And while Max wept, Astaroth listened. Max told the Demon of David's red flowers and how he distilled them into poisons. He divulged how David destroyed the Enemy's ships through the observatory dome and how he'd tricked Prusias by swapping Connor's soul. All these things he revealed and more. The betrayal of his friend was so utterly complete, Max would have dashed himself against the walls were it not for the fetters that bound him.

"Shhh," whispered Astaroth, stroking Max's hair as though to console him. Gradually, the Demon's presence diminished so that Max's mind was his own and he could look upon the Demon's triumphant, smiling face. "Don't feel too guilty, my boy. You've merely confirmed what I suspected. But I'm curious, Max. Did David ever let you touch one of those red flowers?"

Max merely shook his head, his mind still reeling at all he'd revealed.

"Interesting," said Astaroth. "Do you know what they're called? In the Sidh, they're known as *Bláth Mag Balor*—'Balor's Flowers.' You know who Balor is, I presume."

"King of the Fomorians," said Max. "My great-grandfather."

Astaroth chuckled. "Yes, indeed," he said. "Someone's been

researching his family history. Since you know your great-grandfather's identity, I presume you know who killed him."

"Lugh the Long-Handed," Max breathed. "My birth father and Balor's own grandson."

"Precisely," said Astaroth. "And this was no small feat, as Balor was a formidable enemy whose great solitary eye was so poisonous, it killed anything it looked upon."

"I know the story," said Max. "Lugh put out the eye with a sling—"

"And Balor fell dead and the blood from his eye seeped into the earth," Astaroth concluded. "And before Lugh departed this world, he took with him the soil from that place where Balor had fallen. He spread this earth about his gardens at Rodrubân, and soon a red flower grew—*Bláth Mag Balor*. And from this flower, the wise might concoct a poison so deadly that it is a bane to god and demon alike."

From his robes, Astaroth produced one of the red flowers. The deadly thing was suspended in a glowing sphere of energy. Even though the flower was seemingly contained, Max recoiled as if it were a scorpion.

"Do you know what's so infuriating about this little flower?" said the Demon. "The Book of Thoth gives me no power over it. Its origins are in another world, and thus its truename is hidden from me. Now, a clever young Sorcerer might realize this and seek such a thing and spread its seeds about the land as an impediment to my kin. And if this Sorcerer were truly bold and enterprising, he might use such petals to brew a poison of such potency that it could slay every demon on earth . . . even yours truly."

Astaroth peered closely at the flower, then glanced at Max with a sly little smile.

"I suspected this possibility. You merely confirmed it for us, eh?"

Max stared dully ahead, saying nothing.

"One good turn deserves another," Astaroth chuckled. "Shall I tell you the rest of David's plan? It appears he has neglected to share it with you." The Demon eased back as if it was story time. "Now that the young Sorcerer has crafted a poison of sufficient potency, he needs to put his charming plot into action. He will have learned that the nobility of the Four Kingdoms are assembling in this very palace on Walpurgisnacht to commemorate Bram's defeat and the Fall of Solas. And while I have recently kept my whereabouts secret, David will have guessed correctly that this will be the occasion when I will appear and address the aristocracy. And since our mutual friend is unexpectedly bold and exceedingly arrogant, he will choose this moment to strike in the hope of murdering me before my court. . . ."

The Demon's ghostly, beautiful face was contemplative as he gazed at the suspended flower. To Max's surprise, the protective orb surrounding the Blood Petal dissipated, allowing the deadly flower to settle upon Astaroth's bare skin.

"But we have secrets of our own. Ever since I heard tell of *Bláth Mag Balor*, I understood that David had discovered a weapon that could actually hurt me. And through painful, patient exertions, I have prepared myself. And so thorough have been my preparations that no quantity, no concentration of this bane can harm me. I am immune."

With a shrug, the Demon tossed the flower into his mouth as though it were a dandelion. While Astaroth chewed thoughtfully upon it, Mr. Sikes cleared his throat.

"Something troubles you, my dear?" said Astaroth, turning to him.

"My lord knows best," said the imp, "but is it prudent to share all our secrets? *'Pride goeth before destruction,'* and so forth. . . ."

"Well said, Mr. Sikes," said Astaroth dreamily. "As always, you temper play with wisdom. But you must indulge your master, for we are approaching a beautiful moment. Can you envision the instant when David realizes his folly? It will be sublime. And poor Max now knows the very date of his friend's destruction, but can do nothing to save him from the trap. I fancy that is a greater torment than even a baka's whispers. . . ."

Rising from his seat, Astaroth gazed down upon Max's slumped, defeated form with a sympathetic grimace.

"Don't think me heartless," said the Demon. "Part of me will regret devouring David. I will miss his earnest little schemes."

Astaroth bid Max farewell but stopped just short of the door.

"I almost forgot," confessed the Demon. Turning, Astaroth raised a white hand and made a motion as though giving a modified benediction. "Until Walpurgisnacht has passed, you are forbidden to divulge any aspect of this visit or our conversation. You are forbidden to take any action *whatsoever* that might interfere with David Menlo's scheme."

The door closed and the Demon departed.

Again Max was steeped in an utter void of blackness. He wished the passive fetters would dull his mind or that the baka would creep back down to settle on his shoulders and begin its whispers anew. But neither happened, and thus for long hours Max was left to brood upon his betrayal of David and the doom that awaited him.

~ 25 ~

THE SORCERER AND THE SMEE

In the blackness of Prusias's dungeons, Max persevered like some lonely spirit. Hunger and thirst tormented him, but he did not waste away or perish, for there was some insidious magic in the baka that sustained his body even as it destroyed his mind.

Emerging from another nightmare, Max heard a quiet fumbling at the lock. There was illumination—a glimmer of witchfire that peeped through a lantern's sliding panel, revealing a momentary glimpse of a white face hovering outside the cell door.

Max felt the baka stir while he blinked at the figure. It must be Astaroth, he thought. The Demon must have returned to gloat over his victory. . . .

But why would Astaroth bother with a lantern or a key?

Before Max could muse on this, the door opened and the figure slipped inside the cell. The baka hissed as the figure came closer and raised the lantern's shutter so that its light fell upon the prisoner's face. The sudden brightness was painful. With a moan, Max shut his eyes and turned away.

There was a soft thumping noise, and Max felt the baka abruptly stiffen. It was removed from his shoulders, and Max's cheek was suddenly cold as his tormentor's face no longer pressed against his. He heard its body thud into the far corner, but Max knew it was another dream, another nightmare meant to convince him that his ordeal was over. He'd had them before, and they were among the very worst. Of all temptations, hope was cruelest.

Keeping his eyes shut, he refused to answer the voice that gently called his name. His bonds were severed; Max felt them slip away even as the voice continued to whisper. Rough hands took hold of his—a touch that was warm and real and human. The voice was so calm and so determined that at last Max opened his eyes and risked a peek at this most persistent of phantoms.

It was William Cooper.

The Agent's face was just inches away. There was the pale skin and the broken, scarred features and the shoots of gray-blond hair peeking from beneath his black cap.

The Agent patted his hand. "Can you hear me?" he whispered. "It's time to wake up."

But Max could not. He was so tired and so afraid and so very broken.

When Max finally managed a nod—a mere infinitesimal dip of his head—the Agent's blue eyes blazed.

"Good," Cooper whispered. "Lie quiet and let me do the work. I'm getting you out of here."

When Max was lifted, he felt like the little child in his earliest memories. Tipping Max over his left shoulder, Cooper reached down to retrieve the lantern. In his right hand, he held his gruesome kris and something that looked like a compass.

Stepping outside the cell, Cooper stole swiftly into the labyrinth beyond, his movements as stealthy and assured as a panther's.

They moved quickly, but it seemed Cooper's priority was silence. Periodically, he stopped and set Max down, propping him against the rock walls while the Agent studied the thin, disklike instrument in his hand. He allowed no more than a minuscule amount of light to escape from the lantern—just enough to cast a soft glow on the ground immediately ahead.

They had finally started to climb when they heard a shrill, mournful howl. Cooper immediately stopped and closed the lantern. They waited, Max curled against the cool stone in the pitch black. There was a familiar, reassuring pat on his shoulder, and then Cooper padded away to investigate.

After a few minutes, Max thought he heard the Agent returning.

There was a soft clink as something struck the dark lantern. Eager hands scrabbled at it, knocking it over and wrenching its shutter open. Bright light blazed in the darkness. Something scrambled backward, emitted a shrill cry, and seized the lantern, dashing it viciously against the rocks. The lantern's glass broke, and its witch-fire spilled out, forming pearly pools of yellow-white flames.

The creature's eyes, like the egg sacs of a spider, gleamed in the lantern light, wide and unblinking above a broad nose and a thin-lipped mouth that was caked with blood. Its sharp fingers were similarly caked, as if the thing spent its life scrabbling at bare rock looking for food or even shelter from whatever else might stalk such deep places.

It did not need to scrabble or dig for this meal. It stretched toward Max's helpless body.

Steps. Running steps. The thing's head whipped up as a black throwing dagger buried itself in its throat. Cooper arrived a second later, leaping over Max's prone body to crouch over the creature and satisfy himself that it was dead. Once this was done, he unceremoniously swung Max back over his shoulder. More cries sounded shrilly in the darkness, echoing and overlapping upon one another.

"Hide-and-seek is over," Cooper whispered.

And he was off, running with superhuman speed while Max jostled over his back. Instead of staring ahead into the blackness, the Agent focused on his strange compass and its glowing needle.

Cooper ran for hours at this pace, exhibiting almost limitless stamina, before something went wrong. The Agent cursed and slowed.

"Stay in one place," he growled, shaking the compass as though it were malfunctioning.

"Cooper!" Max whispered.

Whirling around, the Agent raised his hand and muttered, *"Solas!"*

An immense light filled the caverns. For the briefest second, Max saw hordes of gaunt, starving creatures closing in upon them.

Now, as Cooper ran, Max saw that every footfall left behind a pool of incandescent flames; the path behind them was soon a blazing minefield that not only stung their pursuers' eyes, but also stuck to their flesh and burned like Greek fire. Shrieks and howls erupted behind them. Dozens of the creatures were burning, but others merely leaped over them or scrambled up the labyrinth's walls. In the firelight, they looked pale and embryonic—a pack of skeletal, ravenous ghouls.

Despite his burden, the Agent was swifter than his pursuers, but they seemed to know where he was going—scores peeled off from the main chase to pursue less dangerous alternatives.

Max feared an ambush.

The creatures' shrieks shook the caverns and echoed in Max's ears. The cries came from all around. A hand snatched at Max's face, its talons snagging in his hair. Cooper's footsteps accelerated. He was running faster and faster, even as Max sensed a crush of bodies pressing closer.

And then . . . open air.

With a final, fiery step, Cooper leaped out of a narrow fissure, his Amplified stride carrying them far out into the gray twilight. . . .

Several of the creatures spilled out of the fissure in pursuit, their momentum carrying them beyond the ledge so that they plummeted screaming into the valley below.

Clutching Max, the Agent kept running even as they fell in a slow arc toward a mountain lake ringed by evergreens. Hundreds of feet they fell, trailing fire like a comet. The wind whipped in Max's face. He tensed for a horrific impact, a deep plunge into icy waters.

But it never happened.

Instead, their descent was controlled. Even as they fell, their trajectory changed so that they skimmed over the lake's placid waters instead of crashing into them. Cooper seemed to be running on both air and water, each step a fiery hiss until they had nearly crossed the lake's entire width. Then, slowing to a walk, the Agent's boots sank into shallow water and he trudged wearily to the far banks.

Propping Max against a fallen tree, the Agent sat utterly still and shut his eyes as though in meditation. Max gazed upon sky and mountains and water and grass—simple things that he did not think he'd ever see again. Evening was falling, and the air was saturated with that quiet, soft light that had inspired painters for centuries. Several deer were drinking at the lake's edge. The moon was just rising. There were no buildings or houses that he could see, no sign of Prusias's palace. Even the fissure from which they'd leaped was now some anonymous shadow high upon the cliff face.

Cooper's eyes opened, and he stood abruptly, as though the minute or two had restored him. Gazing up at the heights from which he'd jumped, the Agent exhaled and gave a low whistle. Max tried to grin, but a part of him remained doubtful that any of this was real. Cooper must have realized the difficulty of acclimating to open air and freedom, for he let Max be. But when the stars emerged, he knelt beside him.

"I know you want to rest," he said. "I do, too. But we've got to get moving again. I think it'd do you good to walk."

At Cooper's urging, Max took his hand and tried to stand. Max's knees buckled a few times, and he was forced to lean against his companion, but within a few minutes, he stood on his own two feet.

"Straighten up," the Agent ordered, his tone sharp.

Max did his best. With a grimace, Cooper looked him up and down.

"You're taller than me," he muttered. "What'd they feed you in there?"

"Nothing," said Max, shrugging with surprise.

But this did not satisfy Cooper, whose grimace indicated a clear belief that incarcerated, malnourished teenagers should not grow taller than their elders. He stalked off.

"Don't be mad," said Max. "I've got good genes. . . ."

"Shut it."

Max grinned. This was unquestionably the real William Cooper.

Stamping his legs to get the blood flowing, Max tottered after him.

Cooper's strange compass had two pointers instead of one, and Cooper seemed to be following the golden needle, which pointed steadily ahead. As Max hounded the Agent and tried to get a better view, he noticed that the green needle was swinging wildly about.

"Why's it doing that?" he asked.

"Because you're moving all over the place," Cooper explained. "That needle points to the quickest path to you. David made this compass—it's how I found you in the dark."

"So that other needle . . . ?"

"Shortest path to him," Cooper answered.

A sense of dread gnawed at Max's conscience—David was nearby. He strained to divulge his conversation with Astaroth, but the words would not form in his brain. Suddenly, the golden needle swung to the left and Cooper halted.

They were standing on a hill crowned with poplars. In a hollow below, sheltered from the wind, was a small campsite with a crackling fire. Descending, they approached the camp, and Max was able to see those gathered around the fire.

It was a group so motley and unexpected that Max's suspicions returned, and again he thought he must be dreaming.

Around the campfire, Max saw a Sorcerer, an ulu, a lymrill, and a strange little creature propped on a pillow. His attention lingered longest on the coppery lymrill, who was peering at him intently. With an anguished mewl, Nick charged.

Max never stood a chance.

Launching himself, the lymrill's dense body promptly flattened Max. Growls, nips, and mewls ensued, accompanied by the maraca-like shaking of his tail and frenzied kneading of bearlike paws. The uninitiated might have suffered a heart attack.

Once Cooper pried Nick away, Maya ventured forward to greet Max. Maya was an ulu, a silvery gazelle-like creature with eyes like molten gold. She was not only David's charge, but also his assistant, as Maya's enchanted blood could be used to translate even the most arcane languages and ciphers. She was a delicate, peaceful creature, and once she'd nuzzled Max, she eased down once again to nibble the grass. Her steward, however, managed only a wan smile and remained seated and wrapped in blankets.

David looked terrible. He was still ghastly pale, but had now grown so thin he appeared little more than a living skeleton. Max might not have even recognized him but for David's eyes, which still exhibited their unmistakable calm and intelligence.

Having greeted his old friends, Max glanced at the mysterious thing lounging on the pillow.

While *thing* seemed an uncharitable term for such a seemingly harmless creature, Max struggled to settle on anything else. He might have assumed it was merely a large yam, but for the fact that it had twisted around to follow the various greetings and reunions. Max soon noticed a golden tuft of hair atop its bullet-shaped head and a mouth set within its midsection. That mouth now spoke, its voice a silky basso that was so incongruous and yet so strangely familiar that Max merely gaped.

"At last, we meet!" exclaimed the lounging gourd.

"Max," said David, "let me introduce Sir Olaf. . . ."

"*Sir Olaf?*" replied Max. "I'm still dreaming. Sir Olaf's a selkie, David. He lives in the Sanctuary lagoon and weighs ten thousand pounds."

"Those were happier days," mused the yam wistfully.

"No," said David, inviting Max to sit. "Sir Olaf is not a selkie; he is a *smee*."

"Um . . . I'm sure I should know this, but what is a smee?" asked Max, peering at the visibly indignant yam. "I never read about one in the compendiums."

"You wouldn't have," replied David. "They're not dangerous per se. . . ."

"But they *are* a right pain," said Cooper, glancing at it. "Parasitic little doppelgängers that are so good at what they do that not even the imitated species can sniff 'em out as fakes."

"How dare you classify me in such a rude and clumsy fashion!" snapped Sir Olaf. His plump form craned to gaze up at Max. "Pay that scar-faced brute no mind. Smees are a proud race, lovingly nourished by Nature's succulent goodness until mighty Providence should see fit to—"

"Meaning, they grow as a grub in the dirt until a big rain washes 'em away," interrupted Cooper.

"The pleasures of language are wasted upon you, sir," the smee griped.

"There will be plenty of time to learn about smees," said David, "but we have more important business. First, let me put some fears to rest. Everyone who was living at the farmhouse is safe. . . ."

Max listened closely as David told him that an imp named Mr. Bonn had visited the farmhouse late one night and pleaded with the residents to leave, as danger might be coming. That very night, the adults had fled with the children to Nix and Valya's house across the valley. They had gone into hiding in the cellar, living on food that was brought by a young goblin.

"Are they still there?" asked Max anxiously.

"Nix and Valya are," replied David. "But I had to move Isabella and the children. They're perfectly safe."

"Where are they?" asked Max.

"At Rowan," replied David, smiling at Max's look of astonishment. "I smuggled them in. Even Ms. Richter was willing to bend the rules for Mina."

"She's a Potential!" Max hissed, as though it was now a dirty word.

David shook his head. "She's much more than that. . . ."

But David changed the subject by asking Cooper for news of more pressing matters.

"The situation along the border is bad," reported Cooper, sipping from a thermos. "War's broken out between Prusias and Aamon in all but name. The raids have been vicious. Sir Alistair thinks they'll declare soon."

"Can Matheus and Natalya accelerate things?" asked David, referencing two other members of the Red Branch.

"Natalya's done all she can without compromising herself," replied Cooper. "Matheus has worked up something promising, but he keeps asking me about Blood Petals. What should I tell him?"

"Nothing," snapped David. "He's supposed to be the best poisons master we have—he can use something else. I don't want anyone even talking about Blood Petals, much less using them on a mission. . . ."

As he said this, Max noticed David's hand stray toward a locked leather case near his pack. Max had seen that case before. It contained the very poisons he intended to use on Astaroth.

Max's conversation with the Demon replayed in his mind, word for word. He wanted to shake David, to scream, to tell him that Astaroth already knew every detail of David's careful plan and that it was doomed to fail.

But he couldn't say a peep.

Unable to comment or even hint at his inner anguish, Max

merely sat and listened. He had never seen this side of David before. Instead of pursuing the path of a nebbish Mystic, David had evolved into a field general. Max could not help but chafe as David and Cooper continued to discuss various news, rumors, and ongoing initiatives. He felt very left out.

And he was not alone.

"You have discussed everyone and everything but *me*," interjected Sir Olaf, stirring irritably. "I've had enough of Zenuvian trade and Aamon's troop movements! It's time we explore *my* role in these undoubtedly grand affairs."

"Before we get to your undoubtedly very critical role," said Max, "I want to hear anything you know about Connor."

"He's fine," replied David evenly. "He's been busy establishing his barony. I've kept tabs on him through Folly and Hubris."

"I saw them," said Max, referring to David's birds. "Or at least one of them—when I was talking to Prusias's imp."

"They kept an eye on you when they could," said David. "There are gaps, of course, but I got a fair picture until you disappeared into the dungeons."

"I don't even know how long I was there," said Max.

"Four and a half months," replied Cooper. "It's mid-April according to the old calendars. Your birthday came and went, but we brought you a gift."

Cooper went to David's pack and retrieved a wrapped bundle. Inside, Max found his father's razor, his brooch from Scathach, and samples of the children's lessons from the farmhouse. It was overwhelming. He did not know what to say and merely handled one after the other, placing each carefully back in the box when he was finished with it. Putting the box aside, he focused on the fire's bright yellow flames.

"I know I've been distant, Max," said David. "Since the Siege, you have tried to help me and to be my friend. For my own reasons,

I have not permitted that. But now I need your help, Max. I need you to make good on your oath."

Max recalled the oath he had taken, the one that Cooper had entrusted to him while they were in the Frankfurt Workshop. It had consisted of only three words: *Protect David Menlo.*

"Remember when I told you there was *no one* I would rather have guarding me?" asked David.

"Yes," said Max quietly.

"I meant it," said David, becoming once again the shy, unassuming boy Max had met on his first day at Rowan. "And I need you to protect me now. Because I've been planning something very carefully, and its time has come. And it will be the hardest, most frightening thing I've ever done. I can't do it without you."

These words were heartbreaking. For Max could not protect his friend from the trap that was waiting; he could only nod and ask how he could help.

David was visibly relieved.

"There is a holy day the demons celebrate called Walpurgisnacht at the end of this month. That night, every demon of any importance will be here in Blys. I have almost everything ready, but I'll need your protection to carry out my plan. And to protect me, you will need a special weapon, something that can harm even the greater spirits."

"Prusias said only a relic can hurt them," replied Max grimly.

"He spoke the truth," said David. "And we have one, but it's broken. I can't fix it, the dvergar can't. . . ."

Reaching into his pack, David brought out the carefully folded bundle that contained the shards of the *gae bolga.*

"You want to find the Fomorian," Max said soberly.

"That's right," David confirmed. "And even with *Ormenheid* and my arts, he will be difficult to reach. The Fomorian is pure

Old Magic, but we have the only living person who has ever found him."

Max glanced at Cooper, who was listening gravely and staring into the fire.

"Are you okay with this?" asked Max.

The smee broke the ensuing silence. "If the brute will not answer, then I will," groused Sir Olaf. "It's one thing to imprison me in my natural state; it's quite another to drag me about against my will. I do *not* wish to seek out an ill-tempered Fomorian and beg favors from him. I shall remain here until you return."

"We might not return," said David. "And we're going to need your help along the way."

"And if I refuse?" demanded Sir Olaf.

"You go right back to Frigga and Helga," said David coolly. "They'd love to see you."

The smee seemed to be reflecting. A moment later, he straightened.

"You know perfectly well they'd squish me."

"I do."

The Tiber gurgled past them in the dark, the waters swollen from the winter thaw and spring floods. As they climbed down the gray banks, Cooper pressed the tiny *Ormenheid* into Max's hand.

"How's she sail?" asked the Agent.

"Very well," said Max. "But I still had a rough passage."

"Here's to a smoother one," said David, standing aside so Max could place the toy-sized ship upon the river.

It began to drift with the current until Max spoke the words that would command it.

"Skina, Ormenheid."

And, as it had upon Rowan's shores, the toy extended through the water, undulating like a golden sea snake, expanding until it had become a full-sized vessel—a Viking ship with room enough for a raiding party.

"What a wonderful thing," observed David, and soon they had all climbed aboard and settled behind its mast and unfurling sail. The oars dipped into the water, and the ship floated motionless, awaiting instruction.

"*Leita*, Isle of Man," Max commanded.

Despite his repeated pleas, the ship remained stubbornly in place.

"Try '*Ellan Vannin*,'" suggested David. "That is what its people called it."

As soon as Max tried those words, the *Ormenheid*'s great oars eased into motion and rowed them swiftly toward the river's delta.

The *Ormenheid* had always been fleet, but with David aboard her, it seemed her enchantments had been greatly enhanced. The vessel now sped over the water as upon a ribbon of impossibly strong currents and favorable winds. And with the little Sorcerer sitting at her prow, the *Ormenheid* was enveloped within a cloaking mist so that she seemed naught but a mistral sweeping across the sea.

By sunrise, they had already left the former islands of Corsica and Sardinia far behind as they sailed south of what used to be France and Spain. Sitting cross-legged at the prow, David hunched over a lantern and pointed the stump of his missing hand at a thin line of gray that suggested the distant coast.

"That's near Connor's lands," said David sleepily. "He's not quite the economic powerhouse he aspires to be, but give him time. . . ."

He laughed, but Max was troubled as he stared out into the gloom.

"What's bothering you?" asked David.

"I hadn't realized before . . . I didn't know that demons

actually eat souls, David. To think of what you had Connor hand over to Prusias . . ."

"Don't lose sleep over it," David replied. "One of the Red Branch is already tracking it down—Peter Varga."

"Varga?" scoffed Max, wrinkling his nose. "He's not in the Red Branch."

"He is now," said David. "Cooper recruited him to replace Vilyak."

Max turned and glared at the sleeping Agent, who appeared almost catatonic beneath a heavy wool blanket. *How could Ronin be in the Red Branch?* Aside from Max's personal feelings, the man was badly injured and could hardly walk.

"I wouldn't trust him to find such a thing," Max scoffed.

David's ghostly face turned toward him. "I would," he said. "It's *his* soul."

"Then . . . David, what is happening to you?" he asked.

"You mean, why do I now look the way I do?" David murmured. "Like a freak?"

"You don't look like a freak," said Max quickly, "but you don't seem . . . yourself. I thought it was because you'd surrendered *your* soul to Prusias."

David chuckled and shook his head. "Prusias would have noticed a swap like that," he explained. "And giving up your soul doesn't make you waste away. Idiots sell their souls for beauty all the time, and they'd be pretty disappointed if this were the result. The simple answer is that I've pushed my limits and it's taken its toll. We both know I'm living on borrowed time. . . ."

With a wan smile, the blond boy tapped at the long, pale scar over his heart. Before Max could ask another question, David spoke gently.

"The hour's late and I have lots to think about," he said. "Get some rest."

And as David said this, Max realized just how tired he really was. Saying good night to his friend, Max crept to the spot where Nick lay sprawled alongside the gunwale. Kicking off his boots, Max gazed up at the stars and succumbed to a lullaby of wind and sea.

By sunset of the second day, they were approaching the strait. Max knew this because he could actually see the dark coastlines, whose opposing cliffs converged to create a narrow passage. Considerable shipping traffic was clustered about this natural gateway—massive galleons, black xebecs, and sleek clippers that skimmed along the shipping lanes.

The *Ormenheid*'s passage had been immensely swift, but now the ship had slowed considerably and cruised through the water at something like a normal speed, even as vyes and pitiful-looking humans stared from their fishing junks. David paid them no heed. He seemed intensely focused, standing at the prow and shielding his eyes from the sun's setting brilliance. Stepping quickly to his pack, David unclasped it and whispered into its depths.

The bag's mouth expanded, and from its depths floated chests and canvas bags and all manner of crates. They arranged themselves along the gunwales, tying themselves into place with sturdy ropes, as though handled by phantom mariners. In a few minutes, the *Ormenheid* looked like an exotic merchant ship laden with treasure.

The smee crowed. "Aha! Deceiving the Enemy, are we? Delightful, absolutely delightful! But will the demons not inquire as to who is master of this ship?"

"They most certainly will," said David. "Which is why we have to hide."

"But surely someone must remain visible . . . ," observed the smee. His thespian's voice trailed away while his body sagged with limp resignation. "It's me, isn't it?"

"Right you are," said David. "You're going to impersonate a demon named Coros."

Max listened attentively as David briefed the smee on a prominent Blyssian merchant, even going so far as to conjure an image of the demon.

"Child's play," said the smee, sounding almost bored. "But I'm a little hurt, David. Why didn't you share the plan with me earlier?"

"Because you've never seen Mad'raast . . ."

David directed them to an enchanted steamer trunk, whose open lid revealed a ladder leading to a sizable cabin. While Max and the others retreated down the ladder, David confirmed several more details with the smee before hurrying after them.

"You're free to transform, Olaf."

"*Sir* Olaf!" insisted the smee, interrupting his voice exercises.

Sighing, David pulled the lid down after him. As soon as the trunk was closed, the roof became perfectly transparent, as though it were made of glass.

"Don't worry," said David, seeing Max's alarm. "This is a jinni-made smuggler's chest. We can see out, but they can't see in. Very useful feature—we'll know if there's trouble."

Holding Nick, Max gazed up at their surroundings. He could see the sky, a bit of the *Ormenheid*'s gunwale, a stout barrel, and now an immensely fat bottom as Coros strode imperiously about the deck in his enormous silk pantaloons.

"David," said Max. "I've actually heard of Coros. He's very well known. Shouldn't we have Sir Olaf impersonate someone less prominent?"

"No," replied David, gazing up. "The fact that Coros is well known and pays exorbitant bribes to facilitate his smuggling makes him an ideal candidate. He's also a coward, which will help explain any fear Sir Olaf might exhibit when he sees Mad'raast."

No sooner had David said this than a shadow fell over the *Ormenheid* as though the sun itself had disappeared. Nick suddenly bristled and squirmed out of Max's arms to tunnel beneath a chair. Moving for a better vantage, Max craned his neck and looked upon Mad'raast.

Initially, Max thought he was simply gazing at the Rock of Gibraltar.

But this rock was moving.

For Mad'raast crouched atop the rock, a mountainous gargoyle of midnight blue. Each of his batlike wings spanned hundreds of feet. They flexed and quivered like a fly-bitten horse as the demon brooded upon his perch and gazed at each passing ship with his orblike eyes.

As they sailed closer, Max saw the gargantuan demon looming over them. Mad'raast suddenly spread his wings, blotting out the vermilion sky, and stretched forth his great arm to seize the *Ormenheid*'s prow.

"Don't panic," said David as the vessel came to a shivering halt.

From their limited vantage, Max could now see only the smee's trembling corpulence and Mad'raast's cruel face leering above the merchant. A cat might have just plucked up a mouse by the tail.

In a hoarse rasp, Mad'raast spoke to Sir Olaf in the demons' tongue and gazed past him to survey the many crates and chests. Max had to admire Sir Olaf's nerve, for although the smee was visibly trembling, he answered straightaway and even appeared to attempt a joke involving a clumsy hornpipe. When this was done, Sir Olaf bowed by way of apology and pointed to a large, reinforced chest.

Apparently, the bribe was accepted.

With an evil leer, the demon swept the chest into his great hand and wagged a warning finger at Coros before releasing the *Ormenheid*'s prow. An aircraft-sized wing swept above the smuggler's chest as the demon turned and clambered back up to his perch.

"That thing works for Prusias?" whispered Max, horrified.

But David only nodded and motioned for quiet.

The *Ormenheid* continued through the strait and out onto the open ocean. When they were beyond sight of land, Sir Olaf tottered over and flung open the smuggler's chest. Max could tell the smee was badly shaken.

"You might have *warned* me," he gasped, clutching his chest. "Dear Lord, what a monster!"

"You were perfect," said David. "In two days we'll reach the Isle of Man, and we couldn't have done it with you. You are a smee among smees."

"So you can even replicate a creature's aura?" asked Max.

"Of course," replied Sir Olaf. "You must understand, good sir, that such unique talents are what crown the illustrious smee as uncontested ruler of the mimicry world."

"But if you're such a good mimic, how'd the selkies find you out?" inquired Max.

"They didn't." Sir Olaf sniffed. "They remained in denial. But Miss Teller started snooping around and published an exposé in the *Tattler*. I was finished! The ki-rin herself marched me to the hedge tunnel and forced me to assume my true form in front of all. I've never been so ashamed."

"*That's* your problem," said Max pointedly.

Defensive indignation returned; the smee's tuft positively bristled. "Pray tell, what exactly is my 'problem'?" inquired the smee.

Max shrugged. "I think you're ashamed of who and what you

are. That's why you're always bragging or pretending to be something else. Have you ever just tried being Sir Olaf the smee?"

Silence. The smee slouched even lower.

"Well, why would I do that?" the dejected thing mused. "I mean, look at me—I look like a yam."

The others disagreed, perhaps a touch too strenuously.

"You're too hard on yourself," said Max, coughing.

"A yam should be so lucky," muttered David.

"I don't even have arms," observed Sir Olaf with sad bewilderment. "Even a starfish has arms."

"Well, what about your golden tuft?" Max exclaimed. "It must be the pride of smeedom!"

"Oh, that. It isn't real."

"Please tell me you're joking," said Max, wincing. "Really?"

"Give it a firm tug, my boy."

Max declined, but the smee insisted. A moment later, Max held a pinch of yellow hairs between his fingers.

"I'll just put it back," said Max, concerned about the strong winds whipping the thing about.

"No," commanded Sir Olaf, his voice resolute. "Carry me astern, good man."

Max did as he was told, scooping the smee into his left hand while he held the tuft in his right. The *Ormenheid* was racing over the sea, already abreast of the Bay of Biscay. At Sir Olaf's direction, Max carried him to the back of the ship, where the smee gazed out at the moonlit wake in quiet contemplation. David and Cooper soon joined them.

Sir Olaf cleared his throat. "You're good chaps," he reflected. "Even Cooper in his own uncouth way. And by Jove, I'm a good chap, too! But it's high time I acted like it. And so I say to you: no more lies, no more lounging on the labor of others. Today, I am proud to be a smee!"

Assuming this was the signal, Max let the golden tuft fly. Its fluttering magnificence soared high upon a gust and managed one majestic loop before plunging into the ocean.

"Sir Olaf," said Max. "We're proud of you."

The smee sighed. "Call me Toby."

~ 26 ~

A SON OF ELATHAN

Without his golden toupee and pretentious airs, Toby was a much more agreeable companion. He sat near the prow, absolutely delighting in the wind and spray while Nick sat near to discourage any hungry seabirds. The *Ormenheid*'s sails were always full, her oars pulled ceaselessly, and she was far too swift to be bothered by any of the piratical xebecs and clippers that cruised the channel separating what had been Britain and Ireland.

"This is all part of the Grand Duchy of Malakos now," said Cooper. "Ben Polk's been scouting it for us. Major commercial center—imports, exports, manufacturing. Actually, you won't believe what he sent me."

"Let me guess," said David. "Shrope Soaps?"

"A whole basket of the stuff," confirmed Cooper. "Hand soaps. Face soaps. Lotions. Shampoos. All wrapped up with paper and bows and stamped with Bellagrog's glaring face. I gave 'em all to Hazel. . . ."

"The hags started a business?" asked Max.

"A thriving business," replied David. "I've seen it from the observatory. The lights are always on at Shrope Hovel. I don't think Bellagrog sleeps."

"Neither does the Fomorian," said Cooper, directing their attention back to a map.

"Did you ever find where he lived?" asked David.

"No," said Cooper. "And if you hadn't been able to spy on him from the observatory, I don't think we'd find it now."

"So what do we do?" asked Max.

"We let him find us," said Cooper softly. "He will soon enough."

Cooper's face remained a stoic mask, but Max knew this was the result of the man's injuries as much as his temperament. His jaw didn't function correctly, and his face had been scorched so badly it looked as though half of it had simply melted away. Whatever neighboring skin was left had been pulled taut to form a mask of overlapping scars and creases.

"The Fomorian ain't like anything I've ever seen before or since," he said quietly. "It's old as the hills and don't want nothing to do with us. If things go quiet—if you feel like someone just stepped on your grave—that means the giant is close."

The Agent swallowed and stared at each of them.

"If that happens, just stay calm," he advised. "Don't yell or point or run—don't alarm it. I made that mistake. Just take a deep breath and let it get a sense of us. Only speak if spoken to."

"And if it doesn't speak?" asked David.

"We get the hell out of there," replied the Agent. "But go slow; running won't make any difference. Don't look back at it. Just go. We won't make it do anything it doesn't want to do."

"What about Nick?" asked Max. "He might do the wrong thing."

Cooper shook his head. "Believe me," he said. "Nick's instincts will be a lot better than ours."

To hear the Agent speak with such trepidation had a powerful effect upon Max. He had seen Cooper tackle unimaginably dangerous situations and foes without the least regard for his life or safety. But now the man's fear was palpable, and their task suddenly seemed much more than a mere waypoint on the road to Walpurgisnacht. Max had been dreading David's fate at Astaroth's hands; now he wondered whether the Demon would even have the chance to spring his trap.

When they finally landed the *Ormenheid* on the isle's gray beach, Toby was eager to set out with them. But the Agent sat with him and explained that they needed to leave the ship behind and asked the smee to do them the honor of looking after both it and Maya. The land was too rocky for the ulu's comfort. She preferred to remain behind and might grow lonely without company. The smee agreed but glanced above at the circling gulls.

"Happy to help," he said. "Delighted. But would it be possible for me to change shape?"

"Of course," said David. "Just keep it reasonable—no pink unicorns."

Leaving Maya and the smee behind, they now hiked up a bluff, Cooper helping David with the steeper sections while Max kept an eye on Nick, who was bounding along and sniffing at the vegetation. There were a few stands of trees, but the immediate landscape was one of rock and lichen, tall grasses and gorse that carpeted the hills and the ridgeline.

It was beautiful, lyrical scenery—browns, grays, and greens with the occasional splash of white sea campion or bright yellow trefoil. The air was cool and wet from gusts of mist that swept in off the sea and flowed over the hills like vaporous rivers. They could see a fair distance along the jagged coastline, but there were no visible buildings or dwellings.

"Do you think demons live here?" asked Max.

"I doubt it," replied Cooper. "If the Fomorian is still in these parts, I think most demons would just avoid it. There's lots of other territory one could claim without so much trouble."

True to Cooper's word, they saw no demons. There were birds, of course, and rabbits and even the occasional deer that peered at them from some inland glade, but no giant. By sundown, they had walked for miles over the hills and heather before dusk swept over the land and they decided to camp.

"Are you sure this is the best way to find it?" asked Max, dragging over an armful of dry tinder. He tossed it on the campfire, sending up fragrant smoke and rosin. Smacking his hands, he sat down on his bedroll and twisted about to see where Nick had gone. The lymrill's eyes shone from the branches of a distant tree, where he lay scouring the ground below like a jaguar. Frustrated by the fruitless search, Max picked clumps of grass and lobbed them into the fire.

"Like I said," replied Cooper, "he'll find us. Now get some sleep."

"But shouldn't someone keep watch for the giant?" inquired Max.

"Be my guest," murmured Cooper drowsily.

Max sat in frustrated silence for several minutes, Cooper

already fast asleep and David consulting a small book full of dense notes. Shaking his head, Max pulled on his boots.

"Going for a walk," he muttered.

Max turned and walked inland, away from the wind and surf and toward the trees where Nick had been lying about in ambush. At least the lymrill's time had been productive, for he was cleaning his paws and poking about the remains of several mice and rabbits. The moon shone in his eyes as he peered at Max and mewled by means of a companionable greeting. Falling in step, the lymrill waddled along beside him, and the two clambered down a hill toward a gully that wound away toward the edge of a forest.

"So," Max mused. "How's the married life?"

The moon climbed as Max walked along the gully and then up to a windswept peak that commanded a view of both the coast and the inland hills. Far off, Max could see their campfire—a tiny beacon of bright flame against the dark countryside. It was a peaceful night and a good place for thinking. Nick wasn't even making his usual array of mewls and snorts but had formed a quiet ball at Max's feet.

As he gazed down at the lymrill's bristling quills, it occurred to him that Nick was actually far more silent and still than he would normally be.

Max listened carefully.

The wind had died away, and not a single birdcall rent the dark. It was a most peculiar sensation, and the only parallel Max could think of was that awful lull before the Siege of Rowan. He turned slowly about, his boots sounding absurdly loud on the stone. His heart was beating like a kettledrum.

The giant was very close.

Nearly an hour passed—an hour of utter quiet and numbing tension. But the giant did not reveal itself, and Max concluded it was best to leave. Scooping the heavy lymrill into his arms, Max descended from the peak. He never looked back at the landscape behind him, but throughout his walk to camp, he felt the presence following him, like Eurydice's ghost.

David was still awake when he returned. Rowan's Sorcerer was sitting cross-legged over what appeared to be an entire ream of very old papers. "How was your hike?" he asked.

Every nerve was begging him to turn around, but Max kept his eyes forward and his voice preternaturally calm. "David, is there anything behind me?"

David's shoulders stiffened and he refused to return Max's stare.

"There is nothing behind you but the woods and the stars and the house of a friend," he answered. "Sit by the fire and put your fears aside."

It was an odd response and delivered with such peculiar emphasis that Max imagined it must be a sort of spell. David never looked up as he spoke the words but gestured stiffly toward Max's bedroll and urged him to sit. Max complied, easing slowly down and laying the lymrill beside him. Nick's eyes peered from behind his thick tail, but he remained absolutely still.

David continued to stare at the fire, his voice soft and placating. "Have I ever told you about Väinämöinen and his magic song?" he asked.

"No."

"It's a good story," said David. "And it's important to remember its teachings. For Väinämöinen was a wizard-hero and wise and humble in his ways. So great were his feats that the people of the far north spoke of his deeds and rejoiced in them. The lone exception was a proud young wizard who was jealous of Väinämöinen and had grown weary of hearing others praise him. And thus, he set out one day, determined to challenge the famous wizard.

When he found Väinämöinen, the young wizard accosted him. And despite the young man's rudeness and discourtesy, the patient elder agreed to hear his words and let him prove his wisdom. But when the young man spoke, he had naught to say but this:

> "*Every roof must have a chimney,*
> *Every fireplace a hearthstone.*
> *Lives of seals are free and merry.*
> *Salmon eat the perch and whiting.*
> *Lapps still plow the land with reindeer.*
> *In your land they plow with horses.*
> *This is some of my great wisdom!*'

"But Väinämöinen merely smiled and asked his challenger to speak of more profound things. And this he tried to do, telling of magic and sea foam, but his knowledge was trifling. And all of these things wise Väinämöinen might have endured until the young sorcerer made this boast:

> "*For 'twas I who plowed the ocean;*
> *Hollowed out the depths of ocean;*
> *When I dug the salmon grottoes,*
> *When I all the lakes created,*
> *When I heaped the mountains round them,*
> *When I piled the rocks around them.*
> *I was present as a hero*
> *When the heavens were created,*
> *When the sky was crystal-pillared,*
> *When was arched the beauteous rainbow,*
> *When the silver sun was planted,*
> *And with stars the heavens were sprinkled.*'

"Then the old wizard grew angry and said the young man was a prince of liars. And beware the wrath of a patient soul, for when Väinämöinen shared his wisdom and sang his songs, the young wizard's arrows flew away as hawks, his horse became as stone, and the upstart himself was swallowed up by the earth until only his head remained to beg forgiveness. . . ."

David's voice trailed away and he put aside his papers. Max remained calm and still, his eyes upon the fire. And as the hours passed, the fire collapsed to embers, and the embers cooled to ash, and the looming presence faded.

Max refused to stir or speak until Nick finally unwound his body from his defensive ball of bristles. Standing, Max finally stretched his limbs and rubbed his hands to combat the morning chill. Without the fire, the campsite was now cool and damp. Cooper was still asleep, his pale face strangely untroubled as the sun rose, its rays filtered by the morning fog. At first, Max thought David was in some sort of trance, but at length he blinked and turned again to his papers.

"Did you see it?" hissed Max. "Was it here all night?"

"It was," said David. "I could see it in the corner of my eye, but I refused to look at him, and I think that was the right decision."

"Why did you tell that story about Väinämöinen?"

"I wanted him to know what I was," said David carefully.

"And so what are you?" laughed Max, only half joking.

"A Sorcerer who respects his elders."

Cooper was stirring. Suddenly, he bolted up and grabbed his canteen. Splashing cold water on his face, he looked sharply at Max and David.

"How long you two been up?" he asked.

"All night," replied Max.

Cooper frowned and glanced at David. "It was here, wasn't it?" said the Agent. "By our camp."

"Yes," replied David. "It stood on the heath beside that stone all night long. I wouldn't look directly at it, but that's where it was. It only left a little while ago."

"He was in my dream," Cooper murmured. "He spoke to me."

"What did he say?" asked David gently.

Cooper was clearly struggling with something; it was several moments before he could answer. "The Fomorian said that we should leave. And he said that he was sorry—sorry to have hurt me all those years ago."

As Cooper spoke, his voice betrayed a jumble of emotions: shock, wonder, grief, and even anger. They played out in every word, every expression. It was clear that he wanted to laugh it off, but the smile promptly died in his eyes and he left the camp. Max and David watched him stride away along the ridgeline, his cap pulled low against the wind.

Max dragged over more firewood, and a minute later, the fire was ablaze with a kettle boiling above it. Instead of returning immediately to his papers, David busied himself with grinding coffee beans. This he did very methodically, holding the grinder in the crook of his right arm while he furiously turned the crank. Moments later, he sipped hot coffee from his thermos and sighed.

"I might periodically leave civilization, but it will never leave me."

Cooper returned well before noon, retracing his steps down the ridgeline while he chewed on wild blackberries. Nodding hello, he leaned down to thump Nick's side and gazed out at an ominous bank of clouds far out over the ocean.

"Are you . . . okay?" asked Max cautiously.

"Don't really know." Cooper shrugged. "Never thought I'd hear that voice again, much less what it had to say. Threw me for a loop, I guess."

"What do you think we should do?" asked David. "Should we stay or go?"

"You get the spear fixed while I was gone?" asked Cooper.

"No," said David.

"Guess we're staying, then," said Cooper, slinging his bedroll over his shoulder. "Let's move camp, eh? Rain coming."

The rain arrived within the hour, a driving storm whose chill soaked into clothes, bones, and spirits. While Nick simply dug a comfortable burrow inside the tent, the three humans sat in a circle and tried to warm themselves while the wind screamed outside and tugged at the stakes.

"Can't you do anything about this?" asked Max, glaring at David.

"This isn't any normal storm." David shivered. "It's been summoned."

"I thought you could do anything!" Max said. "I'm f-freezing!"

"The F-Fomorian's our host," David replied, his teeth chattering. "And if he wants the weather to be this way, then we've just got to deal with it. I can't change anything. I'd insult him if I tried."

There was a flash of lightning, followed immediately by thunder. Peering outside the tent flap, Max could hardly see twenty feet, for the rain and wind were gusting with such ferocity. Overhead, the sky was roiling with heavy, brooding clouds that tumbled about like foaming gray surf. Shivering, Max shut the flap and poked gloomily at their meager fire.

"Clearing up out there?" asked Cooper.

"That's funny," groused Max, wringing out his sweater sleeves.

"Well, I ain't complaining," quipped the Agent, producing a

deck of cards. "Rain's good for my complexion." He tossed the deck to David. "You get first deal."

"I've got one hand."

Ignoring David's acid stare, the Agent merely batted the deck toward Max.

"Right, then. Deal those cards, Max, and let's have ourselves a game."

They played many games throughout the afternoon and well into the evening. Poker, hearts, gin rummy . . . No matter the game, an undeniable truth was revealed: David and Cooper were virtuoso players and Max was not.

He frequently forgot the rules, was hopeless at calculating probabilities, and inadvertently tittered on several occasions when dealt an attractive hand. It became painfully clear that David and Cooper soon regarded Max's imaginary stake as their own private reserve—a readily available sum that might tip the scales in an otherwise even match between the two.

When Cooper ignored yet another bluff, Max sighed. "How do you always make the right guess?"

The Agent shrugged.

"I'm being serious," Max griped. "Would it be easier if I just told you my cards?"

"You already do," said David wearily.

"What am I holding, then?" Max demanded. "Go ahead! Tell me what I'm holding!"

"Two pair," David muttered. "Neither is better than a nine."

Max nearly pulled his hair out. Flinging aside his cards, he collapsed on the soggy blanket with a mind to mope and listen to the never-ending downpour. But there was a significant problem.

The rain had stopped.

Glancing at Nick, Max saw that the lymrill was once again in a compact, bristling mound.

"No one move," said Cooper, laying down his cards. "Keep your heads bowed."

The tent ropes went taut. Something was tugging almost casually at its top. With a shudder, the tent's stakes were wrenched free and dangled uselessly above the grass. Max, Cooper, and David remained huddled on the ground throughout this slow unveiling. From far above them, a voice spoke—deep and powerful as an ocean current.

"I told you to leave."

Nick was trembling so uncontrollably that Max put out a hand to steady him. As he did so, something poked his hand sharply—an unmistakable warning to keep still. The object was the point of an ax, whose blade was the size of a kitchen table. Within its silvery surface, Max saw the giant framed against the moon.

"You may look at me, kinsman."

Turning away from the brutal weapon, Max gazed up at the one who held it.

The Fomorian was even bigger than he'd imagined—far larger than that shadowy specimen he'd glimpsed at the Frankfurt Workshop. This giant must have been fifty feet tall with limbs like several tree trunks lashed together. Max simply did not understand how a being that huge could have gotten so close to their tent without making a sound.

The giant was so tall that it was difficult to see his face clearly in the evening dark. But what Max could glimpse was deeply unsettling. The head was huge and shaggy with a plaited beard not wholly dissimilar from Prusias's. The campfire's light glinted within several eyes and gave a diabolical cast to the giant's grotesque features.

Atop his head were horns similar to a mountain ram; one was broken near its base, and the other curled upon itself like a bony nautilus. While there was undeniable proof of humanity in the creature's basic aspect, his features were far from human. The Fomorian's skull was knotted and ridged; one of his small ears suddenly flicked like a faun's, while his ramlike nostrils and bearded mouth were fused into a shallow muzzle that jutted just enough to hint at some very formidable teeth.

He was clad in overlapping furs and tattered hides, his garb utterly primitive except for a silver armband and torque. Swinging the ax beneath Max's chin, the giant raised his face even higher and considered it.

"You are not Cúchulain," he concluded aloud. "I thought you must be. But now I see that you are not. So answer me, kinsman. Why are you here?"

"We've come because we need your help," replied Max.

"We are here to *beg* your help," said David. "To beg you to mend Cúchulain's spear so that your flesh and blood might use it in a just cause. We know that we trespass, and we ask that you forgive us."

"You ask much," observed the giant. "For upon my lands I have found a man of violence, a kinsman unknown, and a sly, hungry Sorcerer. You are strange visitors and I think perhaps an ill omen. But last night I heard your tale, little thing, and I liked it much, for it had the marks of wisdom."

As he said this, the Fomorian let the ax drift from Max's neck to David's.

"But even a clever fool can tell a wise man's story," he said. "So which are you, little thing? For I might help a wise man, but I will always slay a clever fool."

"How can I prove myself to you?" asked David, sounding very small and young.

And with the ax at his neck, David waited while the Fomorian considered how best to test him.

"We shall make a bargain," the giant concluded. "I would have helped this Väinämöinen in your tale, for he did not just look and listen, but he also saw and he heard. He was a wise man. And so I will ask you a question, little one. If you are indeed wise, you will find its answer. If you are just a clever fool, you will not. The wise man I will help. But I will take the clever fool's head, for such a thing can only do evil."

Max turned to his friend. "David, don't do this," he said pointedly. "There are other ways."

"There's no time for other ways," said David. "Walpurgisnacht is close, and we need his help."

When David agreed to the challenge, the Fomorian lowered himself to the ground so that he sat across from them like some worn and weathered monument. The clouds had departed, and the moonlight shone on the wet heath so that each clinging drop gleamed like a tiny star. And from the rocks and roots came tiny faeries and will-o'-the-wisps that gathered about the Fomorian like moths to a flame. They settled upon his shoulders and horns and beard. Even the grass curled around his hooves, and the trees leaned close to listen. At his command, a great fire sprang up from the wet earth and warmed them while the Fomorian coaxed Nick from his burrow.

"Well met," said the giant, peering at the mystic lymrill and opening his hand. To Max's surprise, Nick promptly waddled onto the enormous, crinkled palm and curled up within it. "It's been too long since I've seen your happy kind among the trees and rocks," said the Fomorian, stroking the lymrill's quills with a thorny finger. "You shall keep me company, and we shall judge if your friend is worthy."

Now that the giant was seated and his face illuminated by the fire, Max could see that he had five eyes. They peered not only from the customary sockets, but also from sockets in the

Fomorian's forehead and cheekbone. A sixth socket was empty— a wrinkled, sunken patch of flesh. The eyes that remained varied in size and in their focus, so that one might have already fixed upon David while another might linger on his companions or the sky.

But soon enough, they were all concentrated upon a single subject. And as the giant stared at David, he stroked the lymrill's coppery quills and issued a surprisingly simple question.

"What is my name, little Sorcerer?"

Having asked his question, the Fomorian leaned back and waited patiently for his answer. Upon hearing the question, David frowned slightly but did not otherwise respond. Max began to despair, for he had never heard David or Cooper or anyone else indicate that this being had a name other than the simple labels that were used. The Fomorian's more famous ancestors—the ones whose names Max had heard—had all perished or departed from this world. Only this one remained.

David sat still, his arms folded in his lap as he leaned forward and studied the Fomorian. Max could tell that David was appraising the giant not as a monster or some forgotten god but as an extension of the wide world beyond—defined not only by the spaces he occupied, but also by those he did not. Throughout this strange contest, Max and Cooper sat off to the side and waited in silent apprehension. The giant did not move, either, but patiently withstood David's scrutiny.

It was nearly dawn when David spoke. "You are a son of Elathan," he declared.

And when David said this, the tiny creatures that had assembled around the Fomorian—the faeries and moss maidens and will-o'-the-wisps—stirred and whispered to one another and gazed up at their master. But the Fomorian remained still and waited for David to continue.

"You are a son of Elathan," David repeated softly. "Elathan, who was brother to both Balor of the Fomorians and Goibniu of the Tuatha Dé Danann. You are a son of Elathan, who was Fomorian but whose face and form were fair like the younger gods to come. You are a son of Elathan, who sired Dagda and Oghma and Bres. You are a son of Elathan, but you are not named with the others, for you resembled your forebears—Cíocal Gricenchos and Neit and Balor—and your father was ashamed to look at you. You are a son of Elathan, and you were banished to live alone beneath the waves until your uncle Goibniu took pity upon you and taught you all his craft. You are a son of Elathan, but you have no name."

And when David said this, the giant bowed his head and set a dozing Nick gently on the grass. And rising once again to his full height, the Fomorian looked down at David with quiet approval.

"I will do as you ask," he said. "But why do you shed tears, little one?"

David stared up at the giant, his face bright and fierce and wet. "If I ever get the Book," he said, "I will return and give you a name."

"And why would you do that?" asked the giant.

"Because it would give you peace." David sniffled.

"If you do that," said the giant, "I will not only consider you wise, but also a giver of wondrous gifts. You are a strange one, little Sorcerer. I have not seen your like before."

Slinging the ax over his back, the Fomorian reached down and scooped them all into his great hands as though they were mere figurines. When they were settled, the giant cupped his hands so that the space inside might have been a snug cave that smelled of earth and sea. And as the Fomorian strode off, Max peered between the fingers and glimpsed miles of heath and wood racing beneath them as though the giant covered the distance in a single stride.

By midday, they had journeyed over the hills and under the sea without ever leaving their shelter within the giant's cupped hands. The Fomorian lived in a vast sea cave, deep beneath water level, and once he'd set them upon a massive table, he brushed bits of seaweed from his beard like so many cobwebs.

Soon the cave was warmed with many fires in many hearths, and the Fomorian set the table with a simple feast. Max devoured everything set before him with a ravenous hunger. Throughout the meal, the giant spoke courteously to Max and David in Old Irish, and asked them about their doings in the wide world. But Cooper remained silent and merely stared about the cave and its reflecting pools and ancient carvings as if their being there were all a dream.

But his attention returned when the meal had finished, for now the Fomorian asked to see the *gae bolga*. Reaching into David's pack, Max lifted out the folded tapestry that enclosed the many shards of black metal and gray bone. Laying the tapestry out upon the table, the giant studied the broken weapon in much the same manner that David had studied him. At length, he lifted the tapestry and funneled the shards into a stone bowl.

"Come with me," he said, carrying the bowl into an adjoining cave that housed a forge and anvil and all the tools of a smith's craft. At the giant's command, a fire was kindled in the forge's hearth—a fire so bright, so intense that only Max could approach it. The others stood apart in the doorway and watched while the Fomorian stalked about his smithy and worked the Old Magic from which he had been made long ago.

The *gae bolga*'s shards were poured into a crucible that the giant held in his bare hands and set within the flames of the massive hearth. The Fomorian did not seem to even feel the fire's heat or the crucible's scorching touch as he held it still and sang over the melting shards. And as he sang, Max watched the giant's shadow flickering upon the cavern wall, its monstrous horns and size so horribly reminiscent of Prusias.

When the Fomorian's song had ended and the shards had melted down, he removed the crucible from the fire and sat upon a bench to stir its contents with his finger. His eyes wandered toward Max. The giant called him closer and lifted him up so that Max stood upon his knee.

"I want you to see something, kinsman," said the Fomorian. "This shall be your weapon and you must know what it is, for brave Cúchulain did not, and much grief did it bring him."

The giant tipped the blistering crucible toward Max so that he could see inside. Sweating and wincing from its heat, Max stood on tiptoe and peered within and witnessed something wholly unexpected.

Within the crucible were no jagged shards or pools of melted metal, but three braids of long black hair. Each of the braids was longer than his arm, and none was remotely singed or even smoking.

"How can that be? Is that really the *gae bolga*?"

"It is," replied the giant. "The most fearsome weapons are not crafted of mere metal and wood—they are made of subtler things, and only the Old Magic can unravel or remake them. These braids are from the Morrígan—a war goddess and a haunter of battlefields."

"That's what the dvergar said," Max whispered. "They said it was her weapon—that it belonged to her. They wouldn't touch it."

"They saw the mark of the Morrígan," said the giant, "but she has never used this weapon; she meant for it to fall into mortal hands and sow strife in its wake. Havoc, blood, and fury are her children, and she would see them prosper."

Reaching into the crucible, the giant picked up the braids

and arranged them carefully upon his great palm so that they lay next to one another.

"It is important that you understand this," he said. "There is no going back with such a weapon. Cúchulain discovered this to his great and everlasting sorrow. Do you truly want me to forge these for you?"

Max considered the giant's words very carefully. In truth, the prospect of having such a weapon frightened him. There had been occasions when Max had not been able to control his temper or his actions—exhilarating and terrifying moments when the Old Magic inside him wanted to sweep away everything in his path.

This weapon would let him do such a thing.

This weapon *wanted* him to do such a thing.

Under different circumstances, Max might have asked the giant to destroy it. But Walpurgisnacht was near, and this weapon might represent the only fighting chance they would have—more so than even David understood.

"I do," said Max. "The time is coming when I will need such a weapon."

The giant nodded sadly as if he had known this would be Max's answer. "Give me your arm," he commanded, setting the braids back within the crucible.

Max did so, and the Fomorian cut his palm with a knife so that Max's blood pattered on the braids and soaked into each in turn.

Ignoring Max's hiss, the giant explained. "The Old Magic is in you," he said. "Your blood will strengthen the crafting and ensure that only you can wield this weapon. If you fall in battle, cousin, this relic dies with you."

Thrusting the crucible within the hearth's white-hot flames, the Fomorian melted down the blood-soaked braids until their true forms dissolved and they mingled into one another so that a single essence was formed. When he finally removed this from the hearth, it appeared as a viscous ball of molten, glowing glass.

Taking up his tools, the Fomorian shaped the mystic alloy, which hissed and sparked at each ringing blow as though it were a living thing. And as he folded the strange substance and hammered it into ever denser, darker forms, the giant resumed his strange, sad song so that the cavern walls hummed and seemed a living partner in the process.

Hours passed while the giant worked with tong and hammer, anvil and chisel. When he was finished and the sweat streamed down his great ramlike face, he set the weapon down to dry and cool upon a clean, white cloth.

The weapon was similar to what Max had used against the grylmhoch—a hybrid of spear and sword, with cruel-looking steel barbs that served as a hand guard. When Max took it up, he realized the broken spear he had claimed from the Red Branch vault had been a mere echo of its storied past. This weapon was whole, and the energy it conferred had intensified tenfold. Max felt a strange combination of delight and terror at his newfound power.

At the giant's insistence, Max tested the weapon upon great blocks of wood and stone and iron. The blade cut through each with such terrible ease it would take some getting used to. The jarring impact that Max normally associated with such blows had largely disappeared—the *gae bolga* merely cut through the material as though it made no distinctions between bone or butter or steel.

"One more," said the Fomorian, rising from his stool and stepping aside so Max could test the blade against the ancient anvil.

"I don't want to ruin it," said Max.

The Fomorian shook his head. "All your strength," he urged.

Max did as the giant told him and gathered himself for the terrible blow that Scathach had taught him in the Sidh. The *gae bolga* lashed against the anvil—and shattered into a hundred pieces. The anvil was unscathed.

"It is as I feared," said the giant, shrugging off Max's dismay. "Your blood imparted some of its properties to the *gae bolga*, but it has not strengthened the weapon's fundamental essence."

The two carefully hunted down each piece of the shattered spear. The shards were melted down once again into the Morrígan's braids, and Max's blood and their essences remingled as the giant sang a different song and made a different weapon.

This time the Fomorian made a longsword whose beautiful blade tapered to a deadly point and whose edge cleaved through wood, stone, and iron as the spear had done before it. But when Max tried the weapon upon the giant's anvil, it shattered as before.

Max slammed the hilt down in frustration and set to retrieving the broken pieces once again. Sweat was streaming down his face; the cave and its forge were intolerably hot, and they were feeding his temper. David and Cooper stood and watched from a distance, peering from the doorway with anxious faces.

When the next weapon, a short sword, was obliterated in the same manner, the giant gazed at the gathered shards and sighed.

"You see what is happening," he murmured, stooping low to show Max the dwindling pile. "Each forging reduces what is left for the next. I fear we may have but one chance remaining before the *gae bolga* is no more. What would you like to do?"

Max saw what the giant saw and it was irrefutable. The volume of material within the crucible was half what they had started with. Whatever the Fomorian forged would be small, and there were no guarantees that it would not break if struck against something as formidable as the giant's anvil. Max was about to answer when he felt a sudden scratch on his leg.

The lymrill had brushed up against him and was half standing with his great claw hooked into Max's pant leg like a cat at a scratching post. Glancing down, Max saw blood spreading upon his pants.

"Nick," he scolded, swatting at the animal's paw. "Go back with David."

But the lymrill held fast and would not let go. Growing impatient, Max bent down to unhook the claw and discipline his stubborn charge. But as he did so, Nick winced at the sudden movement and set to trembling. Max's anger disappeared; he had never seen Nick act this way.

Something was very wrong.

Dropping to one knee, Max gently raised the paw and peered beneath like a parent inspecting a child's palm for a splinter. He caught his breath.

The blood on Max's pants belonged to Nick.

The lymrill was peering intently at him, his small eyes betraying the uncanny intelligence that he conveniently masked whenever he misbehaved. Nick's quills were smoothed back into an earnest, glossy coat so that he looked almost elegant, as if this was a special occasion and nothing but the best would do.

Realizing Nick's intention, Max's heart nearly broke.

"No!" he said sternly, as though a reprimand had ever worked. Turning away from the lymrill's eyes, he reexamined the injured paw. Even as he did so, Nick's claw slid entirely free from its fleshy pad and remained hooked in his pant leg. Max gaped at it—a black claw as long as his finger with a smear of blood at its base.

Another claw slid slowly from Nick's paw, as if nudged by a muscular contraction. It fell to the cavern floor with a metallic clink. The lymrill was trembling, his breath coming in short little bursts. A third claw slid from his paw, followed shortly by another.

"Would someone please help him?" Max yelled, growing frantic. "He's sick."

But Cooper and David stood rooted in the doorway.

"Somebody do something!" Max screamed, his heart sinking as several long quills slid from the spiny ridge along Nick's back. Max shut his eyes and sobbed; the lymrill was coming apart in his arms, and he was helpless to stop it.

The Fomorian's deep, gentle voice spoke in his ear. "Do not look away," the giant urged. "Your friend is giving you the greatest gift he can give. You must honor that sacrifice, cousin. Receive his gift with a full heart. Accept it with all the love and strength with which it has been given. Do not look away, but be present with him."

Max forced himself to return Nick's gaze. And when almost all the quills and claws had fallen and Nick was weakening, Max lay back and eased the trembling lymrill upon his chest so he could sprawl upon him one more time. For that was how they met years ago, when the lymrill had chosen Max to be his steward.

The gesture was not lost on Nick.

An unmistakable gleam of mischief flashed in his dying eyes, and with an anxious snort, he scooted forward so that his chin rested once again upon Max's. And for the better part of an hour, he simply lay there and kneaded his steward's shirt. When the trembling grew too great and his breaths grew too short, the lymrill raised his head and peered at Max one last time.

With a long mewl and a short nip, he said goodbye.

~ 27 ~

An Officiate's Tomb

The sea was hauntingly beautiful. As Max sat at the *Ormenheid*'s prow, he gazed out at rolling waves of silver and platinum. It was one of those serene moments when the waters are lighter than the sky and possess a luminosity all their own. The low canopy of slate-gray clouds had been drizzling since dawn, its patter and the ship's oars the only sounds.

It did not seem possible that Nick was gone. When the lymrill had nipped his nose and lay still, Max's consciousness had drifted into a dreamlike state. He remembered Cooper helping him up while the giant retrieved Nick's body and the gift of his quills and claws. The Agent had led Max into the main cavern while the Fomorian melted the materials down and focused on his craft. Hours passed before the giant finally called to him and asked him to test the weapon he had made. Max had still been in a daze. His motions were so mechanical, he hardly remembered cutting through the wood or the stone or the iron. But he did remember striking the anvil.

Even his grief-stricken soul registered that moment, for there was a terrible sound—a screeching, howling tear as the ancient anvil was destroyed. The impact had sent a brief, stinging jolt up Max's arm, but no more. The weapon remained whole. The Fomorian examined it in detail and could not find the slightest evidence of damage.

The lymrill's gift of his mystic claws and quills might have made the weapon unbreakable, but they also made it homely. There was something appropriate about that, Max reflected. As he stared at the blade, he grew increasingly fond of its unusual features. The Fomorian reported that once Nick's quills and claws had been added to the crucible, the material became stubborn and willful—it simply would not conform to every hammer stroke, and it cooled so quickly that he finally abandoned the effort to make it beautiful.

Like Nick, even the weapon's actual classification was awkward. It was longer than most daggers, but not quite a proper sword. The blade was some eighteen inches. The handle was not encrusted with jewels or wrapped with gold wire, but was simply wound with a worn strip of leather from the hammer that had forged it. The only attention paid to art or ornamentation was a design the giant had etched at the base of the blade: a profile of an Irish wolfhound set against a Celtic sun.

The weapon was all forged of the same remarkable alloy, and Max noted that its color varied significantly depending how the light struck its surface. At first glance, it appeared a gleaming black—like jet or obsidian—but there were other positions when it suddenly shone like silver and still others in which the coppery waves of the lymrill's quills were revealed like the patterns in Damascus steel. No matter how often Max studied the blade, it never presented the same face twice. The weapon seemed a living thing.

In truth it *was* a living thing, and this was bittersweet. Despite his grief over the lymrill's selfless gift, it was some consolation to know that Nick's essence was bound within something Max would always carry. But part of the Morrígan was bound within it too, and the giant had taken great pains to convey the consequent dangers and temptations.

"This blade has a purpose," he had explained. "It has a spirit. We are blessed that part of its spirit comes from you and from your friend's sacrifice, but the greatest presence in this weapon is the Morrígan. It is not just a lymrill that lives within, but also a wolf and a raven that would prowl all the battlefields of all the worlds.

"This weapon can never be broken. The wounds it makes will never heal. There is nothing it cannot pierce and nothing it cannot slay, for its essence will destroy both flesh and spirit. Every ruler and warrior would lust for such a weapon. But the absence of limits is a perilous thing, for this blade will slay gods as well as monsters, friends as well as foes. Should you draw this weapon carelessly—to serve vanity or bloodlust or injustice— the Morrígan will lead you down the path of the conqueror. I forged this for a champion and defender, not a king or tyrant. Do you understand me, cousin?"

Max nodded, but could only promise to do his best. And the giant nodded and placed the blade within its scabbard, whose bronze plates were gilded with wolves and ravens as an appeasement to the goddess who would be watching over this weapon and its bearer. It was a mighty gift, and Max tried to be grateful.

But he had greater appreciation for something else the Fomorian had given him. When it came time to reforge the *gae bolga,* the giant had set aside three of Nick's metallic quills and one claw, and from these remainders, the Fomorian fashioned a Celtic torque that Max now wore around his neck as a tribute to his friend. It was beautiful in its simplicity and shone red-gold even on such a dreary day.

Max sheathed the *gae bolga* and walked back to where the rest of his companions were sitting. They were bundled up and had taken refuge from the drizzle under the single sail. David was cradling the ulu's drowsy head upon his lap while the smee regaled them with every conceivable detail of his uneventful vigil upon the *Ormenheid.* While the smee had been unable to tempt the ulu into real conversation, he'd found her an agreeable companion.

"There's just something about her," he said fondly. "She makes a fellow feel good about himself . . . like new shoes and a haircut, eh?"

"I thought we'd ditched your hair," Max grumbled.

"Figure of speech, dear boy," said the smee. "I know you miss that dear Nick, but try not to be grumpy. We're all on the same side."

Max gave a bitter laugh.

"Spit out whatever's bugging you," said Cooper, flicking his icy eyes toward Max.

Max paced about the deck and debated whether to say anything. But his anger got the best of him. Within seconds, he was ranting semicoherently at the assembled group: Who had made the decision to bring Nick? Had David known what would happen? All these plans and secret plans and lies . . . and now he had lost his charge, his friend, his responsibility. What else would he be asked to sacrifice?

"So toss us overboard," said Cooper softly. "Get it out of your system."

Max just glared at him. "And what did you and the giant talk about?" he demanded. "I noticed when you two disappeared. More secrets?"

"No," said the Agent. "Nothing like that." Peeling off his black cap, Cooper revealed the pale ruins of his scarred scalp and burned, scarecrow features. A wry smile played on his lips. "He offered to fix me up," he explained. "Make me whole again."

Max wanted to stay angry, to vent, to blame. But this was an unexpected revelation.

"He offered to *heal* you? But . . . but why didn't you let him?" asked Max, mouth agape. "I don't understand."

"It was tempting," said Cooper. "I won't pretend it wasn't. Don't think I said a word for twenty minutes when he offered. I used to be ashamed of what had happened to me, my scars . . . the way people looked at me. It reminded me of failure. But I'm not ashamed anymore. I've done good things and bad, and my face ain't pretty, but it's honest and it shows where I've been."

Inviting Max to sit, Cooper reminded him of something he'd said when they were looking for the giant.

"Nick's instincts were better than our instincts. He knew what needed to be done and he did it."

As Max mused upon this, David broke his silence. Throughout Max's tirade, David had held fast and simply listened. But now he spoke.

"Max, I know you're feeling used and you're grieving over Nick. Understand that I would never ask you to make a sacrifice I wasn't willing to make myself. And I would never put you in danger or withhold information needlessly. I have a lot of faith in you. Please have faith in me."

Listening to David's calm, reasoning voice, Max tried to swallow the last of his anger. But it was hard to do. Part of the difficulty lay in pinpointing all the things that were fueling it. Was it grief over Nick? Was it that he felt manipulated? Or was it really the fact that Astaroth was forcing him to watch the slow progression of a doomed plan? He glanced at David's precious case of useless poisons and wanted to fling it into the sea. But whenever such urges came over him, some insidious spell always took hold . . . some governing force that stopped him just short of warning his friend or taking any action that might interfere with David's course.

"I do have faith in you," Max lied. "I'm not going anywhere."

"Good," said David, and the relief on his face was unmistakable. But then the face and manner of the cold strategist returned. "Walpurgisnacht is almost here," he said. "And it's time I shared the plan."

Once they reached the Tiber, they would disembark. Cooper would continue on with the ship and join up with the Red Branch to provoke open war between Prusias and Aamon. This would create distractions and tension, which would help David, Max, and the smee to infiltrate the palace and gain access to the cathedral where the festivities would begin. David intended to get close to Astaroth and then . . .

David opened his case and showed them the bloodred potions in their glass vials.

"But how will you get him to drink it?" asked Max stiffly.

"He'll drink it as a matter of duty," said David. "Hallowmas and Walpurgisnacht are the high holy days for the demons. These nights represent a shift in seasons, a moment of in between when the boundaries between our world and others are thinnest. The demons are strongest at such times."

"And so you intend to attack the demons on the night they're *strongest*?" wondered the smee.

"And all assembled together," added Max.

"Yes," said David. "I won't pretend the circumstances aren't scary, but the demons have certain rituals they perform. By definition, rituals are predictable, and their very predictability allows us to plan their disruption. And fortunately, the demons have one particular ritual that suits our needs very well."

"And what is that?" asked Max.

"Since 1649, Walpurgisnacht has attained even greater significance. In that year and upon that evening, the Enemy destroyed Solas and Astaroth consumed Bram. Thus, for the demons, Walpurgisnacht is of tremendous significance. And how do most celebrations begin?"

"With a toast!" exclaimed the smee. "Bottoms up and all that jolly business."

"Exactly!" David exclaimed, his excitement rising. "The greatest nobles from the Four Kingdoms will toast the Fall of Solas and the defeat of Elias Bram. And I am absolutely confident that Astaroth will use Walpurgisnacht to reinforce the fact that he is the Great God—not Prusias, not Aamon, not Rashaverak, not the Lady Lilith."

"Are any demons actually challenging his rule?" asked Max.

"No," replied David. "None of them remotely rival his power. But Astaroth lets his monarchs rule their kingdoms because he would find that boring. Now that he has the Book of Thoth, he has the opportunity to create new things and reshape the world, and that's where his interests lie. And if the Great God wants to disappear for a while to concentrate on grander matters, so what?"

"But when the cat's away, the mice will play . . . ," Cooper observed.

"That's right," said David. "And the mice have been playing. Prusias and Aamon are on the verge of war. Prusias keeps the Workshop viable despite Astaroth's disdain for technology. Lilith has been signing secret agreements with the witches and infringing on Rashaverak's trade. . . . The intrigues are endless. And I don't think Astaroth really cares overmuch, but every now and again he will reinforce the fact that he is in charge. And he will do so in spectacular fashion . . . kill one and frighten ten thousand, and so on. The four rulers and their braymas use the same tactics in their own territories.

"And I am confident," David continued, "that Astaroth will lead the toast this Walpurgisnacht to commemorate his victories. And when he drinks that toast, we will have him right where we want him."

"What if he doesn't show?" asked Max.

"We will destroy the four kings," replied David coldly. "Even if Astaroth isn't present, we will win a great victory. But I think he'll be there."

Max sighed and rubbed his temples.

"And so how are we going to get in, David?" he snapped, growing incredulous at David's misplaced confidence. "Are we going to waltz through the front door and slip Astaroth a poisoned drink?"

David merely shrugged and looked like a little boy again. "That's exactly what we're going to do. . . ."

The party navigated the strait in identical fashion as before. Into the smuggler's chest they went while a transformed and terrified Toby negotiated with greedy Mad'raast. Another chest of riches was surrendered, and the massive demon clambered back up to his perch.

"I meant to ask before," said Max. "But where are you getting all these jewels?"

"The demons," said David happily. "I've been plundering their ships since Gràvenmuir was raised. I think if you totaled up the sums, I might be history's greatest pirate!"

Max shook his head, his eyes upon the massive demon folding its wings about itself and resuming its leering vigil.

"Do you think Mad'raast will be at Walpurgisnacht?"

"Probably," said David. "He certainly has the rank to receive an invitation."

"Would you guess that Vyndra will be there, David?" asked Max quietly.

"Yes," said David. "Yes . . . I'd imagine so."

Max's roommate seemed on the verge of saying something else but did not. Cooper was not so reticent.

"Your only mission, McDaniels, is to protect David Menlo," he said. "To protect David no matter what. If it's revenge you want, it waits till after."

Max merely gazed out at the blue-gray sea.

By the time they approached the Tiber's mouth, it was late evening, and David's energies were fading. He was leaning wearily against the ship's serpent prow while Maya nuzzled his hand. David sank down, clinging to her neck as though she were a life preserver. Perhaps she was.

"Let's just get it close to shore," he whispered. "We can go overland, and Cooper can sail it farther east. We have to go quickly."

The Agent agreed and commanded the ship to take them toward the nearest landing point. There was an unmistakable urgency to his movements as he tossed David his pack and handed him the smee. Maya stepped shakily from the ship, followed by David.

"You know the place I spoke of?" Cooper asked David. "It's close."

David nodded, gazed up at the fading twilight, and gestured impatiently for the Agent to go. As though pulled by a winch, the *Ormenheid* slid back into the Tyrrhenian Sea and the oars propelled her west. Cooper stood at the deck and raised his hand to them in a silent farewell.

Max was in such a daze he forgot to say goodbye. David's voice snapped him to.

"I'm going to need your help," David said. "I'm weaker than I thought. I'm not sure I can walk all the way."

"Well, let me be of service," piped Toby amiably. "Would a mule do the trick? Something sturdy and sure-footed to navigate these muddy banks?"

"It just might," David admitted.

A minute later, David was sitting upon a well-behaved chestnut mule. Max led Maya, and the four wound their way up the steep banks and bluffs so they could follow the river overland toward the capital.

The hills of Rome had been raised so high and Prusias's palace was so enormous that they could see its brightly lit shapes from many miles away. From their vantage point, they could also see that the roads feeding the city were bright with the lights of carriages making their way to Blys to celebrate the holiday. Around them, Max could see the scattered mausoleums and tombs of the dead from ages past. It was toward one of these that David urged them.

It was set several hundred yards from the road in a quiet glade of cypress and poplar. An image of the sun was carved upon its arch. Passing beneath the arch, they came upon a door of stone that was speckled with moss and lichen. Directing Toby to stand beside it, David reached out his left hand and pressed the door's crumbling seal.

"*Invictus,*" he whispered.

An unfamiliar seal appeared on the door—a set of runes and Roman numerals set around a Celtic sun similar to that which the giant had inscribed on the *gae bolga.* The door swung inward, and they proceeded inside to a circular stone chamber some twenty feet across. The door closed behind them, and Max lit the lantern before helping David down from the mule. The smee resumed his natural shape and soon all four were sitting down upon the cool stone. Max had many questions, but he abstained from asking them until David had had a chance to recover. Instead, he tried to comfort Maya, who could not stop shivering.

"What's the matter with her?" asked Toby. "She wasn't this sick before."

"I don't know," said Max, rummaging through David's pack for Maya's food. He found a small box filled with berries and placed it before her. But the food did not remotely interest the ulu, who merely lay on her side and gazed dully ahead.

"Can you bring her to me?" asked David, his face shining with perspiration.

Max did so, placing the ulu so that her head lay in David's lap. Closing her eyes as though content, she began to doze. David coughed and seemed to gather himself.

"Would you open the door a foot or two?" he asked. "We'll be getting visitors."

Again, Max accommodated him and pushed the heavy stone ajar. The night air seeped into the tomb, along with the sound of crickets. Sitting back down, Max gazed around the tomb at its faded frescoes. They were merely sitting in an antechamber; there was a narrow staircase opposite the door that led down to some other rooms and perhaps to the actual coffin of whatever great person had been buried here.

"What is this place?" asked Max.

"An old safe house," said David. "Our people have been using it for millennia. A family donated it to Solas long ago—before the school was broken."

"What are we going to do here?" asked Max.

"Wait," replied David wearily. "The next stage requires some information I don't yet have."

As David and Maya dozed, Max and the smee sat quietly in the firelit tomb. There was dust and grit upon the floor, the sediment of centuries. How many plans had been hatched inside this tomb? How many wounded or desperate Agents had taken refuge here? If only stones could speak.

Several hours passed before Max heard a sudden chirrup and a fluttering of wings. Toby sat up, blinking sleepily as two birds zoomed into the chamber. They alighted on each of David's shoulders, like hummingbirds with long beaks and delicate bodies of silky blue feathers flecked with bits of yellow. They were Folly and Hubris, David's creations. David's eyelids fluttered as the birds leaned close and seemed to whisper in his ears.

When their message was finished, David nodded and muttered something to them. The pair chirruped, flew about in a swift circle, and sped out of the tomb once again. At David's hoarse request, Max pushed the door closed behind them.

"So," said Toby, padding about anxiously. "What now?"

Lifting Maya's head from his lap, David rose shakily to his feet and retrieved a small pouch of chalk. David conjured a fire— a green-gold trickle of flame that crept around the room's perimeter and filled it with yellow light. Taking his pouch of chalk, David blew upon it so that it scattered from his palm in a great cloud. The chalk fell to the ground in a slow cascade of particles.

But as Max watched, they did not fall randomly. Patterns emerged within the floor's center, growing ever clearer as the chalk settled. A moment later, Max looked upon a simple summoning circle, its geometry and inscriptions perfect in every regard.

"David," said Max. "What are you summoning?"

"A demon."

"I thought we weren't allowed to do such things," Max hissed. "You know—the edicts. Won't this jeopardize Rowan?"

"Possibly," said David. "But I've made it fairly clear that I'm operating against Ms. Richter's wishes. That's why they expelled me. . . ."

"You were expelled?"

"A story for another time," said David gently, his attention focused on the circle. "If you don't mind, I will need you and Toby to remain absolutely quiet for the next hour or so. My strength is failing, and I'm afraid Maya won't be able to help me much longer."

Max did not like any of this. Toby inched into his lap as he took a seat next to Maya. Apparently the smee did not like the idea of a summoning any more than Max did. But the two sat quietly as David walked about the circle and called the demon forth.

And when David spoke the proper incantation and its name, the demon arrived in a flash of light and a whiff of brimstone.

The demon appeared very old and exceedingly irritated. Her body was cronelike, her skin looking jaundiced against her scarlet robes. But it was her face that made Toby surrender an involuntary shriek and bury his face in Max's shoulder. It was covered with pustules, from the pair of rounded horns atop her head all the way down to her chin, from which two living snakes had sprouted and flicked their tongues to taste the air. A single eye, round and unblinking, was set within her brow, and she hissed as she set the eye upon David.

"Are you Cambrylla?" asked David.

The demon laughed and spoke in a woman's voice—amused and sultry and utterly disconnected from the bent, grotesque form within the circle. "I know who *you* are," she purred. "And I know who sits behind you. How dare you insects summon me! Do you have any idea what Astaroth will do to you?"

She laughed, and Max's flesh went clammy.

"You must be very important to threaten us in such haughty fashion," David observed calmly. "One might suppose that Astaroth had just secretly designated you to be his officiate for Walpurgisnacht."

The smile faded from the demon's face. "How could you possibly—"

But David dismissed both the question and her incredulity with a wave. "You will now divulge to me the details of the spoken rites and the garb to be worn by yourself and your attendants."

The demon refused. David spoke a word. The flames about the tomb rose to the ceiling, and it became hot within the room. But while it was merely uncomfortable for Max, the demon floated above the ground and writhed as though racked with pain.

"You cannot refuse me," said David.

Twitching and snarling and gasping in a dozen languages simultaneously, the demon betrayed the secrets of her recent appointment. David listened calmly throughout, but Max could see him shaking as though the strain was growing very great. When the interrogation was over and the demon had spoken the secret words and divulged the dress and manners of the ceremony, David made a sign and she collapsed within the circle.

"Cambrylla, you will remain here until Walpurgisnacht has passed," David commanded. "Not until May Day, not until sunlight strikes this tomb, shall you be free to leave this circle."

The demon scowled at David, but her oozing body shook with laughter. "You think to deceive Astaroth?" she howled. "He sees all, little Sorcerer. He will flay you for your vanity and devour you, body and soul. Back to him you go, little one! Back to Astaroth for you and yours."

She giggled and writhed upon the ground, her joints folding in ways they should not. It was a nauseating sight, and Max wished they could simply dismiss her. But David ignored her mocking laughter and hissing threats. Instead, he turned to the smee.

"Toby," he said. "I need you to take the shape of Cambrylla. And this time, we can't overlook any minor flaws."

"Dear Lord," moaned the smee, peering at the demon.

Minutes later, Toby had transformed and Max grimaced as he stared at Cambrylla in their midst. The smee really was a marvelous mimic and had already imprinted the demon's voice and speech patterns so that the original had finally ceased her mockery lest Toby perfect his impersonation even more. Looking at them both, Max could not detect an iota of difference.

"I can't see auras," he confessed. "How's the aura?"

"Perfect," said David. "Toby, you are truly a smee among smees!"

"Well and good," cackled Toby in Cambrylla's chilling voice. "But when the Demon's turned the little Sorcerer's toes to jelly . . . !" The smee abruptly stopped and gave a short cough. "My apologies," he said in his own melodious baritone. "Once a chap's on a roll, it's just so easy to get lost in the character. Forgive me. Of course, nobody's turning your toes to jelly!"

"No apology necessary," said David. "In fact, I think it would be best if you stayed in character—disgusting as that may be."

"David," said Max. "Please don't tell me you're going to turn me into a demon."

"No," said David. "You and I have easy costumes. We'll be dressed as malakhim."

And saying this, David went to his pack and brought out an entire chest. Rummaging through, he pulled out a pair of hooded black robes and the obsidian death masks with marred, angelic faces. Even this effort seemed to exhaust him. His face had a deathly pallor, and sweat was running freely from his hairline to his chin. Max glanced at Maya and saw that the ulu was also bathed in a cold sweat.

"What's the matter with her?" asked Max, stroking the ulu's clammy head.

"She's dying," replied David with chilling conviction. "Her blood doesn't just help me translate things. It has healing properties, too. And when I overtax myself—as is easy to do—Maya's energies rejuvenate me. Unfortunately, the demands I've been putting on myself this past year have been too much for both of us. She will leave us soon, but we will always be grateful to her. . . ."

And as the demon in the circle began to ridicule his grief, David placed an order of silence upon her. He invited the others to rest, for it was already past midnight and the fateful day had arrived. When the sun set that next evening, the festivities would begin.

But none of them could sleep.

Like any dutiful actor, the smee was focused and reviewing every detail of his upcoming performance—from the greetings given to the doorkeeper to the opening ceremonies themselves. He sat away from them, still looking every bit the hideous demon, as he scribbled notes and whispered various phrases and inflections.

Max sat cross-legged, gazing at the black malakhim mask. Its face was beatific, but there was a crack that ran from temple to chin, marring the face for some past transgression. David had taken pains with every aspect of the costume so that it would cloak Max's aura, as had his helmet and armor in the arena. He and David would accompany the smee, each dressed as a malakhim and holding the ancient rhytons—pouring vessels— that would contain the wine for the ceremonial toast. Max's curiosity became unbearable. He glanced at David, who was sitting several feet away, cradling his charge's delicate head.

Max scooted closer. "Will the poison already be in the wine?" he hissed.

"No," David murmured sleepily. "The elixir must be added to the wine just before it is consumed."

"How do you plan on doing that?"

"Sleight of hand," said David, smiling. "No magic."

Max frowned. David had only one hand and had been reluctant to even deal cards.

"I know what you're thinking," said David. "Have a look."

He passed to Max an artificial hand made of wood. There was nothing enchanted about it or even terribly functional. It might have been a mannequin's hand, the fingers curling so as to hold something. There was something peculiar about the area where the wrist met the forearm, however. All around the wrist were pairs of raised, empty rings, as though to secure any number of slender tubes.

"It can hold six," David said proudly.

"And so you're going to slip your little mixtures in the wine when no one's looking?" asked Max.

David nodded. Max was appalled at the plan's dumb simplicity.

"Won't someone be watching you?"

"Why would they?" asked David. "No, I think all eyes will be on Astaroth."

"I doubt it," said Max. "I'm over a foot taller than you. We're going to look ridiculous standing on either side of Toby."

"I'm going to be wearing special boots," said David. "And I'm not that short."

"I guess you've thought of everything," said Max heavily. "Is there anything else I need to know?"

"Just keep us safe long enough to make our escape," David pleaded. "There is a secret passage behind the altar. The opening is very clever—it can't be detected by magic since it's just an optical illusion that camouflages a narrow exit. If we can clear a path to that tunnel after Astaroth drinks the wine, I think we can get away."

"Won't it be guarded?" asked Max.

"It might," David allowed. "But this is why we got the *gae bolga* reforged. If you give it everything you have, the demons will be in for a shock."

"I hope you're right." Max sighed, touched and amused by David's faith.

With an affectionate smile, David patted Max's sword arm and curled up with Maya to sleep. Within a minute, he was snoring, his nose wheezing with its telltale whistle.

Max stared at his newly forged weapon, its wondrous blade that could pierce heaven and earth. The giant said the *gae bolga* could slay anything. Perhaps he could intervene before David enacted his disastrous plan and strike the Demon down before they bothered with the useless Blood Petals.

It might be their only hope.

The next afternoon, Maya died. They had been restowing their gear when it happened. Within her silent circle, the demon suddenly leaped and cavorted about. She pointed a talon at the ulu, who had been dozing throughout the day and refused to eat. Putting down his case of poisons, David frowned and went to his charge.

He sat with her for some time, holding her head and whispering to her. Finally, he called to Max and asked if he would carry the ulu outside the tomb. He did so, scooping Maya's frail silvery body into his arms and taking her outside into the warm spring day. David followed after, the two boys squinting at the bright daylight.

"I'm sorry, David," said Max. "I don't know what else to say. Do you want me to bury her?"

"Oh no," replied David, sounding distracted. "That's really so nice of you, but it isn't necessary. Let's just lay her by that tree."

"But the insects and animals . . ."

"She won't mind," David assured him. "I think she'd like the idea of being a part of living things. I just didn't want her in that tomb, mocked by that demon. I think that's beneath her."

"I do, too."

When he laid Maya upon the ground, David bowed to her body and then crouched to pat the ulu's silver horns and close her golden eyes. Wiping away a single tear, David stood and turned to Max.

"Can you call for Toby?" he asked. "It's time for us to go."

David did not even bother to address the demon again. When Toby had emerged from the tomb and Max had retrieved the rest of their things, David merely shut the heavy stone door with a dismissive wave of his hand.

"Are we walking to the palace?" asked Max.

"That would never do," David replied. "We will be arriving in style."

Once they were clad in their costumes, the masquerade had officially begun. While David wobbled about and got accustomed to his stiltlike boots, he also surveyed their setting and arranged for transportation.

There was something strangely comforting about the fact that David could retain his sense of humor despite his fear and grief and the awful task ahead. He might have been Cinderella's fairy godmother, and they might have been attending a ball, for they rode in a decadent, gilded coach that had been transformed from a cypress while four squirrels had been conscripted into serving as their team of sleek black horses.

It was not far to Blys; it rose before them, mountainous and beautiful before the setting sun. The awe-stricken smee was so quiet that Max finally touched its oozing, necrotic hand.

"That is absolutely disgusting," he observed.

"Don't blame me," sniffed the smee in Cambrylla's chilling voice. "You're the ones who insisted I take this repulsive form. I never thought I'd actually prefer my native shape."

"Sorry," said Max. "I just want to see how you're doing. I'm guessing you don't have a lot of experience with this kind of thing."

Max did not intend to sound so patronizing. Cambrylla's hideous face turned slowly and grimaced at him.

"Am I to take it that *you* are an old hand at storming demon-filled palaces?"

"W-well, no," stammered Max, "but—"

"I mean, you don't even have to talk!" observed the smee with a bitter laugh. "I have actual lines to remember while you can just stand about like a big galoot! Do you know what they call big, silent galoots in the theater, my boy? They call them 'extras.'"

"Okay, then," said Max, folding his arms and staring out the window.

"Stop bickering," said David. "We're almost there."

Indeed they were.

They were now on the same road Max had traveled with Prusias. The sprawling camps of humans were just ahead, filthy and squalid. Max looked up at the city itself—its towering hills, terraced with dwellings and palaces and gardens. Above all was the main palace, the enormous Coliseum sitting atop the massive pyramid. Atop the Coliseum, positioned so that its rose window faced the setting sun, was the cathedral.

"We have to hurry," said David, his eyes on the sunset, which was reflected in the cathedral's windows. As though in response to his words, the carriage leaped forward, causing all within the road to make way.

Rattling over the Tiber's bridge, they swept up toward the great Mouth of Truth, whose dead-eyed grimace served as the city's entrance. At the gate, an ogre peered inside the carriage and, upon seeing Cambrylla, immediately waved them through.

As David quietly directed the carriage, Max reflected how strange it was to be driving along these familiar streets while wearing the black robes and mask of the malakhim. They had been his companions on his way to the arena and in his silent mansion upon the hill. He wondered if they would accompany Prusias to the festivities. He hoped not. There was something about their silent, expressionless faces that imparted the impression that they were always watching and that they knew more than you imagined. Might they know him by his stance or walk?

Max, you can't think about everything that could go wrong.

Listen to steady Cooper and do your job.

Listen to wise David and have faith.

Listen to beloved Scathach and find the patterns.

The mantras calmed him as the carriage made its way through many districts, pushing through the throngs of vyes and drunken goblins and other shrieking revelers on this greatest of holidays. Cambrylla's leering visage was enough to grant entrance to the most prestigious districts, but there was a problem when they finally reached the palace.

Their invitation had expired.

Apparently, security precautions had mandated that the invitations be reissued. What they had presented was no longer considered valid. The footman—an imp in Elizabethan dress—was unmistakably haughty and superior. Channeling every theatrical impulse, the smee leaped into action.

Emerging from the carriage, Cambrylla hugged her scarlet robes close and bent to address the imperious imp. Max saw her wave the invitation under the imp's nose and gesture angrily at a nearby vye. The vye loped off, and Cambrylla continued to accost the imp, who was now looking profoundly uncomfortable. A moment later, the smee reentered the carriage and they were waved inside.

"How did you do that?" Max hissed.

"Oh, that's no trouble at all," scoffed the smee. "I've bullied and bamboozled my way into more restaurants, clubs, and snooty events than you can imagine. Those people at the ropes are all the same. Told him that I was Astaroth's handpicked officiate and that if he made us one second late, we'd use his empty little brainpan as the wine cup!"

"Toby, that's disgusting," said Max.

"I am *not* Toby," replied the smee loftily. "I am Cambrylla, and that is precisely how one must talk to these people."

Max had never been in this part of the palace before, and the spectacle took his breath away. The spaces were simply enormous, dwarfing even the Frankfurt Workshop. Imps and goblins and vyes were running about, setting up tables and stations for the main feast to come. Meanwhile, the nobles' carriages were directed along a series of internal ramps and causeways that must have been a hundred yards wide.

It was difficult not to gape when their carriage passed a frog-headed creature some thirty feet tall or a black wolf the size of an elephant. Hell had been emptied into Prusias's palace. As they navigated the traffic that was making its way up the ramps and streets within the pyramid, Max gasped as he saw Mad'raast crouching down to speak with King Prusias.

It was an absurd sight. By comparison, Prusias was tiny—a mere man in regal robes speaking to a subordinate that must have been a hundred feet tall. But there was absolutely no mistaking their relative ranks, for Mad'raast looked almost cowed, and Prusias's face was dark with fury. He jabbed his cane under his duke's nose, and Max could not help but notice the huge shadow dancing on the marble walls.

The great red dragon was very close, indeed.

As Max watched real fear creep across Mad'raast's face, he also looked for Mr. Bonn. But there was no sign of him, and Max wondered what had happened to that unusually brave and noble imp. Mr. Bonn had taken tremendous risks to aid Max and provide Cooper with the key that freed him. It worried him that the imp was not with his master on such an important occasion.

But greater worries loomed. Fortunately, these did not include having to wait in lines or jostle among the many carriages and palanquins that vied for entrance to the upper halls. Whenever they were forced to wait, some imp or other elaborately costumed attendant spied their carriage and singled them out so that they could stream past the others and make their way unimpeded. In this manner, they spiraled ever upward.

At last the massive ramp ended and deposited them atop an enormous open, flagged space that fed toward the west front of the cathedral. The wind was howling at such a height, and the setting sun fell full upon the cathedral so that its façade was gold. Below them, Max could see a glimpse of the Coliseum. The huge arena where he had fought and bled and become champion appeared no bigger than a matchbox. No carriages were permitted to approach the cathedral, so they were forced to exit while an imp hopped into the driver's seat and cracked a whip to drive the horses away. Within the costume of the stoic malakhim, Max had to force himself not to crane his neck and gawk at the cathedral's mind-boggling scale.

Even Mad'raast would feel small entering into such a place. As they crossed the open space before the cathedral's entrance, Max tried not to stop and gape. To see the cathedral at a distance inspired awe; to witness these dimensions at such close proximity inspired fear.

This fear was compounded by the acoustics in such a vast interior space. For as they passed beneath the central arch, every sound and footstep was suddenly echoed and amplified so that it seemed both louder and utterly infinitesimal.

The atmosphere was one of intense preparation—the frantic, backstage energies of an opening-night performance. Imps and vyes scurried and hurried about on countless errands. Hundreds of kitsune and other minor daemona streamed in and out of the main archway, clutching belyaëls and cellos and violins.

"There you are!" exclaimed a voice, and Max turned to see

Mr. Bonn hurrying toward them, clutching a dozen scrolls against his chest. He looked to be a wreck, as if the pressures of hosting such an affair and the requisite planning had thoroughly broken him. The frazzled imp wasted no time.

"It is an honor, Countess," he said to Cambrylla. "I have just been informed that the Great God himself will be joining us and that he has selected Your Excellency to serve as his officiate for the opening toast. King Prusias is delighted, of course, and specifically requested that I bid you welcome."

Max noticed that Cambrylla bowed with great care, inclining her head slightly when addressed initially by the imp but bending deeply at the waist when Prusias was mentioned.

"Are you familiar with the officiate's responsibilities?" inquired the imp.

"This is not my first Walpurgisnacht," sneered Cambrylla.

"Of course," muttered Mr. Bonn, bowing hastily. "Please, follow me."

Crying out at musicians and laborers to make way, Mr. Bonn led them into the cathedral.

If Max had felt tiny before, he now ceased to exist. As they proceeded down the seemingly endless nave, his eyes darted about behind their obscuring mask. Eerie voices played around the massive space, in concert with the organ, whose heavy notes issued periodically and made the very air vibrate.

By the time they reached the altar, Mr. Bonn was positively sweating. Max was, too, and he worried about David, who was not only terribly weak, but also trying his best to walk on the equivalent of miniature stilts. Fortunately, there was so much activity and such an air of nervous energy that none had time to gawk at the awkward malakhim stumbling after his hideous countess.

Hurrying over to the altar, the imp lifted a silken cloth and brought forth a golden chalice and two enormous ewers for the wine. Wiping sweat from his brow, the imp handed the chalice to Cambrylla and each of the ewers to Max and David. Sighing, he glanced at the sunlight streaming through the rose window and looked back at the haughty Cambrylla.

"The ceremony will not start for a little while yet," he said. "I'll have your chairs brought."

It was too surreal by half.

Max almost started giggling as three vyes brought three gilded chairs for himself, David, and the smee. They sat behind the altar—impossibly tiny and insignificant—while the sun continued to oet and the musicians hurried to their places. The smee remained in character throughout.

"Must I remind you that we are in a holy setting and must not fidget?"

Max immediately stopped scratching his knee. He was sweating profusely inside his costume. The malakhim robes were heavy, and the mask was as oppressive as the one he'd worn as Bragha Rùn. His heart went out to poor David; just the walk down the nave's aisle must have been an act of sheer will.

So they sat and waited and recovered their strength. One by one the musicians ceased tuning instruments, and behind their screen the choir voices hushed. Only the organ continued playing, the dissonant notes dark and haunting.

The nobles began to enter, filing down the aisles in respectful silence. There were sections marked for each of the rulers, each bearing the standard of the king or queen. Max noted that the followers of Prusias and Aamon were not seated near one another. The more massive nobles—many of whom were the Fomorian's size or even larger—lined the outer walls. Max tried not to stare as Mad'raast settled into an alcove, folding his great wings about himself as though he still sat perched upon the rock.

As hundreds upon hundreds of nobles continued to file in, Max noted that not everyone entered by the door. Far above, he glimpsed ghostly shapes and spirits drifting about the upper reaches of the cathedral, their spectral forms flitting in and out of the thinning shafts of sunlight.

It was immensely unsettling to see the nobles all seated throughout the cathedral in a state of such uninterrupted quiet and stillness. They stared ahead at the altar and the three figures seated behind it. Max felt as though an immense spotlight had been turned upon them. So many eyes and faces of terrible, immortal beings were focused on them. Some beings were nightmarishly fiendish-looking, while their neighbors might be perilously beautiful; others still were hidden behind strange masks and wrappings. The only common denominator among the hideous diversity of faces was their calm, unflinching malevolence. Max was grateful he could not see auras—he might have run screaming from the building.

As a flood of additional guests now filed in, Max silently reviewed the plan.

Astaroth will enter and walk down the central aisle.

Cambrylla will rise to offer him the empty chalice.

David will step forward and pour the Demon a cup of poisoned wine.

Astaroth will be destroyed and Max will cover their escape.

They had a simple plan, a perfect poison, and an ideal position—except for one fatal flaw.

The Demon knew all about it.

Of course, when Astaroth had interrogated him, Max had not known that David would be standing on the altar or that a smee would be impersonating Astaroth's officiate. He had not known all of the minutiae and thus had not been able to divulge every detail to the Demon.

But he had betrayed enough to get them killed.

Astaroth knew that David planned to strike this very evening, and he knew the murder weapon. Even if they managed to poison him with David's elixirs, Max knew the Blood Petals would have no effect.

Every aspect of their evening thus far acquired an increasingly sinister tinge. Had new invitations been issued to parse out the infiltrators' identities? Had the imps and courtiers singled out their carriage and hastened them along to ensure they fell into the Demon's trap? In retrospect, it all seemed an elaborate act to usher the condemned onto their stage.

The sun's final rays dwindled in the great rose window.

Walpurgisnacht had commenced.

~ 28 ~

WALPURGISNACHT

As the sunlight died away, so, too, did the organ music. Instead, a single belyaël started to play a hauntingly beautiful tune. The nobles turned and faced the central aisle as the four monarchs entered and walked down the nave.

The first was Rashaverak, the King of Jakarün. He must have been twelve feet tall and was dressed in robes of golden silk that were at odds with his head, which was that of a balcful red wolf. He wore an iron crown, and every demon bowed as he passed.

Next was Lilith, the demon queen of Zenuvia. She appeared wholly human, a beautiful woman with waves of shining black hair and a chillingly beatific face. The queen wore robes of deepest green and was attended by a pair of elegant kitsune who stood behind her as she took her seat in the front pew.

As Aamon made his eerie, drifting progress down the nave, Max scanned the seats for Vyndra. He found him in Prusias's section of nobles, a fearsome, tigerlike rakshasa dressed in black armor. Max was surprised Prusias would allow his disloyal duke to sit among his devotees; almost everyone knew that Vyndra was in league with Aamon.

But Max did not particularly care about Vyndra's politics: The demon had murdered Max's father in cold blood. And he was standing a mere thirty or forty yards away. . . .

Max tore his attention away only when Prusias approached. If the many traitors and thieves among his delegation bothered the King of Blys, he certainly did not show it. Prusias positively beamed at the demons on either side of him. He looked splendid in his black mail and purple robes, and he was leaning upon his prodigiously powerful cane—a cane that David believed held a page or two from the Book of Thoth.

But as Prusias made his way down the aisle, Max saw he was escorting someone half his size. His guest was a middle-aged human, a woman who wore a jester's costume and who gaped uncomprehendingly about her surroundings.

The woman was David's mother.

And seeing her pitiful, trusting face, Max was almost grateful, because the appalling sight of the demon pretending to fawn over this helpless woman was so infuriating that Max momentarily forgot Vyndra.

He would slay Prusias first.

When things took an ugly turn—and Max had no doubt that they would—he would seek to strike down the King of Blys before he was ultimately overcome. It was the least he could do to that incomparably cruel, grinning figure standing in the front pew, flanked by his malakhim.

Throughout this spectacle, the nobles had stood patiently, and the lone musician continued to play her eerie, hypnotic tune. Max glanced at Toby; if the smee was nervous, he was doing a marvelous job of hiding it. He sat in plain sight, Cambrylla's scabrous hands holding the golden chalice that she would offer to Astaroth.

The belyaël's final note trailed away. A thousand demons promptly stood and turned to face the cathedral's entrance.

The Demon had arrived.

Max knew this before Astaroth had even entered the cathedral, and it had nothing to do with the music or the frightened, attentive expression on every face. It had everything to do with the brilliant white light that was streaming through the open doors and the rose window, growing ever brighter as the Demon approached.

When Astaroth stepped within, Max's heart almost froze once again. There was that overwhelming presence, that clamp upon the will that compelled utter obedience. The Demon wore robes of simple white, but it seemed as though every atom of the Demon's form and vestments radiated light. The silly dream from Max's imprisonment flashed in his mind. *And the moon strikes the ground and rolls away to play with him some other time. . . .*

That other time had come, for as Astaroth approached the altar, he was greater than the moon. He was indeed Lucifer, "the light bearer." The Demon's unveiled presence was so blindingly beautiful and terrible that many demons simply bowed their heads and refused to look directly upon him.

The Demon carried no staff or scepter or even the viper-rod that he often bore as a token of office. The only object he carried was the Book of Thoth. Almost everything about the Demon was white and gold and luminous. The two exceptions were his shining black hair and his dead-black eyes. It was the eyes—those ancient, knowing slits—that had so terrified Max when he'd seen them staring at him from the Rembrandt painting years before. The Demon's eyes had smiled at Max down within Marley Augur's crypt. And those eyes had smiled when Max surrendered the Book.

And they were smiling at Max now.

It was unmistakable—Astaroth was staring right at Max as he walked down the nave. Max would have trembled, would have fainted where he stood, were it not for the Demon's irresistible will, which dominated him and held him rigid. Within his head, Max heard Astaroth's voice speaking to him. Its familiar tones were soft and sibilant and eternally playful.

"*So here we are,*" whispered the Demon. "*I'm so happy you're here. Prusias was enraged over your escape, but I'm flattered that you would take such pains to attend another of my beautiful moments. For you enabled my release from bondage, and you surrendered this precious Book unto me, and now you shall bear witness as I consume your friend and consecrate my rule over this earth. You bring me good fortune, Max McDaniels!*"

Astaroth's voice was so clear that he might have been whispering directly in Max's ear. But the Demon's lips never moved; indeed, his face remained composed and somber. The smile was in the eyes alone.

"*But poor little David,*" observed the Demon. "*He can hardly stand! Without me to prop him up, he should have collapsed long ago. How he trembles! How he shakes on those absurd little boots. He is such a little lamb, as I told him at our first meeting. If his essence did not contribute so wonderfully to my own, I would keep him as a pet. . . .*"

Astaroth was now climbing the shallow steps toward them. His eyes briefly flicked from Max's to his officiate.

"A smee!" chuckled the Demon in Max's head. *"You thought to deceive me with a smee . . . I'm sorry you think so little of me."*

The Demon had reached the top step and was standing before them, blindingly bright.

"Now, Max, I must say a few words to my flock in our own tongue. But never you worry, my love. I shall provide you with a translator."

And as the Demon said this, a gypsy moth flew from the folds of his robe and landed upon Max's shoulder. It was Mr. Sikes, the only servant Astaroth trusted. In his moth form, the imp quickly scuttled inside Max's cowl. Max's instinct was to swat the wretched creature, but his mind and body were not his own. And thus he was forced to watch in a state of silent anguish while the imp's urbane sardonic voice whispered in his ear.

Astaroth bowed to Cambrylla and then turned to face the multitudes. The Demon's voice filled the cathedral as he spoke in the language of the demons.

"My children, welcome to the Halls of Blys, and many thanks to our host, King Prusias. On Walpurgisnacht, we celebrate a sacred evening and commemorate the great moments of our past. . . ."

There was a hissing murmur of assent from the demons.

"For it was on Walpurgisnacht that we did destroy mankind's last great school of magic. On Walpurgisnacht, many of you joined with me to snuff out those humans that would make us serve their vanity. For on this night did Solas fall!"

A great roar from the demons, until Astaroth raised his hand for quiet.

"And on that very night, did we not unite against the one who had been moving against us? And did I not catch him at last and consume him body and soul? Upon this very night, Elias Bram did fall!"

A deafening roar, a chorus of cries shook the very cathedral.

"And on this night, this holy night, I return to stand before you," said Astaroth smoothly. "For I know there are some here who have doubted me. . . ."

All mirth died away. The cathedral became so still that Max could hear his own heartbeat. The imp's antennae scratched against his mask as Mr. Sikes continued to translate. Astaroth's presence before the assembled host became so great, so tangibly powerful, that many demons trembled and hid their faces.

"It is true," he continued. "It grieves me to know that there are doubters. It grieves me that some have the audacity to whisper that the Great God has not returned but has fled with his Book to drift among the cosmos and contemplate the far places. It grieves me that some would ignore my edicts and question my judgments."

Within the first pew, Prusias fidgeted and glanced away. The movement was not lost upon Astaroth, who smiled benevolently at him.

"But I am not a god of judgment," said Astaroth. "I am a god of mercy; I am a god of wisdom; I am a god of truth. For as you sought to deceive me, you have been yourselves deceived. . . ."

And turning, the Demon stared at his false officiate.

Beneath that awful gaze, Cambrylla wilted like a scorched flower. Dropping the chalice, she crumpled to the ground, her limbs shrinking into her robes as smoke rose in little curls. There was a popping sound and a putrid odor as her pustules contracted and burst open. If Max could have looked away, he would have. Astaroth walked somberly to the pile of scarlet silk and thrust his hand within it.

Fishing out the smee, he held Toby aloft by one end of his yamlike body.

"You have the boldness to doubt me and yet you are deceived

by *this*," Astaroth observed wryly. "You permitted a wretched smee to desecrate this holy night and serve as a false officiate! Instead of celebrating our triumphs, you would have witnessed my assassination."

Astaroth shook his head, as though the statement shocked even him.

"For if I was not the Great God, that is surely what would have happened," he declared. "Had I depended on your vigilance or wisdom, I would have been murdered this very night. And it amuses me to see so many of you fools wondering, 'How could this be?' I shall show you. . . ."

The Demon flung Toby dismissively over his shoulder. The helpless smee landed on the altar and curled up like a salted slug. Turning toward David, Astaroth raised his hand like a puppeteer.

David's body was wrenched violently off his feet as though jerked by invisible wires. His mask cracked and fell to the ground and shattered. Astaroth allowed David to move just enough so that the little Sorcerer appeared to struggle, his legs kicking weakly as he was twirled about in the air.

A cry sounded from the audience. Mrs. Menlo had recognized her son and was staring up at him, her mouth agape. One of the malakhim restrained her as she tried to come forward.

"My children," said Astaroth, "this is David Menlo. Some here know of him as Rowan's Sorcerer—he may have even summoned some of you. Others curse him as the plunderer of their fleets. But few know that he is a gardener and a rather gifted alchemist. For it is this impudent boy who has been spreading those pestilential Blood Petals about your lands. But despite his impudence, I must salute him. He not only had the wit to deceive you all, but he also possessed the craft to develop something truly perilous. . . ."

And at Astaroth's playful gesture, David's robes were torn

from his suspended body. He hung in the air wearing his ragged sweater and old trousers—the spectacle compounded by his ridiculous stilts.

"Oh, I wouldn't laugh," said Astaroth, silencing his leering audience. "Years ago, I consumed young David's hand. And while he has not fashioned a terribly inspired replacement, I would direct your attention to the red vials about its wrist. For those vials contain a concoction so dangerous that even a sip would slay the mightiest among you."

Max hoped it would be over soon. He stood absolutely rigid while Mr. Sikes whispered in his ear. David looked so small and so frightened as he hovered limp and helpless above the Demon. Astaroth regarded him as though he were a lecture exhibit.

"But still I am plagued with skeptics," he said with a rueful smile. "I reveal infiltrators in your midst and save you from mortal peril and yet some still retain the temerity to doubt. Very well, I will show you. . . ."

Standing tall, the Demon surveyed the vast cathedral until his eyes fell upon a massive, winged shape that sat brooding in an alcove.

"Ah, the great Mad'raast," exclaimed Astaroth, offering a civil bow. "Come forward, Duke of Lebrim and sentry of the gates, for I have a great honor to bestow upon you."

The fear and anticipation among the demons was palpable as the huge, dark shape slipped from its perch and advanced warily up the nave. Astaroth beckoned playfully at the gargantuan demon as he paused at the final pews.

"Don't be frightened," Astaroth purred. "For I have promised to bestow a great honor upon you, and my word is my bond. For you have failed Prusias, who put his faith in you. It was your responsibility to serve your fellow nobles with vigilance, but you chose instead to serve your greed."

The great demon bowed his horned head and kneeled, his leathery wings folded about him in an attitude of penance.

"You are very good to admit your shame," said Astaroth gently. "I was almost moved to anger, but now see that you are worthy of this honor."

"And what is my honor, Great God?" asked Mad'raast in his deep hiss.

"You shall demonstrate just how dangerous this little Sorcerer is," replied Astaroth. "And by your sacrifice, you shall atone for your greed and offer my flock a gift of wisdom."

The huge, winged demon hesitated, his head still bowed low. "My lord, perhaps there is another—"

"Mad'raast," said Astaroth coldly. "Am I to understand that you are questioning the honor I would grant you? Are you determined to spoil the beautiful death I would bestow despite your failings?"

The demon shook his head gravely and stood to his full, massive height. And at Astaroth's command, David's body jerked and spiraled through the air. His limbs shaking under Astaroth's command, David removed one of the vials and placed it upon Mad'raast's open palm. Bowing low to the Great God, Mad'raast turned and faced his watchful peers.

With a monstrous, defiant cry, the demon swallowed the entire vial.

Its potency was instantly apparent.

Mad'raast's cry suddenly curdled into a hideous, frantic scream. White-hot flames burst from his throat and chest and stomach, sweeping over his body like an inferno. Within seconds, the gargantuan demon had been reduced to a smoldering heap of ashes.

Every demon, every noble looked on in stupefied silence. Glancing at Prusias, Max saw the king leaning forward and staring hard at the remaining vials—ever the opportunist. Astaroth, however, had descended to the mound of fluttering ashes and scooped up a handful.

"Farewell, Mad'raast," said Astaroth, letting the remains sift through his long, sharp-nailed fingers. "We thank you for your gift and can only hope King Prusias will have the wisdom to replace you with someone more attentive."

Ascending to the altar again, the Demon turned and faced his audience.

"You should be grateful to Mad'raast for the lesson he has taught you. For you need me, my children. You have already permitted a Sorcerer to infiltrate your midst, but he is not the only assassin within these walls. For this kingdom's very own champion has returned to exact a vengeance of his own. Look well, Vyndra and Prusias and all my beautiful nobles, for a Red Death has come to claim you."

Mr. Sikes took to the air, fluttering his tiny wings, as Max's robes fell away, along with the mask of the malakhim. Hisses and whispers ran like tremors through the crowd. Max's face was known to the many Blyssian nobles who believed that he had died in the arena. Mr. Sikes settled once more upon Max's shoulder, his sly voice curling like smoke in Max's ear.

"Yes," said Astaroth. "This is Max McDaniels, the very Hound of Rowan whom you thought dead. But Prusias deceived you, my children. For this is not just Max McDaniels, but the very Red Death whom you cheered. The Bragha Rùn whom you believed to be one of us . . ."

Max stood motionless under the collective stare of a thousand demons. Prusias could not help himself; he was staring at Max like a wild animal, a terrible smile on his dark, savage features.

"This is my captive, Great God!" cried the King of Blys.

"Return him to my keeping. I will assure you and all the nobles that he will never raise a hand against our kind."

"My Prusias," said Astaroth gently, "I do not think the nobles would trust such a dangerous one to your care—particularly as you sought to deceive them. I imagine it is obvious to all that you intended to keep the Hound as a very lethal pet. No, I do not think the others would approve if I relinquished him to you."

"My Lord—"

"Be still, Prusias."

Max required no translator to hear the edge in Astaroth's voice. Prusias sat back as though he'd been struck a blow. The king obediently bowed and averted his eyes.

"And so," said the Demon, "this shall be a Walpurgisnacht you shall never forget. For not only have I returned, but I have also shown you the error of your ways, as a good parent should. To consecrate this night, I shall raise a toast to you, my children, and our noble history. While I claim the Sorcerer for myself, I deliver the Hound unto you as my gift. His essence shall forever remind you of this night, when the Great God returned and all doubts were put aside. . . ."

Lowering David slowly, the Demon turned and gazed upon the little Sorcerer with an expression of surprising tenderness.

Mr. Sikes took the opportunity to whisper a message of his own. "Upon the altar you shall go," whispered the imp. "Bound and helpless for all to feast. My lord has promised me the first bite—just enough for me to attain *koukerros*. I shall try not to be greedy, but the others will simply have to wait their turn."

It took all of Max's resolve to move his head against Astaroth's wishes. He moved less than an inch, but it was enough to glimpse the moth upon his shoulder. The rage and fury within Max was surging to frightening levels; the Old Magic howled within him but was held captive by the indomitable will of

Astaroth. Several of the demons were pointing at him; his aura must have been growing, changing into something monstrous.

"Temper, temper," chided Mr. Sikes.

When David had nearly reached the cathedral floor, the Demon strode to the empty scarlet robes of the officiate and plucked up the golden goblet. David was hovering several inches off the ground; his entire body was limp as if his consciousness—and, indeed, his life—was swiftly departing.

"It's almost over, little one," said Astaroth. "But not quite yet. For you have taken great pains to poison my cup, and I would not deprive you of the opportunity. Fill this goblet so I may make my toast."

When the demons realized that Astaroth actually intended to drink David's poison, the cathedral became utterly silent. Max could hardly bear to gaze at his friend as Astaroth forced David's trembling hand to pour vial after vial of the crimson liquid into the goblet. And when this was done, the Demon bowed in mocking gratitude and turned to raise the goblet aloft.

"Behold!" he cried. "The Great God has returned!"

Tipping back his head, Astaroth drained the goblet's contents and grinned with a wild, savage triumph. No flames consumed his body, and the demons roared his name in adulation. Calmly placing the goblet upon the altar, Astaroth clutched the Book of Thoth to his chest. He raised a hand for quiet, and the cathedral fell into obedient silence.

Cupping David's chin, Astaroth raised his head so that the boy could look him in the eye. "Walpurgisnacht has officially commenced, little Sorcerer. Do you have any last words before I consume you?"

David nodded wearily.

"Let's hear them, my love."

"Checkmate."

No translation was necessary.

David spoke in English, and his single word had been perfectly audible in the silent cathedral.

Astaroth blinked. His smile faded, and he made a derisive laugh. "And what is that supposed to—"

With a drunken lurch, Astaroth staggered against the altar. His audience merely stared, unsure of what was happening. Max could hear the demon gasping. The spell holding David up was broken, and the boy collapsed to the floor.

What was happening to Astaroth was not nearly as dramatic as the flames that had consumed Mad'raast, but the demon did appear to be burning. A pearly, vaporous essence was issuing from him, rising like smoke as Astaroth succumbed to a sort of seizure.

"NO!" he cried, clawing frantically at his chest.

The exclamation was not one of pain, but of complete and utter shock. It was a cry of humiliation—for the Demon had been tricked before his entire court. Several nobles rose and approached, creeping cautiously up the steps. Prusias was among them, his expression a strange mixture of fear and delight. He glanced absently at David's motionless body and prodded it aside with his boot.

Astaroth gasped something to Prusias, some plea for aid. But the King of Blys did not pay his Great God any heed.

His eyes were on the Book.

And he was not alone.

The mood in the cathedral had turned; adulation had been replaced by something predatory.

Rashaverak was the first to reach for the Book, a probing swipe.

Astaroth shouted something at the demons in their own

language, but more were coming close—to survey and perhaps to seize upon a very great and unexpected opportunity.

Astaroth clutched the precious relic tighter, shouting at the demons in their own language. But it was in vain. More were venturing near—circling like sharks. And as they approached, Astaroth continued to gasp and writhe within the clinging cloud of pearly mist.

Snarling, Rashaverak made a bolder grab. Sweeping up his cane, Prusias cracked it down upon the wolfen snout, staggering the King of Jakarün and thrusting him aside. Prusias slipped closer to Astaroth, his mad eyes fixed on the golden book.

Boom!

The cathedral's windows shattered as Astaroth flung them all back with some terrible spell. Not a demon lay within fifty feet; even the monarchs had been dashed against the toppled pews and shattered statues.

Moaning, Astaroth clutched the Book closer. The Demon glared down at David with a feral, murderous rage. But there was fear, too. Max saw it spreading like a stain upon the Demon's face.

Looking past him, Max knew Astaroth had good reason to be afraid. The demons were rising once again. Prusias was already walking toward them, his face aglow and utterly insane.

"How the mighty have fallen!" he exclaimed, punctuating each step with his cane. "Has the 'Great God' been deceived?"

He laughed. The rest of the demons said nothing, but closed behind him in an anxious, watchful mob. Astaroth swatted weakly at the mist puffing steadily from his body.

"Stand down, Prusias," he gasped. "I command you."

"I will not," replied the grinning king, arriving at the steps. "Protect me!"

Max was powerless to resist. Commanded by the Demon's will, Max stepped in front of Astaroth and David. Prusias came to a halt upon the steps and stared with amused, malicious glee.

"You should have stayed in my dungeons, Max," he reflected.

Max drew the *gae bolga* from its sheath.

Prusias glanced at the weapon, bemused. "So, you've brought a knife to this little party?" he remarked, licking his lips. "Good for you, lad. But I brought something too. . . ."

Even as he spoke these words, the King of Blys began to grow. The smile never left Prusias's face as the demon transformed grotesquely into something Max had dreaded ever since he'd glimpsed its shadow.

Behold, a great red dragon!

And gazing up, Max looked upon Prusias in his true form. And that form was of a scarlet serpent that stretched the length of the cathedral. The other demons backed hurriedly away as Prusias's massive coils lashed from side to side, sweeping pews and peers aside. But despite the body's monstrous size and violence, Max was transfixed by its heads.

There were now seven of them, seven human heads set atop sinuous necks that had sprouted from the serpent's body. Each was horned and crowned, and bore the familiar, gnashing face of Prusias. One rose higher than all the rest. When it roared, the cathedral trembled.

Max was trembling, too. The *gae bolga* felt alive in his hand, almost straining in its eagerness for battle. Only Astaroth's will prevented Max from lashing out.

A breathless tension filled the cathedral.

Then Prusias attacked.

The spell binding Max's body was broken. All of the energy and rage and fear that had been cresting in him were released.

When the dragon struck, the *gae bolga* flashed like fire as Max slashed it across the demon's throat.

Prusias recoiled frantically from the blow, his face white with shock as blood streamed from the gaping wound. With a great heave, Prusias wrenched his scaly bulk away from the altar and Max. His other heads howled with fury, lashing about and snapping blindly. But the injured head stared, appalled at the hideous weapon in Max's hand.

For the *gae bolga* was screaming now.

It shook in Max's hand, the blade keening like women at a wake. It was a sound to freeze the blood. Many demons backed away, pressing against the outer walls as they sought refuge not only from Prusias, but the weapon that had wounded him.

But not all of the demons were cowards.

With cries and howls, hundreds of them joined the battle. While some stormed toward Astaroth, others from Aamon's and Lilith's camps fell upon Prusias. In a heartbeat, secret factions and alliances were revealed as the cathedral was transformed into a battlefield.

Max leaped forward to meet them, the *gae bolga* shrieking as it cleaved through armor, bone, and spirit with frightful ease. The energies surging through Max were enormous. He became ever wilder, until even Astaroth's voice and commands had faded. Soon there was only the hall and his enemies . . . and Vyndra.

He found the rakshasa in the midst of the fray, battling several of the malakhim. The demon evidently heard Max scream his name. With brutal efficiency, Vyndra clove his attackers in two and whirled to meet Max.

Slipping under the arc of Max's swing, the demon caught him by the throat and slammed him against a pillar. Flames were coursing about the demon's body, searing Max as the two struggled. The demon was much too strong at such close quarters. A frightful blow from a curving saber dazed Max and he barely escaped decapitation. The blade bit into the pillar just above Max's head, sinking deep into the stone. Snarling, the demon held Max at arm's length while he strained to free the blade.

He needn't have bothered.

Prusias's tail shattered the massive stonework like matchsticks. Its force sent Max and Vyndra sprawling as the King of Blys wheeled about and bore down upon them.

In a blink, Vyndra had transformed, becoming a column of living flame that streaked away toward the rafters. But Max had no such tricks up his sleeves. Backing frantically away, he found himself face to face with the King of Blys.

The demon's eyes were blank, unseeing. The Prusias Max had known was gone, his persona given wholly to the monster whose snapping jaws drove Max back toward the altar. It had already devoured dozens of its kind, and its beards were soaked with blood that dripped and hissed upon the marble floor.

One of the heads darted forward, baring its yellow fangs. Max slashed, catching it across its nose. Black blood spurted as it withdrew, but the others converged in a wild snapping and snarling. Max tripped over a fallen musician, rolling away just as Prusias's body surged forward to crush other demons nearby.

Just as Max scrambled to his feet, an arrow struck him in the shoulder.

The impact was like a gunshot, knocking him backward and nearly buckling his knees. Instinctively, he glanced up to glimpse Vyndra as he loosed another arrow from the safety of a balcony far above.

The second arrow struck mere inches from the first and knocked Max flat. Only a desperate parry deflected the next, as

Vyndra now took his time, aiming with deliberation. Crying out, Max stabbed the *gae bolga* into Prusias as a rippling coil threatened to crush him. With a roar, the King of Blys slid away before suddenly doubling back to renew his attack. As he heaved and coiled his body, its bulk momentarily sheltered Max from Vyndra's line of fire. Gritting his teeth, Max wrenched the arrows from his shoulder.

Max's breath came in painful gasps as he flung the arrows away. Prusias's great, bleeding head plunged down at him. This time, he would not be able to evade it. Every hideous detail was visible, from the slavering jaws to the demon's cane embedded within its iron crown.

But just as Prusias was about to seize Max, Vyndra shot another arrow. Instead of striking Max, the deadly shaft pierced Prusias's eye. Bellowing, Prusias whipped about to strike at his assailant.

As the head veered away, Max saw his chance.

Seizing hold of Prusias's tangled beard, Max held tight as the massive head rose high into the air. Below him, Max saw the battle playing out in miniature, the cathedral floor littered with the fallen and those who fed upon them. Holding his ground, Vyndra nocked another arrow.

The demon loosed it just as Prusias annihilated the balcony. The arrow went astray, whistling past Max, who let go of Prusias's beard to seize hold of Vyndra.

He caught the rakshasa about the waist, plunging the *gae bolga* into him. As the pair plummeted down, Vyndra roared with pain and scrabbled wildly to tear the weapon from Max's hand. The blade wailed as it pierced Vyndra's armor and clove the ancient essence beneath.

Frantic, the rakshasa sought escape. Again, his form became

one of smoke and flame as it streaked toward one of the shattered windows. But Max would not let go, clutching the searing shape as though it were a runaway comet.

And as the giant promised, the blade of the Morrígan made no distinction between mortal or immortal, flesh or spirit. It craved them all.

Whether the final scream came from Vyndra or the keening sword, Max could not tell. It did not matter. In a final, fiery burst, Vyndra's essence died and an inconceivable surge of energy flooded into Max.

With an earsplitting howl, Max sprang to the cathedral floor. His body was electric. Astaroth's hold was utterly shattered, consumed by the Old Magic in his blood and the weapon in his hand.

Scathach's words had come true. *"You are the child of Lugh Lamfhada. You are the sun and the storm and master of all the feats I have to teach. You are these things because you must be. . . ."*

As these words flashed in his mind, a light burst forth from him and he shone brighter than the noonday sun. Max was dimly aware of weapons striking out at him, of fearsome spells, of shrieks and pleas. But they were all for naught. He was invincible; he was the wildest demon in Blys.

The *gae bolga* inflicted terrible damage upon those within its reach, its keening reaching a frantic pitch. So swift was Max's assault and so terrifying his aspect that all took flight before him. He heard glass breaking, stone shattering, and the shrieking of fell spirits as he stormed through the hall.

But it was a single word, spoken telepathically, that finally got his attention.

"Max."

The voice was David's.

Whirling around, Max saw David slumped near the altar.

Astaroth lay nearby, still clutching the Book and struggling weakly against the swirling luminescent mist.

David repeated Max's name in the same calm, plaintive tone. It was not unlike Cooper's whispering of his name when the Agent had rescued Max in Prusias's dungeon. But David was not rescuing Max from a cell.

He was rescuing him from the Morrígan.

He was rescuing him from himself.

Max had taken an oath to protect David, and he had nearly forgotten it. Prusias loomed very near to David now, the great wyrm coiling about the cathedral's apse and altar so that David and Astaroth were almost obscured. Even in his wild state, Max realized that Prusias had cut off their escape.

"Max, I need you. . . ."

Max rushed back to the altar, demons fleeing before him. Dashing past the bodies littering the steps, Max finally reached his friend.

David was dying.

The little Sorcerer was lying upon the topmost step, his presence almost overlooked in the pandemonium that had erupted.

He beckoned Max closer. "Get my mother. It's almost time. . . ."

"Where is she?"

David gestured weakly toward a pair of overturned pews. Hurrying over, Max found Mrs. Menlo lying unconscious in the hollow between them. His eyes ever watchful for Prusias, Max dragged her out and slung her over his shoulder.

Running back to the altar, Max saw that the mist above Astaroth was growing brighter, its nimbus coalescing into distinct shapes. Laying Mrs. Menlo next to her son, Max leaped back just as one of Prusias's heads snaked forward to seize him. Its teeth gnashed, just missing as Max dealt three swift blows across its chin. The dragon howled with pain and dashed his head against the wall, bringing huge blocks of masonry crashing down about them.

Shielding the Menlos with his body, Max suddenly spied the smee upon the altar. Toby had curled himself into a ball no larger than a grapefruit. Snatching him with his injured arm, Max stuffed the smee inside his shirt, just as the nearby struggle intensified.

"Get away from me!"

The frantic command came from Astaroth. The Demon lay ten feet away, his back propped against the altar. He was besieged, straining against the enveloping mist, whose tendrils plucked at the Book of Thoth. As Max watched, Astaroth's hand was pried momentarily away and the golden cover was opened. . . .

Max glanced up to see a piece of masonry crashing toward them. Blocking his friends, he deflected it, but a corner still struck him a terrible blow on the head. Staggering, his knees suddenly buckled, and he slumped next to David.

As blood trickled into his eyes, Max glimpsed the Demon as he wrenched the Book of Thoth firmly back into his possession. For a moment, Astaroth's face turned toward him, beautiful and angelic and utterly suffused with hate.

There was a blinding flash of white light, and Max lost consciousness. . . .

He had not imagined death would be quite like this.

It was cold and wet and soothed him with lapping waves that washed over his toes and legs and reached up to his fingertips. And it was quiet and peaceful, a soft symphony of crashing waves and distant gulls.

And it was delightfully blubbery.

As Max moved his head, he felt a pillow of sleek fur.

"I think he's coming to."

Something cool touched Max's face, and he opened his eyes to see David.

The little Sorcerer was smiling down at him.

Max had never seen a picture that captured an expression such as David's. His friend's pale eyes were alight with a quiet radiance, a serenity that exceeded mere happiness. It was an expression of joy, of victory achieved through weary toil and bitter sacrifice.

"Can you hear me?" he asked quietly.

Max nodded, but his head ached terribly.

David urged him to lie still. Max noticed that his friend's deathly appearance seemed to have washed away, and he resembled his old self. Above, the sky was a placid pink, the stars growing faint with the coming dawn.

Twitching his fingers, Max found that he was still clutching the *gae bolga*. He glanced nervously at it, but the blade had gone still and silent. Shifting his weight, he felt the furry headrest ripple beneath him.

"What is this?" he muttered, half turning.

"It's me, you heroic thing," responded Toby. "You cracked your head and needed a pillow, and I can't think of anything more supportive and comforting than a selkie. It's the least I can do after you saved me. Forgive my earlier comments—it would seem you *are* an old hand at storming a palace full of demons." The selkie's body rippled with laughter.

Max grimaced at the sudden movement. "What happened, David?" he said, dazed. "How did you . . . ?"

"Oh, the Fomorian was wrong about me," said David. "I really am a clever fool. . . ."

"I don't understand."

"A wise man would have failed this task," David explained.

"Astaroth would have destroyed him. Only a clever fool could bait him into drinking that goblet."

"But he *knew*!" exclaimed Max, half sitting up. He found that he was finally able to share his betrayal. Astaroth's spell was broken. "David, I told him what would be in that goblet. He made me tell him all about the flowers and your potions. . . ."

"Put your guilt aside," said David. "There was nothing you could have done. And I knew such a thing would occur. In fact, I depended on it. You poisoned Astaroth just as much as I did."

David gently pushed Max back down.

"And you weren't alone," David continued. "I planted information with lots of people and creatures and even demons, hoping that it would eventually trickle to Astaroth. I wanted him to peek at my cards."

"Why?" asked Max.

David shrugged. "That was the only way I could win. Even before Astaroth had the Book, I was never a match for him. I don't have a fraction of his magic. To confront him directly would have been suicide. So I had to fool him—I had to trick him into helping me.

"I provided him with an irresistible opportunity," David continued. "On his holiest day, the 'Great God' could make a grand entrance, destroy his enemies, and demonstrate his superiority to all assembled. Such a prospect would be very appealing to someone like Astaroth. But we could *never* have infiltrated Walpurgisnacht and gotten close to him unless he had enabled it. He complied because he thought we were hapless fools. He thought that *he* was setting the trap."

Max recalled his conversation with Cooper in the Agent's room, their talk of sharps and flats and confidence games.

"I can't believe it," he murmured. "You conned him."

"I'm afraid I did," said David.

"Amazing," observed Max dazedly. "And I'm never playing cards with you again."

David smiled.

"It is undoubtedly the greatest confidence game I've ever heard of," remarked Toby, his voice aglow with admiration. "The opponent! The stakes! The daring! Why, I'm in doubt whether the exalted grand master of smees could have managed such a thing. Hats off to you, dear boy. What an achievement!"

Max frowned at this. "But, David, what have we achieved?"

"Well," said David thoughtfully, "you have avenged your father, and we have struck the Enemy a very powerful blow—one that has sown strife across the four kingdoms."

"But we didn't destroy Astaroth," observed Max. "And he still has the Book."

"Both true," David allowed.

"Then the mission failed," said Max heavily.

David smiled and shook his head. "This was a *rescue* mission, Max. And it succeeded."

Confused, Max said nothing but lay still and watched the sky brightening above him. It was true that they had rescued Mrs. Menlo, but why had David waited until Walpurgisnacht? The gambit seemed needlessly dangerous. It was a lot for Max to process even without his many wounds.

"How is she?" Max murmured.

"My mother?" asked David. "Somewhat bruised and frightened, but she's fine now. I've never seen her happier."

Max smiled, but his emotions were jumbled. His thoughts drifted to Vyndra and the dreams of vengeance that had consumed him. The demon was slain, but the fact offered little solace. Vyndra's death would not bring back Scott McDaniels. As Max pondered these things, David sat patiently beside him, seemingly content to let his friend's mind catch up to all that had happened.

Max recalled the strange mist that had poured from Astaroth once he'd consumed the potions. "David," he murmured. "What was in that goblet?"

"Four vials of Blood Petals," he replied. "And a clever little key."

"What?"

"A key," David repeated. "The fifth vial looked and smelled like the others, but it was an entirely different kind of potion— one that was much more difficult to make. It allowed the prisoner to free himself."

What prisoner? Had they rescued someone other than Mrs. Menlo?

Max was still baffled and groggy, but snippets of memories and events and past conversations formed a clearer picture in his mind. An unmistakable chill ran down his spine. He did not know whether to be elated or terrified.

"David," he whispered, more and more memories flooding back. "How did we escape? Did *you* bring us here?"

David shook his head. Helping Max to his feet, David pointed to a figure standing in the gray-green swells.

"He did."

Only now did Max realize they were on the beach at Rowan. The man in the water was staring out at Brigit's Vigil, whose silhouette stood against the sunrise. He was a large man with a wild mane of steel-gray hair and a thick beard that had always reminded Max of Poseidon.

The man glanced back at David's mother, who stood watching from shore. Wading slowly back to the beach, the man approached and took her hands while she gazed up at him with childlike adoration. His expression stern, he removed the jester headdress and let it drop to the sand.

"Do they know each other?" asked Max.

David cleared his throat. "She's his daughter."

Max tried unsuccessfully to master his shock. "So, he's your—!"

David motioned for quiet. The man was now staring at them. It was a hard appraisal—the guarded look of a wild animal that had just become aware of another's presence.

"Don't speak," whispered David. "He's still adjusting."

Nearly a minute passed before the man's attention drifted toward the chalky cliffs that led to Rowan's campus. Smoothing his daughter's hair, the man took her hand and made for the stairs.

Toby transformed to his native shape and Max scooped him up so the trio could follow. They climbed the steps as the sun peeped over the horizon, turning Rowan's cliffs to gold.

Max felt a rush of joy at seeing Maggie and Old Tom and the ivy-covered Manse. Ahead of them, the man paused to glance at one of the marble statues before he strolled on, studying every detail of Rowan's quiet campus.

It was only when he had nearly reached the Manse that the man seemed to notice Gràvenmuir. He gazed across the qua and solemnly contemplated the demonic embassy. Every windo within the dark, Gothic structure was brightly lit. Sever demons on the grounds were still celebrating Walpurgisnach They ceased their conversations and stared uncertainly at th strange man who studied them from afar.

At the man's silent invitation, Max and David approached He placed his daughter's hand in David's and then turned hi gray eyes to the path that led to Rowan's Sanctuary. Somethin very large was coming toward them.

It was YaYa, the Great Matriarch of Rowan.

The ki-rin was an ancient creature, whose single horn had been broken during the Siege of Solas. While YaYa's appearance was undeniably imposing, Rowan's students had known her only as the gentle black lioness who dozed inside the Warming

Lodge and presided over the Sanctuary with grandmotherly benevolence.

At the moment, the ki-rin did not appear grandmotherly or benevolent. Her expression was so fierce, her bearing so proud that she seemed a different being altogether. She came steadily down the path, her ghostly eyes fixed upon the man, who waited patiently.

YaYa came to a halt, towering over the man as steam poured from her panting mouth. Looking gravely down at him, she dipped her shaggy head by way of salute. For the first time, the man smiled. He reached up to stroke the smooth fur between her great, blind eyes, while the ki-rin nuzzled him like a kitten.

Minutes later, the sun rose above Rowan's cliffs just as Old Tom struck five o'clock. It was May Day, and Walpurgisnacht was over.

As Old Tom's chimes rang across the campus, history's greatest Sorcerer climbed upon the ki-rin's back and urged her toward Gràvenmuir. As the pair approached, Max saw the demons withdraw into the embassy. Even the hideous mummer guards abandoned their post as YaYa stopped at the outer gates. Meek as lambs, the mummers slipped inside.

And when the final chime had sounded, the Sorcerer spread his arms, as though to greet the dawn.

And when he did, the earth shook.

In an avalanche of stone, the entire cliff beneath Gràvenmuir gave way. With an appalling crash, the embassy and all within it were cast down into the sea.

Elias Bram had returned.

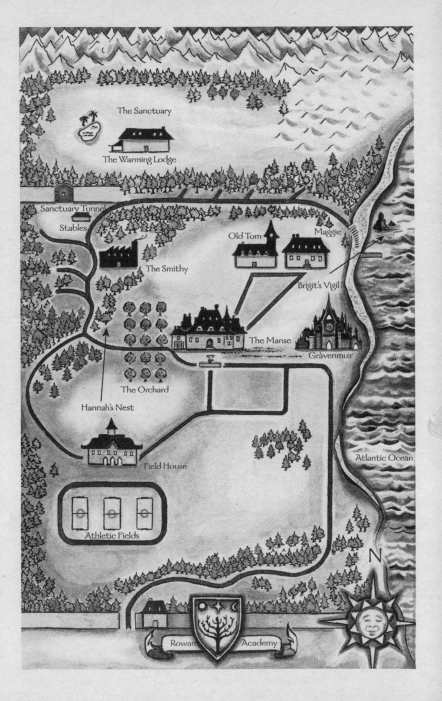

THE KINGDOM OF DRUSIAS

GRAND DUCHIES

1. Blys—Drusias
2. Lebrim—Mad'raast
3. Flarine—Jayna
4. Malakos—Grael
5. Azur—Vyndra
6. Bryllbatha—Unas
7. Raikos—Andras
8. Flolbrymn—Yuga
9. Vrusk—Yva
10. Ascheral—Brolsch

ACKNOWLEDGMENTS

In *The Fiend and the Forge*, Max McDaniels explores a strange new world while confronting demons without and within. The same might be said about writing. But while heroes often face such dangers alone, authors can usually count on help.

This book was more ambitious than its predecessors and I would never have been able to complete it without the unflagging support and encouragement of my wonderful family and close friends. Throughout the process, there were many occasions when I needed to indulge my creative angst and howl at the moon. Their collective willingness to listen, soothe, and provide perspective is a testament to their tolerance and sense of humor. These indulgent souls include my mother, Terry Zimmerman; my siblings, John and Victoria; friends who have known me since I had hair; and my former colleagues and students.

While my friends and family provided invaluable support, many others played a more direct role in bringing the final product into being. The original draft was a monster, some 250,000 words of unfiltered ideas and innumerable plot threads. After all, there was a new world to create, and I was eager to explore every aspect of various cultures, kingdoms, economies, and secondary characters. My editors at Random House, Nick Eliopulos and Schuyler Hooke, did a masterful job of taming this beast, divining my best intentions and shaping the story to match. Nicole de las Heras is the visionary behind the book's beautiful design, while the heroic efforts of Carrie Andrews, Diane João, and Alison Kolani ensured clarity and consistency in the text. As always, Josh and Tracey Adams of Adams Literary provided sound counsel, while Jocelyn Lange ensured that many readers around the world could share Max's adventures in their native languages. As deadlines loomed, these individuals went above and beyond the call of duty, and I'm eternally grateful for their commitment and professionalism.

The final acknowledgment goes to my wife, Danielle Raymond Neff. *The Hound of Rowan* might have sparked our first date, but *The Fiend and the Forge* sparked a marriage. This is my final wedding present, and Danielle has earned it tenfold. If authors are notoriously difficult partners, authors past deadline are insufferable. I have trespassed upon the poor woman's sanity in every conceivable way—keeping inhuman hours, scattering drafts and drawings, raiding her snacks, and subjecting her to every creative impulse, no matter how unformed or silly. She has endured all with saintly patience while contributing many crucial insights regarding the story and characters. She makes me a better man, and she has made this a better book. I am eternally grateful.

ABOUT THE AUTHOR

Henry H. Neff is a former consultant and history teacher from the Chicago area. Today he lives in Montclair, New Jersey, with his wife and young son. You can visit Henry at henryhneff.com.

A SECRET SCHOOL OF MAGIC IS HUMANITY'S LAST DEFENSE!

M ax McDaniels always suspected he was different. When a vision in a Celtic tapestry proves him right, it also pulls Max into an ancient war that threatens all of mankind while awakening magical powers within him.

Play the Game!
Visit RowanAcademy.com